MW00416618

PRAISE FOR
LIBBY LOST AND FOUND

"*Libby Lost and Found* is a story upon a story upon a story, all delightful. One by one, Stephanie Booth's characters are funny, complicated, endearing, and relatable, but then they come together and make magic. This is a book for those of us lucky enough to have ever really, truly fallen in love with one."

—Laurie Frankel, *New York Times* bestselling author of *This Is How It Always Is*

"*Libby Lost and Found* is a hilarious and heart-wrenching debut. Stephanie Booth delivers a charming story of friendship, fandom, and love through the most unreliable of narrators—the titular Libby and her devoted, hilarious disciple, Peanut. Every chapter pulls you deeper into this unexpected narrative, brimming with affection and care. Utterly unique and engrossing, *Libby Lost and Found* is a must-read for anyone who loves getting lost in a good book."

—Elissa Sussman, bestselling author of *Funny You Should Ask*

"When the author of a beloved fantasy series can no longer write, it raises the questions: Who needs that fictional world more: the writer or the fans? And what, actually, is real? Stephanie Booth's writing pops like fireworks as Libby's changing reality crashes into her vibrant, fantastical world. I haven't read a book this full of imagination since *The Night Circus*."

—Erica Bauermeister, *New York Times* bestselling author of *No Two Persons* and *The Scent Keeper*

"An absolute delight!! Clever, engaging, and heartfelt, Stephanie Booth has written a debut novel that packs a punch."

—John Searles, *New York Times* bestselling author
of *Help for the Haunted* and *Her Last Affair*

"Stephanie Booth is a major talent. Her debut is poignant, lyrical, and heartbreakingly funny."

—Dan Zevin, Thurber Prize–winning author
of *The Day I Turned Uncool*

"Step into the imagination of Stephanie Booth, who has crafted a suspenseful story-within-a-story about a bestselling author grappling with a devastating diagnosis and the curious eleven-year-old superfan who helps her complete her final book. Booth's skillful narrative hand gives us exhilarating prose, unexpected turns of events, and a cast of major and minor characters who gradually leave their interior worlds to come together and reveal themselves."

—Esther Crain, author of *The Gilded Age of New York*

"Beautifully written and full of heart...*Libby Lost and Found* is storytelling at its best with high stakes, extraordinary circumstances, and real human emotion at its core."

—Katie Sise, author of *The Vacation Rental*

Libby Lost and Found

STEPHANIE BOOTH

sourcebooks
landmark

Published by Sourcebooks Landmark, an imprint of Sourcebooks
P.O. Box 4410, Naperville, Illinois 60567-4410
(630) 961-3900
sourcebooks.com

Cataloging-in-Publication Data is on file with the Library of Congress.

Printed and bound in the United States of America.
VP 10 9 8 7 6 5 4 3 2 1

ENTER THE WORLD OF
THE FALLING CHILDREN
FROM *NEW YORK TIMES* BESTSELLING AUTHOR
F. T. GOLDHERO!

**WATCH FOR THE FINAL BOOK
THIS CHRISTMAS!**

"An absolute jewel of a fantasy—*Harry Potter* meets *Toy Story*."
—*Publishers Weekly*

"Dazzlingly brilliant... No children's characters are as real to life—or as resolutely beloved—as Everlee, Benjamin, and Huperzine Falling." —*New York Times*

"F. T. Goldhero, whoever you are, the Falling Children have captured our hearts." —*Booklist*

PROLOGUE

The Children are still in the forest. They've been there for weeks now, living off bitter hookroot and rainwater as briny as tears. Huperzine collects both in a sallow gourd that looks suspiciously like a skull, while Benjamin has fashioned a shelter from tree branches and armfuls of dead leaves. Still, it isn't enough. They're cold and hungry and scared.

As far back as they can remember, the Children have relied on Everlee to protect them—she's the bossiest, after all. But for the past thirty-one days, their friend has lain unconscious in the Depths of Despair, her eyes milky and unseeing, her limbs icy to the touch.

"I've fallen and I can't get up," Everlee's T-shirt reads. Under slightly less dire circumstances, the Children would laugh at the coincidence.

"I want to go home." Huperzine bursts into tears, burying their face in their hands. They are only eight and not old enough to realize there is nowhere left to go.

"Shhh!" Benjamin presses his hand over Huperzine's mouth. "He'll hear you."

The Unstopping is nearby. Fear only feeds him, and Huperzine's words are like a Thanksgiving feast.

For once, Benjamin can't think of anything to cheer his friend. He pushes another branch into the fire and listens to it snap.

As the Seer foretold, a lot has happened since the Children fled into this forest of gimcrack and geegaw trees. Neither sun nor moon has risen. Everlee has become stuck fast in a bog that feels like muddy sadness and smells like pig slop. And the Children's beloved Toy Emporium, previously shrunk down and tucked into Benjamin's backpack for safekeeping, has now burned to the ground. All that remains of Pompou's is a painful splinter in Huperzine's right foot.

But something else is wrong, something the Seer hadn't prophesied.

The woods of the OtherWay, usually noisy with the clink of Williwigs' shovels, wisecracking crows, and the creaking axle of the occasional bone grocer's wagon, are empty. The air is still. It's as if the enchanted world of the Children has simply…disappeared.

This isn't good for many reasons, the most obvious that they're waiting to be rescued. In the past, help has always come when the Children needed it most.

Benjamin pulls the last stick of red licorice from his pocket and tears it in two before handing the larger piece to Huperzine, now silently crying into the dirty sleeve of their favorite kitty-cat sweater.

"Ante up," he says, nudging their shoulder.

Huperzine takes a deep shuddering breath. "Ante up."

If the Falling Children have a motto, a call to arms, a secret verbal handshake, this is it.

And for good reason. Since meeting in the bleak fish locker of the Falling Orphanage three years ago, they've endured danger most days. And nights. And in far too many forms to remember, although surely Everlee, with her encyclopedic brain and precise recall, could if she were still able to speak.

The Children have been chained underwater by vengeful sea monkeys, for instance, and nearly bored to death by the heartless View Master's vacation slides. Once, they hacked their way out of a nest of ventriloquist dummies—only to get trapped in a game of Operation because Huperzine was holding their map upside down, but that's beside the point.

The point is, Everlee is the mastermind. The quick study. The deep thinker. Huperzine and Benjamin never make decisions—good decisions—without her.

It's unclear what the Unstopping's spell will do next to Everlee. He traffics in uncertain magic, the most unpredictable kind.

The Depths of Despair could continue to sap Everlee of her desire to live, one breath at a time, until she simply slips beneath the sludgy liquid. Or maybe the Unstopping will rake open Everlee's chest with one spiny fingernail and pluck out her wherewithal, the juiciest part of her soul. It's also possible that the Children's bold, clever friend, who speaks with a British accent when she's asserting herself, could be trapped for eternity inside a small, easily misplaced toy.

Not a clown, Benjamin silently prays. Please, anything but a clown.

Lightning heats the air, followed by a smack of thunder. The rain comes faster now, lashing the canopy of brittle leaves above them.

It is full of words, this rain: Doubt. Worry. Death.

As if on cue, the sky rips open. Always one for a grand entrance, the Unstopping steps through, as easily as a camper climbing out of a tent. What's left of his rotting conscience is safety pinned to the lapel of his tailcoat.

"Who's ready for some fun?" He strikes the heavy rings on his fingers together, and a sour noise tolls through the forest.

Huperzine hurls their licorice to the ground—"Hey, don't waste it!" Benjamin protests—and balls up their small fists. "Don't you lay one grimy finger on us!" Huperzine shouts. "We've got a plan."

Benjamin stops chewing, surprised. Huperzine is a scaredy-cat. Benjamin is more than a little lazy. The idea that they can defeat the all-powerful Unstopping without Everlee is ridiculous.

For the first time in weeks, Benjamin, Huperzine, then even Everlee, sinking ever lower into the gooey Depths of Despair, burst out laughing.

1

Libby hasn't meant to leave the children in the forest this long, but she lost both sets of keys to her apartment and had to call her land-lady, an elderly Japanese woman who confused "key" with *kura*—cooler—and sent an air-conditioning tech instead of a locksmith.

Then there was the morning Libby found herself dozing in the back seat of a town car headed to Manhattan. She couldn't remember why until the driver stopped in front of her publisher's building and expected her to get out.

And there was the entire *week* she forgot the password for her email.

It's now plastered on confetti-colored Post-its scattered around Libby's small apartment.

Everlee.

EVERLEE

Everlee is the password.

Meanwhile, the real Everlee continues to rot in the forest.

Libby has bitten her fingernails to the quick worrying about the Falling Children. It's not just Everlee she's concerned about but Benjamin with his stress eating and sensitive Huperzine, how quickly they fall to tears.

What the Children need is a guardian who looks after them, Libby thinks guiltily. Not someone who's burned their home to the ground and sent them screaming to the gluey Depths of Despair.

Libby isn't cut out to have children, even fictional ones.

She looks at the empty chair beside her, wishing she had someone to tell her otherwise.

Across the wall of the waiting room, the late-afternoon sun takes the shape of a frightened cat. Libby stretches out a hand to calm it. She has spent hours in this snare of taupe and beige chairs when she should have been writing. She should know this cat's name by now.

"Ms. Weeks?"

A nurse in pink scrubs leads her down the hall, not to an exam room like last time but to the neurologist's office. The stiff white carpet sighs beneath Libby's untied running shoes. Diplomas stamp the walls, and the mahogany desk is studded with framed photos, all facing away as if the occupants have seen Libby coming and quickly changed direction.

Only a few clues prove her doctor exists outside this room: a nearly empty jar of peanuts on the corner of the desk; a dog-eared travel guide to Colorado; and kneepads like skateboarders wear, knocked beside a filing cabinet.

Libby feels her brain storing these observations for later use, which is ironic because it's her brain's fault that she's here. Over the past few months, Libby has had lights shined into her eyes and Technicolor pictures taken of the structures inside her head. Vials of blood have been drained from her veins, and during one visit, she was prodded to list all the vegetables she could think of in sixty seconds.

Libby doesn't do well under pressure. All that came to mind was rutabaga.

"Is that even a vegetable?" Libby asked, spinning the top button of her shirt between her fingers.

"It doesn't matter." The doctor typed something into his computer. "Keep going."

Hesitation. Then: "Rutabaga?" Libby asked.

Today, five weeks later, she will officially be told what is preventing her from recalling green beans and Brussels sprouts on demand. But because she does not like waiting—not for food in restaurants, not to "get to know" people, and definitely not for the endings of books, even her own—she has googled her symptoms and deduced the problem herself. She is sure she has a rubbery tumor called a meningioma lurking in her brain.

Fortunately, it can be removed. And if it can be removed through her nose via an endonasal endoscopy, as Libby's online research promised, she will not even need her head shaved.

Libby has the wavy pale hair of a California surfer, although she recently turned forty and has never been on a beach in her life. There are multiple reasons why, including but not limited to sharks, tsunamis, sneaker waves, jellyfish, dune buggy rollovers, and sand in her shoes.

Hair aside, Libby is as tightly wound as the paper she's currently twisting between her sweaty hands. The cheat sheet of vegetables she's brought with her—just in case—has nearly turned to pulp.

Rutabaga is number one, which Libby finds odd because she's still not sure it even *is* a vegetable.

She wishes she'd brought her dog to this appointment. Rolf calms her, lying by her chair, the warm weight of his belly grounding her foot. Nothing upsets him—except UPS drivers—and Libby envies him for it.

When she looks up again, the neurologist is sitting behind his desk. Libby can tell by his eyes that he's been there for a while.

He takes off his glasses, like doctors do when they have bad news, then says many words. She is surprised none of them are "meningioma."

But one is "dementia."

"Excuse me?" Libby sits forward in her chair. "Could you repeat that?"

She puts her hand down to touch Rolf's head, but he isn't there. For a moment, Libby is clutched with fear that she's left him in the waiting room, where anyone—a nurse, a UPS driver, a child obsessed with yellow Labrador retrievers—could claim him as their own.

"Dementia," the doctor says again. "What we call early-onset dementia. You're the youngest case I've seen."

The corners of his mouth turn down in apology.

"It's not a brain tumor?" Libby looks down at the list she's brought. "But there are a hundred and twenty types. Are you sure?"

Nodding, the doctor launches into an explanation. Libby stares at his tasseled loafers peeking out from underneath the desk. They are the usual shoe color, but she is too panicked to recall the word. She only knows it is not meningioma.

Libby's thoughts grow wings and beaks in their haste to flap away from her.

How did I not know?

This isn't happening.

Should I still buy a new toaster?

This isn't happening.

I don't have anyone to tell.

This isn't happening.

Dying has always terrified Libby, but she's expected a bus to come careening wildly around a corner, some forty years from now. She feels betrayed that the process has, in fact, already started. The bus is moving toward her.

Libby presses her sweaty palms together. It's a poor substitute for another person beside her, holding her hand.

"It could take years," the doctor says, trying to help. But because he only knows Libby as his four-thirty patient, not the *real* Libby, he doesn't realize this is the wrong thing to say.

She begins crying, sobbing really, curling into a ball on the chair, her knees pinned to her chest. Her sneakers are caked with mud from the run she took this morning with Rolf. Clumps break free and disappear into the thicket of carpet below.

This is what will happen to you, Libby thinks. *Little by little, you, too, will fall away.*

"Is there someone we can call for you?" The doctor slides a box of tissues toward her. "Do you have family nearby? Or a friend?"

On her knees now, rescuing the lumps of dirt and saving them in the front pocket of her pants, Libby shakes her head.

It isn't hyperbole, as she's prone to. Her foster mother died years ago. She has no partner. No siblings. She doesn't even have friends unless she counts the UPS driver who sometimes shouts, "Jesus, lady! Can you call off your fucking dog?"

Libby only has the Children, and they are trapped in the woods.

And that's when Libby realizes: not only her future but the three Falling Children's lives are in grave danger.

It makes for great suspense, the writer in her can't help thinking. Except for the fact this is not a book. (And it's not a meningioma.) *This* is Libby's life.

Google "F. T. Goldhero Falling Children"

TOP STORIES

Release date of final Falling Children book pushed back

The Falling Children fantasy series has sold nearly 700 million copies worldwide. Now fans must wait another year to learn what fate will befall the beloved fictional orphans. Groton & Sons announced that due to "unforeseen circumstances," F. T. Goldhero's sixth and final book will be postponed...

AP Wire, 5 minutes ago

"We'll try being sweet first": Falling Children fans are losing patience

Tens of thousands of impatient Falling Children fans began a sweet letter-writing campaign today to entice author F. T. Goldhero to finish the long-awaited last book in the series. Their bribe of choice: Red Vines, the favorite snack of Benjamin, the lovably laid-back orphan with a notorious sweet tooth...

Los Angeles Times, 7 minutes ago

F. T. Goldhero, now *you're* being hunted

A Texan billionaire who owes his fortune to pig farming said he will give $1 million to anyone who can unmask F. T. Goldhero, the author of the wildly popular Falling Children series, whose identity is a closely guarded secret. "I hate riddles and I hate waiting," Baron McBroom posted on X this morning. "Lucky I'm rich enough I don't have to do neither. BRING ME FT'S HEAD."

UPI, 10 minutes ago

OLDER ARTICLES

The biggest Falling Children mystery is...who writes them?

It's a publishing recipe for success: Take one captivating plot, turn it into a fantasy series for children (and adults) still mourning the end of *Harry Potter*, add in a real-life mystery (Who's the mastermind behind it?), and allow to simmer in the media spotlight for four magical years...

Time, 6 months ago

Children love the plot; grown-ups relish the real mystery

Like Everlee Falling, Sophie Spiotta, a freckled fourth grader at Chapin, keeps a binder of to-do lists and slips into a posh British accent when nervous. A red butterfly net (Everlee's weapon of choice) hangs at the head of her loft bed. Sophie's mother, Pippa, a hedge fund manager, reads the Falling Children, too. But for her, the "obsessive" fun lies in guessing who pens the books...

NYT, 1 year ago

You'll never hug your teddy bear the same way again

Living inside a toy store is every kid's fantasy—especially if the toys walk, talk, and occasionally drive cars. That's the fizzy, fantastic premise of the Falling Children series. But author F. T. Goldhero isn't playing around. There's a surprisingly existential undertow to the narrative: The dolls, stuffed animals, and tin soldiers are (spoiler alert) damaged souls in need of saving...and it's up to the Children to do so...

USA Today, 2 years ago

I just read the best book EVER and it's for kids

I'm not into fantasy, y'all. *Haaaate* it. And YA? Ewww. So when my roommate was all, "Go get the Falling Children book rn," I went off. Then the cheapskate BOUGHT me a copy, came into my room, and plied me with Blue Dream while I read the first chapter. I admit it, awright? My heart *melted* into an indistinguishable pile of goo. I cried, I laughed, I got lit some more...

Buzzfeed, 4 years ago

2

That night, the diagnosis goes up on a marquee in the facade of Libby's mind, its wide aluminum frame and yellow chase lights blocking the door in her imagination that is supposed to lead straight to the Children.

THE DIAGNOSIS! it reads in commanding black letters.

It's rated R, not because of gratuitous violence or sexual content, but because it will deal with morose adult themes like assisted suicide (although Libby doesn't have anyone yet to assist her). She has waited her whole life to find a partner who'll look at her like *that*. To have a child to read to. To make a friend who gently suggests that she get out of the house more. Now that Libby has proof none of that is on the menu, raising her hand and asking for the check feels like the only logical next step.

The only hesitation she feels about the two giant bottles of Tylenol she ordered online is her beloved, slightly overweight dog, who will find himself without an owner.

Libby studies Rolf sleeping peacefully on her couch. What if he's sent to a kill shelter? What if he escapes the kill shelter and is forced to live on the streets and fend for himself? What if *then*, Rolf accidentally wanders onto the highway and is hit by a stoned teenager trying to drive and tear open a bag of chips at the same time?

Libby can see the boy's glassy, red-rimmed eyes now.

While she's googling "how to keep dog safe after you die," a UPS driver dumps Libby's daily (unmarked) box of fan mail at the door and rings the bell. Rolf trips off the couch, snarling and growling. He has distrusted UPS deliveries since he was a puppy. Libby has always thought of paying an animal communicator to find out why but is too worried it will be her fault.

She drags the box into her apartment and opens it with a pair of fingernail scissors. Who knows where her real scissors are?

Inside are packages after packages of Red Vines. Greeting cards, waxy children's drawings, and ink-smeared postcards spill at her feet:

PLEASE finish the book!

You need to save the Children!

These are for u, Mr. Goldhero, so you will FINISH your book.

Each letter feels like an accusation. *It's your fault the Children are in trouble.* They should come right out and say it.

Libby throws the candy, papers, and fingernail scissors back into the box, then drags it into the corner of her office, where it joins a dozen others.

All anyone cares about are the Children, Libby thinks, grabbing a roll of packing tape. She seals the box until it shines. *She* is insignificant.

Unless she has stories in her head, and right now, Libby has none.

～～～

For the next week, Libby spends most hours curled into a question mark on her bed, wrapped in the lopsided yellow-and-green afghan her foster mother gave her almost two decades ago for her twenty-first birthday.

Vernice had precise pitch and could sing harmony to any song, but it was crocheting she loved, although her skills worsened over time rather than improved. The blanket is pocked with dozens of holes Libby can slide a hand through. She does this most of the day.

Outside, a heat wave has settled over central New Jersey. The ice cream truck cruises Libby's Princeton neighborhood like a patrol car. When she takes Rolf for a walk around the block, the music plinks inside her head. Maybe, Libby considers, because she has fewer thoughts now to serve as insulation.

She pushes on her temples, wondering if it's possible to feel the dementia. Maybe she can coax it to the surface like a splinter. Or pop it like the occasional zit she still gets on her chin. Her head throbs, but that is only because she wishes the ice cream truck would *shhh* and go away.

Dum dum, de dum, de dum.

At night, Libby dreams of the Children, still trapped inside the forest. Huperzine is crying. (Huperzine is always crying.) Benjamin folds his arms across his chest, his hands shoved into his armpits. He looks irritated, but Libby can tell from the way he shifts from one foot to another that he's scared, too.

In the past, grief has oiled the wheels of her writing. It's how she came up with the idea of the Falling Children in the first place. But this is different. Now, when the Children try to speak to Libby, only "blllrggh" or "accck" comes out. Nonsense words.

There *is* one night that Libby hears a new, angry voice ask, "Where is everyone? What am I doing here?"

She sits up in bed.

At first, she's sure someone else has entered the forest. Then she realizes *she* is the one calling out, and this is what Forgetting sounds like.

Fewer than two dozen people know Libby Weeks is the author of the number one bestselling books in the world. That includes her publisher, a tall woman with a port-wine stain and a name Libby can't remember at this very moment. Her editor, who wants to be publisher one day, so she isn't about to tell anyone. A marketing team that regularly posts clues (and red herrings) about F. T. Goldhero on social media. And the legal department, whose interest in Libby is limited to her electronic signature.

The only person Libby told on her own was Vernice, who died a week after the first book came out. She never read it, even though Libby based a character on her.

"Now no offense to you, but you know I like a good romance," Vernice said, quieting her crochet needles long enough to pat Libby's hand.

As far as everyone else is concerned, Libby Weeks is just another middle-aged woman who brings reusable bags to the grocery store. She buys peanut butter and whole wheat bread to toast for breakfast, tomato soup for lunch, and only a handful of chocolate chips for dinner because she is usually hunched over her laptop, writing, Rolf asleep on her feet.

Unless she is out for a run, Libby wears only white shirts with Peter Pan collars, black pants, and gray cardigans, like she wore at private school when she was a kid. The uniform makes her feel she belongs somewhere. Libby's characters may be clever and brave and go on spectacular adventures, but *she* is exceptionally dull.

Except now, she jokes to Rolf, there is the dementia.

That's a conversation starter—if she had anyone to converse with.

Libby "has a whole lot going on in her head and not so much in real life" as Vernice used to say.

That has nothing to do with the Falling Children's success. As far back as she can remember, Libby has felt paralyzed by imagined threats, from a squirrel sitting outside her window (rabies) to eating at a restaurant (food poisoning, earthquake, gunman, server masturbating into her food).

Libby hates to drive. (What if she runs over a squirrel? What if she runs over a squirrel but doesn't kill it?) She hasn't taken a plane since her parents died on a flight to London. Even now, seeing a billboard for an airline brings to mind port-engine failures. (Not to mention bird strikes, terrorists, and tuberculosis germs on the foldout trays.)

If she goes into New York to meet with her publisher, Libby needs an Ambien just to get through the Holland Tunnel. But, because the Ambien makes her groggy, she usually shows up listing and slurring her words.

That, Libby thinks, is what probably inspired Groton & Sons to keep the identity of the Falling Children's author a secret. The real Libby is kind of a disaster.

~

Ten days after the diagnosis, Libby has only been able to write three sentences. They are peculiar and contrived, and the pacing is all wrong, but at least they'll sustain the Children a while longer.

The Unstopping gleefully uncorks Everlee's soul from her body, vowing to hide it somewhere it will never be found. He disappears, and words—actual words—start to rain from the sky. Neither Huperzine nor Benjamin has much of an appetite, and eating the word "hope" isn't nearly as satisfying as feeling it, but they choke down the spiky letters anyway.

As to why it's raining edible words in the OtherWay, Libby has no fucking idea. But at least it's giving the Children a break from eating bitter hookroot, and for that, they can all be grateful.

The outline of the last book Libby did months ago is no help. Under "Chapters 45–50," it only reads, *Figure out.*

Libby resents her past self for shirking such an enormous responsibility. Now Present Libby has to work twice as hard to make up for it.

This morning alone, she has tried to write standing up and lying on her kitchen floor. She has tried typing with her left hand, writing with her eyes closed, and holding on to Rolf's paw for moral support.

Nothing.

Libby knows the Children are suffering, but she can't make it stop.

"This is *not* good" is what Libby's editor says when she calls. Her name is Merry, which Libby finds ironic, because Merry is always in a foul mood. "What is going on with you?"

Libby stares at her computer screen, which is open to a free printable will. *Do you have children, or would you like to provide for any future children?*

"I don't know," she says.

"You need to finish this book," Merry says. "Someone somewhere is going to talk. A million bucks is a million bucks."

The words roll inside Libby's head like marbles. "A million what?"

Merry can't believe she doesn't know. "Baron McBroom? The billionaire who wants F. T. Goldhero's head on a platter?"

Libby's hand instinctively goes to her neck.

"You have got to focus," Merry pleads. "The Internet's blowing up. What still needs to be done?"

Everything, Libby thinks. "Not much more," she lies, biting the fleshy crest of her thumb until it bleeds.

"Will you reconsider working with another writer? You could take your pick. Every book we buy these days is a riff off yours anyway."

"No!" Libby doesn't mean to raise her voice, but she can't imagine anyone but her deciding the fate of the Falling Children. "I'll finish. I only need a few more weeks."

"The sooner, the better," Merry says. "In the meantime, we're having IT scrub you again from the Internet."

Libby reassures her that she's still not on Facebook or Snapchat or TikTok or X, but Merry doesn't let her finish.

"That's not the point." She launches into a tirade about what could happen if F. T. Goldhero's identity is revealed before next spring. It has to do with publicity and the marketing department and the amusement park/six-movie deal that's being finalized—not to mention another podcast launch, TV spin-off, and profits and percentages— Libby can't keep up.

She decides not to tell Merry about the Diagnosis. Instead, she turns back to the will.

"Get to work, lady," Merry says. "You can do this."

"Thank you," Libby says. And then, because she's forgotten who she's talking to, she adds, "You, too."

～

That evening, another UPS delivery arrives. Libby drags the box of Red Vines and letters into her office, which now contains more cardboard than furniture.

Her old rolltop desk is buried under crumpled index cards, crude pencil drawings of the Falling Children, and an oversize map of the OtherWay, the subterranean kingdom where the Children used to have whimsical yet meaningful adventures but where they are now trapped and waiting to die. Pushed to the side, like a cake waiting to cool, is a printout of Libby's almost-finished manuscript.

In the past five Falling Children books, Libby has juggled

dozens of characters and plot points like china plates above her head. Now she needs to carefully catch them, then set a satisfying table for her readers.

Libby has faced narrative challenges before but not so many at once, especially with so much at stake: Everlee needs to escape the vicious spell she's under *and* finally find the parents who abandoned her as a baby. Libby has been dropping clues about them for five books, hoping their identities would eventually come to her. (Spoiler alert: they haven't.)

What will happen to Pompou's Toy Emporium, which Libby tragically burned to the ground two chapters ago? Now all that remains of the Children's beloved home is a splinter in Huperzine's foot. And once the Fallings *do* vanquish the Unstopping—because Libby is a firm believer in happy endings even if her own life will be void of one—what then? How are the Children supposed to grow up and live with boredom and disappointment like everyone else?

The wall behind Libby's desk is covered with hundreds of notes she has written herself over the years, each with its own passionate scribble-scrabble: Williwigs always attack when called "cute," for instance. Or No one can live without a conscience, even the Unstopping. Libby has no memory of writing these reminders or what she's supposed to do with them.

Figure it out, she can hear Past Libby say.

Libby turns off the office light and shuts the door. She crawls into bed with her laptop.

Online at the Falling Children site, fans are arguing again over Huperzine, the most divisive of the Children. Huperzine is prone to well-meaning but poor decisions, like the time they befriended a clearly possessed Baby Alive doll.

My least favorite character I have 2 say, someone complains in the chat. Theyre always falling down and getting stuck or being over-sensitive and saying goofy shit.

Huperzine is trying! Libby types but doesn't send.

Hundreds of threads are devoted to Benjamin. Younger readers share drawings of him on his trusty skateboard, red licorice in hand. Older readers post fan fiction. They are often about Benjamin falling in love with them, although none of them are Benjamin's type.

Where's his romantic love interest? someone demands. He never hooks up.

Maybe he hasn't met the right person yet, types Libby.

Again, she doesn't hit Send.

Because here is another secret Libby is ashamed to share with anyone: although she adores the Falling Children, *real* children, who live outside her head and wield their opinions like spears, frighten her.

～～

That night, Libby can't sleep because her heart is thumping like a—thumping thingy. She puts on her afghan—the holes are so large now, she can slide her arms through and allow the blanket to hang from her shoulders like a dress—and sits at her desk, smoothing her palm over a blank piece of paper. If the Children won't talk to her when she types, maybe she can sneak her way into their world by writing longhand.

Hello, Children, she writes with her favorite brand of cheap ballpoint pen. It's me.

Then she waits.

And waits.

The paper stays blank. So does her imagination.

Anyone there? Libby tries again.

Nothing.

No one.

Libby rests her forehead on the paper, hoping some thoughts, even small ones, will seed into lush green sentences. Instead, she falls asleep. When she wakes hours later, a paper clip is stuck to her lip, and the paper (still blank) is crumpled on the floor, where it belongs.

Sighing, Libby logs back on to the Falling Children message boards.

There's speculation as to who Everlee's parents are (Libby doesn't know yet. Give her a break!), and more than a few readers hope Gran Bere, the closest thing the Falling Children had to a (furry) fairy godparent, will come back from the dead.

Libby still regrets sacrificing Gran in book five.

Gran was a bowlegged teddy bear who smoothed its crisp muslin skirt with its paws when it thought. It doled out honey cookies and wise advice, and it was also a badass. Like the time it pulled a musket from behind its back and warned a pack of bloodthirsty jack-in-the-boxes: "Don't mess with Gran Bere, or it will be the last mess you make."

Libby thinks about resurrection as she scrolls through the message boards. Gran could fix everything.

Then another thread catches her eye: For someone who writes books for children, I sadly think you have forgotten what it is like to be one.

No one asked you, Libby thinks, her cheeks hot.

Still, she clicks on the message.

If you haven't finished the last book by now, then you need MY help, the comment reads.

Let's be honest, it goes on. Children are smarter and stronger than anyone gives us credit for! Sooooo if you are stuck, write me and I will save the day! A line of Falling Children emojis follows: Everlee with her butterfly net, Benjamin eating licorice, Huperzine wiping away their tears. There is also a blue-sky emoji and one of a healthy-looking pink brain.

Libby sits back in her chair and lets the audacity of this message sink in.

For someone who writes books for children, I sadly think you have forgotten what it is like to be one.

She scrolls the replies, fully expecting this commenter to be called out for accusing F. T. Goldhero—*the* F. T. Goldhero!—of being stuck, but there are no comments. Zero. It's as if this message exists only for Libby. She reads it once, twice, three times more.

Then she clicks on the commenter—Time2AnteUp.

Libby has heard that name somewhere before but can't remember where. A note attached to Red Vines? A scribbled signature on the back of a drawing? She picks through her desk drawers, in case the answer lies in there.

Is this what her mind will look like in a few months? Pencil stubs, thumbtacks—why does she have Everlee's name written on Post-its everywhere? Libby has kept a journal about the Falling Children since she first made them up as a kid. To Save, the faded cover reads. She feels like it's mocking her. None of these ideas will save her.

Frustrated, Libby rips page after page from the little red note-book. She snatches up the slips of paper from her desk, computer, phone, refrigerator, shoes. There are keys everywhere as well—duct-taped under her desk, beside the front door, on the hook by Rolf's leash.

She hurls everything into the trash.

The apartment rings with noise.

Rolf looks at her and sighs.

"Don't judge," Libby shouts at her laptop before slamming it shut.

She'll figure out how to finish her book soon, won't she? The answer—*some* answer—will come to mind. It's time that something (or someone) did.

From: Pandora Bixton <Time2AnteUp@blueskiesfamilymedi-cine.net>
To: F. T. Goldhero <FTGoldhero@fallingchildren.com>
Subject: Here's how you will save the Children

Hello, Mr. Goldhero,

It's me, and I am going to keep writing letters and posting messages on your site until you Save. The. Children! There's no reason it should be taking you so long. If you asked me to do it, I could write the last book in DAYS—even faster if I didn't start junior high next week.*

"No, you couldn't. You're 11!" Some people (like my annoying sister) say.

But as you and I both know, children have an extra tank of imagination that adults don't. Think back to when you were my age, and I know you will agree. Plus, in your books, children are the ones who come up with all the good ideas while adults mostly sit around and complain that it's too hard and their backs hurt.

No offense, but even if something hard IS happening to you, it's no reason to make the Falling Children suffer, or cause me to scream on a daily basis with impatience. As you know from my hundreds of previous letters, I have led a HIGHLY unfair life so far. But instead of dwelling on it, I think of the Children, which is what you should be doing, too.

Have you had a chance to read the stories I wrote? I am writing more in my head all the time. You do not have to pay to use any of my ideas, but a character named after me (who does not die a grisly death) would be a nice touch.

En toys speramus,
Your biggest fan in Blue Skies, Colorado, the U.S.A.,
the world, and the UNIVERSE,
Peanut Bixton

* Junior High is not my choice. I would rather eat cold fish at every meal like at the Falling Orphanage.

3

Peanut has always dreamed of the Falling Children, but this summer, they seed her nightmares.

She's watched the *Sink Ng* ship get sucked into a whirlpool of blood and heard the screams of wooden toys hacked to bits with a dull knife. After dreaming she'd been eaten alive by a bone grocer, Peanut woke with three small puncture wounds, in the *exact* line of a fork, on her inner thigh.

"We picked raspberries yesterday, remember?" Jessie said when Peanut shook her awake to show her. "Those are from thorns."

"This is different!" Peanut insisted, chewing a strand of her hair until it crackled. She does this when she is emotional. Her brother calls it her tell.

"Those books aren't real."

"They are to me," Peanut argued. "You don't know because you haven't read them."

Although Jessie is older—and, unlike Peanut, has two eyes that look in the same direction *and* a face free of scars—she has zero imagination. Which is why yesterday, when Peanut asked permission to go on a quest to search for her real parents and Jessie said, "Abso-freaking-lutely not," Peanut knew she must.

When her alarm goes off at 5:20, Peanut quickly dresses in a pair of shorts, Falling Children T-shirt, and tie-dyed knee socks, then tip-toes past Jessie's bedroom and down the stairs. When her father steps outside ten minutes later, she's perched on the front steps, watching the sun spike tangerine.

"Look." Peanut points. "The sky matches my socks."

Her father trips in surprise, grabbing the railing to right himself. "Blast it, child! What on earth are you doing?"

"I got up early to help you."

Scowling in the shadows, over six feet tall, and clutching a worn leather satchel, her father reminds Peanut of a cartoon burglar.

"Did Jessie put you up to this?" he wants to know. "I've been doing this for forty-seven years. I don't need assistance."

Peanut doesn't argue. She knows better, unlike Jessie. Instead, she waits until her father has gone down the porch steps and across the street. And then she follows.

With the distance of a home between them, Peanut traces her father's path down the hill, past farmhouses like their own and yards flecked with pygmy goats and rusted trucks. At the bottom lies a grid of tidy pink and purple Victorians, built by high rollers who struck it big in Blue Skies' now-deserted silver mine.

If Peanut squints, she can pretend she's walking through Dark Crevice, the town where the Falling Children are from. She can almost convince herself that Pompou's Toy Emporium will run to catch up once she turns the corner. Like a loyal dog, it hates to be left behind.

Her father leaves a box of blood glucose test strips on Annie Yolen's porch swing and retrieves a container of foamy pee from the Canbys' mailbox. (Peanut is not a doctor, but even she can tell that's not normal.)

At the corner of Dennis and Main, she hangs upside down from a tree branch, her hair sweeping the sidewalk, while her father checks if Mrs. Breen's in labor yet. This same intersection is where Peanut will catch the bus to Cross Creek Junior High next week.

What happened to that kid's face? she will hear fifty, or maybe a hundred, times.

She has already prepared a spellbinding explanation for people she may want to be friends with and a short, dull version for people she won't.

When her father returns, he's carrying a mug of coffee and two crullers.

"Three centimeters," he says, finally acknowledging Peanut's presence. He doesn't offer her a doughnut.

Downtown is deserted. No mountain bikers or cowboy reenactors or VW buses piled high with inflatable rafts. The narrow red-brick buildings appear to be sleeping, and Peanut is sure she can hear them snoring: the boutiques and breweries, the Shoe Fly and Pig-n-Pancake.

"Did you know that in Dark Crevice, they have a shoe store called the Boot Lace?" she asks her father. "And a little café called the Bear-n-Biscuit?"

He doesn't answer.

"Dark Crevice? Blue Skies? I made a whole list of things that are almost the same. Like"—Peanut counts on her fingers—"they have a really steep hill, we have a really steep hill. They had a magic shop explode, we had that fire once in the bead store, remember? When a customer threw their vape pen away and it caught on fire? Plus," she adds, trying not to brag, but it *is* the truth, "Everlee and I share many similarities."

Her father tucks a prescription for beta-blockers through the police chief's mail slot. "You mean she doesn't know when to stop talking?"

"Yes," Peanut says, deciding to take this as a compliment. "That's exactly right."

They pass the train depot, where Peanut's sister works, and then the redbrick library, with its fat white columns on either side of the front door. Peanut runs her fingers against them as they pass.

Here is another important way she and Everlee Falling are alike: they were both mysteriously abandoned as babies outside their town's library. If not for the Falling Children books, Peanut might view this as a tragic way to enter the world. Now she understands that she—like Everlee—must be marked for greatness. They are both on an Important Quest to find their real parents.

Peanut realizes her father has gotten ahead of her and runs to catch up. Coming up is the only part of Blue Skies that she doesn't like. Before the two-lane road widens into highway squats a mean little wood-shingled house with a toppling chimney and boarded-up windows.

DOLL HOSPITAL reads a peeling clapboard sign out front. People from all over the world used to send their favorite toys here to be fixed by Mr. Greeley. Then, one Halloween, the year Peanut was born, trick-or-treaters found his lifeless body on the porch.

"The toys did it," whisper all the kids who read the Falling Children.

"His son did it," say the adults, who think Mr. Greeley's then-teenage son gave him a heart attack and ran off to Mexico. (Or is it New Mexico? One of those two.)

You're going to die, police found spray-painted onto the mailbox but couldn't prove who wrote it. Now time—or maybe the widow who still lives there but *whom Peanut has never seen*—has skinned the phrase down to just *die*.

It's like something out of a Falling Children book. Or, well, the fifth one. That's when things started getting creepy.

"Don't be silly," Peanut's father says when she points this out. "Mrs. Greeley's a sick woman."

But because he doesn't say anything about the son and Jessie speeds, her eyes glued to the road, when they drive past, Peanut is sure one of the stories is real.

Today there's more proof: a naked doll, its head slumped and bare legs twisted sideways, tied to the chicken wire fence in front of the house. Xs have been carved into its eyes, and its mouth sewn shut with fishing line.

The hair on the back of Peanut's neck stands up.

In book five, this is how the Unstopping announces that he's returned to Dark Crevice.

Peanut holds her breath until the tortured doll is out of sight. Not until her father drops a tube of acne cream into the McAvoys' mailbox and Peanut hears it thump the bottom does she remember why she got up so early.

"Today I would like to go to the Little Diamond Saloon. Not to drink," she says quickly, since her father sometimes treats victims of their bar fights. "But on a fact-finding mission."

From the pocket of her shorts, Peanut pulls out the ad from *The Blue Skies Gazette* she spotted yesterday while Jessie was reading her horoscope.

LITTLE DIAMOND SALOON NOW SELLS VESPER NESTER ALE. COME JOIN US! it reads.

Her father looks at it, his eyebrows knitted together, then back at Peanut. "What on earth are you yammering about?"

"Vesper Nester Ale," Peanut says, unable to contain her excitement.

Then she remembers: although her father is a medical doctor who can deliver babies and stitch wounds and, twice, has shown up at Blue

Skies Elementary to pull a pencil eraser from a third grader's nose, he is not a Falling Children fan. (Or even a reader of the books.)

Peanut starts from the beginning. "When the Falling Children want to send secret messages, they rearrange the letters of words. Like, Pompou's Toy Emporium is Mommie Poop Out Syrup. It's called an anagram."

"I know what anagrams are, Peanut."

Peanut waves the newspaper ad. "Then you understand how key it is that I descend upon the Little Diamond Saloon."

She knows he will not rearrange the letters in his head, so she does it for him.

"Vesper Nester Ale rearranges to 'Everlee's parents!'"

Peanut is extremely good at anagrams.

"It's because I'm always on the lookout for a magical-sounding phrase," she explains to her father. "Sometimes, I just know when I've found one. My fingers feel like they've fallen asleep, and I can hear my heart beat in my ears. It's okay if you haven't felt like that before," she adds graciously. "I have a special bond with the Children."

Peanut's father sighs. But before he can tell her to stop talking, she rushes on. "Since Everlee was abandoned at the library as a baby just like me, this may be a clue for me to find my real parents. What if"— she pauses theatrically and feels her heart thrum in her ears—"our parents are one and the same?"

"I will not go inside the saloon," she promises. "I will only look sharply at the patrons and await more clues. And I won't be by myself. Nancee is back from female-empowerment camp, and she can go with me."

"How can twelve weeks of summer camp cost fourteen thousand dollars?" her father says, focusing on the wrong thing. "Did they sprinkle gold flakes on the child's oatmeal?"

Peanut doesn't know. She doesn't have her own phone, so she hasn't texted or talked to Nancee for the past three months. And she's not on Instagram because Jessie makes her share an account. (Jessie named it, too—@Pnut_Butter_n_Jessie, which just shows how awful she is.)

Jessie doesn't like Peanut being friends with Nancee. She hasn't forgotten the time Nancee super-glued a ten-dollar bill to the sidewalk downtown, then livestreamed people (mostly Jessie) struggling to pry it free. "You need to find a new friend," Jessie, red-faced, tells Peanut in the video. She said the same thing when Peanut asked to go to the Little Diamond Saloon with Nancee today.

"So you see," Peanut tells her father, "I *have* to go."

"'Have to' means you have no choice," he corrects. "You *want* to go. There's a difference."

"So? Jessie shouldn't be the one to always tell me what to do." *Just because you don't want to*, she silently adds.

Peanut is halfway up Cojones Hill, the asphalt rising before her like a drawbridge, when she realizes her father is no longer beside her.

Turning, she sees him a good twenty paces behind, his hands on his knees, breathing heavily.

"Are you having a heart attack?" she calls. "Because in book one, Everlee has to do chest compressions on Gladys, the cruel headmistress at the orphanage, so I know how to do them."

"I require only peace and quiet." Her father, his forehead and neck lit with sweat, points up the hill. "For pity's sake, go home."

Peanut doesn't move. This is too important.

Channeling Everlee in book three, when she pleads for the vicious Williwig king to save Benjamin's life, Peanut drops to one knee, presses a hand to her heart, and bows her head.

31

"Patience, sir!" she cries in a loud, clear voice. She has pretty much all the lines in every Falling Children book memorized. "I would not ask if this were not of paramount consequence. My heart teeters on a tightrope, and I beg you: provide it safe passage across."

The beauty of the words makes Peanut shiver. F. T. Goldhero is a genius.

Her father doesn't smile, but he does briefly meet Peanut's good eye before his gaze travels to her scar.

"Fine," he tells it. "Go."

"Thank you, oh, munificent mortal, thank you!"

She gives her father a low bow. There's no point trying for a hug. "He saves his bedside manner for his patients," Jessie likes to say. It is a joke—but not really.

Sprinting up the rest of the hill, Peanut cuts through the McVays' orchard. She weaves through rows of trees, young Stayman apples swaying overhead like ornaments, the wind ruffling her hair.

Peanut isn't sure what she would do without the Falling Children. They are her life.

4

When Libby opens her browser the following day, headlines about F. T. Goldhero detonate onto the screen:

FALLING CHILDREN BOOK DELAYED AGAIN AND FANS AREN'T HAVING IT

F. T. GOLDHERO: BIGGEST PUBLISHING SCAM OF ALL TIME?

"WATCH YOUR BACK, GOLDHERO!" HUNT FOR ELUSIVE AUTHOR HEATS UP

A slideshow trending on X suggests F. T. Goldhero is a famous person hiding in plain sight. The twelve photogenic candidates include a reality TV star with blindingly white teeth, a teen Instagram poet who once posted, "Ima magic, kidz/the only, words i read/are mine own," and a literary wunderkind from South Korea. In her picture, Seo-yun wears a sweater covered in pink cats but doesn't smile.

She *would* be a good F. T. Goldhero, thinks Libby.

Much better than herself, a former adjunct English instructor at Camden County Community College fired for not "adequately engaging" her students. Plus, Libby blinks in photos.

If the whole world knew F. T. Goldhero shops in the girls' department at 2Cool4SchoolUniforms.com and cranks Tone Loc when she runs, they would love Everlee, Benjamin, and Huperzine just a little bit less.

~ ~

Two weeks after the Diagnosis, Libby wakes one morning filled with certainty that her doctor has made a mistake.

Today Libby's mind is a clean glass pitcher ready to fill. Today she is hopeful—no, she is convinced—that she can write a chapter. Maybe two.

Hang on, Everlee, she thinks. *I'm coming.*

But first, Rolf.

Libby pulls on running tights and a tank top, finds two matching socks, and ties back her hair. Then, for the first time in days, she goes out her door and off her block.

The muggy August heat licks her skin. Across from the Princeton campus, new freshmen, some still wearing their name tags from orientation, drift in and out of the shops on Nassau Street.

"Sorry," Libby says, flinching when they brush against her.

Libby applied to Princeton but didn't get in, even with her tragic family history. "It's just as well," Vernice assured her at the time. "You don't do well under pressure."

Which is still true.

But today there has been a miracle of sorts in Libby's brain. She can feel it. She is lucid and coherent and sharp as a tack, and she remembers all those words.

We'll see, the committee in her head says, unconvinced. Its members are wearing gray wigs and black robes and are suspicious of miracles. They are also waiting outside *The Diagnosis,* popcorn in hand, ready for that film to roll.

I need a good cry, Libby hears one confide.

Despite the heat and traffic, she flies through the four-mile run to the dog park. Rolf, ecstatic to have more than five minutes of exercise, easily keeps up.

Once inside the chain-link fence, Libby unhooks his leash and throws a dirty tennis ball she finds on the ground. Rolf gamely fetches. He has the gait of a heavy horse, cantering on his return, and Libby wipes slobber off his chin and kisses his head.

She doesn't know what she would do without Rolf. He is every-thing she aspires to be: Steady. Friendly. Unworried.

When the dementia kills her, maybe she can come back as a dog. Maybe Rolf will come back as a human and take care of her. Libby is privately liking this idea when a man with close-cropped graying hair and wire-framed glasses approaches. Under one arm, he carries a bored corgi like a football.

"Great dog," he notes, bending down to ruffle Rolf's ears.

It's difficult for Libby to talk to strangers because she expects them all to be serial killers.

"Thank you," she says, already taking a step back and looking toward the gate.

"What's his name?" When she tells him, the man laughs. "Everyone loves the Falling Children, huh?"

When Groton & Sons allowed Libby to choose her pseudonym, she simply rearranged the letters of "Rolf the Dog." She never thought fans would care enough to unravel it. Luckily, it's considered a throwaway ana-gram for "F. T. Goldhero." Libby has seen news stories about a Canadian machinist named Dogle Forth who had his house broken into—twice.

Libby looks down, suddenly worried that something is giving away her secret, but all she sees is a smear of peanut butter on the front of her tank top.

"I'm Glenn, by the way," the man says, extending his hand. He gestures to the khaki pants and oxford cloth shirt he's wearing. "About to go to work."

"Libby." She reluctantly shakes his hand. "About to go home."

"You live around here?"

Libby looks around the park. It's empty, save for her and the possible serial killer. "No," she lies. "I'm visiting my sister." She points to the parking lot. "She's in her car. Waiting. Because she's a policeman. Woman," she clarifies.

Unfortunately, Glenn finds this interesting. "Oh, yeah? Where you from?"

"Hawaii," lies Libby.

"Which island?" He looks impressed. She should have said Arkansas and wonders if it's too late to switch.

Libby hesitates. She's never been to Hawaii. (Sharks, volcanoes, pineapple.)

Glenn mistakes her paranoia for a reluctance to flirt.

"Am I asking too many questions?" He winks. "It's a job hazard. I'm a journalist."

Libby recognizes the name of the website he works for, only because the listicles about the Falling Children make her cringe: "10 Times Everlee Was Probably Totally on Her Period," for instance.

"We're expanding into investigative reporting," Glenn says. "Everyone's got a secret, right?"

When Rolf chooses that moment to crouch in the far corner of the dog park, Libby silently thanks him.

She takes her time picking up after Rolf, but after she throws the bag into the trash, Glenn lurks in the corner, holding his corgi, watching her.

Quickly, Libby ducks out the opposite gate that leads through the area for small dogs. She is almost to the parking lot when she hears Glenn shouting. He waves the arm that's not wrapped around his dog.

"Hey!" he yells. "Get back here!"

Serial killer. She *knew* it.

Taking out her phone, Libby pretends to make a call.

Glenn fast walks to the edge of the gated area, still waving. Fear marches into Libby's chest. Switching on her music, she begins to sprint, "Funky Cold Medina" pounding in her ears. If she closes her eyes, she can hear Vernice singing backup.

At stoplights, Libby turns, half expecting to see Glenn, still holding that damned corgi, coming after her. But there is only the usual August traffic, every third car a station wagon bloated with body pillows and rolled-up *Abbey Road* posters.

Libby is coated in sweat when she finally stops in front of a beige Victorian neatly drawn and quartered into apartments, one of which is hers. There is no creeper van behind her.

You always expect the worst, she chides herself.

It is not until Libby is in the shower, shampoo lathered into her long hair, soap stinging her eyes, that a realization comes to her. It starts at the small of her spine before firing like a missile into her brain:

She forgot Rolf at the dog park.

5

"We're going to Little Diamond," Peanut says when Nancee answers her phone.

"Don't you want to know how my female-empowerment camp was?" Nancee asks. "I lost eleven pounds. I haven't had Takis in three weeks. They made me square dance."

"Tell me later."

Peanut knows Nancee won't like this answer, but once Nancee starts talking about herself, it's hard to get her to stop. Peanut explains the ad she saw yesterday and how "Vesper Nester Ale"—she loves how magical that sounds!—rearranges to "Everlee's parents."

"Oh." Nancee pauses. "You're still doing this?"

"Doing what? Searching for my rightful birth parents? Uh, *yes*." Peanut doesn't like Nancee's tone.

"If this ad were a message to you, wouldn't the anagram be 'Peanut's parents'?"

"No, because Peanut is only my nickname." Peanut is irked that she has to remind Nancee. Her real name is Pandora, but no one ever calls her that, except teachers on the first day of school and her father when he is "in a mood."

When Peanut explains that the next bus to the old mining town leaves in less than an hour, Nancee pauses. "I sort of have other plans."

Peanut almost laughs. Since kindergarten, she and Nancee have only been friends with each other. Plus, Nancee got home from female-empowerment camp this morning. How has she had time to talk to anyone but her parents?

"Because I have a phone like everyone else in the world?" Nancee says. "Rosemary Carver wants me to go to the lake."

Now Peanut does laugh. A) Nancee hasn't been to the lake since she tried tubing in fourth grade and fractured her tailbone, and B) Rosemary Carver called her Butt Crack because of that.

"She's a lot nicer since she had cancer," Nancee insists. "We're supertight now."

Peanut doesn't believe it. With or without a brain tumor, Rosemary is too wicked to be friends with anyone. But the bus to Little Diamond is leaving soon, and she doesn't have time to debate.

"Meet me at the bus stop," she orders and hangs up before Nancee can back out.

When Peanut turns around, Jessie is watching her, her hands on her hips. She's dressed in a long-sleeve calico blouse and muslin skirt, a bonnet tied tight under her chin. A lifetime ago, Jessie hoped to become Blue Skies' first female doctor, but she bombed the SATs and barely graduated from high school, so now she works for the Great Train Robbery.

Six days a week, four times each day, actors dressed as cowboys draw fake pistols and pretend to rob tourists on the steam train that rattles across Gilkey Gulch. Jessie's role is "Frantic Mother." When the wind is just right, Peanut can sit on the front porch and hear her sister scream, "My baby! My baby!"

She isn't convincing. And since it only pays $11.25 an hour, Jessie still lives at home.

"By the time I was twenty-six, I'd graduated medical school, purchased this house from my parents, and taken over Doc Yates's practice," their father says when Jessie complains her hair smells like gunpowder. "Apparently, I adopted the wrong child."

"Wrong children," Jessie corrects. "Buzz isn't a doctor either."

Their father doesn't have an answer for that. Buzz has always been his favorite.

"I told you yesterday," Jessie tells Peanut. "I'm done with these little adventures."

"He's not." Peanut points into the kitchen, where their father is finishing a bowl of oatmeal. "He said I could go."

Jessie has a heart-shaped face and wide green eyes. Her long hair's the color of new pennies. Even angry, she is pretty.

Peanut watches her stomp into the kitchen. She can't hear the whole argument, only a few words here and there. It sounds like:

"You're making things harder—"

"Enough."

"She can't keep—"

"Lower your voice."

"What if she—"

"She won't."

"But what if—"

"*Stop.*"

"If I were you," their father says, scraping his chair back from the table and handing Jessie his empty bowl, "I'd choose my battles carefully."

"Choose my battles?" Jessie circles the kitchen, slamming cabinets and drawers. "Oh, I'll choose my battles all right." Still, she waits to say this until their father is upstairs, the bathroom door has shut, and water glugs through the pipes.

"I'll be fine," Peanut tells her. "You always think something bad is going to happen to me, and it's not. Plus"—she pats her Falling Children backpack—"I've got bear spray. And Nancee."

Jessie rolls her eyes.

"I could find my real parents," insists Peanut.

"Yeah?" Jessie stabs a handful of knives into the dishwasher. "Be careful what you wish for. It might come true."

It's a quote from the Falling Children, but no surprise, Jessie has mangled it.

~ ~

Before heading to the bus stop, Peanut follows the grassy slope of their side yard to the small butter-colored cottage next door. The doorbell lets out a tired burp to announce her arrival, but Peanut's brother doesn't answer.

When Buzz was eleven, his real parents died a gruesome death. "It's all good" is all he's ever said about it, but Peanut thinks that's a lie.

Even after Peanut's father adopted him, Buzz never moved out of this house or packed up his parents' things. There are still three toothbrushes in the holder by the bathroom sink.

Plus, "it's all good" is what Buzz said in the hospital when Peanut told him that the video of his wipeout (EPIC fail: Squirrel Keeper eats skater's LUNCH) had gone viral.

In the spring, a video crew had come to film Buzz land a back-side 5–0 down a thirty-five-stair rail—and while eating a roast-beef hoagie, his signature move. On his fifth try, when he was halfway down the railing, a squirrel came out of nowhere and sat at the bottom. Buzz swerved to miss it. The squirrel ran off with the sand-wich, and Buzz got a concussion, dislocated his shoulder, and cracked his shin bone. Their father said it will be a long time, if ever, before Buzz can skate again.

As far as Peanut knows, Buzz hasn't left his house since he came home from the hospital. Or turned on the lights, even when the physical therapist stopped by as a favor to their father. Each time Peanut drops off a homemade get-well card or one of Jessie's gloopy casseroles, she has to wear a headlamp so she doesn't trip over the front step.

"Give it time," Peanut has heard their father tell Buzz over the phone.

"Give him time," he tells Peanut when he catches her pounding on Buzz's door, hoping to goad him into opening it.

A few weeks ago, Jessie used their emergency key and went inside to make sure Buzz wasn't lying dead on the floor, but she only made things worse.

"So what if you can't skate anymore?" Peanut heard her say. "It's not like you're Tony Hawk. Now you can finally grow up and get a real job."

(Peanut wasn't eavesdropping. She was "listening to the wind," as Everlee likes to put it.)

"You're a fucking piece of work," Buzz, clearly not dead, said. "Leave. I mean it."

Peanut had never heard her brother raise his voice before then, not even the time their father accidentally drove over his foot.

He may also have started crying.

"Leave him alone," Jessie told Peanut. "He'll figure it out on his own."

But that was twenty-two days ago, and Peanut still hasn't seen her brother. She presses the doorbell again and again (and again), but Buzz doesn't come to the door or shout at her to go away.

Like usual, Jessie is wrong.

~

Only one other person is waiting at the bus stop: a teenager with pink streaks in her hair who's wearing a crop top, jean cutoffs, and gold flip-flops. As Peanut gets closer, the girl looks up from her phone.

It's Nancee.

"You look different," Peanut says. She doesn't mean for it to come out as an accusation. It just does.

"Yeah, well, you don't," Nancee says.

Her grape toenail polish glitters in the sun.

Peanut looks down at her own pale legs and tie-dyed socks. The dark hairs on her knees look frizzier than usual, and she licks her index finger and smooths them flat.

Nancee stares. "I forgot how little you are."

Peanut rolls her shoulders back and lifts her chin so she is almost even with Nancee's shoulder. "I'm not that much shorter than you."

"I mean that you seem younger."

Peanut doesn't see why that's a bad thing. "It's the Falling Children, not the Falling Adults," she points out.

"Never mind." Nancee puts on her sunglasses, which are shaped like red hearts, as the bus pulls into view. "Forget I said anything."

Unfortunately for her, Peanut has an extremely good memory.

~

Over the next half hour, the bus winds higher into the mountains, making stops at places only tourists choose to go. A creek to pan for fool's gold. The hot springs that stink of eggs and patchouli. A campground whining with mosquitos. Little Diamond, just above the tree line, is the last stop.

Like Blue Skies, it was once a booming mining town. But when the gold dried up, the prospectors didn't stick around and open dance studios and saltwater taffy stores. They just left.

It's hard for Peanut to believe that two thousand gold miners once lived in Little Diamond. There's not much reason to come here now except to ride an ATV through the mountain pass or have a picture taken in the wooden cabin that once served as the jail. A pair of donkeys stands dolefully behind a split-rail fence, their tails flicking at flies.

"So what do we do now?" Nancee says, once the bus trundles away in a plume of exhaust. The air is colder here, the ground scratchy and dry.

"Find the saloon." Peanut heads toward a framed map of the town.

Only two streets remain of Little Diamond. Peanut sees a town hall sagging at its waist and a long-shuttered schoolhouse. Outside the general store, wind chimes and racks of aqua-colored T-shirts twist in the breeze.

Peanut finds the saloon on the map. "Come on," she says and leads Nancee, who is texting on her phone, across the wide street. Somewhere, fiddle music plays.

"Have you ever been here before?" Peanut asks.

Nancee looks up. "I dunno. Maybe when we moved here. The general store sells jelly beans, I'm pretty sure."

Tourists speaking German walk by and snap pictures.

Peanut feels her pulse quicken when she spots the slanted porch of the saloon. There is even a VESPER NESTER ALE sign in the window! She has always believed her fate is somehow linked to Everlee Falling. If she can find Everlee's parents, Peanut is convinced she will learn the fate of her own.

But the doors of the Little Diamond Saloon are locked, and the inside is dark. CLOSED BY ORDER OF THE HEALTH DEPARTMENT, a yellow sign taped to the door reads.

Peanut pulls on the door handle, unwilling to believe it.

"Why are they closed?" she cries.

A man riding by on an ATV cups his hand around his mouth. "Hepatitis outbreak, girls. If you want ice cream, go to the general store."

"Well, I guess we should go back," Nancee says, not even trying to look disappointed.

"Not so fast," Peanut says in what is truly an incredible British accent. She points to the dumpster behind the saloon. "Our work here is not done."

Unzipping her backpack, she triumphantly pulls out a pair of blue latex gloves she took from her father's clinic.

"OMG, seriously?" Nancee asks.

"I didn't come all this way to be squeamish," Peanut says, snapping on the gloves. "I came to be thorough." (Book four.)

Putting on her headlamp—actually, it's Buzz's really good camping one, which she sneaked out of the garage, but when is he going to need it?—Peanut scrambles over the side of the dumpster. If there's anything here that can help reveal her true parents, she will find it.

Nancee goes to the general store twice—once for a Popsicle, next for a pound bag of jelly beans. She eats them on the stoop, sighing loudly, while Peanut rips opens one trash bag after another.

"What are you even looking for?" Nancee calls after nearly an hour has passed.

"I don't know yet." Peanut shakes out a soggy receipt for a hot dog. "I'll know it when I see it."

Nancee goes back to her phone.

"Did you know Rosemary's family has a cabin? It isn't that far from here," she says a while later. "She invited a bunch of people over today. Even high schoolers. She's friends with everybody."

Not everybody.

Peanut bangs her fist on the side of the dumpster to get Nancee's attention. "Look, are you going to help me or not?"

"Help you do what?" Nancee pulls a black jelly bean from her mouth and throws it onto the ground. "You're just making stuff up."

Peanut doesn't like this post–female-empowerment camp attitude. Pre–female-empowerment camp Nancee would still have been sitting on the stoop eating candy, but she wouldn't have complained about it.

"It's possible my real parents are being held prisoner," Peanut says defensively. "Or they could have been given a potion that erased their memory of me. Like in book five, when Everlee forgets Benjamin and Huperzine because she's—"

Nancee makes a noise of frustration. "God! Rosemary is right. It's like you *want* to be an outcast. You are not a book character, Peanut! You are not Everlee Falling."

Peanut doesn't look up. The beam of her headlamp has found what could be a glinting shard of onyx, loosed from a magic amulet... (Book one.)

"You don't know everything about me," she tells Nancee.

"Oh yeah? I know that's not onyx. It's the jelly bean I spit out."

Peanut's scar pulls tight like it does when she's angry. "One day, I'll find my real parents," she says, "and then you'll be sorry."

"Whatever." Standing, Nancee brushes crumbs from the creases of her shorts and waves to a red SUV slowing in front of the general store. Hip-hop music and the bare arms of cool kids untangle from the windows.

Before she climbs into the back seat, Nancee turns. For a moment, Peanut thinks she's going to apologize. Then someone asks, "Dude, is that kid's face for real?"

Nancee just laughs.

6

Libby flies from the shower, her skin glassy with soap, shampoo burning her eyes. She grabs her sweaty running clothes from the bathroom floor and yanks them back on.

Her mind is lurching—she can feel it, the extension of a ladder slipping, stuttering, crashing down. Rolf is gone. *Rolf is gone.* What has she done?

The panic makes everything worse. At the front door, Libby stops and whistles for her dog. She checks every room in her apartment. Then she goes outside and calls his name.

It is a while before Libby remembers why she's wearing wet clothes. Rolf is gone.

She sends him a telepathic message. *I'm coming. Please still be there. Please.*

Somewhere inside her, the Children think she's talking to them. Cheers rise.

It's about time, Benjamin complains good-naturedly. *I'm starving.*

Are you going to wake Everlee when you come? Huperzine wants to know. *Are you going to save her?*

Not now, Libby scolds. *Not. Now.*

She runs up and down both sides of Greenwich Street, hitting the key fob for her car because she can't remember where she parked the monstrous thing.

After the first Falling Children book made the *New York Times* bestseller list, Libby allowed herself one indulgence. She bought the safest SUV on the market—a hulking something-or-other with seats that heat and cool and a dashboard that makes conversation but never seems satisfied with Libby's replies. Libby hates driving and hates the car. One day, she will donate it to charity, but not now.

She dials 911 as she heads back to the dog park on foot.

As the phone rings, Libby envisions all the terrible fates that could befall Rolf.

Children who chase and kick and throw sticks.

Animal control, where impatient strangers with rough hands will shove him into a dark locked crate and give him a new name that doesn't fit, like "Mickey."

Satanists who slice open the bellies of stray dogs at midnight and feast on their organs.

By the time a dispatcher comes on the line, Libby can barely speak above the sound of her heart.

"My dog." She swallows. "Please—my dog! He's gone!"

"Your dog was stolen, ma'am?" the dispatcher asks in a slow, reasonable voice. Libby wonders if all dispatchers have their voices tested during the hiring process. She would never pass. Her voice is reedy and full of panic. She is an eleven-year-old in a forty-year-old body.

"I don't know!" Libby is sprinting now. Her shoes are untied, her soapy hair slapping the back of her neck. "Probably. Maybe? I don't know. I left him at the dog park."

"You left him there? Ma'am, this number is for emergencies only."

"This *is* an emergency!"

Nassau Street is mobbed with college students. Libby bumps through the line snaking out the door of PJ's Pancakes, knocking one woman's copy of *The Falling Children Fall Behind* onto the sidewalk.

"Excuse you, bitch," its owner says.

Long invisible fingernails scrape Libby's chest—the beginning of a panic attack.

"This *is* an emergency," she says into her phone. "Please! I need a ride to the dog park."

"Ma'am, this is not a taxi service."

The dispatcher begins to lecture Libby on how she is preventing "real" people from getting help. Libby is desperate to hang up, lest the woman trace the call and have her arrested.

She keeps the phone to her ear as she starts to run. "Okay," she says, picking up speed. "I'm sorry. Thank you."

Even with her shoes untied, Libby makes good time. *Rolf*, she thinks with every twinge in her hamstrings. She wills him to wait for her, to not panic, to not get into a car with a stranger.

A truck honks as Libby ignores a DON'T WALK sign and darts across the last intersection.

The dog park is busier than this morning. She sees big dogs, small dogs, not-very-attractive dogs, dogs running, dogs sniffing, one dog lunging after a Frisbee. No Rolf.

The only thing in her life she cares about—the only *real* thing—is gone.

~~~

Libby spends nearly two hours combing the area, whistling and calling for Rolf and asking possible serial killers if they have seen a patient yellow Lab about yea high and very sweet.

No one has.

Twice, out of the corner of her eye, she thinks she's spotted him—on a leash, in a car—and her heart nearly explodes with joy. Then she gets closer and realizes she's seen a Rottweiler or a bag of groceries with bananas curving out the top.

Libby trudges home. She will google "how to find lost dog" and do whatever it takes to get Rolf back. She will offer her SUV as a reward. She will even preemptively reveal herself as F. T. Goldhero, although doing so means being sued for millions of dollars. Libby is wary of the idea of being a public figure, a bottomless receptacle for everyone's expectations and appraisals. But for Rolf, she will swallow them like fire. She wants him back. Even more than she wants the dementia gone.

In her haste to leave, Libby left the front door of her apartment ajar. She panics that someone walked in and stole her manuscript or is hiding under her bed, waiting to slit her throat. It takes her nearly an hour to thoroughly search the apartment, a pair of scissors in one hand, a dulled disposable razor in the other, before she feels certain she is alone.

Then she feels worse.

～～

Libby is determinedly calling every animal rescue site in the state of New Jersey when there's a knock on her door. At first, she thinks she imagined it.

No one *ever* knocks on her door. Even when Vernice was alive, she would wait downstairs for Libby.

Looking through the peephole, Libby is horrified to recognize the gray-haired reporter from the dog park, still holding his corgi.

She dials "91" on her phone before pulling open the door *this* much. Then she puts the phone to her ear and pretends she's in the middle of a conversation. "Oh yes, police. Yes."

Libby's heart jackhammers inside her chest. She wonders if this is the particular terror people feel right before they die.

It takes her a moment to realize Rolf is standing next to the man, a jump rope looped around his collar as a makeshift leash.

"Oh my God! You found him!" Libby drops to her knees and embraces her dog, burying her face into the scruff of his neck.

Rolf isn't one for demonstrations. He jumps onto the couch and circles three times before settling into his usual spot.

"You found him!" Tears stream down Libby's face. "Thank you!"

Rolf closes his eyes, exhausted, but Glenn and the corgi both look at Libby with the same hostile expression.

"You left the park without him," Glenn accuses. "He doesn't have a tag. If he weren't microchipped, he would have ended up at animal control."

"I know," Libby says, wiping her face with the sleeve of her sweatshirt. Her breath comes in little spurts, like air from a bellows. "I—was—so—worried."

"But you *left* him there," Glenn says, his voice rising. "Were you trying to abandon him? Is that why you said you lived in Hawaii? Because if you don't want him, I'm not leaving him here. Let him have a chance with a family that actually wants him."

"It was a mistake. I do want—" She looks at her dog and can't remember his name. "I've just been—sick."

Her voice shakes.

This is why Everlee Falling *never* cries. Not even when the Unstopping tried to gouge out her eyes and replace them with glass ones from a doll.

Glenn looks like he's not sure what to think. He puts his corgi down—and it can walk just fine, Libby sees, as it wanders into the kitchen and helps itself to Rolf's water bowl—and hands her a box of tissues from the coffee table.

"Things—everything—is really hard right now," Libby says, although he hasn't asked for an explanation. She wipes her nose.

"Yeah, I hear you." Glenn sighs. "My wife asked me for a divorce. Six years, we were together. She took my son and moved to the shore. Now I only get to see him twice a month. Less this fall since peewee football's starting."

"That's awful," Libby says. "Peewee" is a terrible-sounding word, the equivalent of a goose honk. She will never use it in her books.

"You have kids?" asks Glenn.

Libby lifts her shoulders. She does, doesn't she?

"Then you know how fast they grow away from you. You don't see them for a week, they become a different person."

Libby nods. "I'm sorry," she says.

Glenn gives a sour laugh. "Yeah, well, you know what they say. 'If we only lived in sunshine, we'd get soaked by the sight of storm clouds.'"

It's Libby's favorite Benjamin Falling quote, and it's an extraordinary feeling to hear his words coming out of a real person's mouth, being said to *her*.

Before she can think, *Oh no, this is a* bad *idea*, she leans over and kisses Glenn. He has stiff thin lips; it's a little like kissing a mannequin.

Libby can't remember the last time she had sex, but she is sure it was like this: sudden and awkward, and she started it.

"Well" is all Glenn says afterward.

He disappears into the bathroom. Libby swipes her hand across the floor, collecting chains of dust between her fingers.

Rolf opens his eyes and studies her.

"I will find you a good home, I promise," Libby tells him.

She's unsure how much time passes before she realizes Glenn hasn't returned. The corgi—what's its name? She can only come up with "Shorty"—is curled up peacefully next to Rolf.

Is it possible that she has two dogs, one that she doesn't like all that much?

How many dogs do I look like I have? she rehearses asking Glenn. But after rounding the corner into the hallway, Libby stops. Glenn is standing in the doorway to her office.

He is staring, his mouth agape, his leather belt still unbuckled.

For a moment, she sees it through his eyes: the pencil sketches of the Falling Children at every age; hundreds of neon-pink and purple Post-its, each listing a plot point for book six, covering the walls; the obsessively detailed map of the OtherWay; boxes of fan mail; and open half-empty packages of Red Vines... Has she been *eating* them?

Please F. T. Goldhero, finish the book!

Where are the Children?

"This isn't what it looks like," Libby says.

Unfortunately, that's exactly what Everlee would say.

7

Peanut is so stung by Nancee's departure that she loses track of time. She waits at the bus stop, pacing with her arms crossed like Everlee does when she's betrayed (books one through five) before it occurs to her: she's the only one waiting.

The sky is the color of a soft potato. Every now and then, a gust of wind slaps the back of Peanut's neck.

"Do you know when the next bus is?" she asks the woman pulling racks of T-shirts inside the general store.

"No more today." The woman stares at Peanut's scar, then quickly looks away. "It's Sunday."

"Sunday?" Peanut repeats.

The woman makes a sound of impatience. "No more bus," she says loudly, holding her hands like stop signs. "No more. Bus all done."

She disappears inside the store, slamming the door and flipping a CLOSED sign.

"You don't have to act like a bone grocer," Peanut mutters. It's a Falling Children reference that Nancee would appreciate—if Nancee were still there.

For lack of a better plan, Peanut decides to walk home. The mountain road is steeper on foot. Her sneakers slip on the pea-sized gravel, and she's forced to take baby steps to keep from falling. At the first hairpin curve, Peanut peeks over the side of the mountain. All she can see are pine trees. The town of Blue Skies is miles away, thousands of feet down.

The longer she walks, the more certain Peanut becomes that everything that's happened today is not Nancee's fault but Jessie's.

Jessie should have let her get a phone years ago. Instead, Peanut is walking eight miles home alone. She's no closer to finding her real parents. And (she looks up at the blackened sky) it's about to storm. A Jeep with a Texas license plate roars around the curve, spraying gravel at Peanut's legs.

"Jack-in-the-box balls!" she yells.

In her head, she taps furiously on a keyboard:

Dear Mr. Goldhero,

I am writing to inform you that as of one hour ago, I no longer have a best friend. Or any friends at all, except for Everlee, Benjamin and Huperzine Falling. I am also madder than I have ever been at Jessie, a.k.a. Queen of the Bone Grocers. Would you kindly let me know if you have any jobs for children in the castle where I assume you live?

Here's what I can do VERY well:

1. Write. (As you know, since I send you stories all the time.)

2. Proofread spelling errers.

3. Dust. (I don't like to, but I will.)

4. Weed gardens if you tell me what flowers to keep.

5. Read. (For instance, I could help you read your fan mail because I'm sure you get tons.)

Also, I do not take up a lot of space, eat very much, or need to be told to wake up in the morning.

Most importantly, I am excellent company (despite what SOME people may think).

~·~

The clouds have torn open by the time Peanut reaches the turnoff for Lake Salida, still five miles outside Blue Skies. Rain beats at her shoulders and drips into her eyes.

To distract herself, Peanut sings as loudly as she can:

O Williwig, O Williwig,
We pledge to stay by thee.
Through life and death or souls bereft,
We'll fight. We'll never flee.

As she starts the next, lesser-known verse of the Williwig anthem, Peanut realizes a car has quietly hummed onto the narrow shoulder beside her. She stops singing when she realizes it's an old dark hearse with fins that remind her of bat wings.

C U Soon the front license plate reads.

It is exactly like the car the Unstopping—the Children's sworn enemy—drives.

The driver's window slides down.

"You look like you need a ride," someone says.

The driver is wearing a hooded sweatshirt, so Peanut can't see his face.

"Things are only going to get worse," he says when she doesn't answer.

Popcorn-sized hail drops from the sky. Sharp bits of ice nick Peanut's cheeks.

"Where you headed?"

"Blue Skies," Peanut answers, holding her arms over her head. She has to shout to be heard over the weather.

The passenger door flicks open. "Get in."

Peanut doesn't move. She's not supposed to take rides from strangers. But the rain is coming steadily, and Peanut's clothes and shoes are soaked through. Lightning scratches the sky, and she can hear her teeth chatter.

She takes a step closer to the car. The leather seat inside looks comfortable and dry.

Don't you dare, Jessie warns inside Peanut's head. *Peanut Bixton, you will be in so much troub—*

Peanut doesn't give the voice a chance to finish. It's Jessie's fault that she's in this mess.

I have bear spray, she thinks—in a British accent, like Everlee uses when she's trying not to feel scared—and climbs in.

The driver is dressed in loose black pants and a baggy gray sweatshirt with frayed sleeves. Stringy hair juts out from under his hood. On each of his fingers is a thick silver ring bearing a crow talon.

Like the Unstopping.

When he catches Peanut staring, the man clicks his rings together to make a strange, sour sound. Then he adjusts the vents so musty air blows into her face and she has to look away.

The car slides around two, then three switchbacks.

"How long you lived in BS?" the man asks.

"Forever," says Peanut. "I was entrusted there as a baby."

She likes that this story is part of her. Yes, it's twisted and sad, but it's also intriguing. She wasn't just born in a hospital like everyone else. She was *found.*

"I was secreted away in an earthen cave behind the library," Peanut explains. She uses her most captivating voice. "Two teenagers walking by heard my pitiful cries that fateful August night. They shoveled dirt away, and there I was, weak and bleeding—but alive. 'Small as a peanut,' that's what my brother said. I was in an incubator in the hospital for sixty-two days."

The man glances over, but the rain outside prevents Peanut from seeing the features of his face. "Someone fucking buried you alive?"

"No," Peanut says impatiently. Adults never understand this story on the first try. "Someone *put* me in the ground for safekeeping. I'm destined for greatness," she adds.

"That scar on your face, too?"

"Yes." Peanut can tell he's testing her. "I believe it's how my real parents will recognize me."

She runs her fingertips over the toughened skin on her cheek. It's the first thing anyone notices about her. Why else would it be there?

"Funny coincidence that your story's just like Everlee Falling," the man says.

Peanut shrugs. "Maybe Everlee Falling's story is just like mine."

The driver lets out a bitter laugh. "Like a wise man once said, we become the stories we tell ourselves."

"It wasn't a *wise* man," Peanut corrects. "The Unstopping says it in book three."

"You don't think he's wise?" the driver asks. "That's because you're only, what, eight?"

"I'm eleven." Peanut sits up straighter. "But I'd think that no matter what age I was."

They pass the Boggy Creek farm stand and a billboard for Mr. Mandelbrot's organ lessons, although he's been dead for years.

"Why are you going to Blue Skies?" she asks.

The driver doesn't answer right away. They pass two more mile markers before he says, "Let's call it a life-or-death situation."

"Have you ever been there before?"

"BS High, class of 2005."

That's a year before Jessie (barely) graduated.

"Jessica Bixton? Now there's a name I haven't heard in years." He strokes his chin. "She ever talk about Orson?"

Peanut knows everyone in town, including the names of their horses and what they say to their prized pumpkins to make them grow faster. She's never heard of an Orson.

"Yeah?" Orson looks over. "I bet you've heard of the Murder House and how I killed my dad and left his sorry ass on the porch on Halloween night."

A drop of rain—or is it sweat?—rolls into the hollow of Peanut's neck.

"So that's—I mean, those stories—they're real?"

At the traffic light in front of the Shoe Fly, the hearse rolls to a stop. A red glow soaks into the car.

"Oh, they're real, all right," the man says. Leaning closer, he slowly traces a fingertip over her scar, considering something. "You, I'm not so sure about."

Under the streetlights, his face inches from hers, Peanut can finally see under the hood of his sweatshirt. She can make out translucent skin, sunken cheekbones, and eyes as black as buttons. And not just an eye on either side of his nose. Peanut inhales sharply. She is sure that she sees dozens of eyes embedded in his cheeks and forehead and neck—like the Unstopping.

As the car begins to move again, Peanut throws open the door and hurls herself out. She lands in the gutter, her knees smacking the concrete.

"Hey! What the hell are you doing?"

Peanut doesn't answer. Tearing down Second Street, pumping her arms at her sides, she splashes through puddles chilled from the storm. This is not the same cozy downtown she saw this morning with her father. The dark entrance of each store gapes like a mouth. The alleys reek of skunk. Where is everyone?

"Come back here!"

What if he doesn't only look like the Unstopping? What if he *is* the Unstopping? Hands shaking, Peanut unzips her backpack, pulls out the bear spray, and releases the safety lever.

They're real all right. You, I'm not so sure about.

Peanut barrels up the steep concrete steps that lead to her neighborhood. Does he think she's lying about being left for dead as a baby? That she willed this ugly scar on her cheek, a perfect half-moon of a shovel blade, into existence?

At the top of the staircase, Peanut glances over her shoulder. No one is there. But as she turns toward home, someone grabs her arm.

"Watch it!"

Squeezing her eyes shut, Peanut presses the trigger on her bear spray. Too late, she realizes it's not the Unstopping. It's her brother.

Buzz doubles over, coughing and gagging. The paper sack of groceries he's carrying drops to the ground. Apples, a party-size bag of Flamin' Hot Dill Pickle potato chips, and dozens of candy bars scatter over the wet road.

"What the fuck." He swipes at his eyes.

"He was chasing me!" The bear spray needles Peanut's lungs. "I jumped out of his car, and now he's chasing me!"

She sprints back to the stairs to look over the railing.

"What are you talking about?" Buzz scoops water from a puddle and splashes it into his eyes.

"The Unstopping! From the books! He's real!" Peanut swipes at her nose. "I don't know how, but he is! He's alive, and I—I think he's here for me! And the eyes? I saw them! All the eyes from his victims. He ate their souls, and now they're trapped inside him for eternity!"

Buzz tries to say something but is interrupted by another coughing fit.

"He wasn't going to stop the car. And then he didn't think my scar was real, so he *touched* it, and I had to jump out and run, and now he's coming after me!"

As Peanut babbles, she realizes how unlikely this sounds, like someone recounting a bad dream. It also occurs to her how awful her brother looks, and not only because she's doused him with bear spray. His brown hair falls into his eyes and stubble covers his chin. Under his (now swollen) eyes are gray lines, and then there is the heavy splint that covers his right leg from calf to hip and the cane he uses to pull himself up.

"No one's coming after you." Buzz limps toward an apple beginning to roll downhill. He isn't fast enough, and it trundles out of sight.

"How do you know?"

"Because nothing happens in this town," he says, splashing more water in his eyes. "Except for whatever shit you make up."

Peanut hears a tapping noise and realizes her teeth are chattering.

"But he was creepy! He had all these crow talons on his fingers and big, baggy clothes like he was hiding something underneath. He told me the Murder House was real, that he *did* kill his dad and leave him out for the trick-or-treaters!"

That gets Buzz's attention. "You got a ride with Orson Greeley?"

"He's not Orson anymore. He's the Unstopping. Are you not listening to me?"

"No. Now would you go home already? Who was baked enough to give you bear spray anyway?"

Peanut picks up a candy bar still lying in the gutter. It's soggy, but she knows Buzz will eat it anyway. "You were, last Christmas, although you didn't give it to me until February, and it wasn't even wrapped."

She expects Buzz to have a comeback—*Be glad you got anything*, maybe—but he is already limping toward home.

"What does the Unstopping want with me?" Peanut asks, following him. "Do you think he knows I'm a close confidante of F. T. Goldhero? Because if so, he may want to crack open my soul like a clam and suck out the juicy part."

In the Falling Children books, this is called "wherewithal." The more imagination someone has, the richer and juicier it is.

"And I have a *lot* of juice," she tells Buzz.

"No shit. Now go inside." He starts across the lawn to his house, hoisting the broken bag of groceries to his other arm. "And stay away from Orson Greeley."

"But what if he really is the Unstopping?" Peanut calls after him. "Then we need to confront him!"

"Like the bone dudes you thought you saw at the Fourth of July parade?" Buzz asks without turning around. "Or the time you had me take all the stuffed animals out of your room because you were sure one of them had gone 'rogue'?" He uses air quotes. "Or the—"

"They're bone grocers. Not dudes. F. T. Goldhero would never say, 'bone dudes.'"

"Whatever."

The freedom Buzz has—to buy a zillion candy bars at the grocery store, to go months without turning on his lights, to completely *embarrass* Peanut with childish memories after she's come face-to-face with the Unstopping (maybe)—infuriates her. She doesn't care if Buzz is twenty-six and she's only eleven.

"You're not supposed to curse in front of me, and you just said the s-word and the f-word approximately a million times!" she shouts after him. "And since you got home from the hospital, I've given you premier access to my prize-winning stories and tried to keep you company, and you haven't even said '*thank you.*' Even if you didn't see the Unstopping with your own eyes, methinks, kind sir, that you should believe something uncanny is unfolding in our wee pretty crook of the universe!"

(Book five, last page, last paragraph, last line.)

"Oh, I believe all right," Buzz says, and Peanut hears his front door slam closed, just as Jessie—furious, her eyes blazing, not in the mood to listen—opens theirs.

8

Two days later, Glenn appears at Libby's front door. He says he was "in the area."

"So, what's going on here?" He cranes his neck to look into her apartment. "Anything interesting?" And then in a lower voice, he adds, "Is he here?"

"No."

Libby is holding her laptop. She snaps it closed so he can't see the article up on the screen: 7 SOLUTIONS FOR STAYING STRONG WITH EARLY ALZHEIMER'S, it's called. She resents the breezy alliteration of each subhead. *Always stay active! Do things day by day!* Libby can't remember the others.

It's hard to tell how much Glenn believes her story of being a personal assistant to F. T. Goldhero, not with the way his eyes search for clues.

"What's he like?" Glenn wants to know. He nudges past her into the apartment, setting down his corgi. "I picture a distinguished gentleman with white hair—you know, a Richard Harris type."

"You should go," Libby says. She doesn't like the way he touches her things, like items in a store he has no intent to buy.

"What's this for?" Glenn picks up the small red notebook Libby left on the couch. To Save, the cover reads.

He starts to flip through it. "Is there stuff in here for the next book?"

"That's mine." Libby reaches for the journal, but Glenn has already dropped it and is staring at the sketch pad lying open on the coffee table.

Blue Skies, Libby wrote on one page. She doodled what the town might look like: whimsically named stores surrounded by trees and mountains, a hilly park with a pond, Victorian homes with stained glass doors and porch swings.

"You from here?" Glenn asks.

"No." Libby pulls the paper to her chest. "Mr. Goldhero has—a friend there."

"How did you even get this job?" Glenn steps closer, rubbing the Peter Pan collar of her white shirt between his fingers. "And what's up with the schoolgirl outfit? Does he make you wear a uniform?"

"No." Libby worries Glenn has asked these questions before. If so, she can't remember how she answered.

"Have you thought some more about giving me an interview? You could be famous."

Libby makes a face. "I don't want to be famous."

Her phone beeps.

Donate brain to dementia research is the reminder.

It's a joke, right?

"You should go," she tells Glenn, smoothing her hair. "I have a—thing."

He takes his time walking to the door.

"I'm not giving up," he says before he leaves. "I'm going to be the one to break this story."

As if Libby's life is an egg.

"F. T. Goldhero is a beloved author," Glenn goes on. "People deserve to know who he is. He can't stay hidden for the rest of his life."

"You'd be surprised," Libby says.

She shuts and locks the door.

～•～

Later, though, she isn't sure this is an accurate memory.

One, because she is not an assertive person. (If she were, she never would have signed such a rotten contract with Groton & Sons.)

Two, because later that day, Libby gets a text from Glenn. She doesn't remember giving him her number.

Three, the text reads, *You won't be sorry trust me.*

She squints at the emoji he's included, not sure if it's an eggplant or a rutabaga. Did she agree to sleep with Glenn again? It's disturbing that this is the best-case scenario. But Libby's palms are sweaty. It's as if her body knows what her brain has forgotten.

Somewhere, a giant sand timer has turned over. (Much like the oversize hourglass in book three.) If Libby doesn't start—and finish—writing soon, the Falling Children will stay trapped forever. And who knows how long she has before her brain turns to mush instead of mushy around the edges?

Libby has seen Dr. Whatsit twice more. Each time he's refused to tell her.

"I don't have an exact date," he says, washing his hands in the exam room sink although he never touches her.

"Can you guess?" Libby wants to know. "Please? If you're wrong, I won't remember."

"We don't have real answers yet, Libby," he says, drying his hands with a towel. "Everyone is different. Try to take things day by day."

She *is* trying. Every day, for eight, nine, ten, eleven hours, Libby sits in front of her computer and stares at the screen. Her fingers curl over the keys, waiting for inspiration.

She isn't sure how much harder she can try.

～～

Reluctantly, Libby fills the prescription Dr. Whatsit gives her. She is reluctant because he admits he has "mixed feelings" about this particular drug, which may help lessen her symptoms. "Let's see how you do" is what he says, handing her the blue slip. His handwriting looks like a rat stepped in ink, then scuttled across the page.

"I will tell you," he goes on, "some of my patients do experience severe side effects."

He lists them on his fingers: Diarrhea. Vomiting. Hallucinations. Insomnia.

"Still," he says as he leaves the exam room, "it can't hurt."

But it does. Once the drug gets into her system, Libby's brain feels hijacked. She sees Vernice's ghost in the kitchen, cracking open a can of Dr Pepper. And when the UPS driver comes each evening, dropping another heavy box in front of her door, Libby hits the floor and covers her head, sure a bomb has gone off.

She spends several nights awake, listening to shopping carts rumbling by on the sidewalk and the *tick-tick-tick* of the WALK sign on the corner. Fused together, they sound like a burglar breaking into her apartment. Libby spends another two days curled on the bathroom floor, exhausted and retching into the toilet.

Is the medicine protecting the still-healthy parts of her brain? Does it matter if she's otherwise incapacitated?

Once she's able to detach herself from the cold fat neck of the toilet, Libby hurls Dr. Whatsit's pills into the trash. But the insomnia and nausea don't immediately disappear. And the following night, when she finds herself tossing and turning in bed so vehemently that Rolf actually growls at her to stop, Libby gives up. Wrapping herself in one of Vernice's blankets, she goes into her office and sits at her desk.

On her computer, the Falling Children website, with its state-of-the-art animation, lights up like a carnival. There is a lush, interactive rendering of Pompou's four-story Toy Emporium, with its funny thatched roof and arched windows that serve as its eyes. Children around the world click in and out of the cozy rooms that evoke Santa's workshop if the Mad Hatter had been in charge. Visitors can design a stuffed animal that best houses their soul, help Benjamin make a pan of magical fudge (hoozleberry or buttered licorice?), learn to curse in Teddy Bear, or take a quiz that declares which Falling Child they're most like.

Libby has taken this quiz four times, three times intentionally lying, and each time she has been dubbed a Huperzine.

She scrolls through the news feed.

Red Vine Rallies, in which fans dress up like Falling Children characters and urge F. T. Goldhero to finish the last book, are taking place across the globe. Libby watches a live stream of one at the San Francisco Zoo. The "Children" are her age, wearing extravagant costumes and singing karaoke while a group of chimpanzees looks on, terrified. She will not finish the book faster for them.

The billionaire pig farmer from Texas swears he's "knee-deep in incriminatin' pig shit" when it comes to unveiling F. T. Goldhero.

This would make Libby more nervous if he didn't repeatedly refer to F. T. Goldhero as "the Most Wanted *Man* in the World."

She scrolls through the message boards.

So pissed at FT stop making us wait u sadist!

I used to love FT but damm I could use a million bucks...

Remember, Time2AnteUp has written, I know how the Falling Children should end.

"Sure you do," Libby mutters. "Because it's just so easy."

Still, she props her chin on her fist and reads the new story Time2AnteUp has posted. It's not bad.

In fact, it's very, very good.

If the Unstopping were real, of *course* he would have grown up in a doll hospital. And killed his father and run away from home, only to return on a stormy night more than ten years later.

Yaaaas queen, reads one comment. Gave me chills.

U sure you're not FT lol?!?!?

Libby crafts a snippy response in her head. *As F. T. Goldhero's personal assistant, I assure you this was definitely NOT written by everyone's favorite author who has spent the last four years eating, sleeping, and breathing the Falling Children and, as a result, has no life beyond them.*

Which gives her an idea.

Honestly, it's the best one she's had in days, aside from eating peanut butter right from the jar so she doesn't need to go to the store for more bread.

The sun is spreading outside Libby's office window by the time she finishes the email. Looking at the symbols on her keyboard, Libby is momentarily unsure that she remembers how to hit Send.

She hopes that isn't a sign.

To: <Time2AnteUp@blueskiesfamilymedicine.net>
From: <iamlibbyweeks@gmail.com>
Subject: URGENT: From the confidential desk of Mr. F. T. Goldhero

Dear "Time2AnteUp"—
Allow me to introduce myself. I am the personal assistant to Mr. F. T. Goldhero.

Mr. Goldhero has asked me to discreetly reach out to a select handful of fans around the world for their predictions about the last and final book of the Falling Children. What do you think will happen, especially in the last 5 chapters?

He is curious to see your ideas, as clearly thought out as possible. What fates await not just Everlee, Benjamin, and Huperzine, but minor characters?

As you can imagine, Mr. Goldhero works very efficiently. He has the books mapped out to the very last detail (as all writers do) and is nearly done, of course. This is simply a heartfelt gesture to listen to Mr. Goldhero's biggest fans.

We do hope you will participate. Because of the mystery surrounding the book, we will need you to sign and return the attached document. It states that you will NOT mention or share this letter with anyone...and if you do, a wagon of cranky Williwigs may show up at your house and throw bowls of cold bitter hookroot porridge at your door! (And you and your family will be liable for a substantial fine, which is more money than most human beings make in a lifetime.)

Thank you for your speedy reply. I look forward to hearing from you in the near future.

STEPHANIE BOOTH

En toys speramus,

Libby Weeks

Personal assistant to F. T. Goldhero

9

"There," Libby sits back in her chair and calls to the Children. "I'm going to get you out of there. Really. This time, for sure."

There is no response from the forest where she has left them trapped by the Unstopping—only the occasional whimper of a thirsty forgotten tree. Even the stream has dried to a bloody crust.

Dr. Whatsit is there, too, taking notes on his computer.

"The Children. They won't let me in," Libby tells him, trying to explain. She is embarrassed that she has dragged him into her imagination. "But maybe someone else can; does that make sense?"

I can tell it's important to you, says Dr. Whatsit.

Libby has not yet told the Children that she is sick. Or wants to die. She doesn't want them to think it's their fault, although surely, they know something is wrong. She has caught them sneaking sideways glances at one another—when she accidentally referred to the Unstopping as the "Unmoving" for an entire chapter, for instance, or forgot Everlee's allergy to shellfish and had her wolf down a plate of clams.

Libby wonders where the Children are and what they overhear when she is at the doctor's office.

I will only share with others what you authorize me to, says Dr. Whatsit.

Libby authorizes nothing. But they can't be underestimated, those Children.

She hopes they know in their make-believe hearts that she would never abandon them. Not on purpose anyway.

10

Peanut spends the next few days lying on her back in the tree house behind Buzz's house. If she half closes her eyes and stares into the leafy green canopy above her, she can pretend she's in the dome-shaped garden at the tip-top of Pompou's. At any moment, Huperzine will burst in, asking a question about solar plexes, the hibernation stuffed animals enter when they're placed directly in the sun. Or Benjamin, his mouth buckling with Sweet Tarts, asking, "*Wmant wmone?*"

Imagining the Falling Children is all Peanut can do since she's grounded. Jessie punished her for hitchhiking by taking away not only her measly allotment of screen time but her Falling Children books. That includes the audiobooks read by a famous British actor. His Huperzine is lispier than it should be, but his Benjamin is perfect.

"I need those!" Peanut shouted as Jessie yanked the books, one by one, off Peanut's shelf. "They're my wherewithal!"

Jessie didn't understand the reference.

"My sustenance," Peanut had to explain. "My lifeline. They feed my soul."

"Then you should have thought of that before you decided to hitchhike," Jessie said. "You are a *child.*"

Bracing the tower of books with her chin, Jessie swept past Peanut and out the room. "One day, you'll thank me," she said.

That time is not now.

Despite the kiln-like heat of the tree house, Peanut takes out a piece of paper and pen.

Dear Mr. Goldhero,

Two important things have happened since my last letter.

1. Late last night, when everyone in my house was sleeping, I posted a new story about the Unstopping to your website. But I think you should know: it's not fiction. What you read REALLY happened. The Unstopping is here, in my town.

(Or well, he COULD be.)

As you'll see from my story, I successfully escaped him— for now.

2. Jessie, aka No Better than a Bone Grocer, has grounded me for "hitchhiking." I have tried to explain how LUCKY I was to have gotten away, yet she has never read your books plus has zero imagination.

I am not the same without the Falling Children! I know you feel the same way.

PS. As a very strange coincidence, the Unstopping says he went to high school with my sister! What do you think that means?

When Peanut rereads her letter, she wonders if Nancee *has* been overtaken by the Unstopping. She and Peanut have had plenty of arguments over the years, but Nancee has always eventually conceded that Peanut is right. Peanut has a nightstand full of Falling

Children drawings, rainbow loom bracelets, and homemade slime to prove it.

But this time, Nancee hasn't dropped off a peace offering. It's been two days, a record that makes Peanut's stomach feel like a bull's-eye. Tomorrow is their first day of junior high. For the first time in six years, Peanut will walk into school alone.

She traces the scar on her cheek. It starts just under her eyelashes and curves to her mouth.

I'm real all right, the Unstopping told her. *You, I'm not so sure about.*

Peanut sees her brother limp onto his back porch. Although it's late afternoon, Buzz is still in a T-shirt and boxers. He leans on the railing, considering something. Then, as Peanut watches from her perch, he drains the beer he's holding, hurls the green bottle into the woods, and uses the f-word.

"Hey!" Peanut shouts. "That's littering! And you're not supposed to curse around me."

Buzz looks up, startled. He makes a noise that sounds like the f-word again, then limps back into his house and slams the door.

~~~

When Jessie calls her to set the table for dinner, Peanut agrees only because she wants her books back.

And "desperate difficulties call for devious measures," as Everlee likes to say.

Still, Peanut doesn't speak to Jessie, even when they sit across from each other at the table. And she only doles out one-syllable words to her father, since she resents him for going along with Jessie's cruel and unusual punishment.

The only person Peanut does acknowledge is their neighbor. Buzz and Jessie call her Mrs. Halfchap since she always wears leather chaps but doesn't own a horse.

"An old mare once said they'd slim my calves, and she was right" is how Mrs. Halfchap explains it. She gave up a career as a lawyer to become an animal communicator, but *perplexingly*, as Everlee would say, none of the animals she's communicated with bothered to mention that her husband had kidney cancer.

Peanut's father calls animal telepathy "woo-woo science." He doesn't care what cats think and says no horse should dare tell him how to dress. Yet every time he goes to check on Mr. Halfchap, he insists Mrs. Halfchap come for dinner.

"Dying is hardest on the people watching it happen," Peanut's father says.

Mrs. Halfchap is hard of hearing, but Peanut doesn't mind. Mrs. Halfchap is a fan of the Falling Children, too, so at least Peanut has a *peer* to speak with.

"Did you hear how I escaped the Unstopping?" Peanut asks Mrs. Halfchap as Jessie slices the pork roast. "He's real."

"Not this again," Jessie says.

Mrs. Halfchap looks from Peanut to Jessie. "Who's real, sweet thing?"

"Nobody," Jessie says loudly. "Peanut's making up stories."

I wish I made you up, Peanut thinks.

"I love a good romance," Mrs. Halfchap says brightly. "Even a tragic one, like the Unstopping and Lucy Parker."

In book three, it was revealed that the Unstopping was once a quiet boy who'd fallen in love with a carousel maker able to carve uncertain magic from single blocks of wood. Lucy Parker was the Unstopping's exact opposite—"the human equivalent of a sunny spring day"—and always surrounded by lifelike painted horses bedecked with ribbons and jewels. When Lucy's conscience became infected with a spell that threatened to turn her into a cruel and heinous villain, the Unstopping selflessly gave her his. He took her sick one instead (because no one can live without a conscience) and tried to keep the evil at bay by pinning it to the lapel of his tailcoat. Still, it turned him *really* evil. And then Lucy, who was about to have his baby, died anyway.

"It gives me goose bumps every time I think about it," Mrs. Halfchap says, wiping her eyes. "Two unlikelys secretly falling in love against the odds."

Peanut's father clears his throat. "For pity's sake, girl"—he turns to Jessie—"must you douse every meal in sodium chloride?"

"What's that?" Mrs. Halfchap cups her ear.

"We all need to be on the lookout for the Unstopping." Peanut points to the raised red flag on the mailbox outside. "He's gaining strength. I can feel it. I'm sending an official warning to F. T. Goldhero."

"That's who you should be on the lookout for," Jessie says, looking at their father as she vigorously salts her food. "Find that F.T. freak so we can get a million bucks."

"He's not a freak." Peanut scowls.

Their father pulls the shaker from Jessie's hand. "Well, whoever or whatever he is, with a bounty that large, the mysterious Mr. Goldhero can't stay hidden much longer."

"For a million bucks?" says Jessie. "*I'd* turn him in for half that."

She looks around the kitchen, and Peanut follows her gaze: the strawberries worn thin on the kitchen wallpaper, a duct-taped lamp on the counter, the chipped yellow linoleum, and the rip in the screen door.

"Yes," their father says, "I imagine you would."

Jessie puts down her fork. "What's that supposed to mean?"

Mrs. Halfchap looks around the table, smiling. "Who says what, dearie?"

When the kitchen phone rings, Peanut races to answer it. "Hello?"

In case it's Nancee, she makes her voice sound both busy and impatient.

No one is there.

"Hello?" Peanut says again.

This time there's a muffled sound, like someone's trying to speak but has a hand clamped over their mouth.

Peanut is about to hang up when an old, frail voice asks, "Pandora Bixton?"

"Yes?"

"Do you know who this is?"

"No."

The voice drops to a whisper. "Why, but you've been searching for me for years."

Without thinking, Peanut touches her scar.

"I've been waiting." The woman starts to cry. "Waiting for the right time to tell you the truth. About me. About you. About—us."

Peanut has dreamed of this moment her whole life. Now that it's happening, she feels lifted out of her body. She floats to the ceiling and looks down at the dining room table, where Jessie and her father are arguing. Mrs. Halfchap is watching their lips, trying to follow along.

"Do you want to know the truth? Why you were left for dead?"

Peanut nods, pressing the receiver tightly to her ear.

"Deep down, I think you already know. Listen to me." There's a choking sound on the other end of the phone. Peanut's mother struggles to speak. "You have always been—"

Special. Magical. Powerful.

"Say it," breathes Peanut.

"A little loser *freak!*"

It takes Peanut a moment to process the words, to close her mouth and blink her eyes, and then another few seconds to recognize two distinct howls of laughter coming from the phone.

One she knows by heart.

"Nancee! This is your meanest prank ever."

"So?" Nancee says, still laughing. "You got me grounded! Jessie called my mom and said I ditched you. And then my mom called Rosemary's mom, so *she* got in trouble."

"Shaming people about their birth isn't funny. It's—shaming!"

Nancee hesitates, like she may be about to apologize. Then Peanut hears the phone switch off speaker mode.

"Stop trying to guilt us," Rosemary says. "You brought this on yourself. And if you don't stay away from us? We'll bury your ugly ass again."

There's a gasp from the background. Nancee squeals, "I can't believe you really said it!" and the call ends.

Peanut's left holding the receiver, Rosemary's words beating in her head as fast as the dial tone.

Jessie comes into the kitchen, carrying a stack of plates mounded with uneaten pork roast. "What did Nancee do now?"

"Nothing."

"You don't look like it was nothing."

Peanut doesn't feel like arguing. Or standing there while Jessie tries to guess what's wrong.

"Is this about me calling her mom? Because she was mad at Nancee already."

"I don't feel good," Peanut says, and lucky for her, Mrs. Halfchap hears that and clucks from the dining room, "A little bird was just telling me a storm is on the way."

~~~

In her bedroom, Peanut automatically reaches for her bookshelf, but her Falling Children books—even the extra copy of book two she found at a yard sale, the pages scribbled over with orange crayon—are gone. Instead, she gathers an armload of stuffed animals—her favorite three bears, a stuffed toucan, a monkey, and two small brown dogs—and squeezes them tightly as she curls up on her bed.

It's what Everlee does when she finds out the truth, that toys aren't playthings. Inside each is the soul of a dead person—villains, abusers, killers, and thieves—who are too damaged to be reincarnated and released into the world. Mr. Pompou safely hid them away until they learned to love. For some souls, that takes *centuries.*

When Everlee holds the toys against her heart and whispers *"pax vobis"*—"You're safe" in Latin—their souls grow lighter. But thinking about Nancee and Rosemary and school starting tomorrow, Peanut feels weighted with dread.

~~~

Peanut's father knocks on her bedroom door much later, long after she's given up hope that anyone would.

"There's always a 'lie' in what we believe, an 'if' in life, and an 'end' in friends," he says. He fills the doorway of her room but doesn't step inside.

Peanut stares at her empty shelves. "That doesn't make me feel better."

"I'm not trying to make you feel better. I'm dispensing advice."

"I don't want to go to junior high. It's not going to teach me any-thing I want to know."

She expects her father to say, *I do lots of things I don't want to do*, a phrase that usually ends in a story about pinworms, but he surprises her.

"Well," he says, fishing his hand into his suit pocket, "maybe this will help."

Historically, Peanut's father does not give gifts—not good ones anyway. For birthdays, she gets something from his supply closet, like a handful of eczema cream samples.

Peanut does not have eczema.

But this time, he hands her a smartphone. Peanut cradles it in her palm like a baby bird. It's the most grown-up thing she's ever owned.

Pushing the home button, she's surprised to see an old photo of her, Buzz, and Jessie at the lake.

Peanut looks up at her father. "You're giving me Jessie's phone?"

"I'll have someone at the office wipe it clean, and you can have it after school tomorrow."

Although a tiny portion of Peanut feels guilty, the rest of her resists the urge to laugh, or clap, or at least thrust her fist into the air and shout, *Vin-di-ca-tion!*

"What did Jessie say when you took it?" she can't help asking. "Is she fuming mad? Did you see sparks shoot from her heart and hurtle toward you at the speed of a thousand wind-up cars?" (Huperzine, fed up in book one.)

Peanut can't make out her father's expression.

"No one said parenting was easy," he says and shuts off her light.

11

Gnawing her thumbnail, Libby refreshes her inbox again. She can't understand it. Her email was, if she does say so herself, intriguing.

True, her goal is to steal—no, Libby points a finger at Rolf as if *he's* accused her of this and needs to be schooled—she prefers "be inspired by"—this random child's stories. So why hasn't the random child replied?

Libby goes to the kitchen for a piece of toast, then sees a knife in the sink already stippled with peanut butter.

YOU ALREADY ATE BREAKFAST! she scribbles on a Post-it note, so furiously that the pen rips the paper. She slaps the accusation onto her forearm. But the air is hot and sticky because Libby may have accidentally broken her air conditioner again. The square of paper sails off her arm and onto the floor.

Libby sits again at her desk and rereads the email she, "F. T. Goldhero's personal assistant," wrote. Any fan would be thrilled to receive it.

She scrolls through the Falling Children forum again to see if there's another prolific fan she can contact. There's no shortage of passion and enthusiasm, but nobody knows the Children as well as Time2AnteUp.

AnteUp4God thinks the books mean that Satan's coming

soon. FaChiAI keeps posting, Benjamin's a robot yall just wait. TheeeSeXpert only posts graphic stories about Everlee losing her virginity.

Dozens of new conversations are not so much about the Children as F. T. Goldhero. Fans are forming small armies—Electric Love, Pompous and Circumstance, the Grrreat Williwig Brigade—to find him and split the million-dollar prize.

One new query makes Libby's palms prick cold: Journalist seeks interviews with employees of F.T. Goldhero.

As loyal fans, it reads, you deserve the truth.

Do you know someone who works for the world's most reclusive author? Do you clean his pool? Gas up his private jet? My DMs are open. All tips confidential.

Replies pop up on the screen like moles in a carnival game.

Me wanna read, someone writes.

Itz about time I'm fucking sick of this secrety shit

KIDNAP F.T. AND MAKE HIM FUCKING WRITE TIL HIS FINGERS BLEED

Chewing her cuticle until it does weep blood, Libby returns to the Sent folder of her inbox and searches for her email to the child whose name she's now forgetting. She will send a follow-up note, letting them know to reply ASAP or this incredible honor will be lost and F. T. Goldhero will be forced to reach out to *another* lucky fan. "Competition puts spurs to every horse," as Gran Bere liked to say.

Before Libby killed off Gran Bere.

But the email is not in Libby's Sent folder. Or her inbox. Panicked, she digs through her real trash just in case. It's not there either.

Libby rests her head on the counter. All the things she has to do—and soon, right away, now—pelt her like stones:

Save the children.

Find Rolf a new home.

Give her money to charity.

Take her life.

Save, find, give, take.

She repeats the instructions in her mind—*save, find, give, take*—then tattoos them in Sharpie on her forearm.

Libby is so distracted by her handiwork that she forgets to keep looking for the lost email. It is another two days—and two dozen texts from Glenn, which include both pleas to come over and vague threats ("the truth is going to come out one way or another")—before she stumbles across the note in her Drafts folder.

She never sent it.

URRRGENTE!! Libby adds to the subject line. She thinks she might have spelled that wrong but can't remember how to check.

Send! Libby commands, as if uttering an incantation. She hits Send again for good measure. Then again. And again.

Afterward, she adds two more instructions to her arm.

"Send" comes first. Which she has done, so she stripes it off.

Is that the right word?

The next, after Glenn shows up again and rings her doorbell, is *Hide*.

12

On the first day of school, Peanut dresses in a black Falling Children T-shirt and shorts, Falling Children socks, and Falling Children sneakers that are really for little kids but Peanut's feet are small enough to still fit. She shimmers with the silver emblem of Pompou's Toy Emporium.

When that doesn't make her stomach stop churning, Peanut climbs back under her covers. The sparrows outside her window chatter smugly about their long unplanned days.

"Come on, P. First day," says Jessie from the doorway.

"I'm not going." Peanut hadn't really decided this until the words came out of her mouth. She likes how they sound.

"Well, if you want your lovely new phone"—Jessie yanks back the blanket—"you better."

Sitting up, her hair clicking with static, Peanut angrily points to her empty bookshelf. "How do you expect me to go anywhere when you've taken hostage the only things I truly love in this world?"

Jessie looks at her in disbelief. "You're not taking six seven-hundred-page books with you to school."

"Correct," Peanut says. "I'm only taking five. Mr. Goldhero is still hard at work on the sixth."

Muttering under her breath, Jessie retrieves the books from her bedroom and thumps them onto Peanut's bed. "Fine. Take your weight set. Now get up."

"Don't listen to her," Peanut whispers to the books. She strokes the gold lettering on their spines. "She hasn't even read you."

Jessie curses some more when she realizes Peanut's missed the bus and has to be driven to school. Their father calls Mrs. Halfchap for a ride to the hospital so Jessie can take Peanut in his old wood-paneled Wagoneer.

The truck smells like eggs when it goes up or down hills. Peanut tries to keep herself from getting carsick by naming wildflowers as they pass: There's globe mallow and monkshood, catchfly and beardtongues. Droopy purple bells are her favorite, since that's also the name of a short-tempered rocking horse the Falling Children befriend.

Has F. T. Goldhero been to Blue Skies before?

At the stop sign by the Murder House, Peanut looks for the hearse. It isn't there. The steep driveway looks as overgrown as ever. The doll with its dead eyes and sewn-shut mouth slumps from the fence.

Peanut cranes her neck to catch a glimpse of the pollen-covered porch. Just as the car begins to move again, she thinks she sees the front door creak open.

"Did you see that?" Peanut turns in her seat.

"See what?" Jessie's squinting, applying mascara in the rearview mirror as she drives.

"Someone was watching us." Peanut points, but the old doll hospital is already shrinking from sight.

"I didn't see anything."

Peanut feeds a thick strand of hair into her mouth and begins to chew. "Do you think there are bags of mutilated stuffed animals in there?"

She shudders, recalling the mangled toys the Children discover in the Unstopping's lair in book two.

"I've told you a billion times, no one lives there anymore." Jessie puts away the mascara and starts on her lipstick. Just Your Imagination, it's called.

Peanut folds her arms. "That's not what Orson Greeley said."

Jessie looks over, her lips only halfway colored in. "What did you say?"

"Orson Greeley drove me home from Little Diamond. I told you."

"No," Jessie says evenly. "You told me it was a man who reminded you of the Unstopping."

"He does." Peanut chews, hands-free, on her hair. It makes a pleasing squeak between her back molars. "He said he knows you," she adds. "He asked if you'd told me about him."

"There's nothing to tell," Jessie says. "Stay away from him."

She cranks up the classic-rock station, which is fine with Peanut. The song that's on, "Free Fallin'," makes her think about the Children. As they head down the steep incline into Wild Cat Canyon, the Wagoneer starts to reek of scrambled eggs. To keep from gagging, Peanut unzips her backpack and takes out a book.

This is a book four day, for sure.

~ ~

Cross Creek Junior High squats like a dog on a parcel of dried brown grass. When Jessie can't find a parking space, she pulls onto the sidewalk out front, narrowly missing a fire hydrant.

"Have a great day," she says.

"That's what everyone tells the Squirrel Keeper right before he loses his magical tasseled cap." Peanut points to the paragraph where this happens.

"You're not a squirrel."

Jessie walks around to open Peanut's door. Even though she's dressed for today's train robbery and wearing makeup applied while driving forty miles per hour, people stare.

It's a different kind of stare than Peanut gets. Once, in front of the Dollarama at the Cross Creek Mall, a modeling agent from Denver stopped Jessie and gave her his business card.

"With those eyes, you could see the world," he said.

But Jessie never called.

"Who would take care of you?" she said to Peanut, like it was her fault.

Jessie tries to give Peanut a hug, but Peanut squirms out of the way. People are watching, and everyone looks worse beside Jessie.

Peanut's legs feel unsteady as she walks up the steps into the building. This is the first time in six years—over half her life—Nancee hasn't been by her side on the first day of school.

Inside the maze of lockers and drinking fountains are boys with cracking voices and girls in crop tops. Instead of kittens and smiling vegetables staring out from the hallway posters, Peanut sees pictures of teenagers vaping and lying down on railroad tracks.

Is this what she has to look forward to?

Not until after the first bell screams overhead does Peanut locate her homeroom. The teacher, a tall woman with severe black bangs and circles of rouge on her cheeks like a clown, stops talking as she walks in.

"So nice of you to join us," she says, clasping her hands in mock gratitude.

Peanut takes a seat at the only empty desk. Unfortunately, it's in the front row. MRS. HADER: TEACHER OF THE YEAR reads a dusty plaque on the wall. The award is a decade old and not even from this school.

"As I was saying, class," Mrs. Hader goes on, "this isn't elementary school anymore. You will be treated like adults. And it's not okay for adults to show up late for work now, is it? You would be fired."

She looks at Peanut and makes a slicing motion across her neck, letting her tongue loll to one side. The entire class—except for Peanut—laughs.

"Now, quickly, go around the room and tell me." Mrs. Hader claps. "What is the most important thing about you?"

A few boys list their favorite football teams. One girl with freckles says she's been to Reno.

"I became an empowered female this summer," a familiar voice says from the back of the class, and when Peanut turns, she sees Nancee.

Rosemary is beside her. Over the summer, she let her blond hair grow out and dyed the tips red. She is wearing the same Falling Children T-shirt as Peanut.

"So I'm a survivor of this rare brain cancer called a meningioma," Rosemary says when it's her turn. "I had this special surgery where they take out the tumor through your nose. That's why I didn't lose my hair." She smooths it over her shoulders. "My dad said once I was better, he'd throw the biggest Red Vine Rally on the planet. We're even asking F. T. Goldhero to come 'cause I'm like *the* biggest fan of the Falling Children ever," she adds. "I adore those books."

Peanut clenches her fists under her desk. The Falling Children are *her* books. Or well, not *her* books because she didn't write them, but they're the most special thing in *her* life, not bone grocer–y Rosemary's. She wishes the brain tumor really had killed her.

And then Peanut realizes: she's said this aloud.

Everyone is staring. And not with interest, but as if she's a china doll whose throat has cracked open so a snake can slither out. (Book five, *super*-creepy.)

"It's the little Bixton," Mrs. Hader says. "I had your—Jessie when I taught at the high school. That was memorable."

"I'm adopted," Peanut tries to clarify, but Mrs. Hader ignores her.

"So let me get this straight. You think only one person is allowed to like a book? F. T. Goldhero wouldn't like that. Neither would his bank account." She draws her finger across her neck and sticks out her tongue again.

"That's not what I meant." Peanut frowns. "I just know the Children best."

"I was the first person in Blue Skies to get a copy of books two through five," says Rosemary.

Peanut silently curses Jessie for not allowing her to stay up till midnight for the book releases. Jessie went to Pretzky's Books for her, then allowed people to pay five dollars apiece to cut in line.

"You still have the book. I don't see what the big deal is," she told Peanut each time, proudly counting her stacks of cash. But this, *this* is the big deal!

"I want my Red Vine Rally to set a world record, so you guys all have to be there," Rosemary goes on. "I bet this is going to be where F. T. Goldhero finally reveals himself."

When the class cheers, Nancee blushes as if the approval is for her as well.

"He won't come," Peanut says loudly. "He's hard at work on his book and has a lot on his mind. I know because I've written F. T. Goldhero every week for nearly five years."

Ricky McAvoy, whose father is Blue Skies' dentist, calls, "Okay, stan."

Everyone but Peanut laughs.

"Has Mr. Goldhero ever written back?" Mrs. Hader wants to know.

"Not yet." Peanut lifts her chin. "But he will."

"Isn't it interesting," Mrs. Hader muses, "how certain books capture the world's attention, even if they're not well written? I mean, how many times have we seen toys come to life?" She extends her arms. "They come to life all the time in the movies!"

"But that's not what the books are about," Peanut says. "The toys house damaged souls that need to be redeemed before they're reincarnated. If not, they'll turn into murderers and terrorists and liars and really, really bad people."

"Thanks for the spoilers, dwerp," someone calls out.

Peanut can tell Mrs. Hader's not listening because she says, "Class, since you have not yet entered the world of literature, I'm sure these books may seem exciting. But when you're ancient like me"—she drags her finger across her neck again—"you understand it's just marketing that's driving this YA juggernaut. Who *wouldn't* want to find F. T. Goldhero and make a million smackeroos?" She lifts her shoulders. "Maybe we should make that our class project. We'll all get rich off the Falling Children!"

There are claps and whoops. Ricky McAvoy puts his fingers in his mouth and whistles.

Peanut turns to look at Rosemary, who's laughing and nodding. She is definitely *not* the biggest fan ever of the Children.

But Peanut is. She raises her hand, and when Mrs. Hader ignores her, Peanut stands.

"I object," she says, cupping her hands around her mouth.

"We've gotten offtrack." Mrs. Hader's still smiling, but her lips tighten like a drawstring. "Take your seat." She points.

Peanut doesn't. "F. T. Goldhero doesn't want to be found. He doesn't like all this attention. He doesn't want people to care more about him than the Children."

"How do you know?" someone asks. "You don't know him."

"I wouldn't worry about what F. T. Goldhero wants," Mrs. Hader agrees. "My guess is"—she looks around the room for dramatic effect—"he's AI."

Peanut can feel her pulse toggle back and forth in her neck. It sounds like, *Don't just stand there. Don't just stand there. Don't just—*

With one magnificent kick, she pushes her desk onto the floor.

"Take it back," she says, her hands on her hips.

The class is suddenly so still that Peanut can hear her breath whistling a little through her nose.

"Just because you can't write books as good as the Falling Children doesn't mean F. T. Goldhero can't either," she says. "He is a bona fide genius, and he is my friend, and he is *real*."

Mrs. Hader's anger burns into Peanut. "I thank you for providing your classmates with a valuable life lesson. It apparently runs in your family." She turns to address the rest of the students. "See, friends? This is exactly how *not* to act in middle school."

Throwing open the door, Mrs. Hader points to the hallway. "Out."

"But you were the one who—"

"*Out.*"

Peanut has been in trouble with teachers before—and each time the reason can be traced back to the Children—but the first day of school is new. She drops to the waxy black-and-white tile of the hallway, wishing she'd thought to grab her backpack. At least then she could read.

Outside, Peanut hears an ice cream truck. Her stomach rumbles.

Dear F. T. Goldhero, she thinks, dragging her finger across a row of dusty yearbooks on the shelf beside her. *My new school is an absolute bomb of an abomination, as Everlee would say...*

Angrily, Peanut yanks out one of the oldest volumes. *Cross Creek Chickpeas: Cooking with Success!* the cover reads. Smiling garbanzo beans tumble into a pot of boiling water.

She flicks through pages of girls with souffléd bangs and boys in parachute pants. None of the last names are familiar: *Kura, Merry, Park, Ups.*

But when Peanut gets to the section of eighth graders, she sees one that is.

Orson Greeley.

The picture Peanut finds isn't a younger version of the man who gave her a ride. There's only a sad moon-faced boy with acne splattered across his cheeks like paint. Even from the shoulders up, Peanut can tell his clothes are hand-me-downs.

"I'M A LOSER," someone has scribbled in a voice bubble next to his name.

For a moment, Peanut forgets about Mrs. Hader. This is like that chapter in book two when Everlee finds an old picture of the Unstopping and realizes that residue from his soul is stuck inside the image, like gum in the tread of a shoe.

Licking her lips, Peanut leans closer to the page. Tapping the picture three times with her thumb, middle finger, and pinky—just like Everlee does—she whispers, "*Indicare locandis.*"

Reveal what houses you.

The bell rings. Classroom doors swing wide. Students flood the hallways. Peanut stares at the picture, holding her breath.

Nothing happens. The doughy boy stares at her.

"*Indicare locandis,*" she tries again, more urgently this time.

This time, one of the Unstopping's eyes looks right at her, while the other glances down the hall, waiting.

Peanut slams the yearbook shut and hurls it into the hall, as far as she can. Someone stumbles over it. The smack their body makes when they hit the floor makes Peanut flinch.

It's Rosemary. And when she lifts her head and looks back at Peanut, she's screaming and holding her nose. Blood drips between her fingers.

"Oh my God!" Nancee drops her backpack and kneels next to Rosemary. "You tripped her on purpose!" She looks at Peanut, her eyes wide.

"No, I didn't!" Peanut gets to her feet. "It was an accident. There was this picture—it was giving me a message."

Nancee looks disgusted. "Don't fake news me. I saw you!"

"I'm not!" *And that's not a verb,* Peanut starts to add, but Mrs. Hader suddenly has a hold of her arm and is steering her down the hall to the principal's office.

"A little piece of advice, friend," she says, emphasizing the word. "This isn't going to end the way you were hoping."

13

"Suspended? A week? On the first day of school?" Jessie is so angry that she can only speak in questions on the drive home. "How could you bully Rosemary? With her brain cancer?"

Peanut can only speak in exclamations. "I wasn't bullying her! I told you! It was an accident!"

But like Mrs. Hader, the principal, and Rosemary's parents, Jessie doesn't hear what she's saying.

She doesn't even trust Peanut to stay home alone while she goes back to work at the train robbery.

"Who knows what else you're going to do?" Jessie fumes.

She brings Peanut instead to their father's office, swishing through the shallow sea of toddlers in the waiting room in her long skirt and prairie boots, Peanut trudging in her wake.

"Aren't you supposed to be in school, Pandora?" Old Mr. Foster looks up from his tattered copy of the *Princeton Business Journal.*

"She's not herself today." Jessie pushes Peanut into their father's office. "Don't go anywhere," she says. "Don't touch anything. Just *sit.*"

"Don't you want to hear my side of the story?" Peanut asks.

"No," Jessie says and slams the door.

"Bone grocer," mutters Peanut.

An old picture of her father frowns at her from the wall.

"Stop judging me," she tells it.

Peanut picks her way through the medical oddities her father collects. There's a vintage hernia belt she used to sneak on for fun when she was younger and a Civil War amputation kit with rusted knives. The walls are similarly crowded with sloppy watercolors and needlepointed thank-yous her father has accepted instead of payment over the years.

On the desk is a picture of Peanut's father and Buzz at the snowy top of Engineer Peak. There are no pictures of Peanut or Jessie. Peanut tries to look inside his desk drawers for one, but they're locked.

She swivels in her father's lumpy leather chair, doodling eyes on one of his prescription pads. Peanut thinks about calling Nancee and insisting she didn't break Rosemary's nose on purpose. Nancee should know Peanut would never violate the code of Pompou's:

Never harm when you can help. Never stop when you can go. Never wrong when you can right.

Her father's secretary sticks her head in the door. Despite her name, Bitty is a large woman with strong leathery hands and a voice like gravel.

"Your dad just got off the phone with the principal," she says. "He was coming to talk to you, but Annie Yolen passed out in her crawl space again. He'll be a while."

When Peanut becomes an adult, she will never pretend adopt a child she doesn't have time for.

She drops her forehead onto the desk hard enough that she sees, if not stars exactly, then the beginnings of stars—molecular clouds. And that's when Peanut spots Jessie's phone plugged into the outlet by her feet.

In seconds, Peanut finds Nancee and Rosemary online—they're dancing and rapping and jumping into a lake while they hold hands and scream. In selfies, they wear dog ears or flower crowns and pout. Despite the trove of videos and photos and stories and comments and texts, there's zero evidence Nancee has ever been friends with Peanut. There isn't even a picture of the time Peanut accidentally slipped in a mud puddle and a corn snake slithered into her hair, when instead of pulling it off right away, Nancee said, "OMG, I am so taking a picture of this."

It's like Peanut doesn't exist.

She clicks on the newest video that @RoRoFallingChild has posted to Instagram. In it, Rosemary is lying on a hospital bed, a white bandage taped over her nose.

"Y'all, I was bullied at school today," she says into the camera, tears bedazzling her blue eyes. "And I'm a cancer survivor!"

But it's the neon-pink hashtag, stamped across the screen, that holds Peanut's attention: #Idontbelieveinrevenge

It's from a speech Everlee gives Benjamin in book one after the Unstopping orders Rock 'Em Sock 'Em Robots to knock out his best friend, Kenji. Benjamin is distraught and wants to race after the Unstopping right *now* and confront him.

"No, not now," Everlee says, holding him back. "I don't believe in revenge, but I *do* believe in justice. The difference," she whispers, "is that your enemies never see justice coming."

Over two hundred people have watched Rosemary's video so far.

"Was Ms. Yolen three sheets to the wind again?" Peanut hears Bitty ask down the hall.

"If you mean three-fourths into a bottle of whiskey, then yes," Peanut's father says.

When Peanut ducks under the desk to replace the phone, she's startled to see she has fourteen new emails. Each contains the same subject line:

URRRGENTE: From the office of F. T. Goldhero.

From the office of F. T. Goldhero?

Urrrrgente?

Peanut's throat feels squeezed by an invisible hand.

Quickly, before her father opens the door, Peanut clicks on the first email.

Her first (fleeting) thought is that her dream has come true. Then a more sensible explanation takes over: Rosemary's playing another prank. #Idontbelieveinrevenge

Peanut hits reply.

OMG, her thumbs jab the screen. I never dreamed I'd hear from you. What an incredible HONOR.

Sadly, she continues, I can't email my stories. They're far too valuable and a hacker might steal them. If you want to read them, you'll have to fly your private jet into my town (I'm sure you know where that is) and meet me at The Pig-n-Pancake at 7pm on Sunday. Trust me. I'll be READY for you.

And by "ready," Peanut means she will have Silly String, water balloons, a Nerf gun, and her new phone to film Rosemary and whatever cruel prank she is planning.

This doesn't violate the code of the Falling Children, she tells herself. Like Gran Bere says, "There are two types of people in the world. Those who eat the cookie when it crumbles—and those who choke."

14

The plane is crowded with children.

Libby studies their faces as she inches her way down the center aisle, her carry-on clutched to her chest.

You are not mine, she thinks.

Or you, or you, or you.

How has she lived her entire adult life alone?

For days, for weeks, for years, she has only sat in her apartment and written. And although the Falling Children have thrived (present dire circumstances excepted), Libby hasn't. Her life is crowded with imaginary people, not real ones.

No friend who insisted on driving her to the airport. No partner to whisper an inside joke about carry-ons. No baby to hold in the crook of her arm.

Instead, Libby has two bottles of Tylenol tucked away in her suitcase.

Most children in the cabin are holding one of the five Falling Children books. They are reading, being read to, or tracing small sticky fingers over the gilded cover.

The adults on the plane are glued to their phones or iPads or laptops or seat-back screens. From the snatches of conversation she overhears, Libby knows what's on the news.

"Man, a million bucks?"

"They'll find him."

"What if he's, like, on this plane?"

Libby is trembling by the time she finds her seat in the thirty-third row. Her imagination doesn't help by quickly cycling through a batch of worst-case scenarios: hijackers, deadly germs on the fold-out trays, angry drunk breaking into the cockpit, computer software malfunction...

Someone across the aisle is wearing a sad-emoji sweatshirt, dabbing their eyes with a tissue and Libby wonders if seats have been assigned according to life happiness.

She hoists Rolf, who is reluctantly wearing a bright purple "Service Animal" vest purchased for $29.95 online, into the middle seat. The elderly man on the aisle gives them both a wary look.

After preemptively wrapping each of her fingers in Band-Aids—otherwise, she will have no fingernails left by the time they land, trust her on this—Libby pays for a glass of white wine and in-flight Wi-Fi.

She gulps the Chardonnay quickly, like medicine, then spends the rest of the five-hour flight to Colorado googling "F. T. Goldhero" on her phone. Each time, she expects an unflattering photo of herself to pop up and everyone on the plane to suddenly look over, recognizing her rumpled gray cardigan and five-year-old black flats. Their faces will fall like cakes, Libby thinks.

Is that even an expression?

She searches it on her phone while the man in the aisle seat fights Rolf for the arm rest. Rolf is intent on lying down, but there's not enough room. Still, he slides onto his elbows and gives it a try before hiking himself back up to a seated position. Drool swings from his mouth.

"We don't travel much," Libby tells the man. When he looks unmoved, she adds, "It's an emergency. We had no choice."

The wine slurs Libby's words, making her sound like the snake in the Garden of Eden. "How do youoooo think they asssssignnn sssssseats?"

The man hunches away.

As the plane rolls and bumps through the clouds, Libby checks and rechecks the time on her phone. When the flight attendant comes by again with a drink cart, Libby orders a cup of water, no ice, for Rolf, which she holds so he can noisily drink.

Spit flies everywhere. Libby mops it up as best as she can and avoids her seatmate's glare.

"I don't travel much," she apologizes again. "My parents died on a plane."

Correction: her parents died in a plane *crash*, on a Wednesday. Libby can still vividly recall being pulled out of her sixth-grade English class and given the news by the headmaster. She looks down at her white shirt and dark pants. She was even wearing the same clothes.

Three decades is a long time to abstain from flying, which explains why Libby had no idea what to do when she walked through the metal detector at the airport and had to be instructed to take off her shoes. She isn't entirely sure where her suitcase went or how she'll get it when she lands in the little town of Cross Creek, Colorado.

"Enjoy your flight," the gate agent told Libby as she entered the skyway, Rolf gripped to her side.

Libby only wants to survive it.

~~~

Halfway through the trip, Libby can't wait any longer. She must go to the bathroom. *Thirty-three C,* she tells herself, staring at the seat number. *Thirty-three C, thirty-three C, thirty-three C.* She types it into her phone.

Rolf comes with her. But that means he needs to step onto the man's lap so he can jump down into the aisle, and the man is sleeping and startles a little when ninety-two pounds of dog presses into his thighs.

Then Rolf is too big to comfortably fit into the bathroom, so Libby has him sit outside the door while she sits on the toilet and holds his leash. A flight attendant with curly hair and a kerchief tied around her neck like a bandit doesn't like this idea and calls it a "safety hazard."

"Rolf's very sweet," Libby assures her. "He would never bite anyone."

"He could trip them," the bandit challenges.

"Then can you watch him?" Libby asks, handing her the leash. "I'll be right back."

But she isn't. Because after Libby finally figures out how to flush the toilet, which takes a while, she stares at the door. There's no knob. How did she close it in the first place?

More importantly, how does she get out?

Libby can feel rings of panic clinking faster inside her. She runs her hand over the door, looking for a keyhole or button to press, but there's only a protruding metal grip. When she presses and twists it, again and again, nothing happens.

"Hello," Libby calls as loudly as she can. "Hello?"

She starts to knock, then pound, on the door to get someone's attention. Rolf, realizing she's in trouble, begins to bark and scratch from the other side.

"Help!" Libby calls. "I need help!"

The next thing she sees is the curly-haired flight attendant and her kerchief sliding the door open.

"Thank you," Libby says, near tears. She's grateful when the woman escorts her back to her seat because she can't remember where it is.

"You and your service dog need to remain here until we land," the flight attendant says.

Libby sinks low into her chair.

Children stare.

They are not her children.

Squeezing her eyes shut, Libby wishes that every seat on the plane were inhabited by a character from the Falling Children books like the Little People of Abacus or Jenny dolls, whose thoughts smell like small filled tarts. She imagines Benjamin sneaking sodas off the flight attendant's cart and Everlee using binoculars to look out the window, identifying bodies of water so she knows exactly where they are in the sky. Huperzine would be worried, as Huperzine always is.

What if we crash? What if we lose our luggage? What if she—pointing to Libby—*gets stuck in the bathroom again?*

Huperzine's dialogue is always the easiest for Libby to write.

~ —— ~

By the time the plane lands in Denver, Libby has written herself a cheat sheet—everything she needs to do to safely walk out the skyway, into the terminal, to the town of Blue Skies, and safely back home. The writing is Lilliputian, so the man sitting next to Rolf can't read it. Libby's hand is cramped from the effort.

Gripping the cocktail napkin, she watches each row of passengers slowly get to their feet, pull their carry-ons from the bins, cradle their Falling Children books, and disappear into the skyway.

They make it look easy, Libby thinks.

In her pocket is a hundred-dollar bill. As the man in the aisle seat stands to get his bag, Libby carefully drops it onto his seat cushion.

Aside from running, dropping money is the only hobby Libby has.

She likes witnessing the delight of someone who's found a hundred-dollar bill thrown into their path. She pretends they are looking that way at her.

"Excuse me." She points. "I think you left something?"

It's the least Libby can do since the man put up with Rolf throughout the flight, not to mention her. She's pretty sure she cried most of the way.

The man looks down but doesn't pick up the bill.

"That's yours, isn't it?" She tries not to sound too eager.

"Because you think everyone over the age of sixty-five must rely on others for financial support? Or is too frail and incompetent to still be working a full-time job?" he asks Libby, unsmiling. "Perhaps you should get to know a person before you presume what they need."

"I don't," she says quickly. "I mean I should. I just thought it would be nice—I mean—"

But the man is already leaving the row.

Libby is so ashamed that she forgets to follow her list. And that means that although "get suitcase from overhead bin" is number one, she doesn't do it.

～～

Libby has never been to Denver. She has never been farther west than Pennsylvania, where she went to a bereavement camp the year after her parents died. It was supposed to distract Libby from being lonely, but she spent most of her time alone in the infirmary because by that point, she was homesick for Vernice.

Which is why in book two, Everlee discovers a pile of rusted toys buried underneath the infirmary at *her* summer camp and realizes the counselors there are secretly working for the Unstopping. When Libby doesn't like something, she rarely changes her mind.

After several false starts on the monorail in which she gets off at each terminal and wanders until someone directs her back on, Libby catches the shuttle to the car-rental hub. She's dreading the drive to Blue Skies, but Uber drivers (potential serial killers, pickpockets, people who want to make small talk) scare her more.

As she's paying for her economy model, Libby asks the clerk how to get to Blue Skies.

"You a mountain biker?" he asks, smoothing a map that is all green, green, green.

She shakes her head.

"Hiker?"

"No."

"Climb—"

"I'm nothing."

"Well, they still have a good old-fashioned train robbery," he assures her. He winds his pencil through a blob of national forest and over a rocky crag of mountains. "It's about three hours from here. Four if you get stuck behind a tourist. No offense," he adds.

Three hours? How did Libby not know this?

"I thought Blue Skis—"

"Blue Skies," he corrects.

"—was a half hour away." She fumbles to find the itinerary on her phone.

"If you fly into Cross Creek," the man explains. "Not from here."

Libby taps every app on her phone but can't find her flight information. It doesn't matter. She either got off at the wrong airport, missed her second flight, or both.

"It's a pretty drive," the man assures her. "Nothing, really, between here and there."

Libby nods, pretending that she, too, thinks this is a good thing.

Then she pays extra for GPS so she can at least have a voice in the car to keep her company—or, well, a voice other than what's in her head.

~~~~~

The sky outside is chewy and bluey like taffy. (Are those the right words?) Clutching the steering wheel with both hands and driving at the only speed that feels safe—glacial—Libby follows the disembodied GPS voice out of Denver and to Boulder.

Blue skies, Blue skies, Blue skies, she's written on scraps of paper. The words cover the dashboard, passenger seat, her lap.

This isn't so bad, Libby thinks as she snails past the university. The wrought iron gates and austere brick buildings remind her of Princeton. The pancake house on the main drag looks reassuringly like the one by her home.

And then without warning, the road narrows. The nose of the Camry she's rented points toward the sky, and Libby finds herself driving up, up, up into the mountains. Paved road turns to silver dust, and the sky disappears behind fat-needled pine trees.

Occasionally, Libby sees a mountain biker or chipmunk. Other than that, the road is deserted.

A new and complicated fear plays in Libby's head like a movie she would never pay to see. First, she'll get a flat tire, not know how to change it, and be forced to spend the night in the car, freezing and hungry. Next, in the pitch-black hours of the morning, a rabid bear will smash through the car window. (Libby is not sure exactly how, only that one will.) Lastly, Rolf will die a painful, bloody death trying to protect her.

Libby watches this happen several times in her head, each version a little more gratuitously violent than the last. Not until her heart jackrabbits in her chest and the rabbit is viciously murdered, too, does she take mercy on herself and turn on the radio for distraction. Unfortunately, it's an AM station, and the static only makes the news more dire.

Earthquake! Shooting! School bus overturn!

Smacking the dial with her hand, Libby is trying to turn it off, turn all of it off, when the newscaster announces, "A Texan millionaire says he's received over a hundred thousand leads about the identity of bestselling fantasy author F. T. Goldhero."

Libby leans her forehead against the steering wheel.

"This is proof that the good Lord wants F. T. Goldhero to be found," announces Baron McBroom. He has a voice thick like cream gravy. "And once he is, I tell you that he will be held accountable for his sins, which I believe include both greed and sloth."

She passes a sign for Blue Skies, followed by one for Mr. Mandelbrot's organ lessons and the Great Train Robbery, which promises to be a "hair-raisin', gun-totin' adventure!"

"I don't think we'll have to wait much longer for the big reveal," agrees a university professor who specializes in backlash against anonymous authors. "Fans are frustrated. They want their book. And they're beginning to feel F. T. Goldhero is toying with them, pardon the pun. Instead of wanting to protect him, my guess is that it will be a loyal fan who turns him in. In fact, if I were F.T. and wanted to avert a crisis, I would—"

Libby doesn't hear the rest.

The mountains fall apart like curtains, and there, in a valley below, lies the picturesque town of Blue Skies.

Libby slams on the brakes, and Rolf falls off the back seat.

She has an eerie feeling that she has seen this town somewhere before.

15

Behind rows of Victorian houses painted the soft-boiled shades of Easter eggs, Libby finds a steepled church, an undulating green park, and a stream chuckling under a stone bridge. Redbrick buildings with glass storefronts line the streets of downtown: Whatsit's Antiques, with an array of old medical equipment in the front window. An appliance store specializing in Japanese air conditioners. WE CUT KEYS! a tidy sign on the door reads. Stores sell (Falling Children) ice cream, (Falling Children) books, (Falling Children) T-shirts...

Overlooking city hall stands a towering outdoor clock, although the hands have stopped. Just past it, concrete stairs are cut into the side of the mountain.

Something about this town unsettles Libby. She wants to get the child's stories and go home.

The Pig-n-Pancake restaurant is tucked away on a side street. Mountain bikes fill the rack out front, and the sidewalk bobbles with people carrying orange life vests or paddles. Occasionally, someone strolls by in chaps and a Stetson, leading a horse.

Libby checks her phone. She has time to reapply her ChapStick or smooth the wrinkles in her sweater. Her hair could stand to be brushed and new Band-Aids applied to hide her ten raw cuticles.

But Libby is not used to leaving home for longer than a trip to the grocery store or her publisher. She is exhausted.

Setting the timer on her phone for twenty minutes, but what she will later realize is two hours, Libby climbs into the back seat and falls asleep, using Rolf as a pillow.

~ ~

Knock-knocks, the big Toucan Sam–like creatures from book one, are Libby's least favorite characters in the Falling Children series. They're twee and predictable and tell terrible jokes. When Libby is stressed, they flap into her dreams and embarrass her.

"What do you call an alligator wearing a vest?"

"An investigator!"

"Why should you never trust a pig?"

"Because they're bound to squeal!"

In her sleep, Libby attempts to shoo the gawky creatures away.

"Knock, knock!" They gather around, pushing her with their hard yellow beaks. "Knock, knock!"

Irritated, Libby does the only thing she can to get rid of them: she wakes up.

"Knock, knock," says the doughy-faced policeman outside the car. He raps on her window with his reusable coffee cup. *Knock, knock.*

To her credit, Libby doesn't scream, although she does startle so much that she thumps her head against the opposite door.

"You're sleeping in a no-parking zone, ma'am," the cop says.

Libby can't figure out how to lower the window, so she opens the door, smacking his belly. "I am?"

He nods and gestures toward the license plate. "From Texas, eh? I'm no fan of the Cowboys."

Libby has always had a fear of being wrongly accused of a crime and locked away in prison for the rest of her life. This is exactly how she sees it happening.

Pulling a ticket book from his pocket, the cop thumbs through until he finds a clean page. "License and registration, please," he says, not looking at her.

Libby climbs into the front seat, then freezes, her hands on the steering wheel. *Where would those be? What do they look like?*

Slowly, she opens the console between the seats.

What is she looking for again?

She can't—

Remember, the weary synapses in her brain chorus. *We know.*

"I don't think I have them just *now*," Libby says. She hopes the inflection makes it sound like whatever he asked for will be delivered any moment.

The cop sighs. He looks a little longingly at the restaurant behind him, where a line has formed at the front door. "Go ahead and get out of the car, ma'am."

"Now?" Libby asks.

"Yes," he says, more firmly. "I would say now."

She is half-in, half-out of the car when a voice cries, "Wait!"

At first, Libby thinks it comes from her. Then the officer turns and looks down the street.

A small girl with a wild nest of black hair and something stuck to her face that resembles Silly Putty runs toward the car. She is dragging a red wagon full of water balloons, two cans of Silly String, a Nerf gun, and what look like…fireworks.

"Don't write her a ticket, Freddy!" the girl says breathlessly. "She's here for me, to see me."

She presses her face to the car window. "You're Mrs. Weeks, aren't you?" she asks, talking so fast that beads of spit fly onto the glass. "I thought it was a joke, but it's not, is it? It's really you! This is your car."

Libby nods, although she can't stop staring. The girl has a narrow, delicate nose and full lips, but her right eye doesn't track along with her left. Instead, it gazes off to the side like it's considering something else. And her face—on the right side of her face, the letter C appears to have melted onto her skin.

"Who is this, Peanut?" The cop turns to her. "She a friend of yours?"

"Yes!" The girl bounces on the toes of her Falling Children sneakers. She's also wearing a Falling Children T-shirt, black leggings with shorts (Huperzine's go-to ensemble), and three athletic socks fashioned into a tie around her neck, à la Benjamin when he's trying to dress up.

Libby feels a rush of admiration when the girl stamps her foot and says, "You can't write her a ticket because she's here for me. She came all the way from New York City."

The cop takes a step closer to the car. Libby can feel him taking in Rolf. The mostly empty bag of baby carrots she apparently shared with him during the drive. The Band-Aids covering all ten of her fingers. When did she put those on?

"And what brings you to Blue Skies?" he wants to know.

"She has information about my real mother," Peanut says before Libby can speak. "She may be able to help me find her."

"Your real mother?"

"Yes." Peanut nods. "We have an appointment to discuss it. In here." She points at the Pig-n-Pancake behind them.

"Fido, too?"

Peanut looks surprised to see Rolf but nods anyway.

"All right then, you go right on inside." Freddy opens the car door for Libby. "Come on, Texas."

Rolf comes, too, farting as he slips down from the back seat.

"Thank you for protecting and serving our town," Peanut calls, grabbing Libby's wrist and pulling her past the line of people waiting to get into the restaurant. "Have a nice day!"

"Oh, I'm not going anywhere," Freddy says, pulling out his phone. "I'm calling Jessie."

~ ~

The interior of the Pig-n-Pancake is unexpectedly narrow, as if someone has taken a normal-sized restaurant and squeezed it between their hands. Black-and-white tiles crisscross the floor, and Elvis Presley bumps from a jukebox in the corner.

Peanut elbows past customers in line—"They're just tourists," she explains—and leads Libby to an empty booth by the bathroom.

"My dad's the only doctor in town," she says by way of explanation, waving enthusiastically to a stout woman behind the counter who is slicing an apple pie. "That's the owner. She has an irritable uterus."

Forks scrape plates. Timers bleat in the kitchen. A milkshake machine drones. Libby starts to cover her ears, but Peanut leans over the chipped Formica table and grabs her wrists.

"What's he like?"

Libby recoils. She isn't used to being touched. "What's who like?"

"F. T. Goldhero," Peanut whispers excitedly. "I love him! I love him so much. I love the Children. And the books. I—" The eye looking at Libby shines. "What's he like in real life?"

"Shy. Quiet." Libby pulls the sleeves of her sweater over her hands and sits on them. "Not used to being around people."

"Does he live in a castle?" Peanut wants to know.

114

Libby nods. "In England. A castle with turrets and battlements and a stable full of steeds."

"I knew it!" Peanut bounces up and down. "And is this his dog?"

Libby looks down to see Rolf tenderly licking a crack in the floor. "Yes," she says. "I also dog sit. It's part of my job."

Coffee mugs slam onto tables. A hand dryer roars inside the bathroom. Behind the swinging doors of the kitchen, someone named Renato is berated for not loading the dishwasher fast enough.

"My abuela podria hacerlo mas rapido."

It's not helping that the girl speaks at record speed. In a matter of seconds, she's mentioned how she almost didn't come because she thought Libby's email was a cruel prank. There's something about a mean teacher who once was Teacher of the Year when she was at the high school but definitely not anymore, a cancer survivor with an ulterior motive, a father who adopted three children but really only likes one, and how she's not allergic to peanuts but was a very tiny, sickly baby, born premature and buried alive—just like Everlee!

Libby's head swims.

"Does F. T. Goldhero read all my letters?" Peanut pauses. "Do you think he likes me?"

Libby is relieved that she doesn't have to answer. A woman who is not the waitress is next to their table. She has a sheath of long red hair, pearl-like skin, and green eyes, which she smallens—is that the right word?—at Peanut.

"What is going on?"

Peanut's unscarred cheek turns bright with guilt. "Nothing."

The woman glares at Libby. "Who are you?"

"Nobody," say Peanut and Libby at the same time.

The woman waits for a better answer.

"She's a friend I met online," Peanut tries again. "Talking about the Falling Children."

It's the wrong thing to say, of course.

"Someone you met *online*?" The woman's eyes widen.

"It's okay," Peanut insists. "She just wants to see my stories."

"Your *what*?" She turns to Libby. "What kind of sicko are you to prey on an innocent little kid?"

"Th-this is the only time I've preyed," Libby stammers. "I mean, I'm *not* preying. But you have every right to be concerned." She pats her pockets, wishing for another hundred-dollar bill. "If I had a daughter, I'd feel the same way."

Peanut makes a face. "This is Jessie. She's my sister."

"I know what you must be thinking," Libby tries again, "But I work for"—she slides closer so Jessie can read her lips—"F. T. Goldhero."

"You?" Libby feels the woman rate her puckered sweater, slept-in-a-car hair and the dog at her feet. Rolf has now rolled onto his side so servers have to step over him with platters of French toast. "*You* work for the biggest writer in the world?"

"Yes." Libby nods. "He's my boss. In the castle where he lives. That has turrets and steeds and—"

"Get up, Peanut," Jessie says. "We're leaving."

But Peanut isn't paying attention. She's tapping away furiously at her phone. Typical iScreen generation, Libby thinks, liking her less.

"In a second," Peanut says. "Hold on."

"No, *now*."

"Okay, okay. Give me a second," Peanut slumps so far down in the booth that she disappears from view.

"Peanut!" Jessie thunders.

"I'm coming! My shoe fell off. You don't want me to walk home without it, do you?"

Jessie throws up her hands. "Unbelievable," she says. "This whole thing."

When Peanut finally sits up, she extends a hand toward Libby. "It was a pleasure to make your acquaintance," she says in a British accent.

Libby is startled to feel a folded napkin press against her palm. It's exactly like the one Everlee gives the One-Eyed Duke in book two, when the Children plot to rescue him from the *Sink Ng* ship. Libby doesn't need to unfold it to know what it will say:

Don't move. Stay here. Help is on the way.

~ ⁓

The owner of the irritable uterus, a woman with a gray ponytail that reaches her waist and a faded tattoo of Tweety and Sylvester on her bicep, delivers pancakes that Libby doesn't remember ordering.

"You know," the woman says, leaning down to chuck Rolf under the chin, "dogs aren't allowed in here unless they're helper animals."

Rolf's "service animal" vest is long gone. "He helps me," Libby says.

She pats the booth so Rolf can jump up. It's a tight squeeze, and he manages to knock over a glass of water and get syrup on his tail. Otherwise, he's content to sit beside her, lapping up pancakes as she cuts them for him.

Libby knows people are staring but doesn't raise her eyes to confirm.

"There's less to look at when your eyes don't look back" as Gran Bere used to say.

Before Libby painfully and unnecessarily killed Gran Bere.

"Am I here for you?" someone asks.

The guy standing by her table is tall and lanky with green eyes and brown hair that flops into them. The front of his T-shirt has a hole the size of a half-dollar. Even scowling, he is handsome.

A grown-up Benjamin, Libby can't help thinking.

"No." She smiles, extracting a napkin from inside Rolf's cheek. "Definitely not."

He doesn't leave. "Peanut said I was supposed to get you. I'm Buzz. Her brother."

Libby isn't getting a serial killer vibe from him. Still, she explains that she doesn't go to people's houses.

"Ever?" Buzz asks.

"No. Never."

The owner with the irritable something—attitude?—points to the last pancake on Libby's plate. "You want to take the rest home, hon?"

Before she can answer, Buzz is sitting across from Libby, folding it into his mouth in one bite. "My toaster's broken," he says when he sees her staring.

"You don't make pancakes in a toaster," says Libby. She pauses. "Do you?"

"I do."

"I'm sorry," Libby says. "And you are here because?"

"You tell me."

Each of his answers feels like a bent key being jammed into a lock and confirms what Libby already knows: she never should have left her apartment. Time2AnteUp can't help her.

Libby doesn't like being questioned by the police. Or eating in public. In a wave of panic, she suddenly realizes she has no idea where her suitcase is.

What about me? Everlee pipes up angrily from the Depths of Despair. *I'm dying here.*

"You can be such an asshole sometimes," Libby tells her, rubbing her forehead.

"You don't even know me," Buzz says, insulted. He pulls the tab off a coffee creamer and throws it back like a shot.

Something about the move strikes Libby as familiar. It's as if she's watched him do this hundreds of times before, maybe even handed a creamer to him. If Benjamin doesn't do shots of International Delight in the books, he really should.

"Are you sure?" she asks.

"Yeah." Buzz wipes his mouth with a napkin and stands. "Definitely not."

Message from Jessie Bixton SOS! At pig n pcake need u right now!!!!!!!!

Fuck you

Not Jessie it's me Peanut on her phone come NOW 2 get someone URGENT!

nancy can walk home

No! PM Electrics helpers here BIG secret so shhhh. Or well be cursed.

shes Libby and has a dog take them 2 ur house Ill b there soon

busy

No ur not! You have to help! this is my DESTINY!! i know it

If u squash my dream Ill never forgive u!!!!!!!!!!!!

EVER

pleaaaaaaaaaaaaaaase

fine but u owe me

You wont be sorry

Something BIGS going to happen I CAN FEEL IT

16

"Your obsession with those books is going to get you in trouble."

Peanut runs to keep up with Jessie's angry strides. "No, it's not."

True, it would make more sense if F. T. Goldhero's assistant had a business card and carried a leather briefcase instead of a dog. Peanut wasn't expecting this small skittish woman whose hair kept slipping loose from its bun and who kept patting her pockets like she lost her car keys. And what was up with all the Band-Aids on her fingers?

Yet this only makes Peanut love F. T. Goldhero even more. He cares more about who people are on the inside, which means Peanut has a chance, too.

"What do you need from me?" she asked Ms. Weeks eagerly. "I have lots of ideas about how the last book ends. They're at home because, well, I didn't think your email was real, no offense. *Urrrgente* is a misspelling, unless you meant it to be in Spanish. Did you? That's why I had the water balloons. But I can show you," she added. "I can go home right now and get my stories and show you."

The woman took a sip of coffee and looked left, right, left before answering. "Yes, please," she whispered. "I don't have—I mean, Mr. Goldhero doesn't have—a lot of time."

Peanut can't wait to show Ms. Weeks her stories. She wonders if she'll read them over the phone to F. T. Goldhero.

Bloody brilliant! he'll exclaim. *Why didn't I think of that? Fly this prodigy to my castle!*

And when she arrives via private jet, Peanut will find not only F. T. Goldhero but the Falling Children, because she is still holding out hope that they are secretly *real*, and they will help her find her parents.

They've been in front of you the whole time, Everlee will announce after making one of her topographical Maps of Corroboration. And from the middle will rise—well, whatever her real parents look like.

"...And by the way, I want my phone back," Jessie demands, letting the screen door of their house slam behind her. "You never should have gotten it after tripping Rosemary Carver."

"I didn't trip her. I told you."

"Hand it over." Jessie holds out her palm.

Peanut pulls the phone to her chest. "No."

Jessie tries to grab it, but Peanut darts around the couch, leaps over the coffee table, and tears up the stairs.

"Stop telling me what to do all the time!" she screams. "You're not my mother!"

She bumps into her father on the landing. Mrs. Halfchap is with him. Her half chaps are in her hands, not around her calves, and both she and Peanut's father are sweating on their foreheads.

"Thank you for persuading that squirrel to vacate our attic—" her father is saying, his face red from the heat. "For pity's sake, what is all this ruckus?"

"Peanut met a stranger off the Internet." Jessie crosses her arms over her chest.

"She's not a stranger," Peanut insists. "She works for F. T. Goldhero!"

Their father mops his brow with a handkerchief. "What on earth are you talking about?"

"F. T. Goldhero told her to email me! But I'm not supposed to tell you, or I'll be in trouble!"

This doesn't have the effect Peanut thought it would.

"Oh, my," says Mrs. Halfchap, touching the orange kidney cancer pin on her blouse. Two of her buttons are undone, and Peanut looks away so she doesn't have to see Mrs. Halfchap's big beige bra.

"Let me see this email." Peanut's father puts on his reading glasses and holds Peanut's phone an arm's length away. "How did this person get your contact information?" he asks after he reads it.

"She's on some site about the Falling Children that I keep saying she shouldn't be on," Jessie interjects.

"What's that about the Children?" Mrs. Halfchap asks.

Everyone ignores her.

"Why would a published author send an assistant to speak to minors without their legal guardian present?" Peanut's father asks. He places the phone on the windowsill.

"Maybe"—Peanut looks in turn at each of them—"because adults ruin everything!"

Which is true.

"If F. T. Goldhero wanted ideas, wouldn't he ask you to submit them on the Internet? And wouldn't his invitation come from an official email address?"

"Exactly!" Jessie throws up her hands.

"And F. T. Goldhero doesn't need ideas," clucks Mrs. Halfchap. "A little bird once told me he doesn't do anything *but* write."

Peanut shoots her a dirty look. She likes Mrs. Halfchap better when she can't hear.

"From what I've heard, everyone is searching for Mr. Goldhero, whoever he may be." Her father shakes his head. "I can't imagine he'd be dimwitted enough to send requests to random fans, then arrange to meet them in public. Think of the time involved. And the cost. Not to mention the chance he'll be discovered."

"But—"

"I believe, Peanut, that you've been had. And"—he raises his hand to silence her protest—"you're fortunate this didn't end on a worse note."

"But—"

"I want my phone back, and she should be grounded for real," Jessie says. "You don't just meet up with strangers from the Internet."

Their father nods. "For once, I agree with Jessie."

Peanut's eyes itch, and she can tell she is about to cry. She doesn't like to cry.

In second grade, she and Nancee rubbed onions on their cheeks while they looked in the mirror. Nancee continued to look like Nancee except a little wet around the eyes, but Peanut's eyes shrank into peach pits, and her nose doubled in size.

"You look like an ugly baby!" Nancee howled with laughter.

Peanut hasn't cried since and isn't about to now.

"*Tuum arca clausa!*" she shouts instead at Jessie.

Mrs. Halfchap gasps.

"May your box stay closed!" is the worst thing one lost soul can say to another: you can't move on to a higher realm of existence if there's no one to love you, and no one can love you if they can't ever *see* you.

Jessie makes a face. "You and those books," she says. "Ugh."

17

For hours, Peanut lies motionless on the floor of her bedroom, anger encasing her in amber.

If her father weren't so busy with his patients and hospital rounds and files, he could actually spend time with her instead of letting Jessie be in charge. Not once has he helped Peanut try to find her parents. Not once has he played along when she guesses who they could be. And he's never told Jessie *oh, hush!* when she complains, "Are we still doing this?"

9:04 p.m.

Did Buzz really go get F. T. Goldhero's assistant? Peanut tries to send Ms. Weeks a telepathic message.

Don't go, she thinks. *You need me.*

Downstairs, Jessie and their father are arguing again.

"It's not normal!" Jessie insists.

"It's to be expected," he says.

Peanut knows she is "it."

She opens her door and screams, "I can hear you!" Then, after turning off her light, she climbs into bed, still fully dressed, and waits.

～–～

By midnight, Peanut can only hear the ceiling fan whirring in Jessie's bedroom and the occasional *yip* of a coyote looking for company.

Taking care to avoid the stairs that creak, she sneaks downstairs and feels her way into the kitchen.

The window above the sink looks on to Buzz's house. Lights shine from every window, but that doesn't mean anything. What if Ms. Weeks already left?

Stop being such a Huperzine, she scolds herself, searching the front hall for her sneakers. *She's there. She has to be.*

Like Everlee assures Benjamin at the end of book one, "Sometimes it's okay to believe and not know why."

Peanut has her hand on the doorknob, ready to slip outside, when she hears Jessie outside on the porch. "What are you doing here?" she asks.

Peanut freezes.

"Surprise, surprise," someone else drawls.

Peanut's never known Jessie to have a boyfriend, only the occasional date with a tourist. Nancee thinks that's because then they aren't around long enough to get to know the *real* Jessie, who's a control freak and a complainer and lies to people right to their faces.

"You've…changed," Peanut hears Jessie say.

"Looks like I've missed a lot. Maybe you want to catch me up."

Peanut recognizes the voice. Her heart, and the sprinkler across the street, go *tick-tick-tick.*

She doesn't need to crack the front door—although she does—to confirm: the black hearse is parked in the driveway.

"Some other time," Jessie says, but now she sounds scared. "It's late."

"What's it been—ten years, maybe a little more?"

"I don't know. Maybe." Jessie pauses. "Are you back for good?"

Peanut can hear Orson Greeley thunking down the porch steps. A car door slams, and Peanut hears the engine rumble to life.

"Good or bad," he calls. "I haven't decided yet."

Headlights find Peanut through the window and flicker through her.

Before she can move, the front door opens.

"What are you doing?" Jessie says when she sees Peanut there. She is out of breath, her eyes darting around the room. "Why are you down here?"

Peanut freezes. "I don't know."

"Are you spying on me?" Jessie's eyes pulse. "What did you hear?"

"Nothing, I—"

Her sister points upstairs. "You need to go back to bed and stay there until morning. I mean it, Peanut."

Ms. Weeks may be waiting next door, but something about the way Jessie says this takes Peanut aback. Jessie's words are not a punishment so much as a warning.

Peanut doesn't argue. But she won't go to school in the morning, she decides as she heads back upstairs. Instead, she'll go next door to the Cross Creek Airport or to every hotel within a hundred miles, whatever it takes to track down Ms. Weeks.

Good or bad, I haven't decided yet, she hears Orson Greeley in her head. Something makes Peanut look outside her window. Sure enough, there is the hearse, parked across the street. Waiting, although Peanut has no idea for what—or for whom.

18

Libby leaves the diner with Buzz, only because she can't remember where she put the keys to her rental car or at which hotel she
made a reservation. *Did* she make a reservation? After the trip to
the airport, the plane ride, and the long drive here, it's a relief to
have someone—even if it is a stranger—open the door, point, and
say, "This way."

Buzz uses a cane, limping like his right leg is made of wood, and
every few feet, he turns and glares as if he knows she's thinking this.

Libby averts her eyes, watching instead the stores they pass. In
case he does turn out to be a serial killer, she'll need to explain to
the police where to rescue her. THE LICORICE PARLOR. GIBBON'S
GROCERIES. TEE-SHIRT TIME. An unnamed souvenir shop where
tourists dress in Wild West costumes and pay to have daguerreotypes
taken beside a stagecoach.

She stops in front of a video rental store, chunky VHS boxes for
Beverly Hills Cop and *Airplane* in the window. FREE BEANIE BABY
WITH 100TH RENTAL, a sign says.

"What year is it?" she asks, bewildered.

"Here? Perpetually 1987."

"Like the town in the Falling Children books?"

"Don't know." Buzz lifts his shoulders. "Haven't read them."

The street dead-ends at a narrow cement staircase cut into the hill. Buzz gestures for Libby and Rolf to go first. She stops counting steps at thirty because it's hard for her to count and climb at the same time.

At the top, Libby finds herself in a neighborhood of old farmhouses and wide unfenced yards. Leafy trees frame the sky, and the air is silhouetted with apples. Libby inhales. Wherever she is, it's quite pretty.

Buzz is still making his way up the stairs, gripping the metal railing with one hand, his cane in the other. By the top, his T-shirt is dotted with sweat. "There," he says, pointing to a tidy cottage across the street.

The front door is unlocked and the lights on. Buzz flops onto the living room couch and, using both hands, hoists his right leg onto the coffee table, narrowly missing a bowl half-full of milk. A few soggy rafts of cereal slosh back and forth inside it.

"Fuck," he says, massaging his hip. Then, remembering Libby, he gestures. "Sit wherever."

The couch is littered with skate magazines, a bird-watching guide, binoculars, prescription bottles, and empty energy drinks. Two nearby chairs are heaped with crumpled beer cans. Wedged into the carpet between them is an ashtray with a half-smoked joint rolled as fat as a cigar. A walker lies upside down against the fireplace, as if it has been thrown there.

Pushing a few peanut butter cracker wrappers out of the way with her foot, Libby chooses to stand.

On the flat-screen TV above the mantel, a skinny kid with shaggy brown hair jumps onto a skateboard and flies down a stair railing while eating what looks like a roast-beef hoagie. He spins into the air, chewing, before landing easily at the bottom.

"Is that you?" Libby squints.

"Not anymore." Buzz shuts off the TV, then shakes a blue pill from one of the prescription bottles and swallows it dry.

"You don't skateboard anymore?"

"No, I don't 'skateboard anymore.'" He puts air quotes around the phrase, although there's no need. "Look, do you know when Peanut's coming? I've got things to do."

Libby doubts that. She is pretty sure the only thing he has on his agenda is sitting here, watching old videos, drinking beer, and throwing the empty cans at the two chairs opposite the couch.

She's less certain who Peanut is.

"Peanut," Buzz repeats. "The kid you came here to see?"

Libby waits for her brain to catch up.

Nothing happens.

Buzz pulls a phone from his pocket and texts. Then he stares at the screen and waits for a reply. When one doesn't come, he makes a call.

"Where's Peanut?" he asks instead of saying hello.

At the answer, Buzz throws his phone onto the coffee table. It slides across, landing in an old takeout container.

"Why is this fucking happening to me?" He closes his eyes and squeezes the bridge of his nose. For a moment, Libby thinks he's crying.

"Are you—okay?" she asks.

Buzz looks up. "What's your name again? Mrs.—"

"Me?" She touches her chest. "I'm Libby."

How awful that she feels a sense of pride for remembering this.

"Peanut's grounded," he says. "She's not coming over. Do you remember how to get back to your car? I'll tell you how to get to a hotel. Or you can take the highway and go into Cross Creek. There's more places to stay there." He picks up a hospital bill from the floor and holds it out. "If you write Peanut a note, I'll give it to her next time I see her. Whenever that is."

It's too much information. "Say that again?" Libby blinks.

Buzz gives more details the second time: First, take a left, cross the street, wonky steps, look for the video store, remember the Beanie Babies? Take another left past the fountain. It's a cowboy, and he has his hand stuck in his pants, don't ask, whoever made this town had a twisted sense of humor...

Panic won't help, Libby tells herself. *What you need is to pay attention.*

It's what Everlee says to Huperzine in book two, when they're trying to outrun the Hide-Behinds. While Everlee quickly maps out an elaborate plan in the dirt, Huperzine breathes into a paper bag to try to stop hyperventilating.

Libby makes a fist and taps it against her forehead. *Calm down*, she begs both herself and Huperzine.

But it's the wrong verb because what she really needs to do is *remember*.

Buzz is watching her. Libby doesn't like to be watched.

"You want me to walk you back?"

She can tell he wants her to say no.

"No. I just—" She doesn't want to have a panic attack in front of him. "May I use your—"

Libby follows the direction he points, picking her way over crumpled socks, candy wrappers, and a bowl of old SpaghettiOs, which Rolf stops to polish off.

In the bathroom mirror, Libby's eyes are blue-yellow marbles of worry, her hair mostly out of its bun. She looks like someone who's rolled off an emotional precipice and has yet to hit bottom.

Paying attention so she doesn't repeat what happened in the airplane bathroom, Libby carefully shuts and locks the door. First, squeeze lock thingy with (trembling) fingers. B, turn to the left. Number three, let go.

Then she sits on the pink tile floor, her back against the cabinet, and studies her phone. Surely she wrote a note to herself about what she needed to do in this tiny town. Surely she planned ahead, knowing at some point, she'd lose the plot—again. But Libby can't remember the password to unlock her phone.

She runs her finger over the screen.

Her password's always Everlee, but this is a number pad. Libby tries the easiest combinations she can think of:

1234

5678

33C?

And just like that, her phone, assuming Libby is not Libby but someone with evil tendencies, maybe a Hide-Behind who has leapt out of the pages of—which book were they in?—shuts down for good.

"No." Libby jabs her finger at the dark screen. "This can't be happening."

She stands and pulls at the door, but it's locked. She's locked in. Libby pulls the knob as hard as she can, then tries to slide the door sideways like she saw a flight attendant in a movie do once. Nothing happens. Hand to her chest, trying to tamp down the panic—although really, she is swimming in it now, like a cold sea—Libby pounds on the door.

"Let me out! Please! Is anyone there? Let me out!"

Rolf barks from the other side.

"Please!" Libby feels as if the Unstopping has unleashed his giant wooden snake, the Cipher of Naught, on her. She can feel it curling the slats of its venomous tail around her throat. Any second, its scaly, poorly painted head will slink closer, hating her with its yellow eyes, preparing to sink its long fangs into her flesh. "Can anyone hear me?" She kicks at the door. "Please don't leave me!"

"Take it easy," a weary voice says from the other side. "I'm here, all right?"

19

The next thing Libby remembers, it's seven o'clock. Not p.m., but seven in the morning, according to the clock next to her bed. Sunlight paints her cheek.

Libby can't remember the last time she slept so soundly, despite a long, drawn-out stress dream. It was an embarrassing caper where she actually *got* on an airplane—she smiles at the absurdity—and traveled to some tiny mountain town in order to steal a fan's stories about the Children.

Along the way, Libby misplaced her manuscript of the last book. Which, of course, would mean losing years of hard work and being unmasked as F. T. Goldhero.

Thank God she woke up.

Libby's mouth is stale, but her head feels clearer, that's the important part. She taps her temples. She can feel space up there— fresh air again. *Today,* she thinks with excitement, *is going to be a good writing day.*

Kicking back the still-warm sheets, Libby stands and stretches. First, she'll go for a run with Rolf. Then she'll have a spoonful of peanut butter. Next, she'll write—all day.

It's only then that Libby notices the row of skateboards lined against the far wall. And the bookshelf jammed with bearings and bushings, gloves and tubes of shoe goo. There is a tall oak dresser, the drawers decorated with faded Stüssy stickers.

Peeking through the window blinds, Libby sees mountains rising in the distance. Her heart doesn't just sink. It plummets and plunges and all those other things.

~~~

Buzz—so she remembers him, at least—is sitting at the kitchen table, wearing a faded red T-shirt and jeans. His bare feet rest on Rolf's back. Rolf beats his tail against the worn linoleum when he sees Libby but doesn't get up.

Traitor, she thinks.

"I can't believe I'm really here," she says, wrapping her arms around herself.

Libby feels her breath coming in shallow, fast spurts, the way it had at Dr. Whatsit's office when he gave her the diagnosis.

Buzz looks up from the newspaper.

"I've never seen someone so wasted, they couldn't unlock a bathroom door." He finishes his yogurt and tosses the container at the trash can. It lands next to it, rolling alongside several others. "And I've seen some pretty fucked-up shit. Do you remember me taking the door off the hinges?"

Libby doesn't remember, but she's guessing there was lots of crying involved.

"You're lucky I didn't call the cops."

She is curious as to why he didn't. *She* would have if someone went into her bathroom, then forgot how to get out.

"Did I—say anything I shouldn't have?" she asks, feeling color twist into her cheeks.

Buzz unpeels the wrapper from a candy bar and looks at her, considering. "I don't know," he says finally, taking a bite. "I wasn't listening."

Libby takes stock of the small kitchen, with its flowered wallpaper and framed paintings of birds. Dirty dishes pile in the sink. A fine sheen of crumbs covers the counters like a dusting of snow.

"I have the same refrigerator in my apartment," she says.

"Who are you?" Buzz asks. "Seriously."

She lifts her shoulders. "Nobody."

"Then why are you here to see Peanut?"

Libby gives a small cough and begins the spiel she practiced on Rolf. "I work as a personal assistant for F. T. Goldhero. As a tribute to his fans, we're asking children around the world to weigh in on how the series will end."

"So there's this thing called the Internet," Buzz says, raising an eyebrow. "Your boss doesn't believe in email?"

Libby is grateful that he's given her the answer. "He doesn't use a computer unless he has to. And even then, he types with gloves on."

"Gloves."

"Not winter ones," Libby says. "Latex. Like a surgeon wears."

Silently, she apologizes to the imaginary F. T. Goldhero.

"Don't take this the wrong way," Buzz says as he limps to the counter and drops a piece of bread into the toaster. He has to smack the lever down several times before it stays put. "You don't seem like an assistant."

Libby runs a hand through her hair, feeling the tangles. "I just woke up," she says. "And I've been traveling." She looks around. "Did I bring my suitcase in? A green carry-on?"

"No."

"Did you see me with a suitcase?"

Buzz gestures to Rolf. "Only him."

Libby sinks into a chair. This is just like her dream—except worse, because now she has to live with the consequences. She tries to remember exactly what is in her suitcase: Underwear. Dog food for sure. Shampoo. Running shoes. The little red notebook she takes everywhere, even though most of the pages are now missing. And her printout of the manuscript for the last book.

Libby drops her forehead onto the table. Crumbs nick her skin. "This isn't happening," she says.

She can feel Buzz watching her.

"What is it you want exactly?" he asks.

A new brain, Libby thinks.

"My suitcase," she says aloud, but she is too drained to sound like she means it. Maybe it doesn't matter anymore.

"I mean, what do you want from Peanut."

"Writing's so much easier when you're a kid." Libby can't keep the jealousy out of her voice.

"You're a writer, too?"

Libby wonders if he's trying to catch her in a lie. "Not lately."

They look at each other. Libby pulls the sleeves of her sweater over her hands. It would be easier to stare back if he were doughy and soft, with little round glasses. Like the Speelgoedmaker from book three, she explains.

"I don't know who that is," Buzz says. "I'm not into fantasy crap."

"If you say so," says Libby, offended.

The toaster lets out a feeble beep.

"You want breakfast?" Buzz slides a plate of blackened toast and mostly empty jar of grape jam in front of her. "Hope you like it well done."

Libby doesn't have an opinion. Thanks to the plaques and tangles in her brain, she can't taste much anymore. She cracks the crust between her fingers, pretending to be interested in something outside the window so Buzz stops talking to her.

The backyard drops into a soft pocket of woods. A trail emerges from the other side like a dusty tail, before winding up another steep slope of green. Is it a hill or a mountain? Libby doesn't know. She watches someone make their way up the trail—a long-haired man dressed in baggy black pants and a dusty oversize tailcoat that swings when he walks.

He's using a crooked walking stick that reminds Libby a little of the Staff of Consequence in book four. But he doesn't seem to be exerting himself, so, she thinks, maybe it *is* called a hill.

When the man reaches the top, he turns and waves. It feels like he's waving right at Libby, but she's inside the house.

Isn't she?

Tentatively, Libby reaches out her hand to touch the window. The glass is warm under her palm. A dead fly lies trapped between the screen and storm pane. When she looks back up at the hill, the waving man is gone.

"Do you know anyone who wears a borrowed conscience on the outside of their clothes?"

Buzz looks at her. "Do I what?"

She points. "There was a man—"

"What the fuck's a borrowed conscience?"

"It looks like an appendix," Libby says, reaching for a pair of binoculars on the table, "but it tells you right from wrong."

"Why would I borrow one?"

"There was a man—" She holds the binoculars up to her eyes.

"Other way."

Buzz flips them, and the woods transform into an army of green-whiskered pine trees. Libby is suddenly so close that she can see the craggy lips worn into their trunks. Everlee would know what they are whispering. Libby can only pretend. *Go home, go home, go home.*

She doesn't see the man.

"What's that?" Libby points to what looks like part of a tree house. It is exactly halfway there, as if someone began dreaming of it, then woke up in a cold sweat.

"My dad and I started that," says Buzz. "It was supposed to be a half-pipe."

"Why didn't you finish?"

"He died." Buzz shrugs. "Both my parents." He holds out his palm. "You can still feel the splinter from when we were trying to build it."

Libby gingerly touches his skin but can't feel anything. "I'm sorry," she says.

The trees are talking faster now. *This, this, this,* Libby reads their lips.

She is close, *so* close to something she needs to save the Falling Children. She has no idea what.

⌐＿〜

They wait for Peanut.

Buzz flips through the sports section of the local paper, although Libby senses that he's watching her more than reading. He hands her the rest of the *Blue Skies Gazette*, but reading has become hard for Libby. Her attention lopes away like a horse.

SEPTIC TRUCK OVERTURNS. *I'll never save the Children.* LOOSE BOVINE PIGS OUT AT WEDDING. *What if I can't find my suitcase?*

The revelation that it's not just her suitcase that's missing but her manuscript hits Libby like, well, a septic truck overturning on top of her.

Think, Libby begs herself. But instead of concentrating on the real problem at hand—*Where is the manuscript? The manuscript is missing. It's missing, do you understand?*—Libby's hands continue holding the newspaper, and her eyes continue reading the words on the page.

TIME RUNNING OUT FOR F. T. GOLDHERO, another headline reads. *Time is running out!*

Libby reads the words again, tapping them with her finger. She looks up at Buzz. "What does this mean?"

He looks over. "It ate the whole fucking wedding cake. It's like a six-hundred-pound pig."

"No, this." She points. "They're saying they know where F. T. Goldhero lives." She follows the text with her finger. "That his personal assistant lives near the Princeton campus."

It's likely that F. T. Goldhero lives at least part-time in the area as well, says the source, Glenn somebody. *While he spends time crafting the books, his low-level assistant handles administrative duties like responding to fan mail.*

Low level?

"Rude," Libby says under her breath. "I never should have slept with you, Glenn. And definitely not twice."

She closes her eyes in an attempt to steady the room.

"Who's Glenn?" Buzz asks.

Libby pretends she didn't hear him. "Do you have a phone?" she asks.

He points to an old yellow rotary dial on the wall. Libby doesn't touch it. She has no idea where to put her fingers.

"Do you have one that I can…?" She makes a jabbing motion with her index finger.

Buzz hands her his iPhone. The sliding door to the back deck is open—thank God—so Libby doesn't have to figure out how to thingy it. She slips through into a burst of birdsong and sunlight. Rolf follows.

"City and listing, please?" the operator asks.

Libby's mind goes blank. It is a lovely white blank, like a snowflake, only without the intricate patterns. She would describe it as peaceful if not for the fact that it affixes itself firmly over her memory.

"Breathe," she tells herself, sitting on the wooden deck. Libby exhales slowly, as long and hard as she can, trying to blow the white out of the way.

"City and listing, please?" the operator asks again.

"Glenn—" Libby stops. She can't remember his last name. Has she ever known it? Has she ever asked?

"Excuse me?"

"Glenn with the beard," she tries again, seeing him clearly in her mind. "And a corgi. I think his last name starts with a B? Or maybe a C?"

Closing her eyes, Libby tries to retrieve anything more specific.

"I know he's in Princeton." She squeezes the bridge of her nose. "And he has a wife who just moved to Belmar."

"I need a full name, ma'am," the operator says, unimpressed.

"Could you just give me a few names to try? Please?"

The operator disconnects.

Libby realizes Buzz's phone screen is cracked in the corner. She hopes she didn't do that.

Not until Rolf beats his tail excitedly does Libby realize Buzz is standing in the doorway, eating her leftover toast.

"You want me to call someone for you?" he asks uncertainly.

"I can't remember." She hands back his phone. "I can't remember anything."

141

"Then you think I should call, like, a hospital?"

Libby blinks back tears, but she can't blink fast enough. They ski down her cheeks. "No."

"Family?"

"No."

"Friend? Neighbor? That guy, Glenn?"

Does he fit into any of those categories?

Libby drops her head into her hands. There are the Children to rescue—where is her suitcase?—she needs to get home. Why isn't her phone working?

She desperately wants to take a shower, but the door to the bathroom is off its hinges.

"Has your life ever been so shitty that you just want to hide from the real world and never come out?" she hears herself ask.

Libby is surprised when Buzz slides down next to her. The brace on his leg looks hot and itchy.

He flicks the last fragment of toast over the edge of the deck. Black specks launch into the air. "Yeah," he says, "it has."

20

In the morning, Jessie tries to make peace with blueberry pancakes, Peanut's favorite. She pulled ripe berries from the bushes behind their house and warmed up the maple syrup.

Peanut jams the handle of a fork into the tall stack of pancakes. Then she scribbles I *hate you* on a flag of paper and presses it onto the tines.

"Lovely," says Jessie. "Very mature."

Pushing past her, Peanut takes the last grapefruit from the refrigerator. She hates the sour fruit, but if she doesn't eat it, Jessie will. She eats nothing but grapefruit two days a week to make sure she fits into her Train Robbery corset.

"You can't stay mad at me forever," Jessie says, watching Peanut hack at the grapefruit with a butter knife.

Oh yes, I can, Peanut thinks.

"I've only ever done what's best for you."

Peanut viciously spoons out a pulpy segment of grapefruit and forces herself to swallow it.

"I wish I'd had someone looking out for me at your age," Jessie goes on. "I'm trying to prevent you from making the same mistakes I did."

Peanut throws the barely touched grapefruit into the trash so Jessie can't even have the leftovers. Then she grabs her backpack and heads to the door.

"Peanut, wait."

"What?" she asks in her iciest voice. She is Everlee in the Falling Orphanage, confronting the cruel headmistress who deprives the children of meals, warm beds, socks in the wintertime...

But unlike Gladys, Jessie wants to give Peanut a hug.

"I hate fighting with you," she says into Peanut's hair.

For a moment, Peanut relents. Jessie smells like pancakes. Her arms are warm. Then she thinks of F. T. Goldhero's assistant and finds the strength to wriggle free.

"Then don't be such a Gladys."

~

Outside, bumblebees spiral in cursive loops above the lilac bushes. The Graysons' chickens chatter as they scratch for worms in the dirt. The streets in the fancy historic district are being repaved, and as Peanut walks down the hill to the bus stop, she breathes in the sludgy-sweet scent of hot tar.

Once Peanut is sure Jessie isn't watching from the porch, she cuts back through the McVays' orchard, glad she wore a green Falling Children T-shirt today so she blends in.

Her stories make her backpack heavy, but it's a good weight, like armor on a knight. Crouching low, Peanut ducks around the opposite side of the Graysons' house.

Jessie will surely be in the bathroom now, finishing the last layer of her makeup and pinning her hair into an upsweep. She likes to practice her lines in the bathroom mirror: *Please! My baby! Give me back my baby!*

Still, Peanut stays low as she creeps between her neighbors' houses. The last thing she needs is for Mr. Halfchap, still dying in bed, to open a window and ask, *Have you seen my wife?*

Buzz's yellow house comes into view. He does nothing to maintain it, but still it's one of the tidiest houses on the hill. That's because their father cuts the grass and Jessie plants tulip bulbs each fall. Something about Buzz makes people want to do things for him.

Which is why Peanut doesn't feel the least bit guilty about asking him to save F. T. Goldhero's assistant. He's long overdue to pay it forward, so it might as well be to her.

The backpack smacking against her spine, Peanut sneaks up Buzz's driveway.

"Sorry for the delay," she practices saying, "but you'll find these stories worth the wait."

She is trying it out with a British accent when Buzz comes to the door. He looks cranky.

Peanut's heart sinks. "She's not here anymore, is she?"

"Not all here." Buzz steps outside, closing the front door behind him. "What the hell, Peanut? Where'd you find her?"

"I told you, she works for F. T. Goldhero. She wants my stories." She pats her backpack.

"You can't just bring home rando people you met online."

"Technically, I didn't," Peanut points out. "*You* did."

Buzz doesn't laugh. "You know what I mean."

"She's not a rando. She works for F. T. Goldhero, the most creative, imaginative person in the world!" Peanut pushes past him into the house. "I'll do the talking," she says. "A spoonful of sugar in a lake goes unnoticed. In a pond, it kills the fish."

"What's that supposed to mean?"

Peanut looks at him reproachfully. "You really need to read the books."

Buzz's house is worse than Peanut has ever seen it—all mounds of dirty laundry and slimy food wrappers on the floor. The bathroom door is off its hinges, lying on its side in the hallway.

"You didn't clean up?"

"No." Buzz makes air quotes. "I didn't 'clean up.'"

Libby is at the kitchen table. Her chin rests on her fist, and she's staring out the window at the woods beyond. There is an unnatural stillness about her, and when she turns toward Peanut, it's like she's fighting an invisible undercurrent.

"I'm here!" announces Peanut.

Buzz picks an old plastic jack-o'-lantern off the fridge and combs through the contents before lifting out a roll of Smarties. Then he leans back against the counter and unwraps the candy like he's settling in for a show.

"I'm glad you're here," Libby tells Peanut. "I need to go home."

Peanut shoots Buzz a resentful glance. "I wouldn't want to sleep here either."

"And you have your—" Libby flips her hands back and forth like pages in a book.

"Stories? Yes!" Peanut drops her backpack onto the table. "Ta-da!" she says and pulls out the hundred or so pages she has. Some are written on notebook paper. Others are typed in her favorite fonts like *Brush Script MT* and *Snell Roundhand*.

"You wrote all these?"

Peanut warms under her astonishment. "I've been writing about the Falling Children since the first book came out when I was seven and a half," she says. "I even have stories about what happens after they vanquish the Unstopping and become grown-ups."

When Libby doesn't reply, Peanut keeps going. "I write first thing in the morning, and sometimes, if I have a really good idea at night, I get up and write it down. And when I don't have school, I go outside and write." She points to the woods outside the window. "In the tree house. You can't really see it that well from here, but it's my best writing spot."

"Is it?" Libby smiles ruefully.

"It's not a tree house," Buzz says.

"But I can write anywhere," Peanut says quickly, in case F. T. Goldhero invites especially gifted children to write at his castle. "And super fast. Once, I finished a story in, like, two hours. And that includes checking for spelling errors. Although," she adds, "I rarely find any."

"You make it sound so easy." Libby's mouth twists. Peanut isn't sure it's a smile, but this is her favorite subject, so she barrels ahead.

"It is for me. I know the Falling Children. It's like they're living in my mind, and I can visit them anytime I want."

Peanut hopes she sounds confident but not braggy. She's still figuring out the fine line between the two. Whenever she's taken a quiz about it online, her score always includes advice like, *Eat a slice of humble pie, girlfriend!*

Libby stares at Peanut's stories.

"Read them." Peanut settles into a chair. "I can wait."

Libby doesn't read. Instead, she looks around, as if someone might be listening, then lowers her voice. "Is there anything in here about what to do if the Cipher of Naught gets free again?"

"No." Peanut laughs. "Why would there be? The Children grabbed it by its tail and trapped it for eternity." She glances at Buzz. "It's a big wooden snake. You wouldn't like it."

Libby frowns. "Then what about—Mean Li'l Bebe?"

With her cruel heart and soul-shattering cries, Mean Li'l Bebe is one of the scariest parts of the entire series. Luckily, in book five, Everlee lured the baby doll into a fun house mirror, which Benjamin and Huperzine then smashed into a billion pieces. There's no way Mean Li'l Bebe could recover from that.

"But what if she did?" Libby asks. "And what if the Unstopping captured Everlee with uncertain magic, and dropped her into the

Depths of Despair, and is now trying to harvest her soul?" She bites her lip. "Then what?" she asks. "What would you do?"

When Peanut looks at Buzz, he raises an eyebrow as if to say, *See? Told you.*

She looks back at Libby, noticing for the first time the spot of jam on her sweater and the bony crests of her shoulders, the way she nervously taps her right index finger on the table. Her socks (one gray, one bright pink) don't match.

Last March, when there was a freak blizzard after a 90-degree day, Mr. Harland, who owns the local oil company, undressed in the middle of the street and ran naked through downtown. He waved his arms, ranting about how people who burned fossil fuels today would be fossils under the sea tomorrow. His wife stopped him from plunging into the icy river by promising him a vacation in Hawaii, but she really just took him to the hospital and left him there.

Something in Libby's voice reminds Peanut of Mr. Harland.

"F. T. Goldhero wouldn't do any of those things to the Children—not without knowing exactly how to save them," she says slowly.

"All I know is, if one of them dies, all of them should," Libby says. "The despair—they couldn't bear it. *I* couldn't bear it. Maybe you could help me figure out how to do it quickly."

Peanut stands. "I don't have any stories like that," she says. "I love the Children."

"Me, too," Libby says, too quickly.

There is no way this woman can work for F. T. Goldhero. Peanut shoves her stories into her backpack, even as Libby pleads, "No, leave them! I'll still read them. I just need…" She curves her thumbs and index fingers into circles and holds them over her eyes.

Peanut is shaking from anger now as much as disappointment. As if being left for dead as a baby wasn't bad enough, there's Orson

Greeley trying to abduct her in his hearse, and now this lady, who is clearly no friend of the Children.

"I tried to tell you," Buzz says, following her to the front door.

Peanut feels her heart folding in on itself like a little paper box.

"Stop talking to people on the Internet, all right?" Buzz says. "Jesus."

She stares at the holes in his T-shirt. "Please don't tell Jessie."

"Why would I?" Buzz yawns. "I'm kicking her out and going back to bed. You want me to find you a ride to school?"

She shakes her head.

But when Buzz opens the door, Peanut can't bear the thought of going through it. Outside are Nancee and Rosemary and the moist dog-food smell of the school cafeteria. Out that door is her father and his arm's-length disinterest and Jessie and, well, everything about Jessie.

Peanut catches sight of herself in the mirror. Her right eye is swiveled sideways, straining to look back into the kitchen. Her cheek sags under the weight of her scar.

Peanut leans her head against Buzz's chest.

"Take it easy," he says, surprised. He claps her shoulder a few times. "It's all good."

Buzz is a terrible liar.

21

Halfway between her house and Buzz's, slipped into the narrow crack between wet cool grass and hot dry sidewalk, Peanut spies a crumpled wad of paper. She picks it up automatically, thinking it's another one of Buzz's junky wrappers that he should have put into the trash.

It's not. It's a napkin with the name of an airline printed in the corner. And on it is written a list, the handwriting spiky, black, and so small, it could have been written by the stuffed dormouse that Huperzine befriends in book one. To remember! it is titled.

1. Get suitcase from overhead compartment.
2. DO NOT FORGET ABOUT ROLF THE DOG.
3. Get rental car.
4. Pay extra for GPS. Do not cheap out!
5. Drive to town.
6. Be charming (TRY?) and act normal. You are the assistant (hired by Cyndie Herod-Huntlee! haha) so act like one! Pencil behind ear. Brisk manner while speaking. British accent? Practice first. DO NOT STARE OFF.
7. Casually (casually!) drop in conversation how children may be/are definitely in serious

danger. Ask: "Hmmm how would you fix?" Don't be weird. Please.

8. Take v. good notes. Better: Record conversation! (Figure out how to on phone.)
9. Thank profusely. Shake hands. Promise autographed copy.
10. Drive to airport (USE GPS!) and take flight home. You can do it!
11. DO NOT FORGET ROLF.
12. Carry suitcase onto plane. Get from overhead compartment once you land.
13. Take cab home from airport. (Key inside zipped compartment of carry-on.)
14. SAVE THE CHILDREN.

Peanut's head spins. The list is uncannily similar to the one Everlee writes on her forearm in fine-tip permanent marker in book four, after the Unstopping slips her a poison that will slowly erase her memory.

"To remember!" that fourteen-point list is titled, too, although it contains things like "Swallow a teaspoon of bilge water from the *Sink Ng* Ship" and "Convince the Squirrel Keeper to give you one of his whiskers." Once Everlee does everything, she realizes the list is actually a spell of uncertain magic. Her memory is restored.

Peanut's good eye speeds through the list again. Her heart rocks faster.

While most of her mind has been reading the words, a small part of her brain has been working on something else, something Peanut didn't ask it to.

Cyndie Herod-Huntlee (ha ha)
Cyndie Herod-Huntlee?

Peanut flings her backpack onto the sidewalk and, kneeling, digs out a pencil and a piece of paper.

Cyndie Herod-Huntlee

Peanut pushes up her glasses. Rearranged, the words could be "cheerily hued tendon." Or "Lenore hided chutney."

But it is also…

The Children need you.

Peanut is a believer of hunches and gut instincts. Like when she decided to sit next to Nancee in kindergarten. And how she just knows her real parents have an excellent explanation for abandoning her as a baby.

Tearing back to Buzz's, Peanut pounds on the door. When he unlocks it, she pushes past him.

"Mrs. Weeks? Mrs. Weeks!" Peanut has always wanted to be breathless for a reason other than PE, and it has happened today and feels as good—no, *better*—than she dreamed.

"What's going on?" Buzz follows her into the kitchen.

Libby is still at the table, gloomily tracing one finger through a pile of crumbs. *HELP*, she has written.

Peanut thrusts the limp napkin into her face. "It's you," she announces. She shakes the paper. "*You're* F. T. Goldhero."

22

"I thought F. T. Goldhero was a dude."

Peanut looks at Buzz, disgusted. "Women are extremely great writers, too. Look at me!"

Libby squints at the napkin. She doesn't remember writing the list—or following those directions. Life would have been easier, though, if she had.

Cyndie Herod-Huntlee, she notices. *Good one.*

"Is it you?" Peanut asks. "It is, isn't it?"

Libby bites her thumbnail, considering her options. But that becomes too confusing, like trying to think of a color she's never seen before, so she raises her shoulders and says, "You can't tell anyone. Please?"

The little girl looks as if she might faint. She drops to her knees and gazes rapturously at Libby. "You have the best imagination of anyone I know," she says on a breath. "I wish I were you."

"Don't say that." Libby makes a face.

"Aw, come on." Buzz swipes the newspaper off the table and skims the article about F. T. Goldhero, although there's no picture to compare Libby to, only words. "That's not you," he announces. "No way."

"See?" Libby agrees. "Now you see the problem."

And not even the biggest one.

"Look, if you're really F. M. Goldhero—"

"F.T.," corrects Peanut.

"—then prove it," he challenges. "Prove you are F. *T.* Goldhero. Show us something only he would know."

"Like?" Libby asks.

"Like your bank account," he challenges. "Then I'll fucking believe you."

"I don't remember the password."

Libby isn't trying to be coy, but she can tell Buzz thinks so. "So show me your checkbook," he says. "Or your wallet. I'm easy."

"It's not like her credit cards are going to say 'F. T. Goldhero.' Or she walks around with hundreds of dollars," Peanut says scornfully.

"Well, sometimes I do." Libby pats her pockets. "But I gave them away already. I like to drop them on the ground sometimes. You know, as a surprise?"

"Riiiight." Buzz pulls his old laptop off the counter and sets it in front of her. "In that case, check your email."

"My—email?"

"Yeah. You have emails from your 'fancy banks,' right?" he says, making air quotes. "Or your lawyer. Or fans or whatnot. So open your email. Let's see it."

"My email," Libby repeats.

"We swear we won't read anything confidential," Peanut adds, glaring at Buzz.

Libby stares at the dozens of icons on the computer screen, the colorful circles and letters, and a tiny little camera, and appropriately enough, a question mark. Buzz tosses another sleeve of Sweet Tarts into his mouth and rests one arm on the back of her chair, waiting.

"I'll open Gmail." Peanut tries to help. "Everyone has Gmail."

She pushes a few buttons and gets to Buzz's email account. His inbox, Libby sees, is line after line of past-due hospital bills and threats from collection agencies.

Peanut sees them, too. "Why aren't you paying your bills? Are you out of money?"

"This isn't about me." Buzz leans over and quickly logs out.

Libby is left staring at two blank pipes for her username and password.

She stares for a while.

"Here's the email address you wrote me from," Peanut says, typing it in.

iamlibbyweeks@gmail.com

"Oh," Libby says, pleased at how nicely that fits into the space. "Thank you."

She bites her bottom lip and tries to think of the password that comes next.

Rolf. Benjamin. Huperzine. FallingChildren. Fa1lingch1ildren. Falling_Children. FallingChildren3.

Password incorrect, it responds each time.

Libby feels she's failing a test.

Gran Bere, she tries. She loves Gran Bere. She imagines it waddling into this kitchen, putting its paws onto its thick hips and saying, *What in dear heaven's name is this fine furry mess?*

Libby can't believe she killed off Grand Bere. She is a horrible person.

Horrible person, she types into the bar.

Password incorrect.

Then Libby gets an idea. It blooms like a thingy from the middle of her thing-brain.

"Who's the bossy one?" she asks Peanut. "The one in charge."

Peanut looks confused. "You mean Jessie?"

"No. In the books."

"Everlee?" Peanut looks shocked that Libby doesn't know this, but Libby is already typing.

Everlee.

Everlee is the password.

Her inbox opens, and Libby sits back in the kitchen chair, exhausted from the effort but grinning as widely as if she's found the secret entrance to the OtherWay and convinced the notoriously foul-tempered Squirrel Keeper to let her through.

Inside are tens of thousands of fan letters, forwarded from Groton & Sons, that still need to be answered:

The Children saved my life!!

Thank you, from the mother of a very sick child

Pls read: Everlee helped me leave my husband

You make me feel less alone!!!

"Wow," Buzz says, surprised. "People really like you."

"Not me," Libby clarifies. "The Children."

It doesn't take long to find several emails from Peanut. Besides her reply to Libby's *URRRGENTE* request, she has recently written:

Don't forget! Ante Up

You need to think like a kid to save the Children

READ: I am the good idea you need

"It's you." Peanut claps. "It's you! It's you! It's you!"

Libby navigates past emails from Merry@grotonbooks.com titled things like Did you change your personal email? URGENT: PLS CALL, and Where are you?

She has also written dozens of emails to herself, using the subject lines as reminders. Scrolling down, she reads, Turn off stove, Almost out of dog food, and Tell Dr. Whatsit getting worse.

"What's getting worse?" asks Buzz.

"Nothing." Libby hastily clicks to the following page.

Save the children. Save the Children. URGENT: Save the children.

Buzz lets out a low whistle. '"So," he says, "if someone turns you in, they really get a million bucks?"

"You better not." Peanut's eyes narrow.

"It's a joke." Buzz flops into a chair, hooking his leg over the arm. "But," he says to Libby, "I still don't get why you're here."

Maybe at one point, Libby had planned something articulate to say if she was found out, but she—*Can't remember*, the Children chorus inside her head. *We know.*

"I was sick for a while," she says. "It affected my—" She taps her head.

"Writing? Like writer's block? You can't write?" Peanut looks worried. "When will it go away?"

Once I kill myself, Libby thinks.

"Soon," she says, thinking of her Tylenol.

"What you said before." Peanut frowns. "Is that true? Are the Children really in mortal danger in the last book?"

She ticks off the offenses Libby mentioned earlier—the Cipher of Naught and Mean L'il Bebe, resurrected and stronger than ever. Everlee trapped by the Unstopping in the Depths of Despair.

"Sort of?" Libby says. "Maybe?"

"But why?" Peanut raises her voice. "Why did you do that? How *could* you do that?"

Libby feels her face warm. "It just—happened."

"Ease up, P," Buzz says. "It's not like they're real."

"Maybe *you're* not real," Peanut says.

"It's not as bad as it sounds," Libby lies. "I need a little help. That's all."

"I *will* help you." Peanut pinches her scar excitedly. "And you can stay here instead of a hotel so Baron McBroom doesn't swoop down like a Knock-Knock and find you."

"Stay here?" Buzz gestures to the messy living room. "But I'm busy."

Libby thinks of the bathroom missing a door. "I don't—"

"Buzz won't tell anyone, don't worry. He'll protect the Children." Peanut shoots him a warning look. "He just doesn't know he wants to yet."

She elbows her brother until he extends his hand.

Libby hesitates. She doesn't like shaking hands. Her palms are always sticky with sweat, even first thing in the morning. "Worry runs inside you like sap," Vernice used to cluck. Or was it Gran Bere talking to Huperzine?

Buzz's palm is as dry and smooth as paper.

Feeling it against her own, Libby is reminded of when the first Falling Children book was published.

The Children, very young then, had safely escaped the orphanage and outsmarted the Unstopping (for the time being). By the last chapter, Everlee, Benjamin, and Huperzine had moved into Pompou's Toy Emporium, living among joyful whirling tops and marionettes that did the cancan and toy trains that happily shrank them down and transported them anywhere in the world.

Libby felt such gratitude that the Children had welcomed her into their world. In real life, Vernice was dying of cancer, and Libby had been fired by the community college. She had three hundred dollars in her bank account and four hundred dollars' worth of bills on her desk.

Despite that—or maybe because of it—the Children became more real than anything in Libby's own life. Out of her imagination sprang flesh and bone. More importantly, their story became a place for her to hide.

Libby takes in the sunny cluttered kitchen; the girl with a misshapen face in front of her, chewing a frizzy strand of hair; the lumpy mountains outside the window; and Buzz's hand in her own. She can do it again, can't she?

23

"What need do we first?"

Peanut is so excited that her tongue trips over her words.

True, F. T. Goldhero is nothing like she imagined, but if he were, *she* wouldn't be here asking for Peanut's help.

Peanut wants nothing more than to pull her backpack more tightly onto her shoulders and parachute into the last book, where the Children are apparently choking down way too much bitter hook-root and feeling doomed.

"Where is it? Can I read it?"

Libby chews her thumbnail for a while. Then she looks at Buzz. "It's in my suitcase."

"The one that's lost?" he asks.

"Lost? It can't be lost!" Peanut smooths out the napkin—which, by the way, she is keeping *forever*—and points to number one on the list. "Wasn't it there when you landed in Cross Creek?"

Libby shakes her head. "I accidentally got off in Denver."

"What was the accident?" Buzz asks under his breath.

Peanut ignores him. "Then I bet your bag is in Cross Creek." She tears to the front door and gestures for them both to follow. "Come on! Hurry up! We have to go get it!"

"Don't look at me." Buzz holds up his hands. "I don't do Cross Creek."

"It's only a half hour away!"

"I don't care if it's five minutes," Buzz says. "Everything about that town sucks."

Peanut pulls her brother into the laundry room for a private conference.

"If someone else finds that suitcase, I'll never get a chance to save the Children," she whispers fiercely. "The entire series will end with gruesome death and deep sadness and the poor little Williwigs being tortured, one by one, by the Unstopping."

At Buzz's expression, Peanut adds, "They're a little like Ewoks but so cute that they make your heart melt in your mouth like candy."

"So?"

"So you should care!"

He shrugs. "I don't."

"Well, then too bad because you don't have anything else to do! You're sitting here, feeling sorry for yourself. It's annoying."

"And what is it you'd like me to be doing instead of"—he uses air quotes—"'sitting here'?"

"Drive us to the airport," Peanut says. "Call me in sick to school. And give me the emergency credit card Daddy gave you." She reaches for his wallet on the counter. "Because I know he did."

Buzz slaps her hand away. "What for?"

Sometimes Peanut feels her brother has fallen off his skateboard one time too many. "So I can buy things to make F. T. Goldhero feel better."

"Like—flowers?"

"Like medicine and stuff. Things to help her write so she can save the Children."

"Or plan B: I make one phone call and become a full-on millionaire."

"Trust me, you will be repaid a thousand times over in karma, my good man." Peanut puts her hands together and bows like the Sightless Kendama the children rescue in book four.

Buzz sighs. "I'd rather have a million bucks," he says.

Peanut opens the laundry door. She can't help clapping when she sees Libby still sitting there. F. T. Goldhero is real. The Falling Children are *real*.

She knew it.

～～

On the way to Libby's rental car, Peanut borrows Buzz's phone and googles "writers block" and "cure."

Tens of thousands of solutions pop up. How easy was that? Peanut marvels. She is surprised (and a *smidge* disappointed, if she's being completely honest) that Libby didn't do this already.

Peanut looks up to see Mr. Pretzky, who owns the bookstore downtown, washing his car with a hose that doesn't quite reach. The water splatters into a puddle on the driveway, which he then attempts to kick onto his soapy tires. Why do adults always make things harder than they need to be?

At an online store for natural remedies, Peanut adds vitamin B, an herb called ashwagandha, and a bottle of something called MegaMindPower Extra Plus to a shopping cart. Something is bound to do the trick and certainly all these things together. Maybe they can be mixed into a smoothie.

What will F. T. Goldhero be like when she feels better? Peanut sneaks a look at Libby. Maybe she usually *does* wear a skirt-suit and carry a briefcase. Maybe when she gets rid of her writer's block, her British accent will come back.

Before they reach the bottom of the staircase, Peanut has spent over three hundred dollars on products. True, it is a lot of money, "but you can't put a price tag on friends, even imaginary ones," as Gran Bere says. Peanut pays extra to have all seven products arrive at Buzz's the next day. Hopefully, they'll start working fast.

Meanwhile, she mentally combs through the Falling Children series, trying to remember every single good thing that might help save the Children. There is the Jumping Jack and his ability to *sproing* through time. Frozen Charlotte, the mysterious fortune-telling doll with chattering teeth whom the Children rescued from under the lake. The Conjurer of Rokenbok, who originally built the passage from Pompou's to the OtherWay.

Peanut has no idea how anyone can cut the Children free from the Unstopping's notoriously uncertain magic, but maybe Libby is using *hyperbole*, she thinks. In real life, there is always a way to escape.

As they pass the train depot, a throng of excited tourists already lined up to board, Peanut ducks to the other side of Buzz. She has enough to think about it right now. She doesn't want to face Jessie, too.

24

Small problem: Libby can't remember where she parked her car.

"It's a big silver SUV," she says, thinking of her obnoxious car at home. "Ugly and talky, with big hips. The seats are always hot."

Buzz reads the tag attached to the rental key. "It's a blue Camry."

Peanut trails behind them, her head bowed to her phone. The sidewalks downtown are crowded with people carrying kayak paddles or fishing gear or loops of climbing rope. Road bikers flash by in a blur of smooth legs and neon nylon. Twice—or maybe three times—as Libby starts to cross a street, Buzz throws his arm out like a safety rail to prevent her and Rolf from getting creamed.

"You can hear them coming," he says after the second—or maybe the third—time. "The tires press the pavement."

"You bike?" Libby asks, not able to picture him in tight shorts and click-clacky shoes.

"No," he says, "I just know the sound of an accident when I hear one."

To prove his point, he holds out his arm a third—or fourth—time and prevents her from stepping off the curb as more bikers streak past.

"Watch out," one of them calls.

"Fuck you," Buzz says.

The rental car is still parked in front of the Pig-n-Pancake, two tickets curled like eyelashes under the windshield wipers.

"But I didn't do anything wrong," Libby says. "Did I?"

"You have a Texas license plate." Buzz pulls the papers loose and throws them into the back seat next to Rolf.

"Freddy? The police chief? He hates the Cowboys," Peanut explains, sliding in as well.

Libby's heart sinks. She'll never remember to pay them, and then what? A suspended license, contentious court case, jail?

She's grateful Buzz offers to drive so she can continue her mental list of worst-case scenarios. This will take a while:

Being framed for a crime she didn't commit. Once in prison, brutally shivved by her cellmate. Given solitary confinement, only to have an apocalyptic natural disaster strike that leaves her dying of starvation, thirst, and fear in a locked, dank cell...

"Man, did you get the smallest car you could?" Buzz pushes the seat back. "If I were you, I'd be cruising around in a Rolls-Royce."

"No, you wouldn't," Peanut says from the back seat. "You don't go anywhere anymore. You didn't even come over for my birthday, and I'm next door."

"I've got a lot going on."

"No, you don't. He doesn't have anything," Peanut tells Libby. "He sleeps all day, then litters in his underwear. This is good for him, that he's getting a break from wallowing in misery."

Buzz glares at her in the rearview mirror.

"I'm not judging you," Peanut says reasonably. "No one should drown in the Depths of Despair."

She has to explain to him that the Depths of Despair is an infinitely deep oozy bog of sadness and grief. The Children were almost trapped in it for good in book one. (The Knock-Knocks plucked them out and flew them to safety; literally, the annoying birds' only redeeming quality.)

"If you don't get out in time, the regret and misery yank you under," Peanut tells Buzz. She presses down on his shoulders with all her might so he understands. "All you want to do anymore is lie there and close your eyes. Like what you've been doing."

"Would you stop?" Buzz says, trying to move out of her grip.

"Oooh! The Knock-Knocks have a good joke about that. How do you get an astronaut's baby to stop crying?" Peanut taps Libby's shoulder. "You know this one."

Libby smiles and nods like she does.

"You *rocket*!" Peanut collapses, laughing, onto the back of Buzz's seat. "Get it? You rock—"

Not until Buzz hits the brakes and threatens to turn the car around does Peanut finally return to her phone.

The seat belt tightens around Libby's shoulder as they leave town and merge onto a curly two-lane road. Everything here is oversize: the pillowy sky, the heat of the sun, the bearded, big-bellied motorcycle riders who roar past on the double yellow line. As the car skates around another sharp curve, tree branches lean into the car and snatch at Libby.

What did you do to the Children?

What will you do?

You're sick.

Sick.

Libby wonders if she really wants her manuscript back. Maybe she lost it on purpose.

Closing her eyes, Libby imagines that everything is back to normal. Not her life—she doesn't have enough of one—but the Children's. She is right there with them, gazing up at the shelves of Pompou's, crowded with laughing, somersaulting toys. She can imagine the feel of Benjamin's hand and Huperzine's arm linked through hers as they wave to the Squirrel Keeper and cross through the underground passage to the magical OtherWay.

Come on. Everlee turns back and laughs. *There's nothing here to be scared of.* She stops when she spies Libby. *Except,* she says slowly, *for you.*

Libby's eyes flick open. She hears gunshots.

"Help!" a woman screams. "Help! Somebody help!"

"What was that?"

Buzz is flipping through the radio stations. Country. Static. Spanish. An ad. "What was what?" He doesn't look up.

In the back seat, Peanut scrolls through her phone.

"Please! Someone help my baby!" The voice is frantic.

Country. Static. Christian rock. An ad.

"That!" Libby cranes her neck to see where the screams are coming from. Halfway up the mountain, a sinister black train hurtles along a track, cowboys on horseback galloping in pursuit. A red-haired woman, leaning out of a window, screams, "Help me! Somebody, please!"

"Oh my God." Libby points. "There's—"

"The Great Train Robbery. It happens every hour." Peanut yawns.

"The—what?"

"You get on this steam train that goes up the mountain," Buzz explains, "and right before you pass out from boredom, actors lean in the windows with fake pistols and pretend to steal your shit."

Libby laughs out loud, thinking he's kidding.

"Oh, no. It's real."

"Really?" Libby can't stop laughing but isn't sure why.

"It's true," says Peanut. "Once, Jessie told me they took this man's iPad and accidentally dropped it on the tracks."

"That wasn't an accident," Buzz says, almost smiling. "He was from Texas."

Libby's cheeks are wet with tears, and her stomach aches. She can't remember the last time she laughed so hard—maybe not since book two, she says, when Gran Bere de-pants the owner of a rival toy store that's trying to put Pompou's out of business. Naturally, he turns out to be working for the Unstopping.

"I love that part." Peanut claps.

"How long ago was that?" Buzz wants to know.

"Two years ago," guesses Libby, still laughing.

"Don't you do anything besides write?"

She looks down at her hands. Her right finger is calloused and crooked from leaning against a pen. "No," Libby says. "I only do one thing."

Buzz shifts in his seat, wincing as he repositions his hurt leg. "Well," he allows, "that's one more than me."

~ ~

They don't talk for the rest of the drive. Buzz shakes his head and says, "Fucking Cross Creek," under his breath each time they pass a sign for the town. Rolf hangs his head out the back seat window, reveling in the musk of deer. And Peanut stays glued to her phone, occasionally saying things like, "This is perfect!" or "We should try this, too."

The Cross Creek Airport is a stucco building, the size of an elementary school, with a tiled Spanish roof and a sign out front that reads Señor Cactus Bar and Grill Now Cerrado.

There is one check-in area, one line for security, and one gate for arrivals and departures, which lies just past a sagging Mr. Pibb machine. Behind the baggage-claim counter, see-through lockers are crammed with unclaimed suitcases, forgotten fly-fishing reels, and skis.

The clerk reminds Libby of the pirouetting elf on the label of her favorite brand of peanut butter. Except instead of a handful of unshelled peanuts, he holds a pack of Camels and stares longingly at the parking lot. I EAT WILLIWIGS FOR DINNER his knit cap reads.

"But they're so cute!" Peanut protests.

The clerk taps his cigarettes on the counter. "What do you need?"

Libby waits for someone to answer before realizing Buzz and Peanut expect it to be her.

"I'm missing something." She makes the shape with her hands.

"Claim ticket?"

Libby shakes her head. "I never claimed it. I lost it."

She leans over the counter, trying to spot her bag inside one of the locked compartments. If this were a Falling Children book, the right door would click open. Her bag would simply float through the air and into her arms. Peanut must be thinking the same thing. Her arms are already outstretched, her eyes closed.

Nothing happens.

"Can't help you without a ticket." The clerk cracks open a pack of nicotine gum and tosses a few squares into his mouth.

"Can you look and see?" Libby asks. "It's green." (She thinks.) "And important."

"More than important," echoes Peanut. "Like, urgent. Like, lives depend on it."

The clerk looks at Peanut's scar, then back to his computer screen. On the bottom is a taped pink note. At first, Libby's mind plays a trick on her. *Everlee is the password,* she thinks it reads.

She moves closer.

EVERYONE MUST PRESENT CLAIM TICKET, it says.

As Libby turns her gaze to survey the airport—she really is in one, isn't she?—she spies her bag, shoved onto a shelf above the clerk's head.

"There." She points. "That's it! See? The tag looks like Rolf."

She gestures to the real dog standing beside her, licking the side of the counter.

"Can we see it?" Peanut bounces on her toes, hands clasped together. "Please? It's hers! Please? Please?"

"See it all you want." The clerk unlocks the locker and gestures at the bag but doesn't take it out. "You still need a claim ticket."

"Oh, come on," Buzz says, finally speaking up. "Why would anyone ask for a bag that's not theirs?"

The guy raises his hands. "Happens all the time, bro. What planet are you from?"

"See? This is why I hate Cross Creek," Buzz tells Libby. "Everyone's a prick. The first time I made a kickflip frontside boardslide, one of their cops arrested me for skating in the church parking lot. In Blue Skies! It wasn't even his town. He wasn't even on duty. I was fucking *six*."

"Buzz!" Peanut scolds. "Stop cursing in front of me."

"I knew I knew you from somewhere!" The clerk snaps his fingers. "Squill Boy! I laughed my ass off at that video. That squirrel taking your sandwich? Man, that wipeout was—"

"Epic," Buzz says. "I know. I was there."

"He *bested* your balls." The clerk pantomimes a fall. "If that had been me grinding those stairs, I would have flattened the little tree rat."

"Well, it wasn't you," says Buzz. Color creeps into his neck.

Libby wishes she were the type of person to always have a snappy comeback or at least a hand buzzer at the ready. She is not. Even the first tender shoots of conflict make her tongue freeze and her fingers grow cold.

Jamming her hands into the pockets of her sweater, Libby is surprised to feel a wad of paper.

"Figures Squill Boy is from *Boo-hoo* Skies." The clerk laughs. "In Cross Creek, we don't cave to shit little squirrels. You choked, man."

"Excuse me?" Libby smooths the hundred-dollar bill onto the counter. "Will this help?"

He eyes it. "With what?"

"With—everything?"

The clerk plucks the bill off the counter and shoves it into his shirt pocket. "Take your freaking bag, Squill Boy." He gestures. "You ain't got nothin' else going on."

"What comes around, goes across," Peanut pipes up in Williwig. It sounds like, *Grr, grr, gr-yah! Grrrrr—*

"Don't," Buzz says. "Just—don't."

Libby can't remember how to deploy the suitcase handle, so she clutches the bag to her chest, exiting quickly in case the clerk changes his mind. Peanut skips along beside her.

"So that's what you do, huh?" Buzz says once they get outside. He limps to catch up. "Throw a bunch of bills around to get what you want? Like Mr. Monopoly?"

"No," Libby says, surprised.

"A hundred bucks might not be a lot to you one-percenters, but to the rest of us peasants, it is. You paid him off for being an a-hole."

"I was trying to help."

"If I were a gazillionaire, I'd toss money around, too," Peanut pipes up. "I'd rent a giant hot-air balloon and shake hundred-dollar bills over everyone. Except people I don't like."

"I haven't made gazillions," Libby tells Buzz.

Besides the dementia, the fact she sometimes pretends her dog is her boyfriend, and a few other things currently eluding her recall, here is something else in Libby's Top Five Embarrassments: she signed a horrendous contract with her publisher. "Horrendous" not being an actual legal term but what she came to conclude when more and more copies of the books sold, T-shirts and key chains and magnets were licensed, and yet she still received the same modest amount each time she turned in a new manuscript.

"Your lawyer let you sign that?" Buzz looks skeptical.

Libby nods, thinking of Vernice's friend's cousin's stepson, a first-year law student who'd flipped through the contract at a Fourth of July BBQ. "Looks good to me, shorty." He'd shrugged, handing back the papers, fingerprinted with rib sauce.

"It's fine. The important thing is that they were published," Libby lies.

"But they're the best books in the *world*." Peanut looks incredulous.

"You get some sort of bonus, though, right?" Buzz wants to know. "When you're done?"

Libby nods, and if she looks excited, it's only because she's remembering one of the missing humiliations. "Once the real F. T. Goldhero is revealed. After the last book comes out."

"What do you mean, the 'real' one?" Peanut asks.

"They want someone who's more—I don't know." Libby looks down at the permanent marker on her hand. Her sweat has turned the words into a storm cloud. "F. T. Goldhero–like?"

"It's okay," she says at their expressions. "I'm better with words than people. And I don't like having my picture taken. I blink."

Buzz takes the suitcase from her. "So you write all these books, and they're not going to give you credit?"

"And you're not fighting back?" Peanut asks. "You have to!"

"It's fine," Libby lies, lies—she is a liar. "It's better this way. Really. I don't need attention."

"It's not about attention; it's about getting what you deserve," Buzz says. "All those emails you have—those people are writing to *you*."

Tomato, tom-ah-to, Libby means to say. Instead, what comes out is "ruta, rutabaga."

Buzz places the bag next to the car. Like magic, the handle periscopes down.

"That elf was right," Libby says, trying to change the subject. She points to the luggage tag. "This does look more like a mastiff."

"Wait!" Peanuts stops Buzz before he lifts the bag into the trunk. "Are you a hundred percent totally sure the book's really in there?"

Libby isn't 100 percent totally sure about anything.

She drops to her knees and unzips the bag.

Dog food for Rolf. Wool socks. Three identical white shirts with Peter Pan collars. Three pairs of black pants. Seven lacy purple bras and matching panties that she can't remember owning. Eye drops. A dozen ballpoint pens. Her little red notebook. Underneath two jumbo bottles of Tylenol—*What am I planning to do with those?* Libby wonders—is a thick sheaf of rubber-banded paper, the corners crinkled and a coffee stain shaped like a bird flying across the first page.

The Falling Children Find Their Way Home, it reads.

"There you are," Libby greets it.

She lifts it out as carefully as a baby, a lump of pride in her throat. "It's my only copy," she says.

"Then put it back," Buzz says, alarmed.

"No, no, no! Give it to me!" Peanut bounces on her toes. "Can I start reading it? Please! I'll be so careful. So, so careful!" She presses her hands together. "Please? I'll sit in the car where you can watch me, and I won't show anyone."

Libby hesitates. Not even her editor has seen this draft. Or did she, and she didn't like it and asked Libby to start over from scratch? She presses her lips together, trying to remember.

"Please?" Peanut is now strapped into the back seat of the car, her arms outstretched like she wants to give Libby—or the pages—a hug. "I'll read right here and so fast. You can watch me. Please?"

"She stops talking when she's reading," Buzz says.

When Libby still doesn't move, he adds, "It's why you're here, right? To have her help you? The sooner you finish, the sooner you can go home."

Slowly, Libby holds out the manuscript.

"It's like Christmas for toys," Peanut whispers. She looks like she might faint.

Libby feels she might, too. Buzz lifts her suitcase into the trunk, but she's forgotten to zip it. The contents—her unremarkable cardigans and grape-colored bras, an appointment card from Dr. Whatsit and those ominous Tylenol bottles, and pens, so many pens—rain down at her feet. It's like the contents of her brain.

25

After they pass a sign that reads Blue Skies 7 miles, the gas light flicks on. Its yellow eye winks at Libby from the dashboard.

Buzz shrugs when she points it out. "We probably have enough," he says. "If not, we can hitch a ride."

But then what? thinks Libby.

In her head, fears stack like Jenga blocks, and out of habit, she lists them under her breath: escaped criminals, police chase, shootout, jumping from a moving car, lost in the woods, bear—ferocious bear, loyal Rolf bleeding at her feet...

Buzz does a U-turn and pulls into the only gas station they've passed on the otherwise solitary road. "It's not bear season," he says as he turns off the engine. "Just so you know."

Peanut is so busy reading that she doesn't look up.

Libby gets out and stretches, surprised to find they're surrounded by yellow and purple wildflowers. It's the prettiest gas station she's ever been to, even if the bathroom around back is tagged with Falling Children graffiti—*The Unstopping is here*—and the toilet appears not to have been flushed for several days. At least there's a door that closes but doesn't lock.

Exiting the restroom, Libby goes left instead of right. She ends up in a small kitchen that reminds her of her own at home—doesn't she have the same worn red pot holders?—before making her way to the store. The man behind the counter has a bushy black beard, glasses, and belly: a Middle Eastern Santa Claus in a Grateful Dead shirt and puka necklace.

"Look who finally left his house," he says when Buzz comes inside to pay.

"Hey, Lou."

Libby spins a rack of paperbacks in the corner. Copies of *The Falling Children* stare up at her like puppies in a pet store. *Me. Pick me.*

She touches each of their covers, hoping they go to good homes.

"Saw my first northern goshawk last weekend," Lou says. "Real pretty but fierce as all get out. Took down a mallard right there at the pond."

"No shit." Buzz looks impressed.

"It's always the ones you least expect. Mrs. Halfchap said they were fighting over me." Lou points outside. "You finally trade in that skateboard of yours for a car?"

"Nah."

Libby, now arranging the Falling Children books in numerical order with the covers facing out, feels Buzz look over.

"It's hers."

"Did he tell you how we met?" Lou calls. "My first day here, I caught him stealing a pregnancy test." He lets out a wheezy, wet laugh. "Fifteen years old! That was a good one for the crime log."

"Yeah, good times." Buzz turns to leave, but the handle of his cane catches the gum machine and sends it crashing to the ground. Gumballs hit the floor and crack in every direction. Buzz's neck turns the same shade as the red ones.

Libby bends down to help corral them.

"I didn't lose my virginity until college," she says to make him feel better. "To my creative-writing professor. And," she adds, as they drop the gumballs back into the globe, "I still got a D."

"I don't think it was because of me," Libby says quickly. She rubs her sticky hands against her pants. "My short stories weren't that good. I kept trying to write ones set in Victorian England, but I hadn't done enough research. Honestly, I probably deserved an F. I think the D was just for effort. Because I tried."

Stop talking, she orders herself.

"With the plot," she feels compelled to clarify. "Not having sex. Although I did then, too." She clears her throat. "Try, I mean."

Buzz heads for the door. "Thanks, Lou. You can put the gas on Dr. B's tab."

"Don't be a stranger," Lou calls. To Libby, he says, "You, too, Church Bell."

It's Victorian slang for a chatty woman. Lou looks pleased at Libby's surprise.

"One of my masters is in Victorian studies," he explains.

She follows Buzz to a rusted vending machine on the side of the building. It's filled with off-brand candy—Señor Mints and Kick Kack bars.

"I've never seen any of these before." Libby points to a tube of brightly wrapped cookies. "Moreos?"

"They don't eat those in Victorian England?"

"What was that thing you were talking about?" she asks, changing the subject. "The thing that killed a duck?"

"A goshawk?" Buzz blows a piece of lint off a quarter before sliding it into the slot. "It's like a hawk but fiercer. No one ever sees them. I have, but I'm like the only one in town. Or was."

"You bird-watch?"

Buzz pulls a lever, and a package of Moreos slides out. "What's so funny about that?"

"Nothing."

He rips the package with his teeth and hands her a cookie.

"And who's Dr. B?"

"Dr. Bixton," Buzz says. "He adopted me after my parents died."

"You don't call him 'Dad'?"

He shrugs. "I was eleven when it happened. I already had a dad."

"My parents died when I was eleven, too," Libby says, surprised. "They were in a plane crash." She can still remember the news footage, how pieces of the crumpled airliner bobbed among open luggage and magazines and seat cushions in the Atlantic. "They were estranged from their families—which is putting it mildly, really. Nobody wanted me, so I went into foster care."

"That sucks."

"It did, but I got lucky." Libby thinks of Vernice and the warm lopsided blankets she crocheted and how she hummed, not yelled, when she got angry. The way she snuggled extra syllables into words: "may-on-naise" and "Christ-o-mas."

"That's one way to look at it," Buzz drops more change into the machine. "Most people would say it wasn't fucking fair that their parents died and their families didn't step up. Or"—he gives her a sideways glance—"that they should have gotten an A instead of a C for boning their teacher."

"It was a D," she says. Then she asks, "What about you?"

"What about me? I never banged a teacher."

"No, I mean—how'd you end up with—" She gestures to the car, where she can just see the top of Peanut's frizzy head in the back seat.

"Dr. B. never had kids of his own. Took in Jessie as a baby after her mom skipped town, then took me in. And then"—he sighs—"Peanut came along."

"You're like the Falling Children. Three orphans who mysteriously find themselves—"

"No," Buzz says. "We're not." He bites into a Five Musketeers, then maybe realizing his abrupt tone, offers her the other half.

"May I ask—only if you feel like saying—I don't usually meet—How did your parents…?" She feels greedy for wanting to know.

"Abducted by aliens," Buzz deadpans.

Libby stares. "They were abducted by—"

"I'm teasing." Buzz starts to limp toward the car. "They spontaneously combusted."

"What?"

"Joking. They were eaten by a shark."

"Ha," Libby says, catching on to the game.

"I'm serious," Buzz says over his shoulder. "My mom fell off a boat in the Florida Keys, and my dad jumped in to save her."

Libby swallows the wad of stale gummy chocolate in her mouth. "That's the worst thing I've ever heard."

She does not mention that she has always been terrified of being devoured by a hungry shark, sometimes even when she is on land.

Buzz gives her a confused smile. "It's not a contest."

"I know, I meant—"

"Everyone has their own shit. Just in different flavors."

Before she can stop herself, Libby recites, "Black licorice. Pig slop. Bitter melon. Blood."

"Let me guess, the Falling Children?"

"No, it's from me—the taste grief leaves in your mouth. Every book, I add it in, and each time my editor cuts it. She thinks it's too sad." She tosses the rest of her candy into a patch of wildflowers. "I am too sad."

Neither Peanut nor Rolf looks up when they get back to the car.

"Brought you Moreos," Buzz says, dropping the blue package onto Peanut's lap.

Peanut shushes him. "I'm reading."

"Must be good." Buzz looks over at Libby.

She doesn't answer. Partly because she's decided to stop talking altogether; she's terrible at writing her own dialogue. But mostly because her brain has decided that now would be an excellent time for a panic attack. Libby's pulse has begun hammering in her wrists, and she can't feel her face. An invisible hand tightens around her throat.

Calm down, Libby tells herself. She squeezes the slick fabric of the seat belt between her fingers as if that will prevent her from hyperventilating.

"After my parents died, I looked for them everywhere," Buzz says abruptly. He hooks his thumbs onto the bottom of the steering wheel. "Like, where do you fucking go when you die? One minute you're there, the next you're not. You go somewhere, right?"

Libby doesn't answer. She never has panic attacks when there is something to panic about. They happen hours, days, sometimes weeks after her anxiety spikes—a buildup of stress hormones erupting in her brain like a messy baking soda volcano.

"Right after they died, I started seeing these two crows hanging out all the time," Buzz is saying. "At the funeral. Outside my window. At the park. I swear it was the same two birds."

Libby is overcome with a wave of nausea. What if she's actually having a heart attack? Should she ask to go to a hospital? What if she doesn't say anything and dies right here in the car? Which would be more embarrassing? Libby watches her sweaty fingers curl into fists.

"I wanted them to be my parents so fucking bad, like they'd come back to keep an eye on me. People don't magically turn into birds, though," Buzz adds, "in case you were wondering."

His disappointment reaches Libby, even if she can't catch her breath. "They do in my books," she says.

Buzz starts the car. "Yeah." He gives a short laugh. "Of course, they do."

The seat belt warning signal shrieks in agreement.

Sick. Sick. Sick.

Libby pretends to be overcome by a cough, hoping Buzz won't notice she is opening and closing her hands, raising and lowering her shoulders, breathing in for four and out for—

"You need to strap in," he says.

"Oh, right." She studies the strap in her hand. *I am dying*, she thinks.

Buzz pulls forward.

The beeping doesn't stop.

Libby would turn up the radio to drown out the sound, but she can't remember how to.

Buzz brakes at the exit and looks at her, waiting.

Closing her eyes, Libby wishes everything around her—including the incessant beeping—would *stop*. Why is it her mind that has to? Why can't everything else?

"I don't feel that well," Libby says.

Her voice sounds far away.

She can feel Buzz watching her.

"Here," he finally says. Leaning over, he pulls the seat belt around Libby's waist and clicks it into place. She is acutely aware of the weight of his body across her own.

"Ohhh." Libby draws out the word to fill the awkward silence.

If it weren't for the Children, she would swallow her hundreds of Tylenol gel capsules (*that's* what they're for!) right now. There's no other reason to stick around and see how helpless she is and how much worse this disease will make her.

The glitter-eyed crows in the parking lot hop away in agreement.

26

"I don't get it," Benjamin says, turning the disposable camera around in his hands. "I'm supposed to take pictures with this thing, then just throw it away?"

"It helps fill the land." Huperzine nods. "I learned in school that the earth is like an inner tube. We have to keep stuffing it with trash to keep it from deflating."

Benjamin stops. "You learned that in Williwig School. Those bears don't know anything."

"Yes, they do!"

"No. They don't. Their brains are literally stuffing. Back me up here, Everlee."

Everlee, a few strides in front of them, doesn't answer. Although it's midday on a Saturday, the sun beating hot above them, the streets of Dark Crevice are deserted. No cars. No pedestrians. No cat dozing in the bookstore window...

"They should have made this camera edible, not disposable. You take your pictures, then eat your camera." Benjamin grins at the thought. "Now that's the ticket!"

Everlee snatches the toy camera out of his hand.

"Hey!" he protests.

"Huperzine, where did you get this?" Everlee demands. "Who gave it to you?"

"Just some creepy clown," Huperzine says. "He really wanted me to have it. For free."

Benjamin groans.

"What?" Huperzine looks anxiously at him, then Everlee. "What did I do now?"

"Look." Everlee motions for Benjamin to look through the viewfinder.

When he does, he sees the town of Dark Crevice like it usually is on a steamy Wednesday in August. There's Gladys, the beak-nosed headmistress from the orphanage, leaving the grocery with her usual soggy parcel of warm day-old fish. People walking their dogs. The mailman juggling a tower of twine-wrapped packages. "Invisible Touch" booms from the open door of the frozen yogurt shop.

Confused, Benjamin puts down the camera to witness the deserted street again. "I don't get it. Where'd everyone go?"

Everlee shakes her head. "Nowhere," she says. "It's us. We've gone somewhere."

At the sound of her voice, a door creaks open, and a small doll peeks out. Its eyes have been blacked out with marker, its mouth sewn shut with shiny black fishing line.

"Oh no." Huperzine's bottom lip trembles.

Benjamin puts a protective arm around them. He eyes the yogurt shop and wonders if he has time to run inside and help himself before things take a turn for the worse.

"You're hiding something, aren't you?" Everlee asks the doll.

It's an unnecessary question. For one, the doll's unable to speak. And deep down, Everlee already knows the answer.

~ ~

"Will you get out already?"

Blinking, Peanut looks up at her brother. She feels sick and woozy, like the time she spent the night at Nancee's and they ate an entire tub of strawberry frosting *and* a bag of french fries. It takes Peanut another few seconds to realize she's no longer in Dark Crevice with the Children but the driveway of Buzz's house.

"I'm not done."

"So? Go home before Jessie shows up," Buzz says.

Reluctantly, Peanut climbs out of the car, clutching the manuscript to her chest. "What's the doll hiding?" she asks Libby. "When do we find out?"

"You have to keep reading," Libby says vaguely.

"I still have five hundred and one more pages. If you let me take them home, I won't show anyone, I swear. I'll be really careful and bring them back in the morning. I promise."

Libby watches Rolf take a long pee in the grass.

"If I finish the book tonight, we can figure out the ending tomorrow," Peanut adds.

"Tomorrow." Libby nods.

Peanut decides that's a yes. Especially because at the bottom of the hill, she can see Jessie trudging up the sidewalk. Her hair is askew, and her shirt is splattered with mud. One of the cowboys must have pulled her out of the train window and onto their horse again to show off.

"Thank you," Peanut calls to Libby before racing home. "You can trust me."

"To do what?" is the last thing she hears Libby ask.

～～

From 3:30 to 6:00 p.m., Peanut reads. Her head hurts, and her bones ping from sitting in the same position on her bed, but the story is too suspenseful for her to care. When Jessie insists that she come downstairs for dinner, the Unstopping has bound everyone in Dark Crevice with their dreams. The townspeople lie motionless in their homes or in the streets, useless expressions on their faces, their wrists and ankles tethered with silver filaments of want.

"How could you!" Everlee shouts when she comes face-to-face with the Unstopping in front of the video store. Trembling with rage, she swings at him with her butterfly net. "What gives you the right to be so cruel?"

The Unstopping grabs the net and easily snaps it between two fingers. "You foolish girl." He smiles his slippery smile. "I have something special planned for you. Who's ready for some fun?"

He clinks his rings together, summoning uncertain magic. But before it appears, the Unstopping is attacked by his own murder of taxidermied crows. They swoop toward him in a dense black cloud, pecking his hands and pulling at his stringy hair with their talons. The Unstopping has recently ordered them to wear little bow ties and jaunty hats, and they are mad.

"Run!" Everlee bellows at Benjamin and Huperzine. She points to the forest. "It's the only place where we'll be safe."

Run, Peanut begs. *Run!*

"Dinner!" Jessie calls. "I'm not asking again."

Peanut stows the manuscript under her pillow and stomps downstairs. "I'm not hungry. I told you." Jessie tries to feel her forehead, but Peanut slides out of reach. "I'm not sick. I just don't want to eat."

She thinks of the Children racing into the forest, the Unstopping on their heels. It's not that far from Dark Crevice. How long will it take them to reach it? Five minutes? Ten? Will they be there by now? They *have* to stay safe.

"What are you doing up there?" Jessie calls as Peanut tears back upstairs.

"Nothing! Eat without me."

"Fine," Jessie says. "But if you get hungry later, you're going to have to eat bitter hookroot."

Peanut stops dead on the stairs. Slowly, she turns around. "What did you say?"

"I said," Jessie says more loudly, "if you get hungry later, all you can have is saltines."

That's definitely not what Peanut heard, but the Children are waiting.

—⁓ ⁓—

From 6:10 to 8:10 p.m., Peanut reads. Her head pounds from not eating or drinking anything but Moreos since lunchtime, and her muscles feel waspish from lack of use. The Children made it to the forest and successfully stayed hidden from view when some of the Unstopping's henchmen—plastic dolls with the real heads of sharks—marched past. But now they're in trouble again.

While looking for fresh water, Huperzine accidentally fell to the bottom of an abandoned Unwish Well. Everything they don't want to come true—a tornado, flash flood, the Jack-in-the-Box Army coming back to life—is happening.

Huperzine has a *lot* of worries.

Benjamin, meanwhile, has been kidnapped by a resurrected-and-stronger-than-ever Mean L'il Bebe. Under her power, he trance walks to the edge of the OtherWay and contemplates throwing himself into the Abyss of Nothingness, which smells like a metal trash can on a hot August day.

"Do it," L'il Bebe croons. "This is no life worth living. End it."

At the very last minute, the Squirrel Keeper intervenes. He leaps from a tree and lands directly on top of Benjamin, throwing him off-balance and breaking Mean L'il Bebe's spell (and Benjamin's leg) at the same time.

"You owe me, you furless imbecile," pants the Squirrel Keeper, breathing his nut-juice breath into Benjamin's face. "The things I have to do around here to keep things running smoothly! It's odious! Revolting. Beyond the pale."

"Why'd you save me?" Benjamin is too astonished to realize how much his leg hurts. "You hate us. Me, Everlee, Zine—we drive you nuts."

The Squirrel Keeper finishes grooming his tail, then stands on his fat hind legs and sniffs the air. "There are things at stake more important than you or me." He gestures to the Abyss. Nothingness is churning, sloshing, spilling onto the bank. "It's rising, have you noticed? We don't have much time."

Benjamin's stomach rumbles with fear. "Time for what?"

~ ~

"Peanut?"

The door to Peanut's bedroom opens, and her father pokes his head in.

"What?" Peanut feels she's been shaken out of a deep, blissful sleep.

"You were so quiet at dinner. I came to check on you."

"I wasn't *at* dinner!" Peanut kicks her legs in frustration and papers go everywhere. Papers. *The* papers.

She has forgotten to hide the Children.

A page lands at her father's feet, and he bends down to pick it up. "What's all this?"

"Nothing." Peanut snatches it out of his hand. "A girl at school wrote a story and asked me to read it."

"She's quite a prolific writer," her father says. "There are hundreds of pages here."

"Over six hundred, and she's not done yet," Peanut says. "She wants me to help her finish."

"I suppose this has to do with the Falling Family then."

"Falling Children," Peanut says through gritted teeth, but he's stopped listening.

"Head downstairs and get some food so Jessie stops fretting that you're withering away."

I don't care if she frets. Go away! Peanut wants to say. But if she challenges her father, she'll get a lecture about how elders should be respected. Sometimes she thinks this is the only reason he adopted children: to ensure a captive audience.

"I'm fine," she tells him.

"Well then, don't stay up too late." He pats her head.

"How can I?" Peanut grumbles. "Jessie screams at me if I do. She screams about everything."

"She's only trying to do what's best for you."

Peanut doesn't answer. Jessie doesn't know what she needs.

Pinching the scar on her cheek, she returns to the Children.

~~~

From 8:15 to 9:00 p.m., Peanut reads. Her head throbs, and she badly has to pee, but she can't bear to leave the Children. Nothingness continues to rise menacingly toward the forest, but none of the creatures who live there will admit they're in danger. Getting water one morning, Everlee leans over a brook and sees not her reflection but that of the Unstopping. He knows where they are. To protect Huperzine and Benjamin, Everlee doesn't return to their camp. She sets out alone, searching for a way to defeat him.

Naturally, Huperzine and Benjamin are frantic that Everlee is missing. Reluctantly—because bad things always happen when they do this—they split up to go look for her.

Inside an abandoned nest of ventriloquist dummies, all clacking jaws and splintery arms, Huperzine finds a mysterious book with their name on it.

Unfortunately, it's in such dreadful shape that some of the words have sprouted wings and stingers. Angrily, they buzz toward Huperzine, jabbing their face and neck before spiraling to the ground and collapsing.

Huperzine is covered in ink and hives by the time they get the book shut. But something about the book calls to them—as in, really *calls their name*—so they wrap it sturdily in twine and take it with them.

Many miles away, at the opposite edge of the forest, Benjamin discovers a giant bonfire. As he creeps closer, he realizes it's Pompou's, their beloved toy store.

"Why are you doing this?" Benjamin bellows at the Unstopping, who stands nearby, looking pleased. Trains and tops and stuffed animals scramble off the shelves and flee toward the doors, but the Unstopping has locked them with the vilest, strongest magic: the uncertain kind.

Boom, boom, boom.

Jessie pounds on Peanut's door. "It's past bedtime. Turn out your light."

"I'm not tired." Peanut can't take her eyes off the page, even when Jessie comes into her room. How could this happen to Pompou's? It's like *heaven* burning. And who is going to save Everlee? Is she going to die?

Peanut feels like she might throw up.

"It doesn't matter." Jessie lifts the curtain and looks up and down the street. "It's bedtime, and I have things to do." She tests the window lock.

"So go do them."

"I mean it, Peanut. Lights, now."

Once Jessie shuts the door, Peanut gropes under the bed for her flashlight. In all the years she's stayed up late to be with the Falling Children, Jessie's never caught on. That's because she has no idea what it's like to get swept up in a book, how it can become more real than real life.

Under the covers, Peanut turns the next page. And then the next.

"Help!" Benjamin shouts into the passage that leads from the OtherWay to the real world. His arms are full of the weakest toys, the ones the Unstopping desires the most: the scratched and stained stuffed animals, an ugly doll with two cracked eyes, the heart puzzle missing its red center piece. "Can anyone hear me?"

Yes, Peanut thinks. *I am right here.*

~~~

At 11:48 Peanut's eyes are full of tears, and her stomach lurches like the time Buzz bought her a fried Mars bar at the country fair and *then* she had a hot dog with relish. But this time, she's sick from grief. At page 521, the story simply...ends.

It's like a doctor walking out of open-heart surgery. A pilot parachuting from a crowded passenger jet. A mother abandoning her baby.

The Unstopping has captured Everlee and vows to kill her as slowly and painfully as possible. While Benjamin and Huperzine watch, he gleefully throws her into the Depths of Despair. Who knows what the Unstopping's uncertain magic will do next?

"We have a plan!" Huperzine shouts defiantly at the Unstopping. But it is a desperate bluff; anyone can see that.

There is no one left to help rescue the Children. The Unstopping has used Nothingness to empty the forest of its magical creatures and wise, advice-giving trees. The few surviving stuffed animals that made it out of Pompou's alive have gone rogue.

The heavy book Huperzine has been lugging around this whole time is still an enigma. "Save us!" they plead, shaking it.

A few letters come loose and flutter to the ground.

A N T E U P, they jeer.

Angrily, Huperzine kicks them aside.

"This has been a long time coming, hasn't it?" the Unstopping sneers.

"You can't kill Everlee for good!" Benjamin says.

Fear and frustration fuel the Unstopping, and he telescopes before the Children's eyes. "Good or bad," he calls down. "I haven't decided yet."

And then with a terrible shriek, Everlee's wherewithal, the juicy plasma of imagination that resides deep within the soul, begins draining from her body.

"Nooo!" Benjamin screams.

Those are the last words on the page.

Switching off her flashlight, Peanut lies in the dark.

Is Everlee dead? She can't be dead.

Rolling onto her stomach, Peanut bites the edge of her pillow to keep from crying. Peanut's love of the Children is so strong, it must be in her blood. She aches to find her real parents. They would be just as outraged to learn how the Falling Children's story ends.

Where are you? Peanut sends a telepathic message to her parents. *Why aren't you trying to find me?*

She lies very still on her bed, listening for a response.

That's when Peanut hears noises downstairs.

At first, she thinks Jessie is exercising, doing a kickboxing video or jumping around with filled water bottles because she can't afford dumbbells.

192

But when Peanut opens her bedroom door and tiptoes down to the landing, she can hear grunting and what sounds like furniture bumping the wall.

Peanut's mouth goes dry. It sounds like the video Nancee played on her phone after asking, "Siri, what's sex like?" Peanut covered her eyes at the seven-second mark, but she heard the rest.

The noises become louder.

As she turns to run back upstairs, Peanut reaches for the banister but miscalculates. Her hand knocks a photograph of Buzz off the wall. It thumps and clatters down one, two, three steps.

Peanut freezes.

From downstairs, someone says, "Shhh!"

Peanut's brain won't let her match the voice to a name.

There is more urgent whispering. Peanut stays rooted to the spot, willing herself not to breathe.

After several agonizing minutes, the sounds start again, quieter and slower this time.

Peanut races back to bed and burrows under her covers. The harder she tries to not to think about what she's heard, the more she does.

"Once you know something, you can't just unknow it." Benjamin Falling, book five.

Seventeen minutes later, Peanut is still awake when the front door opens. She can hear the dark ruffle of a car engine.

She doesn't have to go to the window to confirm: it belongs to Orson Greeley.

27

Libby stays asleep until midnight. Is that good for an insomniac? She drums her fingers against her ribs and tries to do the math.

Moonlight smokes the window, casting a ladder-shaped shadow across the ceiling. Taking it as a sign that she should climb out of bed, she throws back the sheets and heads down the hall toward her office.

Instead, she ends up in Buzz's bedroom.

At first, Libby thinks he is sprawled on top of the blankets in a fur coat. Then she realizes it's Rolf. Buzz isn't there.

"Pssst!" she gestures to Rolf.

He opens one eye and regards her but doesn't get up.

Well, Libby thinks, trying to look at the bright side, at least she's found a new home for Rolf after she kills herself.

After heating a glass of tea in the microwave—she doesn't trust herself to use the stove, whose burners are crusted with neon cheese powder anyway—Libby sits at the table and opens Buzz's laptop.

How can she save the Children? She will freewrite until her subconscious gives up the answer—even if it takes hours. What else does she have to do?

But instead of opening a Word document, Libby launches the Internet browser. The screen explodes with headlines:

EXCLUSIVE: Details leak about last Falling Children book

"Evil Wins": Shocking finale planned for Falling Children

Falling Children die, fans revolt: "This is betrayal"

Boiling water scalds the roof of Libby's mouth.

The first article contains a picture of the wall in her office, a messy, elaborate patchwork of plot points for the last book. Luckily, thanks to Libby's tiny, sloppy handwriting, many of the words look like 

Still, the reporter—a Glenn somebody—attempts to translate.

"There's no question this will be a much darker, angrier, 'adult' book," he writes. "F. T. Goldhero has made the stunning decision to resurrect nearly every villain from the past five books, while indicating some, maybe all, of the Children will meet a grisly end."

A professor of child psychology at Stanford warns that if any of the Falling Children die, "children across the globe will be needlessly traumatized."

He points out that in twelve hours, an online petition—"Save the Children"—has already racked up nearly 4 million signatures. #Dontyoudare and #KillFTNottheChildren are trending on social media.

"Is Goldhero resentful of hiding? Pressuring his publisher for more money? Clamoring to write more 'adult' fare?" questions Glenn. "What's clear is that he no longer cares about giving these beloved characters the happy ending they, and fans, deserve."

Hands trembling, mouth burning, hot water dripping off the table and into her lap, Libby struggles to remember the right username and password for her email. It takes dozens of tries.

Once she cracks the code—Everlee is a good password, she should remember that—Libby tries to think of what to write to Glenn.

You have it all wrong! is as far as she gets before realizing that her editor, Merry, has flooded her inbox with messages:

Trying to call but no answer. Pls call

Call me ASAP

Did you change your phone?

URGENT: We HAVE to talk. Today.

URGENT: Meeting with legal

URGENT: Potential leak

URGENT: Did you talk to reporter? Legal needs to know

LIBBY, WHERE ARE YOU???

Libby can't deal with this right now. She clicks onto a news site.

EXCLUSIVE: Details Leak About Last Falling Children Book

"Evil Wins": Shocking Finale Planned for Falling Children

Falling Children Die, Fans Revolt: "This is Betrayal"

Libby is horrified. Who took a picture of her dry-erase board?

Grateful that her inbox is open—is this starting to feel a little familiar? She can't tell—Libby types "Merry" into the search bar. Her editor's emails pop like corn.

Libby's fingers can't keep up with her thoughts. Instead of *I don't have my phone,* I don't have my thing appears on the screen.

Instead of *Someone's convinced that I'm F. T. Goldhero's personal assistant,* she writes, Something else is wrong with the Children, something besides me.

After rereading the message, Libby deletes it.

The rest of her inbox mostly contains invitations to date Russian women. There's also a note from Glenn that came a week ago and is marked "read."

Heads up, reads the subject line.

Look, Libby, I know you're risk averse, but F. T. Goldhero is
a public figure. Fans deserve to know who he is. If you don't
come through with an interview, I'll keep releasing the details
I have already. Don't take this personally. It's how life works.

Libby reads the email twice, biting her nails until she can feel
drops of blood release into her mouth. She doesn't like being called
risk averse, even though it's true. What else does Glenn know?

2 deleted messages in this thread, reads the screen. But they're
gone from the trash folder, gone from Libby's memory.

She longs for a webcam in her apartment. Libby needs to see that
her coffee mug is still on her desk and the hostas in her kitchen, which
she hopefully remembered to water, are turning their leafy faces toward
the late-summer sun. That her four pillows are arranged just so on her
bed. That there are no signs someone besides her has been there.

A run would stop Libby's thoughts from snapping their teeth so
loudly, but she doesn't trust the dark outside the window, this strange
little town, herself.

She paces next to the dish thingy. Libby would pay millions of dollars
to think clearly again—even for a few days. She would give anything.

It's not enough movement. She needs more. Libby snatches up
trash from the counters. Bottles and wrappers and takeout containers
and newspapers. She fills the trash can under the kitchen sink.

Her brain likes this, she can tell. It's like finding the one spot where
a vicious dragon likes to be scratched.

Using bleach and an old sponge she finds under the sink, Libby
scrubs the counters and floor and mostly bare refrigerator. The
kitchen gleams. Libby's brain purrs.

It's nearly 3:00 a.m. by the time she finishes. After throwing the empty gallon of bleach into the trash, she sits and composes an email to Merry.

Long story but book almost done. Pages ready soon! I'm in Blue Skies Colorado for another few days.

Only after she hits Send does Libby realize she has addressed the email to Glenn.

28

Libby wakes at the sound of the screen door chuffing open. Buzz stops short when he sees her on the couch.

"What are you doing?"

"I couldn't sleep." Libby sits up, her hands going straight to her earrings. She turns both of them, like she's winding herself up.

The cuckoo clock on the wall—*Has that been here the whole time?*—calls twice.

Libby is about to ask where Buzz has been—his face is flushed and sweaty, the skull on his T-shirt is sticking to his chest—when he notices the kitchen. "Jesus. What'd you do?"

Libby looks at the sparkling linoleum and scrubbed and cleared countertops, the alphabetized stacks of bills and carefully aligned glasses in the drying rack.

"Cleaned it?" Her fingerprints are smooth from bleach.

"You didn't have to do that," he says, dropping into the chair next to her.

"I know." Libby puts her head back down on Rolf, covering a yawn. "But I like to."

"To clean?" Buzz looks at her in disbelief. "That's fucked up."

Libby is too tired to be embarrassed. "Probably," she says.

The next time she wakes, the room is bathed with sunlight, dust motes shimmering in the air like the shy wind-up fireflies the Children meet at Pompou's in book one. The doorbell's ringing, and Rolf, his ears pinned and teeth bared, races toward the door.

"UPS," Libby predicts. And sure enough, when Buzz comes into the room a few minutes later, he's carrying a tower of small boxes, each pockmarked with dog slobber and bite marks.

"What does he have against UPS?"

Libby can't remember.

"Well, maybe this'll help." Buzz jabs open the first box with a fork from the kitchen. He seems cheery this morning and even whistles a few bars of a song she doesn't recognize. "Some tasty krill oil. Noni juice, whatever a noni is. Fish oil, ginseng, some acetyl-L-carnitine." He lifts something that resembles a car battery. "Or we can, uh, hot-wire your brain, I guess?"

Libby pulls out a box of lemon-balm tea and a bottle of Huperzine A, a brilliant name she hopes she remembers to use for a character one day. "What is all this?"

"Peanut ordered it. To get rid of your writer's block."

"Will it work?" Libby lines up the containers like soldiers. Is it possible Dr. Whatsit doesn't know everything about her condition? That he forgot to google "dementia" to see what remedies exist besides the ones he learned about in med school?

Buzz twists the cap off a bottle and sniffs the contents. "Can't hurt, right?" He shakes a vitamin E capsule into her palm.

When she hesitates, he throws one into his own mouth. "Ante up."

Libby can't taste anything, but the pill is the size of a toy battleship. It runs aground near her tonsils.

Buzz uncaps the bottle of noni juice, takes a swig of the murky green liquid, and hands it to her. "This isn't any better," he says hoarsely.

Libby is choking the stringy juice down when Peanut comes in, looking troubled. She is wearing a white T-shirt that reads POMPOU'S IS MAGICAL. Her hair frizzes in a triangle around her face.

"You shaved." She frowns at Buzz. "And took a shower."

"Yeah? So?"

"It looks weird," Peanut says.

"So don't look at me."

Peanut points to the kitchen, dazzling with cleanliness. "And why'd you do that?"

"I didn't."

"It was me," Libby says, raising her hand from the couch.

Peanut turns to face her but doesn't smile. "I finished the book," she announces, pinching her scar.

Her tone catches Libby off guard. When was the last time she asked anyone to critique her writing? For years, she's only received lavish bouquets from her publisher, adoring notes from fans, and five-star raves from reviewers.

Stupendous.

Magical.

An instant children's classic.

The work of a compassionate genius.

Your books changed my life, Mr. Electric.

Peanut hugs Libby's rubber-banded manuscript to her chest. "It's like you were trying to punish the Children."

Out of all the things Libby expected her to say—and honestly, they are all variations of *it was so good, I didn't want it to end!*—this is not one.

"Me?" Libby puts her hand on her chest. "That's the last thing I want."

"I can't think of any way to save them," Peanut says fiercely, like this is Libby's fault, too. "I thought about it all night. There's nothing!"

She counts on her fingers. "There can't be a Return Charm because they used the last one in book two. They can't go back in time because the *Sink Ng* ship was sunk. Everything magical in the forest has disappeared. Gran Bere's ghost is gone. Huperzine and Benjamin are lost in the forest and getting weaker. You burned Pompou's to the ground! And Everlee is *dying*."

Libby smooths her hair, not sure what to say. She can't remember half the plot points Peanut has mentioned.

"You need to fix this!" Peanut's scar twists with anger. "You can't end the book like this. The Children can't die! None of them! It's not fair!"

Life isn't fair, Libby wants to agree, but that feels like an ugly truth a child should learn from their parent.

"Jeez, take it easy, P," Buzz interjects. "That's why she's here. To get your help."

"But I can't do it!" Peanut is shouting now. "You don't understand. She's ruined *everything*."

"Well, we've got noni juice now," Buzz says, shaking the bottle.

Peanut storms from the living room. The front door slams. Libby's face burns.

Not because she is humiliated, although there is that, but because she knows Peanut is right. Underneath all her good intentions and hand wringing, maybe Libby does want the Children to suffer as much as she is.

29

Peanut is so lost in her thoughts that she doesn't hear Rick, the owner of the alpaca ranch, coast down the hill behind her on his recumbent bike. He has to swerve so he doesn't hit her.

"Look alive!" he shouts.

"I'll look however I want!" Peanut shouts back.

She kicks a rock across the road. Every time she tries to think about the Children, she thinks about the noises coming from her living room last night instead. Or how Buzz shaved like something special is going to happen.

Ice grows in the pit of Peanut's stomach.

"Where fear lies, there trouble lies," is the first thing the Unstopping ever whispers to Everlee.

A knot of kids waits for the Cross Creek bus. Peanut has known each of them since she was a baby. They're not friends, but they depend on her father when they're sick or hurt themselves.

"Doctor B," they call him. The boys show him their report cards and soccer trophies; the girls give him hugs. They ignore Peanut, but she's never cared. Since kindergarten, Peanut has had Nancee. One best friend is all she's needed.

Now she has no one. And the Children will be gone soon, too.

"Did you get extra homework because you busted up Rosemary's face?" Ricky McAvoy asks.

When he flicks his thumb and index finger at the papers in her hands, Peanut realizes: she's still carrying Libby's manuscript.

The school bus hurtles around the corner. Peanut freezes, not sure what to do. She can't go to school with Libby's manuscript. She promised to keep the Children safe, and no matter how disappointed she is in Libby, she will.

But their lives are hanging by a thread, a voice inside Peanut points out.

And if she does go to school, the voice adds, she could show the manuscript to Nancee. Although Peanut is the Falling Children's number one fan, Nancee is surely in the top two thousand. In Colorado, at least. Maybe she'll figure out how to save the Children. Or, well, inspire Peanut to have a brilliant idea.

Peanut doesn't recognize the bus driver. He looks at her face, not even trying to hide his curiosity.

"Hey, you was that baby who was buried alive, weren't you? I remember those eyes from the newspaper photo." He shakes his head. "That was something awful. My whole family prayed for you."

"Thank you," Peanut says stiffly.

He starts the engine, raising his voice so she can still hear him. "What kind of mother dumps her baby like a worthless piece of trash? They ever found out who did that to you?"

Even over the roar of the motor, Peanut can tell everyone on the bus has stopped talking. They turn toward her like maybe she has something to say.

"Not yet," she announces. "But I will."

"Good girl. That's the spirit." The bus driver nods.

From the back of the bus, Ricky circles his finger around his ear.

Peanut feels she's missed a month of school instead of six days. Haikus and long division quizzes are thumbtacked to a bulletin board, and the rows of desks have evolved into a circle. The only thing that feels familiar is how Mrs. Hader's nostrils flare when she sees Peanut.

"Class," she announces after the bell rings. "Once you have gotten in trouble with me, you are on thin ice for the rest of the year. That means," she says, looking at Peanut, "that you should watch your step." She draws a slow finger across her neck.

From the corner of her eye, Peanut sees Rosemary, her nose protected with a white bandage. Next to her is Nancee.

Peanut fiddles with the corners of the manuscript. She put it under her math book so no one can see, but it's like trying to hide a roll of toilet paper under a thimble.

When Mrs. Hader breaks the class into groups to discuss rising plot and action, Peanut takes the manuscript with her. So long as she carries it everywhere, nothing can happen to it, she tells herself.

The other kids in her group discuss the book they've been reading in class. It's something about an old, dying woman who spends her last days talking to people who aren't really there. Peanut isn't listening. Partly because the book sounds depressing—Peanut is annoyed when adults don't try to help themselves—but mostly because Nancee has gotten a pass for the bathroom.

Peanut shoots her hand into the air.

Mrs. Hader ignores it.

Peanut waves her hand.

Mrs. Hader pretends she doesn't see it.

Peanut snaps her fingers.

Mrs. Hader turns on a little radio at her desk.

"I have to go the bathroom!" Peanut finally jumps up, still clutching the manuscript. "Right now. It's an emergency."

The teacher gives her a stony look. "Wait until Nancee comes back."

"But—"

"Sit down, Peanut. If you have such a tiny bladder, I suggest you look into diapers."

The class erupts into laughter.

Scowling, Peanut sits.

"She *so* hates you," says Marcy Beamer, who always smells like horses.

"Careful," Ricky McAvoy says, "or Peanut will bust your nose next."

"What's an unreliable narrator?" Mrs. Hader calls from the front of the room. "Is there one in this book? How do we know?"

When Mrs. Hader turns toward the board, Peanut slips from her chair and bolts out the back door of the classroom.

The hallway floor is as treacherously waxed as ever. Peanut slides over the checkerboard squares, around the corner, and into the closest girls' bathroom.

It's empty save for five sinks, dripping in unison, and the smell of banana-cream Juuls. The radiator in the corner lets out a steamy belch.

There is another noise, too—a rustling from one of the stalls.

"Nancee?"

The rustling stops.

"Nancee! This is an emergency. I need to talk to you!"

The door to the last stall cracks open, and Nancee peeks out. She's holding a marshmallow-fluff sandwich, her mouth and chin smeared white.

"Don't tell Rosemary," she says, her eyes wide like a rabbit's. "She doesn't eat added sugar."

Peanut pushes her way into the stall. "Never mind Rosemary. There's a bigger problem. Like, the worst problem ever."

"I'm not supposed to talk to you." Nancee's breath sparks with sugar.

"This is an emergency. It's about the Children. They're all going to die!"

Nancee takes another bite. "That's just some lame rumor going around."

"No, it's for real." Peanut lowers her voice. "F. T. Goldhero can't write anymore, so she—I mean, he," she corrects herself, "wants to kill them all off."

Nancee looks confused. "What do you mean he can't write anymore? Like he broke his hands?"

"No, like he ran out of imagination."

"That'll never happen." Nancee sucks the filling from her sandwich. "He's a genius."

"But sometimes geniuses get sick," Peanut insists. "Or need help."

"Where'd you hear this?" Nancee is suddenly suspicious.

Peanut's holding the last book so tightly that the corners slice into her palms. She looks at Nancee's sticky double chin and the freckle just below her left eye.

Here, she could say. *Read.*

Everything could go back to normal.

"Are you making stuff up to talk to me?" Nancee says. "Because if so, that's sad."

"So is Rosemary threatening me on social media."

"Only boomers say 'social media.'"

"It's still mean," Peanut hisses. "And you're a cyberbully, and you're lucky I have a skin as tough and resilient as a Williwig's. Otherwise, you'd get expelled."

"It's not me," Nancee says defensively. "It was Rosemary's idea. And I don't blame her. Not after what you did to her face."

"I didn't do anything! I told you, it was an acc—"

"Have you seen her nose?" Nancee throws her empty ziplock bag into the toilet. "It's so un-Rosemary now. She's even having to stop modeling."

But Peanut is no longer listening. Partly because Mrs. Hader is now in the bathroom, booming, "Pandora Bixton? Are you in here?" But mostly because Peanut's instinct was right. Talking to Nancee *has* given her an idea of what she can do to help Libby, so Libby can save the Children.

*It's so **un**-Rosemary now. She's even having to **stop** modeling.*

It is dangerous and terrifying and *perfect*.

30

"That's the lamest f-ing idea I've ever heard."

"No, it's not." Peanut folds her arms.

Buzz turns to Libby. "The old lady who used to live there? No one's seen her in like a decade. She's dead or nuts or both."

"But the Unstopping lives there now, too," Peanut insists. "He told me when he gave me a ride home."

"Orson Greeley is not the Unstopping."

"You didn't see him!" Peanut pulls at her face. "He had eyes everywhere. And this tooth?" She points to one of her canines. "Just like the Unstopping, it's a little tiny baby tooth! He's using uncertain magic to prevent you from finishing your book. I know it."

"Your imagination is dangerous," Buzz says, eating a Mumps bar in two bites.

"Then why is that creepy doll tied up in front of his house?" Peanut challenges. "I'm not imagining that."

"Some kid probably put it up for a prank." Buzz lifts his shoulders. "How should I know?"

"You can't know. You haven't read the books. But I have." Peanut points to Libby. "And she's F. T. Goldhero. She's not scared of anything, are you? Not when you feel okay, right?"

Libby smiles. She likes being thought of as intrepid, although it's a color that's all wrong for her—like sunflower yellow. She can't even reread the part in book four when the Children find a dusty old kaleidoscope. When they hold it up to the light, they realize it's the Unstopping's secret dungeon. Trapped inside are dozens of forgotten stuffed animals, cotton leaking from their open bellies, glass eyes hanging loose, tire tracks lining their once-smiling faces.

Still, Libby reminds herself, she has nothing to lose. This morning, she couldn't figure out how to work the toaster. Buzz had to do it for her. Later, after she worked up the courage to shower, even with the door still off its hinges, Libby couldn't remember how to button her shirt.

"You're, uh, coming loose there," Buzz said, averting his eyes when she came into the kitchen.

"These buttons, they never work," Libby said. "Do you have a stapler?"

He ended up buttoning the shirt for her, Libby's eyes trained on Rolf sleeping on the floor and not Buzz's hands next to her breasts. She hadn't even attempted to put on a bra, with its slippery straps and fiddly hooks.

Buzz looks over at Libby. She can tell he wants her to say no, she won't go look for the Unstopping—is shaking his head and mouthing it even. *No.*

"But we need a quest that seems like a bad idea!" Peanut insists. "The Children never get anywhere without one."

"Here's an idea," Buzz says. "How about you sit down and write the freaking ending to the book?" He gestures to the manuscript Peanut has brought back, along with a handwritten apology to Libby for her "emotional outburst" this morning before school.

"What outburst?" Libby said, sniffing the few limp blooms of bittercress that Peanut handed her as well. "You don't need to apologize to me."

Peanut beamed. "See?" she says to Buzz. "I told you she'd understand."

"We could write," Peanut says now, looking at Libby. "Or we could fix the book *and* you by bravely confronting the Unstopping." She squeezes her hands together. "I know you're under some type of spell. I just know it."

"Enough." Buzz points to the clock. "Get home before Jessie does."

Peanut drags herself off the couch. "Why can't I move in with you? She's a heartless creature who only exists to pummel my dreams."

"More walking, less talking." Buzz points to the door. "Go."

"Will you think about it?" Peanut begs Libby. "Please? I know this is a good idea."

"Of course," Libby says. "Sure."

After the front door slams, Buzz asks, "You're not serious, are you?"

Libby has no idea what he's talking about. She's too busy picking a staple out of the front of her shirt. "Serious about what?"

~~~

How long has Libby been in this house, this town, this world? She's fuzzy on the details, but besides the kitchen, she's now cleaned both bathrooms, the living room, and the dining room.

"You don't have to do that," Buzz says each time he catches her on the floor with her sponge and bucket of bleach water, but Libby likes to clean.

She can scrub, wipe, and polish even though she can't remember how to save the Children—or put the cap back onto the bleach container. When she accidentally knocks it over in the pantry later that afternoon, Buzz mops it up with a pile of dirty T-shirts, but the air still fills with fumes.

"It'll air out." Buzz limps to the screen door and slides it open as far as it will go.

Libby follows him outside, her eyes and nose burning.

Buzz flops into a patio chair, a cloud of pollen rising from the cushion. "You bleached your hair," he points out when she takes the seat next to him.

"I what?"

"Your hair. You bleached it." He leans over and separates a strand of Libby's hair, just above her ear, and holds it out so she can see. Sure enough, it's dramatically lighter than the rest.

"It doesn't look bad," Buzz says.

Libby knows he's being polite. Like when she accidentally sat on the TV remote and sent the volume up, up, up and couldn't get it to go down again.

"I got it," he said.

Or when she left the water running in the kitchen sink. "Happens." He shrugged.

"You're kinder than I expected you to be," Libby says.

She means it as a compliment, but Buzz doesn't take it that way. "What's that supposed to mean?"

Libby lifts her shoulders. "Most of my adult characters turn out to be villains. Write what you know and all that."

"Maybe you should get out more."

There's no judgment in his voice. It's an observation, the same way he points west and hands her a pair of binoculars.

"Pygmy nuthatch."

Libby can't find the bird in the lenses but nods and pretends to until Buzz says, "Nah, you're like six feet off." He scrapes his chair closer and lines up the binoculars for her.

"See?" He motions for her to look again. "It's a little guy, blue on top with a white throat and yellow chest."

His arm grazes hers, and Libby feels a rush of embarrassment. How sad that the slightest touch from a stranger makes her grateful.

"Now you see?"

"I do, but I don't see what's so special about it," Libby says. "And that call? It sounds like a rubber duck being squeezed." She mimics the lackluster noise: *wee-bee, wee-bee.*

"What are you talking about?" Buzz looks at her incredulously. "He's fucking awesome. Nuthatches live together in one big family. And help each other build nests. Look how busy he is," he points out, "and he does all that on, like, nine calories a day."

She looks again, but the bird flits into the branches.

"Here." Taking the binoculars, Buzz slides his chair backward to try to find it again. Libby feels strangely exposed, like she has gone out into a snowstorm without a coat.

"What's that wooden thing out there?" she asks, rubbing her arms.

Buzz gives her a sideways glance. "The half-pipe I started to build with my dad? That you asked me about already?"

"I was kidding," Libby lies.

Buzz hangs the binoculars around his neck and stands. "Want to check it out?"

She doesn't move. "Isn't it far away?"

"Nah, just looks that way."

Libby hesitates. "I don't know."

"What do you have to know?" he says easily. "Come on."

Rolf is first to follow Buzz off the deck and down the green slope of the yard. At the back, Buzz pushes open a wooden gate to reveal a waist-high tangle of choke cherries and raspberry bushes.

"I guess I haven't been back here in a while," he admits.

"We can go back," Libby says quickly. "There are probably ticks."

Or spiders, snakes, mountain lions, bears, or serial killers, she thinks.

Buzz actually laughs out loud. "Is there anything you're *not* scared of?"

"No," Libby says, and the honesty of the statement makes her smile.

"Well then," Buzz says, "we might as well go."

Using his cane, he bushwhacks their way to a small deer trail that winds into the belly of the woods, then up and around—Libby isn't paying attention. Her eyes stay on the back of Buzz's red T-shirt, making sure she doesn't lose sight of him.

By the time they reach the base of a sturdy oak, he's sweating through his T-shirt. Burrs cling to his sleeve. Libby reaches over and plucks one off—then one more, so it has a friend.

"Make a wish," she says, cupping both in her hands. From Buzz's expression, she realizes that may not be the right thing to say. She slides the pair of burrs into her pocket instead.

"You first." Buzz points to the two-by-fours nailed into the wizened trunk of the tree and tilted like loose teeth.

When was the last time Libby climbed a tree? (*Concussions, broken arms, broken legs, earthquakes, Timber!* her mind chatters.) Maybe she never has.

"I'll give you a leg up," Buzz says and makes a step with his hands.

Libby is worried she won't remember how to climb. There is so much effort involved, a right-left and a thing-thingy. But her muscles know better than her brain, and she reaches the platform in what feels like no time.

Buzz has more trouble.

"Are you okay?" She leans down to ask when she hears him cursing.

"Fucking squirrel."

After a series of ominous cracking noises, he drags himself onto the platform, rolls onto his back, and closes his eyes. "I'm going to strangle the next squirrel I see, swear to God."

"Look at this place." Libby exhales at the view of the town splayed out below. "It reminds me of Dark Crevice."

"Is that where you're from?"

Libby smiles. "It's where the Falling Children are from. The church with its spindly steeple?" She points. "It reminds me of Pompou's. And look! You can see armies of miniature soldiers—"

"Tourists," Buzz says, "but they can be aggressive."

Cars trundle through the streets like wind-up toys. Even the mountains framing downtown look like they've been formed from homemade green clay.

"Why are they the *Falling* Children?" Buzz asks. "Do they wipe out a lot?"

"No. Or well, Huperzine does, but that's not why." Libby hesitates, wondering how much she should share.

"It's my favorite word," she says. "'Falling' conveys this sense of excitement and danger and feeling out of control. But there's also something so hopeful about it—you can fall in love, for instance. Or into good luck. Or a pile of crisp autumn leaves."

Libby does none of these things. But she likes the *idea* of falling, how she feels when she writes these things, how the words look on the page.

"There's a right way to fall, so you don't get hurt." Buzz gestures to his bad leg. "This wasn't it."

"I could never skateboard," Libby says. "I can only write about it."

They sit for a while without talking. Then Libby jumps up, suddenly panicked. "Rolf! Where's Rolf?"

"He's down there." Buzz points. "Just chilling."

She leans over the edge of the tree house—"Half-pipe," Buzz corrects—and sure enough, there Rolf is, nosing through a pile of dead leaves at the base of the tree.

Libby covers her heart so Buzz can't hear how loudly it's beating. "I lost him once. It was the worst day of my life."

"How'd you get him back?"

The details escape her. "He just—found his way home," she says. Isn't that the way it always happens?

"He's a cool dog," Buzz says. "I never had one."

"Never?"

"Nope. Never."

"Then would you want him to stay here after I die?" Libby hears herself ask. "He likes you. So long as you don't start working for UPS. That would be"—she struggles for the right word and can only come up with—"you know."

"You're dying?" Buzz looks startled. "You said you had writer's block."

"I mean, *if* I die." Libby tries to smile. "One day. In a car or something. Or because of—another thing. Something. We're all dying."

"Yeah, but you better not," Buzz lies back and folds his hands over the bare skin where his T-shirt has come away from his jeans. "Everyone'd lose their shit if F. T. Goldhero died."

"But not *me*," Libby corrects. "Nobody knows me." She watches a bird that's blue on top and has a white throat and yellow belly.

"Another pygmy nuthatch," Buzz says. And then, after a moment has passed, he says, "*I* know."

"You're one person," Libby says. "No offense." She lies next to him, the sun staining her body against the warm wood.

Buzz closes his eyes. "None taken."

The wind slides through the leaves above them. When Buzz turns toward her, the afternoon light flecks his eyes green. "How do you feel about staying here for the rest of your life?"

Libby's fingers tighten around each other like sailor knots. She is not sure what she thinks or feels.

"_____" is all she can come up with.

Buzz gives her a lopsided smile. "I broke a couple of the boards getting up here. What I mean is I don't know how the fuck we're getting down."

31

Someone—Libby can't remember who—once accused her of being "risk averse." It's true that there's a long list of things she's too scared to try, feelings she's too worried to have. Panic and fear are the only emotions solid enough to hold her. The rest crack under her weight like sheets of ice.

Libby does not like to fall.

This explains why the last time she had a relationship, not just a one-night stand, was eleven, almost twelve years ago, with another writing instructor who taught at the same community college. Nick had sold his first novel to a small press and was charming and funny. He had no opinion about Libby until a holiday faculty mixer with an open bar.

After several gin and tonics, mixed by a bartender grimly determined to drain all the bottles by 8:00 p.m., Libby asked Nick for a ride home. They had sex in the back seat of his Kia and then for the rest of the spring semester, until Libby showed him one of her short stories.

"Don't take this personally," Nick said afterward, pushing the stack of papers back toward her, "but very few people have what it takes to be a writer."

He stopped returning her calls after that.

Libby reminds herself of this when she finds herself sitting next to Buzz, so close that she can feel the warmth coming off his skin. She makes herself remember the condescension in Nick's blue eyes (*Were they blue?*) and how he kept them open and looked past her when they kissed.

Libby is too guarded to enjoy romance, even if she were writing it herself. Once they're back inside, she takes the jugs of Tylenol from her suitcase and displays them, labels out, on the nightstand as a reminder: she has more important things to do than wish she were twenty years younger.

And the truth is, twenty-year-old Libby was not much different than the Libby who is forty. Except for the creases beginning to etch themselves onto her forehead.

And the dementia.

You almost forgot, Libby jokes to herself.

She stays in the bedroom, door shut, for the remainder of the evening, alternating between reading about F. T. Goldhero on Buzz's laptop and trying to write. It's like trying to choose whether to be mauled quickly by a hungry lion or tortured slowly by a fatal virus.

Online, love for the Falling Children continues to curdle.

17 Reasons F. T. Goldhero is Dead To Me, one slideshow is titled.

The final FaChi book is going to SUCK, insists a commenter on the Falling Children website. Hundreds of others agree. Their emojis alone make Libby shrink back from the screen.

Glenn's photos of Libby's office have been blown up and dissected for every last clue. An open package of Red Vines on the desk. (*F. T. Goldhero is a selfish pig!*) A crumpled wad of tissues on the floor. (*F. T. Goldhero is a misogynistic slob who expects his housekeeper to pick up his repulsive Man Garbage!*) One enterprising fan has blown up the view outside Libby's office window. He boasts that he will extract metadata from the photo to pinpoint the exact location of the apartment. *(F. T. Goldhero is careless and deserves to be outed!)*

Libby's heart slams against her chest.

She crawls into bed, staring at the Tylenol on the dresser. The sun has begun its drop, and shadows lap at the room.

Is it time?

Give me a sign, she asks the universe.

There is a knock at Libby's door.

"Have something for you." Flipping on the light, Buzz holds up a red box labeled CONCENTRATION MAGIC. "Peanut ordered this for you. Want to magically retrain your brain?" He shakes it and the cards inside *coo-coo-ca-choo*.

"That won't help."

"How do you know? At least try."

How badly does Libby want to save the Children? This feels like a test.

Reluctantly, she follows Buzz into the kitchen. A sandwich waits on the table.

"Nothing plugs a hole in the head like peanut butter." He gestures.

"What's that supposed to mean?"

"That's one of your lines." Buzz points to a frayed paperback of book one on the table. "I got it from the library. It's not bad." He sits next to her. "How'd you come up with the idea anyway?"

Libby picks at the sandwich crust. For years, she's practiced how she would answer this question in an interview, if she were allowed to be revealed as F. T. Goldhero.

I rescued the Children when they needed me most, she will say.

Maybe in a British accent.

It's a pretty idea, like a lavender sweater that brings out Libby's eyes, but it's not the truth.

"I started writing them when I was a kid. After my parents died. I'm not very good at real life," she says, although Buzz must already know that—of course he does. "They gave me somewhere to hide."

Until she ruined it.

Libby thinks of the abandoned forest, Pompou's burned to the ground, the panic in Huperzine's eyes.

"So write something else."

Libby doesn't know anything else. Her whole life is the Children. She's never had her own adventure without them.

"You came here," Buzz points out.

"Yes," Libby sighs. "I came here."

The clock ticks, ticks, ticks. Libby stares at the wall, not sure what comes next.

"Okay," says Buzz, shaking the lid off the game. "Let's do this."

"You can play without me."

"Then it's not a game."

He lays out dozens of cards, each showing a different object: a sunny sky, a ladder, a disembodied foot. Then he turns them upside down, and they take turns trying to make a match.

Buzz gets two pairs in a row: apples and bears. "Piece of cake," he says.

When it's Libby's turn, she doesn't get any.

Buzz gets four matches on his next turn. Libby doesn't get any. She can't remember which cards she's already flipped over or the pictures they reveal.

After Buzz gets another pair, he slides his chair closer to Libby. "Here, I'll help you."

"You don't have to."

Buzz turns a card over anyway. "A goldfish. Remember where we saw the other one?" He leans over her to tap a card. "Try here."

Libby does. "Oh," she says, surprised. "It is another little fish."

"Keep going." Buzz drapes his arm around the back of her chair. "Pick a card, any card."

Tucking a piece of hair behind her ear, Libby slowly turns another. It's a bird with a colorful plumed tail.

"Peacock," Buzz says. "Where's the other?"

Libby wishes his knee weren't touching hers. "I—did I see one?"

"Yeah, you did." Buzz waves his hand over the cards before pausing above one. "Here."

Sure enough, it matches the bird she's holding in her other hand.

"Does this mean I'm winning?" Libby smiles despite herself. "I never win."

"I'm not saying. Now you try."

Only four cards are left on the table. Libby flips the card closest to her. It's a roller skate. "Easy," Buzz says.

Libby is buoyed by his confidence. Of course, she can do this. It's a kids' game. She's looking for a roller skate. The Children will be fine. Only four cards are left.

Outside, a car passes by, bass thumping with "Funky Cold Medina."

"I love this song," Libby says.

She closes her eyes. It's like Vernice is in the kitchen, too, and if Libby turns around, she'll see her standing by the stove, sipping room-temperature Dr Pepper (no ice) while attempting to cook an edible breakfast, but mostly just urging Libby to sing along.

Libby remembers every single word.

Buzz laughs. "That's your favorite song?"

Libby laughs, too. "It's okay. I'm dying alone."

She means it to be funny, but it doesn't come out that way.

Her card slips under the table, and Libby leans over to get it, but Buzz gets there first. When he touches her sleeve, at first she thinks he's pulling a loose thread from her sweater. But then he says something—not a word she recognizes, but "uh" or "ah" or a combination of both—and he kisses her.

Under the table, years between them, somehow they fit. Libby feels something brighter and more spectacular than fireworks. She can see herself as Buzz does, the person maybe she's capable of becoming.

The phone rings.

"Don't get it," Buzz says quickly, as if that were a possibility.

An ancient answering machine clicks on. Libby can't hear the recorded message, but after the beep, she thinks she hears a woman says, "Good evening, it's Donna calling from Dr. Whatsit's office. We've tried calling you three times over the past two weeks to make sure—"

Buzz nearly flips over the table in his haste to get to the machine. "Fucking robocalls," he says, punching one button after another.

Libby stands. She can feel blood draining from her cheeks. "That didn't sound like a robot. It sounded like a real person."

"Yeah," he says. "That's how they get you."

"How does he know I'm here?"

"Who?"

Libby looks at him incredulously. "Did you call my doctor? Did you tell him I was here?"

Buzz looks confused. "No."

"Then why is he calling me?"

"No one's calling you. What did you hear?" Buzz toggles a switch on the machine.

"My doctor!"

"It wasn't your doctor. It was another fucking debt collector trying to get me to pay my hospital bill."

Libby doesn't believe him. She stands, shaking. "Then play it."

The tape on the answering machine sputters backward. But when Buzz hits Play, nothing happens.

"Oh." He shoots Libby a guilty look. "I guess I deleted it."

Libby doesn't know what to think. She tries to stuff the playing cards back into their cardboard sleeve but can't line them up.

"I'll do it," Buzz says, taking them from her, but it only makes Libby feel worse, like she's an old, dotty invalid who needs to be cared for.

Whistling for Rolf, who chooses not to come, she retreats into the bedroom. Libby wishes she could rewind and erase time like the answering machine—or better yet, fast-forward her life so she can finish the book and kill herself already.

She no longer trusts her brain to tell her the truth. Did Dr. Whatsit's office really call? Leaning her head over the side of the bed, she spies a half-eaten bag of Funyuns. Are those hers? Does she *like* them?

Buzz comes and stands in the doorway. "So," he asks, "when the phone rang—what did you think you heard?"

Libby has enough pity for herself. She doesn't need someone else's. "Can we not talk about it? Please—just go."

Buzz takes the bag of onion rings and shuts the door, which is fine with Libby. She's used to being alone. *It's better this way, baby*, she hears Vernice say.

But a few minutes later, when the door pushes open again, Libby feels betrayed at the height her heart leaps.

It's (only) Rolf. He jumps onto the bed, curls into the crook of her legs, and sighs.

Google "Who is Libby Weeks and why am I here"

Your search—"Who is Libby Weeks and why am I here"—did not match any documents.

Suggestions:

- Make sure that all words are spelled correctly.
- Try different keywords.
- Try more general keywords.
- Consider that maybe you don't want to know the answer.

32

Long fingernails scrape Libby's window.

"Wake up," something outside the house whispers. "It's time."

The room is pitch-black, save for a ghastly face, all pale shadows and shiny teeth, behind the windowpane.

The Unstopping.

"Are you ready? I have a plan."

Libby is about to scream—exactly what, she isn't sure—when the ghoulish face whispers, "Libby! It's me!"

Turning on the bedside lamp—after knocking it to the floor first—Libby realizes the figure outside is Peanut, shrouded in a black hoodie. Black shoe polish dots her cheeks and forehead.

"Who did you think I was?" She giggles through the half-cracked window. "You looked so scared."

"What are you doing here?" Libby looks at the clock, which has also fallen to the floor. The hour hand is closer to eleven than ten, but she can't remember what, exactly, that means besides "late."

"I'm getting you so we can confront the Unstopping," Peanut says. When Libby looks at her blankly, Peanut goes on. "I know it's him. You have to be the reason he's here."

"But"—Libby gestures to the dark sky—"don't you think he's—sleeping?"

She doesn't want Peanut to know she's afraid.

"Well, then he'll have to wake up because this is the only time I can go." Peanut sets her mouth like a lever. "And it may be the only true way we can help you."

When Libby hesitates, Peanut says, "In every book, Huperzine or Benjamin don't want to go somewhere. But once Everlee makes them, they realize it's their destiny. And that if they'd gone sooner, it would have been even better."

"Okay," Libby says, mostly so Peanut will stop talking. The volume of words pelts her like rain. "Fine."

She's still fully dressed, so she only has to pull on her sneakers. In case Peanut is right and an idea does come to her, she tucks a pen and her little red notebook into the pocket of her jeans. Then she feels her way to the front hall. From the main bedroom come Rolf's snores. When did he leave her?

Peanut is waiting on the porch, talking as if their conversation was never interrupted.

"—and I have an extra flashlight for you—see, you squeeze this button—and my safety vest." She pulls a wad of neon-yellow mesh from her jacket pocket and shakes it. "We can take turns wearing it. His house, or well, let's say 'lair,' is about a mile away. Or more than that? I'm not sure. I don't like math because it's never about the Children. We can go through the woods or walk next to the highway. You can choose."

"Which is easier?" Libby shivers as she pulls the door closed behind her.

"Definitely neither," Peanut says, misunderstanding. "If we go through the woods, we could get lost—maybe for weeks!—like the

Children are in the forest. But if we take the highway, we get to walk this close"—she holds her palms a few inches apart—"to a steep cliff that's like the Abyss of Nothingness."

Libby looks back at Buzz's house. "Maybe we should—"

"Go one way there and the other back." Peanut beams. "I knew we'd think alike."

They go around the house and through the backyard. It's the same way Libby came with Buzz, but she can't remember if that happened yesterday or a week ago.

As they walk, Peanut tells Libby stories. About playing "Falling Children" out here with her best friend, who's no longer her best friend, but she feels Libby is, if Libby feels the same way. How sometimes tourists take a wrong turn coming down Mount Snaffles and Jessie will sketch a map and sell it to them because Jessie is always looking for ways to make money. How right there, over that hill and down the other one and past that grove of trees, is the library where Peanut was buried alive as a baby—just like Everlee.

"The similarity is truly uncanny," she says.

Libby doesn't answer. Tree branches pull at her sweater. The ground is uneven, and she slows her steps to keep inside the stunted beam of the flashlight.

"We're close," Peanut announces once they emerge onto a deserted two-lane highway.

WELCOME TO BLUE SKIES reads a large sign behind them. The white paint gives off its own light.

Libby follows Peanut over fallen logs and the occasional wayward soda can. On the other side of the shoulder is—nothing. The earth simply drops away.

"See?" Peanut says excitedly. "I told you; we could fall to our deaths in seconds."

Libby moves farther into the road. "Where are we going again?"

"We're already there." Peanut points to a narrow driveway of chewed concrete that leads up a hill. DOLL HOSPITAL a sign reads.

A fence of sagging chicken wire runs parallel to the road. As Libby shines her flashlight over it, she feels a scream building inside her. On the fence, hanging by its neck, is a baby.

Libby moves toward it, her arms outstretched, before she realizes this is not a real infant but a life-size plastic doll. Its pink skin is covered with scratches, and its shaggy hair has been eaten away. Deep black Xs are carved over both its eyes, and its mouth is sewn shut.

"See? Just like in your books," Peanut whispers. "How the Unstopping signals that he's back."

Die is spray-painted orange onto the nearby mailbox.

Peanut motions for Libby to follow her up the driveway, past another sign that reads KEEP OUT.

Libby's heart pumps in her ears. It sounds like, *Bats, rats, murder site—*

"Look!" When Peanut stops short before her, Libby grabs the girl's shoulders to keep from falling. Peanut is so small, almost not there at all.

Ahead is a low-slung house with a punched-sideways chimney. Shingles are missing from the roof, and the screen door hangs from its hinges. Graffiti-sprayed plywood covers the windows. Parked next to the house is a hearse.

Peanut turns and looks at the narrow driveway choked with weeds and potholes. "How'd he get it up here?"

Getting down on her knees, she knocks on the pavement. "It sounds real," she says.

Libby chews her thumbnail. Who shows up at a dangerous stranger's house in the middle of the night? And with a *child*? What is wrong with her?

She shines her flashlight on Peanut. The jeans she's wearing have red hearts embroidered on the back pockets. Peanut should not be making decisions for Libby. Or herself.

"We should go."

"Why?" Peanut stands and looks at her, surprised. "We're on a quest."

"We can do it later, can't we?"

Libby hates how cowardly she sounds. Peanut must feel the same way.

"But don't you want to help the Children?"

Libby has no idea how this girl can be so fearless. She can't remember a time when the universe felt on her side instead of plotting against her. Her stomach churns with herbal supplements and noni juice.

Animal hoarder, trigger-happy gun owner, Satanic cult in the middle of a ritual—

"Come on," Peanut says, and when Libby still hesitates, she lifts a canister of bear spray and a yellow plastic whistle. "Which one do you want?"

Libby takes the whistle.

Up close, the house is worse. Furry cobwebs droop from the eaves. Pipes, coils of copper wire, and an old toilet lie scattered by the front door.

Libby's head hums like a swarm of bees is loose inside it.

"Hold on a second. I need to think," she says, mostly to herself. She takes the notebook from her back pocket and sits down on a tree stump, her head in her hands.

What are they getting themselves into? She needs time to finish listing all the things that could—and probably will—go wrong...

But Peanut is already knocking—four short knocks, three long, which is how the Children summon the Unstopping.

Someone's scrawled an X over the door with orange spray paint.

It creaks open, but no one's there.

"It's just like that scene in your last book," Peanut says.

Libby is thinking the same thing.

33

Inside, their flashlights flick over boxes, slick bags of trash, empty beer cans, and cats. Paper-thin cats are everywhere, their tails twisted into letters. Sleeping. Walking. Eating. Meowing.

Buttery eyes blink at Libby.

"Hello?" Peanut calls.

Clearing her throat, she adds, "'Tis I! Peanut Bixton, come to expose your uncertain evil to our inherent goodness, forcing you to unshackle this woman's imagination from your foul and vicious magic!"

"That sounds good," Libby says. She wishes she had a pencil to write it down.

"You already did," says Peanut. "Remember? In book three, when Everlee—"

"It was a joke," lies Libby.

Peanut smiles. "Good one!"

Libby follows her into a small filthy kitchen. The '80s-era range is missing its knobs. The refrigerator is chained shut. A sign strung from the faucet sink warns STOP.

"Can we go now?" Libby whispers. "No one's here."

"That's good. We can look for ways to defeat him."

Peanut runs her flashlight over the ceiling. A drop of hazy-brown liquid oozes from a crack and splats onto the floor before them.

"Did you see that?" She turns to Libby. "The house is weeping!"

To Libby, it looks like a roof leak, but Peanut has already moved on. "Look for something causing the spell he put on you!"

Libby isn't sure what that would be. She accidentally kicks an empty soda can across the floor, and the cats scatter at the noise. It catches Libby off guard, too, and she stumbles against the wall. The pale pink wallpaper is clammy and—is it pulsing?

"*Welcome to my brain,*" the Unstopping tells the Children in book two. "Don't get lost."

"Please, Peanut." Libby feels sweat in the small of her back. "We need to go."

Peanut doesn't answer. She's peering into the nearest trash bag. Severed doll parts—arms, legs, and scalped heads with frozen smiles—spill to the floor. Then come discarded stuffed animals, their faces chewed and bellies ripped.

"Toys have been killed here," Peanut says, wide-eyed.

"Can we go? Please?"

Peanut looks up, hurt. "I thought you wanted to save the Children."

"I do. But—"

"Then help me look!" Peanut points to a kitchen cabinet. "Check in there."

Libby is mentally rehearsing how to say *we need to go now* more authoritatively—either *we need to go* now or *we* need *to go now*—when she hears a noise. It sounds like crying.

To be honest, it sounds like Libby crying, but her cheeks are dry.

Peanut hears it, too. She tiptoes to a dead-bolted door next to the refrigerator and places her ear next to it. "Who's down there?" she calls.

The crying abruptly stops.

Libby doesn't move, can't move. It's Peanut who slides back the latch and yanks open the door.

Warm air tongues over them.

"Hello?" Peanut flips a light switch, but nothing happens. "Helloooooooo!" she calls again.

Libby grabs Peanut's arm before she can start down the stairs. "Wait! We don't know what's down there!"

"So?" Peanut looks surprised. "Don't you want to find out?" She raises her right index finger and recites the Falling Children motto: "Never harm when you can help. Never stop when you can go. Never wrong when you can right."

Libby definitely doesn't remember writing that. Has she ever followed that advice in her own life?

"What I mean," she says, "is we should call for help."

The crying comes again.

"We *are* the help," says Peanut.

It's another favorite phrase of Everlee's, and before Libby can form an argument in her mind—*They're fictional; this is real!*—Peanut skips down, down, down into the darkness.

"Peanut!"

Who would Libby be if her teeth weren't chattering? If she didn't have a death grip on the banister or a bruising, sick feeling in her stomach? Take away her fear, and what is left on her bones?

Libby minces her way down the stairs. There are too many of them, she realizes. No normal staircase is this long. Fear tucks under her arms like a too-tight raincoat. What if she has another panic attack?

Like the floor above, the basement is a warren of boxes and garbage bags. A dim light in the corner reveals shelves of glass jars. Inside float small eyeless creatures. In her haste to move away, Libby bumps into the cold metal footboard of a bed—then jumps as she realizes someone is in it.

Curled under a sheet is an old woman. Her eyes are open but, unfocused, her body limp, although Libby can see her chest rising and falling underneath her nightgown. She looks…

"Just like the Seer in your books!" Peanut speaks so quickly that spit collects in the corners of her mouth. "Maybe the Unstopping's holding her hostage? To learn what she knows about the future? Maybe she can help us!"

Libby wants to go home.

"Excuse me, madam," Peanut tries. "We're on a quest. Omniscient OtherWay being that you are, I presume you already know the gory details."

The woman doesn't change her gaze or turn her head.

"Can you help us?" Peanut approaches the bed and curtsies, then covers her nose with her hand and, gagging, quickly steps back. "What's that smell? What's wrong with her?"

When Libby doesn't reply, Peanut answers the question herself. "The Unstopping's gotten to her already, hasn't he? He's sucked out her soul!"

She studies a plastic box fastened to the headboard. A string connects it to a clip on the woman's nightgown. "And he's trying to kill us. Look! It's a bomb—just like in the first book!"

A red eye glows from the center of the box. B-SAFE SENTRY read the words above it.

"It's not a bomb," Libby says. "It's an alarm, so someone knows if she gets out of bed."

"That's horrible!" cries Peanut.

Libby doesn't explain that she has seen these bed alarms online. Just like she has seen the yellow signs crisscrossed over the basement windows and door that command STOP. And the cold safety rails on the bed. And the sippy cup on the table. And the pack of adult diapers spilled onto the floor.

"Why is the Unstopping torturing her like this? We have to do something!"

Libby doesn't answer. Peanut is too young to be told that in the real world, the Unstopping isn't one immortal being. He is everywhere—like an invisible disease that consumes people from the inside out.

A door slams.

Footsteps thunder above them, then stop. "Ma, why's your door unlocked? What are you playing at?"

At the sound of his voice, the woman starts to cry again.

"Who's here?" Orson Greeley demands.

Steel-toed boots smack down the stairs. Without agreeing upon it, Libby and Peanut head for the side door that leads outside. Peanut pulls at the yellow safety tape, while Libby yanks at the knob. It won't open.

Angry footsteps, footsteps, footsteps…

That staircase is too long, Libby thinks.

She pulls harder at the knob.

"Push!" Peanut moves Libby aside and opens the door. Cold night air, followed by a half dozen cats, swims past.

Peanut tears outside, but Libby is still standing there, her hand frozen to the doorknob, when tubes of fluorescent light fizzle overhead.

He really does look like the Unstopping is the first thing Libby thinks. Eyes—dozens of flat black eyes—cover Orson Greeley's sunken cheeks and neck.

The second thing Libby realizes is that the Unstopping has a lazy eye like Peanut. It does not look at her.

"What the hell are you doing here?"

Libby can see the basement clearly now. Besides the small twin bed, there's a recliner and flat-screen TV. What looked in the dark like toothless creatures in jars are pickled vegetables. Beets and asparagus and…maybe rutabaga?

She resists the urge to laugh. *I thought we were in a dungeon,* she considers confessing. But there is the Unstopping, slowly widening his mouth into a smile. It isn't a friendly smile. Where his left canine should be is a small baby tooth.

Does one of the tattooed eyes on his neck wink at her? Libby can't tell. The Unstopping sees her staring and cinches his hoodie more tightly.

"You're not supposed to be here."

Frogs and crickets hold court outside. Somewhere, Peanut is waiting, but the questions Libby has root her to the spot.

Why do you want to be the Unstopping?

Did you know I would come here?

Where did you get that baby tooth?

But the one that rises to the surface is "how long has she had dementia?"

She points to the old woman.

Orson steps closer, so close that his face is now inches from her own. Libby can feel his breath on the tip of her nose and see the cold sore jutting from his bottom lip. Red veins web his eyes, but behind them, there is something—someone?—she recognizes.

"Don't you wish you knew," he whispers.

Giving Libby a hard push outside, he slams and locks the basement door behind her.

Her shoulder, where he touched her, is on fire.

"Here!" Peanut's voice comes from far away. "Over here!"

Libby stumbles toward the beam of the flashlight. The panic ricocheting in her chest makes her see spots.

"Wasn't that *awesome!*" Peanut bounces up and down. "I told you, he's supercreepy. And Mrs. Greeley—I mean, the Seer—smelled like bitter hookroot, didn't she? But look! She knew we were coming! She left us a clue!"

Peanut holds up a red notebook, not much bigger than the palm of her hand. On the front, written in blue ballpoint, read the words To Save.

"I ran around to the front, and it was right there, on the ground, like it was waiting for us to find it."

Libby sees two Peanuts, then three, then whatever number comes next. "I don't feel so good," Libby tries to say, but her mouth feels knotted with yarn.

She thinks of the yellowed baby tooth in the Unstopping's mouth. Who was Orson Greeley before he read the Falling Children books? Is his existence her fault?

Don't you wish you knew?

The old shell of a woman—it's me, she thinks.

She stumble-follows Peanut down the uneven driveway, but just before the road, Libby's light catches on the doll strung up on the fence. Up close, its plastic fingers have been gnawed by weather or wildlife—or maybe the Unstopping. Patches of its eyelashes have been picked clean away. From underneath the black Sharpie Xs, one dull, given-up eye gazes at Libby.

"What are you doing?" Peanut asks when Libby kneels on the ground.

Undoing the wire would be easier if Libby could remember which direction turns something loose. Her brain won't tell, so Libby yanks as hard as she can.

Finally, the doll drops to the ground, its head rolling loose from its body. Spiders scuttle from inside it.

"That's better," Libby says, but the truth is, she doesn't want to pick it up.

"Uh-oh," says Peanut. She's not looking at the doll, discarded now on the ground, but Libby's palm, which shines with blood.

"I don't like blood," Libby remembers aloud. *Pain, death, birth…*

The doll head stares at her, its lips pursed with black thread.

Maybe she didn't want to be rescued is the last thought Libby has before she faints.

34

Peanut hammers her fist on Buzz's front door until he opens it, his hair standing wild and his eyes half-shut. "What the freak," he says.

He smells like sleep. He isn't wearing his leg splint, and backlit by the hall light, his scar is worse than hers.

"There's something wrong with Libby." Peanut hops from one foot to the other. "She fainted."

Buzz looks back into the house, scratching the back of his head.

"We went to confront the Unstopping." Peanut's words come out in a rush. "And the Seer was there, possibly being held against her will. I'm not sure exactly, so we didn't break her free just yet." She chews on a piece of her hair. "But then afterward, Libby got a little wavy? And then she sort of collapsed."

Buzz squints. "Start over and speak English."

"Libby passed out on the side of the highway!" Peanut shouts.

Not until the words hang in the air does she absorb the gravity of the situation: She's abandoned a sick grown-up. By the side of the road.

Correction: Peanut has left *F. T. Goldhero* unconscious by the side of the road.

Buzz has already pulled on a pair of shorts and his old Vans high-tops and is sliding the car keys off the table in the front hall. He whistles for Rolf, who emerges, yawning, from the bedroom.

"I tried to shake her," Peanut says defensively. "But she wouldn't wake up. So I hid her under some branches."

In retrospect, she is not sure if this was the best thing to do. Although she did leave the notebook with Libby.

It says "To Save," doesn't it? Peanut assures herself. *That will protect her.*

Unless, of course, the notebook is a trap set by the Unstopping.

Buzz unlocks the car, and Peanut and Rolf climb into the back. They are reversing out of the driveway when someone steps out of the shadows behind them.

Buzz slams on the brakes. Peanut can't help herself: she screams.

Later, she will feel embarrassed by this—Everlee would never scream—but for now, she is annoyed that it's Jessie.

Buzz rolls down the window. "Move."

"Where do you think you're going with Peanut? It's after midnight!"

"This is an emergency!" Peanut says.

"What kind of emergency?" Jessie cranes her neck to look inside the car. "Are you okay? Whose dog is that?"

"She's fine and nobody's," Buzz says. "*Move.*"

"Make me."

Peanut has such hatred at that moment for Jessie. And then Jessie makes it worse by pulling open the passenger door. "Fine. Maybe I'll come, too."

"Whatever."

Although Jessie looks triumphant, Buzz backs so fast out of the driveway that she bumps her head against the door.

They speed down the spine of Cojones Hill and onto the dark

county highway. The windows are down, and the sharp scent of skunk fills the car.

"Where'd you lose her?" Buzz wants to know.

"I didn't lose her. She was right next to me!" Peanut wishes Jessie weren't listening. "But then she cut her hand and passed out."

"Who passed out?" Jessie demands. "Is this about Nancee?"

"*No,*" Buzz and Peanut say together.

When they are almost to the Greeleys, Peanut shakes the back of Buzz's seat. "Here! Stop here!"

He pulls onto the shoulder, gravel pinging the hubcaps.

"See!" Peanut says excitedly, pointing to something orange shining on the ground. "There's my safety whistle."

She swings open her door, but Jessie grabs her wrist before she can climb out. "You know you're not allowed to be over here by yourself. *Ever.*"

"You don't own me." Peanut wriggles free.

"Libby!" Buzz is out of the car now, too. Cupping his hands around his mouth, he shouts, "Hey, Libby!"

"Who's Libby?" Jessie demands.

"Only the most important person in the world," Peanut says, trying get her flashlight to work. She toggles the switch over and over. "The Children need her. They need her to be okay."

"Oh my God." Jessie puts her hands to her head. "Someone tell me what we're doing here."

"Libby is F. T. Goldhero," Buzz says.

"I thought you could keep a secret." Peanut glares.

Buzz ignores her. "Peanut took Libby to the Greeleys. She thinks they're characters from the fucking book."

"I don't think. I *know,*" says Peanut. "And it's not one book. There are five so far."

Jessie's face squeezes like a lemon. People wouldn't think she's "a hot piece," like it's scribbled on the stall of the Allsup's bathroom, if she made this face at them.

"It is off-limits for you to come here; you know that." Jessie bites off each word.

"I didn't do it for me—it was for Libby."

Jessie raises her hand like she's going to slap Peanut. She's never done so before, and Peanut is curious to find out if she'll go through with it, but Buzz steps between them. "Look," he tells Jessie, "either help us find Libby, or sit in the car."

"Fine." Jessie steps into the middle of the road. "If she was right here when you last saw her," she says, "she either went that way"— she points the beam of her light north to Little Diamond—"or downtown."

"Or into the woods, using my special shortcut." Peanut pauses. "Do you think someone figured out who she is and took her to Baron McBroom?"

"Nah," says Buzz, but he frowns like he's thought of that, too.

"So which way?" asks Jessie. "Make a decision already."

"The shortcut through the woods!" Peanut lifts a fist into the air. "That's where the Children would go."

Moonlight smears the trail into the forest.

"See? I knew this was the right way," Peanut says, pointing to a spindly weed tree growing among the pines. "It's like the Skinny Bones in book two."

"No, it's a *tree*." Jessie motions Peanut to go ahead and waits for Buzz to catch up.

"Is this funny to you?" Peanut hears her ask. "Letting her pretend she found F. T. Goldhero?"

"Maybe she did."

"Or maybe you enjoy making everything worse."

"Me?"

Peanut knows Buzz and Jessie used to get along. Jessie has the proof in her bedroom: framed pictures of her and Buzz riding bikes together and squashed into an inner tube at the lake. Peanut has just never seen this in her lifetime.

"You have no idea how hard this has been on me," Jessie says.

Peanut has always believed that Buzz is like the Moreos Lou sells at his gas station. Crunchy and hard on the outside, but squishy once given a chance. But Buzz surprises her.

"Right," he says. "Because, like always, everything is about you."

He limps down the trail, past Peanut, Rolf at his heels.

"What did you do to make him so mad?" Peanut asks Jessie.

All she does is shake her head.

~ ~

Once they're deep in the woods, Peanut can no longer see the moon. Tree branches tangle above them, and the owls and crickets have gone silent.

Peanut only finds the edge of the steep drop-off when her foot slips over the side. Just in time, Buzz grabs her by the ruff of her safety vest.

"This isn't right," he says.

"Don't worry; we can repel down," Peanut says. "I have rope." She shimmies out of her backpack straps.

"No, what I mean is Libby would never come this far in the dark or go down this. She'd be too scared."

"The Children don't get scared!" Peanut starts listing examples on her fingers. "In book one, they drop upside down into a nest of ventriloquist dummies. In book two, they have to play the Wicket, this captivatingly vicious game of croquet—"

"I'm not saying the Children," Buzz says. "I'm talking about Libby."

"Oh." Peanut pauses, surprised. She hasn't thought of Libby as separate from her characters. She feels a sting of jealousy that Buzz may be right, that he may somehow have figured out the answer to this riddle before she has.

"So then where do you think she'd go?" she challenges.

Buzz points. "The other way," he says.

35

Libby isn't sure how she comes to be walking alone through downtown Blue Skies. Is the little town even real? There are so many similarities to Dark Crevice, the peculiar little town where the Children first meet at the Falling Orphanage. A big-bellied sheriff. A bookstore with a fat tortoiseshell cat twitch-sleeping in the window. Both towns are cradled with mountains and forest. Both have a house on the edge of town that you should never, ever enter, although Libby can't recall the reasons why.

She pauses in front of an elaborate fountain.

MAY YOUR BELLY NEVER GRUMBLE. MAY YOUR HEART NEVER ACHE. MAY YOUR HORSE NEVER STUMBLE AND YOUR CINCH NEVER BREAK, reads the plaque below the bronzed cowboy, thumbs hooked into his belt loops, standing at its center.

The words tumble through the cracks in Libby's brain and down into the OtherWay of her imagination.

The bottom of the fountain flickers with coins.

I wish I could save the Children.

I wish I could remember why I'm here.

When she tucks in her hand to borrow a penny, the water swells with blood.

Libby is staring at the deep gash neatly bisecting her palm—*Don't* panic. *Tetanus. Don't panic. Sepsis. Don't panic. Amputation*—when the door of a nearby bar opens. A throng of people empty onto the sidewalk along with laughter and the bracelet jangle of reggae.

WHIPPITY JIM'S, the sign out front says.

Libby stares at the couples, their arms curved around each other's shoulders and waists. Her bloody hand would stain anyone who tried to get close. She pushes it back under the water. Has she lost too much blood? Is she feeling dizzy? She *is* feeling dizzy.

"Libby? Is that you?"

She looks up to see a man with close-cropped graying hair and dark, pressed jeans walking toward her.

"Did you not get my texts? I flew in hours ago." He leans down and gives her a quick peck on the cheek. "Is you-know-who around?"

Before Libby can answer—and who knows, really, what she is about to say—the man grabs her wrist.

"Whoa, what happened to your hand?"

Her fingers are as swollen as gingerroot, her palm zigzagged with blood. She tries to sit, feeling like she might faint, but she is already sitting and nearly collapses backward into the water.

The man catches her elbow. She can't smell his cologne—she can't smell anything anymore—but she is sure he's wearing some.

"Let's get you something for that," he says.

~——~

The floor of Whippity Jim's is gummy and wet. Libby squish-squishes after the man to the bar, where he orders two pints of beer.

"Reopen my tab, would you?" he instructs the bartender, grabbing a stack of cocktail napkins and handing them to Libby. "Name's Glenn."

The name still means nothing to Libby, but at least now she knows what to call him. She drains her beer, wondering when she last had a drink of water. The back of her throat is as raw as if she'd been screaming.

"Could I have another?" She peers into her empty glass.

"That depends." Glenn winks. "What's it worth to you?"

Nailed onto the walls are ancient snowshoes and dusty skis. Music and chatter ricochet off the scuffed wood floors. On TV, the Buffalos are losing. Libby closes her eyes. Her hand throbs.

Don't you wish you knew? the Unstopping asks inside her head.

"So much," she tells Glenn.

He stands and collects their beers. "Let's move outside."

He has to shout to be heard over Bob Marley.

Three little birds
Pitch by my doorstep

Libby follows him to a picnic table by the sidewalk. The sunny-yellow umbrella looks out of place against the black-buckle sky.

"I'm getting old." Glenn smiles. "I couldn't hear a damned thing in there."

Unsnapping the black messenger bag he's carrying, Glenn pulls out a digital tape recorder and sets it on the table between them. "You don't mind, do you?"

Libby has no idea what he would be recording, but she knows instinctively that she does not want, say, a coerced confession on tape. Or her voice sampled on a Japanese pop song.

"Now don't get cold feet on me." Under the table, Glenn presses one of Libby's knees between his own. "I'm your Aldo Fondstun."

"Who?"

"You know. The magician who was friends with the original shop-keeper of Pompou's in book one? Who could find any toy in the world that was lost? Aldo Fondstun, lost and found?" Glenn spreads his arms. "Like how I found Rolf for you?"

Libby blinks. "None of that made any sense."

Glenn looks annoyed, which makes Libby wonder if he's her *husband* and they've been married so long that he can do this openly.

"Look, let's stop playing games." He leans forward. "Why'd you email me if you didn't want me to come all the way out to Buttfuck Egypt?"

Libby lifts her shoulders. The beer makes them feel buoyant. But not her hand, which throbs.

Did she cut it on something in the Unstopping's kitchen? Libby tries to remember what they saw there. A can of tomato soup? Or was that what she had for dinner in her own kitchen?

A small red notebook is next to her on the table. She and Glenn notice it at the same time. To Save.

"Save until when?"

When she doesn't answer, Glenn slides next to her on the bench. "I will do this right, Libby. I deserve to tell this story." He rests his hand over hers. "You can trust me. I think it was fate that I found Rolf. And you."

Glenn pecks at her cheek with his lips, not unlike a crow trying to pick up a morsel of food.

Libby smiles at the analogy, but Glenn misunderstands. He draws her closer and kisses her more.

She tries to feel something—desire, curiosity, enjoyment—but the kiss registers no more emotion in her than Dr. Whatsit's nurse taking her blood pressure at the beginning of each appointment. Libby thinks of Buzz and what it was like to kiss him, the infinitely long hallway of doors it unlocked and opened in her chest. Then she thinks of how cliche that is, a middle-aged woman fantasizing about a younger man. She is glad no one can read her thoughts.

Still, she mentally draws a line through them: ~~She thinks of Buzz and what it was like to kiss him.~~

"Get me face time with your boss?" Glenn murmurs into her ear.

Libby doesn't like the word "murmur." She isn't sure she can trust him. But kissing, passionate or awkward, is normal. It's what people who aren't losing their minds do.

She can pretend she likes Glenn. Libby is better at pretending than living her own life.

I'm glad you're here, she types on a page inside her head. And then, haltingly, she says the words aloud.

36

The neon teacup above the Pig-n-Pancake is dark. The window grate at the train depot ticket booth is down. Libby is not in front of the snow globe store or Gibbon's Grocery. Both are closed.

Where are you? Peanut thinks from the back seat. She clenches her fists. *Come back.*

They circle Blue Skies in Libby's rental car. Peanut has never seen the town this late at night. The houses and stores look flimsy, as if they've been hastily created with cardboard, tempura paint, and tape. One gust of wind, and they may collapse.

"There." Buzz swerves to a stop, pointing to the bar on the opposite side of Main Street. "She's right there."

Relief detonates inside Peanut's chest when she sees Libby. She has forgotten how good it feels to take a deep breath.

You're real. You're here.

Then Jessie ruins it. "Who's that with her?"

An older man—a tourist, not a townie because he's matchy-matchy in crisp jeans and a navy blue knit polo—slides onto the bench beside her. He whispers into her ear, his arm coiling over her shoulder.

"Libby!" Peanut leaps from the car, waving her arms. "Libby!"

She tears down the sidewalk, squeezing past a table of college students wearing Princeton T-shirts.

"We've been looking everywhere for you," Peanut blurts out once she reaches Libby. "I didn't know what to do! I went to get Buzz, and then we didn't know what to do, and it took us a while to find you because I was thinking what the Children would do, not you and"— she takes a breath—"I'm sorry."

Libby looks surprised. "Everything's fine," she says.

"Then who's he?" Peanut can feel the man staring at her scar and pulls her hair over her face to hide it.

"Him?" Libby pauses. "This is Glenn." She says his name firmly, like she's recently mastered it in a different language. "He's a—"

"Friend," the man finishes. But when he removes his arm from around Libby's shoulder, Peanut sees him drop a digital recorder into his bag. "I thought I'd surprise Libby during her work trip," he says. "Who are you, kiddo?"

"Libby's best friend," Peanut says coolly. "And professional colleague."

"Funny little town you got here," Glenn says. But he's not looking at Peanut anymore but Jessie, who has arrived.

"You're hurt." Jessie points to Libby's palm, which is wrapped in a wad of blood-soaked napkins.

"Please don't make me think about it." Libby tries to move her hand out of sight, but Jessie holds her wrist for a closer look.

"You might need stitches," she says. "When was your last tetanus? And does Buzz know you're wearing his sweatshirt? Because now there's blood all over it."

"Daddy can look at her hand when he gets home," Peanut says. "Since you're not a doctor," she adds.

"Who's your dad?" Glenn wants to know. "And apologies, I didn't catch your names."

"We're the Greeleys," Peanut lies. She doesn't like this man with his drill-bit eyes and shiny leather sneakers. She especially doesn't like his tape recorder. "We live out on the main road. People call our house the Murder House."

"Peanut!" Jessie is aghast. "Why would you say that?"

Peanut turns to look at Buzz, confident *he'll* play along—he doesn't trust anyone with clean sneakers—but he's not there.

"Where'd he go?" she asks, whirling around.

Jessie holds up the car keys. "Walking home."

"But—why?"

Peanut doesn't wait to hear Jessie's answer. She may be small for her age, but her birdlike bones make her a fast runner. She's not even out of breath when she catches up with Buzz and Rolf in front of the stationery store. IT'S NEVER TOO EARLY TO SHOP FOR YOUR VALEN-TINE, a sign in the window reads.

"Where are you going?" Peanut flags her arms. "We can't leave Libby!"

"Why? We're not leaving her alone."

"That man can't be trusted. He has a tape recorder! He wants to expose F. T. Goldhero. He could be in cahoots with Baron McBroom!"

"So? She wrote the books. Let her get credit for them."

"But the Children aren't saved. Libby can't be found yet! Then she'll never finish."

"Tell her that."

Peanut narrows her eyes. "Why are you so mad?"

"I'm not mad," Buzz says. "I don't know why I'm here. I want to go home and be fucking left alone."

Peanut looks at Rolf, patiently standing next to her brother. "Then why do you have Libby's dog?"

Buzz and Rolf look at each other. Rolf wags his tail.

"Take him." Buzz shoves the leash at Peanut. "Whatever. I don't care."

Peanut knows that when anyone says this in a Falling Children book, they most certainly *do* care. A lot. In toys, extra care sometimes spills out in the form of cotton batting or little plastic beans.

Peanut watches Buzz start up the stairs cut into the mountain.

"You're not going to turn her in, are you?" she calls.

"Who knows. Maybe. Maybe I already have."

"I don't believe you. And you know why? You sound like Benjamin in book one, when Everlee first invites him to Pompou's, and he says it sounds lame, but—"

"Really, he's scared shitless of dolls," Buzz finishes. "Yeah, I get it, okay?"

Peanut watches him struggle to climb the stairs, pausing after each step to rub his thigh. It's hard to believe he used to fly down this railing while eating a roast-beef hoagie. Even harder to believe he knows anything about the Falling Children.

"You never read," she says, suddenly suspicious. "What are you not telling me?"

"Lots. Leave me alone."

"Fine," Peanut says. "You just cursed about a million times in front of me, so you're not a good role model for a child anyway."

"Not trying to be."

"You're not trying to be *anything*," Peanut shouts, frustrated that he can walk away from her—and their secret mission to help Libby and save the Children—so easily. "Sink back into the Depths of Despair. Whatever. I don't care!"

Buzz doesn't turn around.

~~~

When Peanut gets back to Whippity Jim's, she tugs Libby's sleeve. "We have to go."

"Go?" Libby looks up, confused.

"Home."

When Libby gets unsteadily to her feet, Glenn gives her a peck on the cheek, his hand spread like a starfish on her lower back. "Let me know where you're staying. I'll stop by tomorrow."

"We're busy tomorrow," Peanut interjects. "And the day after that. And the day after that."

"Yeah?" Glenn looks amused. "You Greeley kids have a lot going on."

He chuckles, although Peanut sees nothing funny about it. Or the faded red notebook he's about to slide into his messenger bag.

"That isn't yours," she says.

Glenn pauses, midthievery. His eyes dart right and left. Peanut can tell he's wondering who else is watching and if they will believe a child over an adult.

Before he can decide, she grabs the tiny notebook and shoves it into the waistband of her jeans.

"Amateur," she says.

37

Libby wakes the next morning under a pink gingham comforter. The bedroom she's in is also painted pink. Pink curtains hang from two large windows, and a shaggy pink rug, like the hide of a stuffed animal, covers the wooden floor. Beside the closet is a stack of old teen magazines. BE YOUR BEST SELF, reads a headline on the top cover. DO YOU KNOW WHERE YOU REALLY ARE?

No, thinks Libby, although Rolf, sprawled and snoring across her legs, doesn't seem concerned.

The bedroom door opens, and Peanut's sister comes in with a plate of toast and a cup of tea.

"Room service," she says without enthusiasm.

"Thank you," says Libby. But when she reaches out to take the tray, she winces with pain. A bandage, dotted with blood, covers her palm. "What happened to my hand?" She panics.

"You don't remember? You cut it on something." Jessie hands Libby an ice pack. "My father will take a look once he's back. When's the last time you had a tetanus shot?"

"I have no idea," Libby says. "As a kid?" Which reminds her. She looks around the room. "Where's Peanut?"

"School. You know, because she's only eleven and all," Jessie says pointedly.

"Where's Buzz?"

Jessie crosses her arms. "At home. We thought it was best you come here."

"I'll go back." Libby is already climbing out of bed. "All my things are there."

The pink-framed pictures on the walls and every flat surface make her queasy, as if they're leftover wrappers from candies she's eaten before being fully awake: Jessie. Jessie and Peanut. Peanut. Jessie and Buzz and Peanut. In each photo, Jessie's smile dazzles, Buzz looks irritated, and Peanut...what is different about Peanut?

"We brought everything over." Jessie points to Libby's suitcase standing at attention in the corner. "You're better off here. Trust me."

Libby looks down at the bed, which is not her bed but Jessie's. She looks around the room, which is not her room, with her things, but Jessie's. Libby wants to keep this straight. She does not trust Jessie. Or herself, if she is being honest.

~

Dr. Bixton ducks his head to get through the door. It's an apologetic gesture—his shoulders hunched, his head bowed—but there is nothing contrite about his gaze. His blue eyes, as clear as water, look at Libby as he says, "Tsk, tsk."

He's older than Libby expected—what *did* she expect?—and is wearing a suit and tie, although neither are new nor pressed.

"I hear we have a visitor," he says, setting a well-worn medical bag next to her on the floor. "I'd shake your hand, but I take it that's what I'm here to examine."

"Doctors make me nervous," Libby can't help saying.

Dr. Bixton sits next to her on the bed and eyes her over the top of his half-glasses. "Me, too. That's why I chased the rest of them out of town. Let's see what we have here."

He unwraps the bandage and studies the angry gash on Libby's palm. "How'd you manage this?" he wants to know.

"It happened when she and Peanut were out in the woods in the middle of the night," Jessie says, tattling.

"Is this part of F. T. Goldhero's mystique?" Dr. Bixton gives Libby a probing look. "Urging children to traipse around the forest in the middle of the night?"

"No," Libby says. "Not at all. It was her idea and—"

"Oh, so now you're blaming Peanut?" Jessie asks.

"No, what I meant was—"

But when Dr. Bixton and Jessie both tilt their heads, waiting for her answer, Libby can no longer remember what she meant.

"I'm sorry. I didn't plan for any of this to happen." She gestures around the room like she's the one responsible for the Pepto-Bismol paint, the shaggy rug, and people trapped together in photographs. "I'm not a bad person. I don't have nefarious intentions, I swear."

Good for you, thinking of such big words, Libby tells herself. She even spelled them correctly.

"I needed some help with the book, and Peanut is such a big fan— You can ask Buzz."

"I doubt our friend next door feels much like weighing in" is all Dr. Bixton says. "He's had his own streak of sorry luck."

Libby winces as he cleans her wound and applies skin closure strips, followed by gauze.

"I believe you'll live," he says. "For the time being at least."

She looks at her hand. The pain is tight like a mitten. How is she going to write?

"No needles!" Libby flinches as Dr. Bixton swabs her upper arm with alcohol. "I don't like needles."

"It's a tetanus shot."

Is it, really?

"No, thank you. I don't like any needles." Libby wonders if she's slurring her words. She shouldn't have drunk a beer last night. Or was it two?

"Well," Dr. Bixton says slowly, "you did awfully well seeing as how I already gave it to you."

"A shot? Just—now?"

"Just now."

He turns the swab over to reveal a faint bead of blood. And sure enough, when Libby presses just below her shoulder, the skin there feels tender.

"I guess I'm more tired than I thought," she says, attempting a smile. "There's a lot going on right now."

"It certainly seems that way." Dr. Bixton gathers his bag from the floor. "I was reading about you in the newspaper yesterday. A million-dollar bounty is serious business. I suspect most people would turn you in for far less."

There's an uncomfortable silence. Libby doesn't like that she is lying in bed with a gashed hand and a sore arm and they are standing over her, Jessie with open resentment on her face, Dr. Bixton and his bag of sly needles.

"But you won't," she says uncertainly, "will you?"

Kidnapping, blackmail, other methods of slow, painful torture that I can't think of right now but will fill in later . . .

Dr. Bixton looks at Jessie. "I'd say Ms. Goldhero has found herself among the few people in this world who can keep an enormous secret, wouldn't you agree?"

Jessie doesn't answer. She moves to the window and slams it closed, drowning out the sound of a garbage truck rattling up the street.

"I can't say I'm a fan of dogs," Dr. Bixton says, eyeing Rolf. "But I will ask that you stay here a few days. I'd like to keep an eye on you."

"On my hand, you mean," Libby says, raising it in an awkward salute.

"On your hand," he agrees.

~~~

After Dr. Bixton leaves, Jessie retrieves a set of frayed pink towels from a closet in the hallway and sets them on the bed. "He's scary, isn't he? Imagine growing up with that."

Libby doesn't reply in case it's a trap.

"You might feel better if you shower. You're covered in dirt." Jessie holds up a plastic bag. "I can put this over your hand so it doesn't get wet."

"Are you a nurse?" Libby asks as Jessie efficiently tapes it around her wrist.

"Nope. And not a doctor," she says. "I'm just here."

Jessie points to Libby's suitcase. "Get some clothes and meet me in the bathroom," she instructs. "I'll show you how to use our shower. It's a little wonky."

Everything in Libby's suitcase is carefully folded, even her dirty socks. She wonders if Buzz packed for her.

Jessie is waiting across the hall. The bathroom's apricot tiles and wooden cabinets remind Libby of the one she shared with Vernice growing up.

The hot water faucet is on the right, but Libby should turn it the other way, Jessie explains. Cold water is controlled by the faucet on the left, but Libby will need to turn it clockwise, twice.

"Don't flush the toilet, or you'll lose the hot water. And keep the shower liner closed, or water will leak through the floor."

Hot, right. Cold, left, shower liner something something—

"Does it bother you that you've gotten rich by fooling kids?"

Libby can see why Peanut complains about her sister. Jessie doesn't speak so much as sling words like arrows.

"I'm not falling anyone."

She means to say "fooling," but Jessie doesn't point out her mistake.

"You make kids think that if they don't like their life, they can hold out for something better. That there's this magic world if they want it badly enough. Real life doesn't work that way."

When Libby is too surprised to reply, Jessie shakes her head, disgusted. "Whatever makes you rich, I guess."

"That's not why I write about the Children."

"Why else would you?"

On paper, Libby could describe the loneliness that's punched holes in her entire life, how she's craved not just a family but friends to help her pick out a new toaster—really, it shouldn't be this hard—and a walkable town of people who know her well enough to assign a (gentle) nickname. How her imagination is all she has, and sometimes she doesn't know what it will give her until she is holding it tight inside her hands.

In real life, the shower faucet catches Libby's interest and won't let go. *Hot, right, cold, left?* And there's something about the toilet. She needs to flush it to get the shower to work?

Her thoughts shudder back to the Children suffering in the woods while the world around them fades away, holding out hope that Libby, any second now, will come to the rescue. That the right words will tumble from her brain and Fix Everything.

They must hate her.

Jessie busies herself arranging bottles of lotion on the bathroom counter.

"Well, it's like my dad says," she says finally, "if you've never been hated by your children, then you're not parenting right."

38

By late afternoon, Libby is struggling to breathe. It's not only because her hand throbs and the late-summer heat has stuffed itself, uninvited, into Jessie's pink bedroom. She doesn't belong here. She needs to go home.

In the OtherWay, this feeling would manifest as a sinister toy with a thirst for imagination, especially the kind that radiates, like golden-green light, from young children. Here it's an invisible weight that presses onto Libby's chest.

Pay attention, her brain warns but doesn't offer more help than that. She feels as if she is turning over a thousand puzzle pieces of a long-haired white cat.

When deep breathing doesn't quell her panic, Libby closes her eyes and pretends she's safely back home in her apartment.

Look! she assures herself. *You haven't gone anywhere.*

There, in the corner, is her parents' tall mahogany shelf, books shoved into every conceivable empty space. (The top needs a good dusting, but she's not going to do it now.) Over here is the fat Christmas cactus that hasn't flowered since Vernice died. Libby makes herself feel the dry soil crunch between her fingers.

She can hear the afternoon ice cream truck, the flat hum of the window air conditioner, her twentysomething neighbors next door playing their Xbox... *"Dude!"*

She lies down in *her* bed, on *her* sheets, and puts her head on *her* pillow. "You're home," she tells herself, curling into a ball. "You're already home."

~~~

Almost as soon as she falls asleep, Peanut shakes her awake.

"Dinner," she says. "Aren't you hungry? Come eat."

Groggily, Libby follows the girl downstairs.

Jessie is in the kitchen, along with Dr. Bixton and an older woman with curly hair the color of old candy corn and a pair of suede riding chaps over her purple leggings.

"I am such a fan." The woman pumps Libby's unhurt hand. "Little Peanut, of course, is the biggest. But I read your books to my husband every day. He's dying," she adds.

"But Mrs. Halfchap is here all the time for some reason," Jessie says. "I guess it's my cooking."

She looks sideways at her father.

Libby looks to Dr. Bixton, too. "I thought you weren't going to tell anyone about me."

"Oh, it wasn't him, it was little Rolf." Mrs. Halfchap bends to give the dog a chuck under the chin. "You know he's never been one to keep a secret."

"Just like you," Jessie says under her breath.

"What's that about juice?" Mrs. Halfchap cups her hand around her ear.

"I said," Jessie says more loudly, "it's time to eat."

At the table, Dr. Bixton gestures to a platter of spaghetti and meatballs.

"Please," he says to Libby, "be my guest."

Libby can feel everyone watching as she tries to spoon spaghetti onto her plate. With each attempt, the strands slide back into the serving bowl.

"There are tongs, you know," Jessie points out.

"Right." Libby hastily trades out the utensils. "I didn't see them."

Once everyone has been served, Dr. Bixton touches her elbow. "So," he says, "tell us about yourself. You have a captive audience."

Libby stares at the tangle of food on her plate. She has no idea how she'll eat, save for lowering her mouth and sucking up the noodles like a vacuum attachment. She looks across the table at Mrs. Halfchap. How is she managing it? A flash of silver goes from the woman's mouth to her plate, then repeats. The motion—a silvery flash of tines—is like music. Libby watches, intrigued.

"Libby?" Dr. Bixton asks.

"Yes?"

"Tell us about yourself."

"There's nothing to tell," she says. "I'm not exciting."

"You managed to hide from us for over a week," Dr. Bixton says. "In this small world, that's an impressive feat."

"What did you even do at Buzz's?" Jessie wants to know.

Libby taps her fork against her plate. "I wrote."

"Really? Then why aren't you done with your book yet?"

"It's not her fault," Peanut pipes up. "Buzz kept distracting us. You'll be able to write a lot better here." She nods at Libby.

Dr. Bixton motions to Libby's plate. "You haven't touched your food."

"I'm fine." Libby rubs her eyes. When she opens them again, she has to remind herself that she's not sitting at her kitchen table at home. That is *not* her flowering Christmas cactus in the corner. Or her curtains that need a good shake. That is *not* her mirror that needs to be cleaned, although inside the frame, yes, that is her.

"Look at me. I look so tired."

"I'm sure you are," Dr. Bixton says. He proceeds to assail her with trivia about Blue Skies. His voice hums like her window air conditioner at home.

Libby closes her eyes.

"Let's you and I head outside," Dr. Bixton finally says, patting her arm.

When Libby looks up, she realizes the table has been cleared. Jessie and Peanut are loading the dishwasher. Mrs. Halfchap is gone.

"Can I help?" Libby says, embarrassed.

"Not a whit. That's what children are for," Dr. Bixton says. "You and I can chat."

The living room door slides open onto a back deck. Beyond, silhouetted by the moon, are thick trees and overgrown raspberry bushes, plus a raised garden bed curling with peas. Buzz's house next door is dark.

Taking a seat at the patio table, Libby props her chin onto her hand and stares into the sky. She wishes she knew the constellations, but she only knows the ones in the world of the Falling Children. They are the Child, the Key, the Secret, and the End.

Dr. Bixton places a cup of tea before her. "I've yet to read the books, I regret to say."

Libby points to the sky. "Those things. They're all so pretty."

He pulls out the chair beside her. "The stars, you mean."

"The stars," she agrees.

Libby's about to excuse herself to go to bed when Dr. Bixton says, "I hear you're having trouble writing and remembering things. How long has that been going on?"

His tone reminds her of Dr. Whatsit.

"It's nothing," Libby says. "I'll feel better once this book is done."

Dr. Bixton looks at her over the tops of his glasses. "You didn't answer my question."

Libby can't remember what it was.

"Even to a humble small-town doctor"—Dr. Bixton drips honey for a long while into his tea—"it appears that you're having some cognitive issues."

"Really?" Libby tries to sound surprised. "That would be terrible."

But when she reaches for her tea, it isn't where she thought it would be. Instead of a cup handle, her fingers curve around air.

Dr. Bixton slides the mug closer. "I'm assuming you've spoken to a neurologist?"

"A little," Libby says. "Maybe."

"Ignoring your symptoms won't make them go away."

Minutes pass, and Libby hears a door open, then close at Buzz's house. She waits for another noise—footsteps, a car engine, a whistle, his voice—but nothing comes.

"I'm so—" Libby puts her hand on her heart, trying to find the right word.

"Tired?"

She nods, although that isn't it. She is alone.

"Well, you're battling this illness, that's why. It takes a lot of strength to fight this."

"Am I fighting?" Libby wipes her eyes. "I feel like I'm just—hiding. Pretending that any minute I'm going to finish this book, and everything will be okay."

She looks past the porch, at the dark yard beyond.

"Sometimes we need to tell ourselves a story to prepare for the truth," Dr. Bixton offers. "Peanut knows that quite well, this whole nonsense about finding her parents. Who else have you told?"

"No one." Libby shakes her head. "I don't have anyone *to* tell."

Dr. Bixton leans back in his chair and considers this. "Well, I'll tell you what I tell Annie Yolen when she complains about her diabetes," he says. "I tell her, 'You didn't cause this, and you can't cure it. But you sure can't deal with it alone.'"

"But why is this happening? Why me?"

Dr. Bixton lifts his shoulders. "You'll likely never know."

"I don't like that answer."

"This world is full of answers we don't like. We live with them anyway now, don't we?"

They sit in silence for a moment.

"What would you tell one of your characters, if this was happening to them?" Dr. Bixton asks.

"I don't care!" Libby raises her voice. "I'm tired of writing about the Children. I'm tired of everything being about them. They're not even *real.*"

And then, ashamed, she realizes what she has said.

～～

When Dr. Bixton carries the tray back to the kitchen, Libby follows so she doesn't get turned around and end up in a closet. The kitchen is clean, the dishwasher humming. There is no sign of Jessie or Peanut.

Which reminds Libby.

"Dr. Bixton?" She twists a loop of hair around her finger. Something about him makes her feel like a child. "Sometimes, I accidentally say things that I don't mean to say aloud."

He ties a small yellow apron at his waist and smooths it with his hands. *Just like Grand Bere,* Libby thinks. "I would say that's to be expected."

She isn't making herself clear. Libby can feel the thought slowly dripping away. "What I mean is, outside you said it was nonsense that Peanut was searching for her mother."

"Did I?" His tone is a light breeze to float the topic aside.

When he rolls up his sleeves and begins scrubbing at the sink—"Jessie's dratted spaghetti sauce stains everything it comes into contact with"—she asks, "Do you know who Peanut's mother is?"

Dr. Bixton doesn't look up. "You know, interestingly, we know that in the short term, denial can be a helpful coping mechanism. It's when you stay in it too long that you may find it harder to face reality."

Hunched over the sink, his voice reminds her of Dr. Whatsit's.

Libby takes a step back.

"Who are you?" she asks, suddenly frightened.

Turning off the water, Dr. Bixton faces her. "I am only someone who is trying to help." He sighs. "Let's focus on the present, Libby, shall we?"

Google "FT Goldhero last Falling Children book"

BookTok is calling out the Falling Children for these "annoying" characters

As the sixth and final Falling Children book remains in limbo with no publication date in sight, TikTok users are diving deep into plot twists and characters they're not happy with. #FallingDown is trending. One video about Knock-Knocks has been viewed over 3 million times.

Yahoo! News, 15 minutes ago

Survey: 85% of Falling Children fans would "easily" turn in F. T. Goldhero

The worldwide fan base and appreciation for the "Falling Children" appears to only go so far. A Marist Poll recently surveyed U.S. readers and asked if they would reveal the identity of its author, F. T. Goldhero, for $1M. An overwhelming majority responded...yes! 7%, particularly women ages 30–54 in the Midwest, said they would turn in the author for "less than $500."

EW.com, 2 hours ago

Baron McBroom insists his 96-year-old grandmother make him a grilled cheese during a board meeting, then throws it to the floor and fires EVERYONE for not finding F. T. Goldhero!

Grandmother "exhausted and in tears"
McBroom vows to "destroy" author. "He's playing with us!"

HuffPost, 1 day ago

Are the Falling Children worthy of our obsession?

Sidewalks these days are thronged with drippy-nosed children

artlessly wielding butterfly nets or sticky-tipped, half-chewed Red
Vines. Nor are adults immune to the intoxicating folklore of F. T.
Goldhero. Indeed, I have borne witness to many a middle-aged
friend, tears flowing freely, as they recall the death of beloved teddy
bear/Amma/fierce warrior Gran Bere. Yet after digesting literary
critic Dmitri Lomachenko's new essay, "We *All* Fall Down," my
feelings are going an Other Way...

The New Yorker, 3 days ago

39

"You talk, I'll write." Peanut aims her freshly sharpened pencil toward the paper like a harpoon.

But what Libby wants to talk about has nothing to do with the Children.

"Tell me about when you were a baby," she says. "How were you found?"

Peanut loves this story, but she's told Libby before, and not that long ago. She skips to the highlights: A weak cry from underneath a plot of fresh dirt. A teenager who happened to be in the Right Place at the Right Time. A scar from a curved shovel blade that sets her apart, *and in ways she has yet to fully comprehend.*

"Just like Everlee," Peanut finishes. She writes it on the paper in curlicue letters.

Just like Everlee!

"But the police didn't look for your mother?" Libby asks. "No one saw anything? There wasn't a story in the paper?"

"I already wrote you all that in a letter." Peanut is offended that Libby doesn't remember. "They're boring facts that don't tell the whole story."

Peanut straightens the ream of fine-ruled paper between them. "Okay," she tries again. "How can we free Everlee from the Unstopping's spell? What have you come up with?"

Libby rests her chin on her fist and stares out the window. "I should take Rolf to the dog park," she says.

"We don't have a dog park."

Libby points to herself. "I do."

Peanut scrapes back her chair. She hoped they would find something at the Unstopping's house to cure Libby. Instead, it feels like they've ended up on opposite banks of a wild-moving river: Peanut standing shoulder to shoulder with the Children; Libby absentmindedly poking the rapids with a stick, refusing to hold out her hand so Peanut can yank her across.

"I'm going to the library," Peanut announces. She doesn't want to be irritated with F. T. Goldhero. That would be almost as bad as meeting her mother in real life and hating her. Still, disappointment shakes inside Peanut like a little jar of black sand.

~~~

Three Januarys ago, the roof of the Blue Skies Saloon collapsed during a blizzard. Volunteers dragged the bar's furnishings to the town library for safekeeping. But after the saloon was rebuilt as Whippity Jim's, no one bothered to come back for the swinging doors or long oak bar cratered with bullet holes. Peanut has to squeeze past both in the library foyer. Wheezy music trembles from the player piano.

In the children's room, toddlers race into and out of a plastic playhouse, screaming. Peanut sits cross-legged on the floor underneath a Falling Children poster and carefully removes the little red notebook from her backpack. Just touching it gives her goose bumps.

To Save.

When Peanut first examined it, she was hopeful that it would reveal itself to be magical—like in book one, when the children hide from the Unstopping in the back room of the local butcher shop. Benjamin's grossed out by a pile of knuckle bones, and Huperzine starts to cry because they feel sorry for the cows the bones came from. Then, Everlee remembers that long ago, children used to play jacks with cleaned bones like these.

"They're toys," she insists. *"They can help us!"* And when Everlee clutches a half dozen gnarly bones to her chest, blood juicing down her arms, it's true: the Children are protected.

Peanut loves that scene. It shows that magic can be found anywhere; you just have to look. But most of the notebook pages have been torn out or are blank, except for one page hidden in the middle. In pencil, it reads:

Black licorice
Pig slop
Bitter melon
Blood

"Do you know what this means?" Peanut asked Libby when she first found the list.

Libby shook her head.

Maybe they're ingredients, Peanut thinks. She wonders if the Unstopping drinks this mixture to strengthen his powers, sort of like a smoothie of evilness. Or is it another anagram?

Peanut isn't fond of riddles she can't solve quickly. Staring out the window, she considers how words spring, so easy and alive, from the pages of the Falling Children books.

F. T. Goldhero's words are as real as the purple-cheeked pansies outside, blooming from sidewalk pots. As alive as Mr. Pretzky's fat orange cat, snoring in the window of the bookstore.

When Mrs. Goodwin props open the library's back door, Peanut can smell warm banana bread and fresh coffee from the Pig-n-Pancake. But if she believes hard enough—and she does—she can also smell the Children's hot buttered fudge and celery-nut Restora-Elixir.

She wonders when Orson Greeley transformed from a teenager with greasy hair and dingy hoodies into the Unstopping. What happens to fill someone so full of hate? Is it black licorice, pig slop, bitter melon, and blood?

Shovels *clink* in the garden outside the window, and Peanut flinches. It's only the Library Ladies in their straw hats and matching pink gloves, planting begonias. Still, Peanut closes her eyes and listens for a baby's cries.

When she opens them, a small girl with a runny nose—the librarian's granddaughter—is staring at her scar.

"What?" Peanut moves her hair over it.

"There's a monster in there." Sucking her fingers, the girl points to the playhouse.

"Monsters can't breathe in libraries," Peanut says. (Book one.) "There are too many words."

"This one can," the girl says.

Peanut looks toward the playhouse. Its shutters and door are closed, so she can't see inside.

When she looks up again, the little girl is gone.

The ceiling lights flicker, a sign that the library is ten minutes from closing. Peanut stands and shoves the notebook back into her backpack. "I'm not done with you," she tells it.

And that's when she hears a strangled cry coming from inside the playhouse.

Peanut looks toward the front desk, but the librarian isn't there.

Slowly, she tiptoes toward the sound. Maybe she'll discover a magical creature who needs her help. (Books one through five.) Maybe a character from the OtherWay has come to life—and Blue Skies—to help Libby.

Excitedly, Peanut kicks open the door. *"Indicare locandis!"* *Reveal what houses you.*

"Ow!" a voice cries.

"Nancee?"

Peanut drops to her knees and peers inside the house. Nancee is wearing a black sparkly T-shirt and a pair of jeans shorts that squeeze her in the middle like a tube of toothpaste. Her face is swollen from crying.

"What are you doing?"

"Go away."

Peanut crawls in next to her. There is not much room, but she is small. "Why are you in here?"

"Rosemary's mad at me," Nancee says in a muffled voice.

Peanut feels hope flutter, like a scrap of paper, in her throat. "Why?"

"We sneaked out some of my dad's beers? And my mom found out, and she called the Carvers, and now Rosemary's grounded and won't text me back. She even blocked me on TikTok."

"Maybe you shouldn't have taken the beers," Peanut says.

"They didn't even taste good," Nancee says. "And I had a headache the next day, and my poop smelled like eggs." Tears roll down her cheeks. "I bet Rosemary's hanging out with Kristy Crews. Her mom takes all these pills for her back, so she never knows when Kristy's home." She kicks the wall of the playhouse. "We live in the most boring town ever."

"Maybe it's not as boring as you think," Peanut can't help saying.

"How would you know?" Nancee says bitterly. "Jessie doesn't let you do anything."

"Maybe I'm actually on a Quest of Necessity, and a few short hours ago, a life hung treacherously in the balance."

Nancee makes a face. "I don't want to hear about you playing the Falling Children."

"I'm not playing." Peanut hesitates, wondering if she can trust Nancee. "Do you want to see something?"

"No," Nancee says, but Peanut pretends she doesn't hear. Unzipping her backpack, she dramatically pulls out the notebook.

"Do you know where I got this?" she whispers. "The Murder House. I went there, in the middle of the night. And inside was the Seer, who is quite possibly under the control of the Unstopping. She left this right there on the ground for me to find."

Nancee's eyes flick from the little notebook back to Peanut. "Liar."

"I'm not lying," Peanut says. "Hold it and shut your eyes."

Reluctantly, Nancee accepts the notebook into her hands.

"Can't you feel its uncertain magic?"

"No," says Nancee. She pushes the notebook away.

"I'm not making this up," Peanut insists. "The Children are in the gravest danger of their lives, and they're counting on me to help."

Nancee is quiet for a few minutes. Then she sighs. "Fine. Tell me the story."

Peanut does, although in this version, *she* fainted on the side of the highway.

When she finishes, Nancee nods. "That's a good one. The house? And all those skinny cats? Ewww. But why'd you even *go* there?"

"It's my destiny. And you know what else?" Peanut says, suddenly realizing something. "The Unstopping," she whispers, "has an eye exactly like mine."

She means to say this for dramatic effect, but hearing the words aloud makes Peanut's chest tighten.

Maybe because the only other person she's met with a lazy eye like hers is possibly a murderer. Maybe because seeing him makes Peanut realize her eye probably won't get better as she gets older. Maybe...

"Did you tell Jessie I had nothing to do with this?" Nancee nudges her. "Because otherwise she blames me for everything." Raising her voice, she complains, "Peanut, why do you and that Nancee Coffee make my life so difficult!" She tosses her hair and growls, a perfect imitation of Jessie.

Peanut smiles.

The overhead lights flicker, then, with a dramatic *whump*, turn off. "The library is now closed," the librarian calls in her tired, sweatered voice.

"OMG, we're going to get locked in!" Nancee starts to stand, bumping her head on the plastic playhouse roof.

"Shhh!" Peanut pulls her back down. "I know the alarm code," she whispers. "We can let ourselves out."

"Seriously?" Nancee's eyes widen, first in fear then—*Ah!* Peanut thinks—respect. "OMG, you *are* out of control."

And just like that, they are friends again.

~~~

For the next hour, Nancee and Peanut analyze the few lines of writing inside the notebook.

"Black licorice, pig slop, bitter melon, blood," Nancee muses, tapping each word with her finger. "Black licorice, pig slop—"

"Don't say it aloud!" Peanut cups her hand over the page to hide the words. "What if you summon the Unstopping?"

Nancee nods, mouthing silently this time. *Bitter melon, blood...*

Peanut watches Nancee's index finger, shingled with silver glitter polish, slide across the page. She breathes in the scent of Nancee's baby powder deodorant. Peanut has missed her so much.

"Stop staring." Nancee looks up. "You're creeping me out. What do you think this means?"

Peanut doesn't know. She's already held the page before a mirror and checked for a threatening message from Mean L'il Bebe. She also arranged the notebook on the floor of her bedroom, stuffed animals circling it, in case the purity of their souls could draw out the meaning.

Nancee suddenly gasps.

"Oh my God," she says. "I know what we should do!"

Peanut sits up. "What?"

"You should let me show Rosemary!" Nancee says. "She's so good with puzzles."

"No!" Peanut makes a face. "This is mine."

"No, it's not. You stole it."

"It was *entrusted* to me. And you're not even friends with Rosemary anymore."

"But I could be." Nancee flops her legs over Peanut's. "Please? Let her look. She's smarter than you think."

Peanut doesn't think so. But the weight of Nancee's legs on her own and the fruity gum on her breath make her relent.

"You can take one picture of it," she says, "but you can't tell her where it's from. And you have to call me *if*"—she emphasizes the word—"anything uncanny happens."

Peanut already knows nothing will. This message, these words, are meant for her.

～～

It's after nine o'clock by the time Peanut gets home.

"You can't keep running off!" Jessie insists. "You're a child!" She is still in her muslin skirt and high-necked shirt from work, a streak of red mud across her forehead.

Peanut's good mood evaporates. *I need to do everything I can not to turn into an adult like you,* she thinks.

"Where's Libby?" she asks. "Is she writing?"

"No, she went somewhere with that reporter."

Peanut looks at Jessie in disbelief. "She *what*? Why'd you let her go?"

Jessie throws up her hands. "Apparently, she doesn't listen to me either."

Peanut finds her father in their garage, his head and torso hidden under the hood of an old black truck.

When Vast Robbins, who owned the only auto shop in town, died of emphysema last year, he left his 1944 Jeep to Peanut's father. He's been trying to get it to run ever since, but like he always tells people who ask how it's coming, he's no Vast Robbins.

"Libby shouldn't be with that reporter!" Peanut says instead of hello. "She should be at home."

Her father stands and stretches. "I agree. Libby has some serious health issues that need attention. Getting her home is a wise idea."

"Can I drive your truck to go get her?" Peanut asks eagerly, already looking around for the keys. "I know how. First, you put in the clutch. Then you—"

"I mean," her father says, "we should get Libby back to *her* home."

"But she likes it here." Peanut drops her hands off the invisible steering wheel. "She's always saying how pretty Blue Skies is. And she'd never had Moreos before." Peanut points to Buzz's house next door. "She even laughs at Buzz's jokes, and he's not funny at all."

"However, she's not writing, and isn't that what she came for?"

"Her ideas are gestating," Peanut says stubbornly. "They're in her mind like a little baby, not ready to be born yet."

"If you believe that, I have some real estate next to the Cross County Waste Station to sell you."

Peanut runs her finger over the doorjamb. It looks like a face: big nose, tiny eyes. She wonders if it minds being in the dark most of the time. She won't close the door all the way when she leaves.

"Nancee's friends with me again," she announces.

"When wasn't she?"

"Yesterday? And the day before. For a small but tremendous eternity! Didn't Jessie tell you?"

"I think we've established that Jessie rarely tells me anything."

Her father bends over the open hood again.

"I hate Jessie," Peanut offers. "I wish her soul was trapped in a slimy old doll that no one ever wanted to play with. One that's left outside during the coldest Snowpocalypse, buried—"

"Enough, Peanut."

"She doesn't tell the truth and doesn't have any friends and doesn't read or respect the Children and never even puts the cap back on the toothpaste, so then it—"

"I said, that's enough."

"Don't you ever wonder what your life would be like if you didn't adopt Jessie?" Peanut can't help but ask. "Has she done one good thing in her life? Because I can't think of—"

Peanut doesn't see the wrench leave her father's hand and come flying across the room. It misses her and smacks the little face in the doorjamb. Peanut isn't sure if that's a mistake.

40

"I can't believe this town. The first person I asked, 'Do you know a Punky Brewster kid with a scar?' gave me directions. People *trust* here. It's like the eighties." Glenn holds up a coupon. "Look, I got a free VHS rental. And it came with Dippin' Dots!"

He calls to Jessie, who has retreated into the kitchen after answering the front door. "I hear you're the star attraction of the train robbery."

Jessie glances up from the grapefruit she's halving. "I'm good at pretending."

"So." Glenn turns to Libby and rubs his hands together. "Should we grab dinner?"

Libby doesn't feel like grabbing anything. Her thoughts are bound in cotton, like they're about to be shipped off in a large crate to a museum. But Glenn is insistent.

"Come on. I came all this way."

"Walk downtown to the Clam Box," Jessie suggests. "You probably won't get food poisoning again."

Again?

"I'm fine," Libby says, but Glenn takes hold of her shoulders and steers her toward the door. At first, Libby thinks it's an affectionate gesture. Then she realizes he's trying to intercept Dr. Bixton, coming up the front porch steps, medical bag in hand.

"Hello, sir." Glenn extends his hand. "Libby might have told you about me. Glenn Lawson. Reporter from New York."

"Shame to hear it," Dr. Bixton says, clunking his bag down on the kitchen table. "If you're from east of the Mississippi River, you're considered a yahoo out here."

Glenn pumps his hand. "So be it." He grins.

"What can I do for you?" Dr. Bixton points to a bulge in Glenn's pants pocket. "I can inject something to bring that down but suggest you try an ice pack first."

"Oh, this?" Reddening, Glenn pulls out a digital recorder. "Professional hazard." He toggles a button, and a red light goes off.

Libby follows Glenn's gaze around the house: at a dusty painting of sunflowers on the wall next to the door, a rip in the couch cushion, patches of varnish worn thin on the hardwood floor.

"Lovely home. Very rustic. How long have you lived here?"

"Too long," calls Jessie from the kitchen.

"How long have you been a doctor?" Glenn asks Dr. Bixton.

"Longer than anyone imagines, I expect."

"Any hobbies?" Glenn presses. "Fishing? Hunting? Writing?"

Dr. Bixton smiles politely. "I'm sure the pharmacist downtown would call my scrawl something far less flattering."

Glenn tosses out other questions about the medical school Dr. Bixton attended and the year he graduated, his favorite authors, his favorite toy as a child...

"Libby," Jessie beckons. "Come help me with something."

Libby follows her into the pantry, tripping over a bag of potatoes. Jessie reaches past her to close the door. "Your reporter friend thinks my dad is F. T. Goldhero."

"I know." Libby nods.

"Doesn't that offend you? He doesn't think there's any way it could be you."

"Well, nobody does." Libby pulls her cardigan more tightly around her chest.

"He's using you. Tell him to leave."

Libby closes her eyes. First, she tries to picture Glenn's face because she keeps picturing Aldo Fondstun, for some reason. Then she tries to remember how long it's been since she's heard from the Children. Hours? Days? Weeks?

All she can conjure is the feel of Buzz's hands on her waist, guiding her down from the tree house. "I'd say don't think about falling," he advised. "But it sounds like it's on your mind."

Jessie snaps her fingers. "Hey, I'm trying to help you here." Her mouth is the same heart shape as Peanut's. "Do you even care what's going on?"

Libby needs to get back to real life, which in her case, means the Children.

"It's okay," she tells Jessie. "I'm going to ask Whosit to drive me home."

~~~

Libby is barely down the Bixtons' porch steps before Glenn swings an arm around her shoulders. It means her steps have to slow to match his.

"That's him, isn't it?" he asks in a low voice. "I expected him to be a little more—nuanced. And British. Scottish, at least." He looks at Libby. "How the hell did you land this job?"

"Long story," she says.

They walk downtown to the Clam Box, where dusty fishing nets and bright blue papier-mâché lobsters are nailed to the ceiling. It's not much bigger than Libby's living room at home.

Glenn orders a pint of dark beer, plus a shot of whiskey. "To you," he toasts Libby once they sit down in a booth. "For helping me get the scoop of the fucking century."

He clinks her glass, and the tap water sloshes inside it.

"Two dollars for a pint of microbrew?" Glenn wipes his mouth. "I think I might move here."

A man with a bushy black beard pauses next to their table. HOOKED ON QUACK, his T-shirt reads. A puka necklace peeks out of the crew neck.

"Feeling better?" He puts a hand on Libby's shoulder.

She's never seen him before. "Excuse me?"

"Buzz should have known better than to bring you here on a Friday." He pats her shoulder before retrieving a bag of takeout from the counter. "I have IBS, so I have the shits anyway."

Libby's eyes wander over the half dozen vinyl-backed booths and the framed pictures of cartoon clams on the walls. How often has she been here? How long has she been in this town? Who has food poisoning and doesn't remember it?

All she knows for sure is that the Children are still waiting for her.

They are, aren't they?

Leaning across the table, Libby cups her hand over Glenn's. "Will you take me home?" she asks. "Right now? Please?"

He looks surprised. "We just ordered."

Then, misinterpreting Libby's squeeze of his fingers—and her expression, which is one of transparent desperation—Glenn stands and throws a five on the table.

"Keep the change," he calls.

~ ~

The lobby of the Diamond Boar Hotel resembles a musty Victorian museum. There are horsehair couches with rigid wooden backs and busty mannequins wearing fussy velvet gowns and wilted feathery hats. Every mirror—and there are many—is scalloped, and each lamp is cinched in the middle as if wearing a corset. Atop glass shelves, taxidermied mice, kitted out in impossibly small suspenders and bow ties, nibble Libby with their eyes.

She and Glenn are the only ones inside the elevator. The air inside might be from the Victorian era, too. Libby feels like she's standing in her closet at home, squeezed between her dozen long-sleeved white shirts and gray cardigans. If she closes her eyes, she can hear her empty plastic hangers *tap, tap, tap* against each other.

And then the doors open, and Glenn pulls her into his room.

The sex is like a gulp of water or maybe air—not enjoyable so much as necessary. Libby uses it to stop thinking. She doesn't want to think about her plastic hangers. Or what she's been doing this past week—or is it longer? She doesn't want to think about how she can no longer think, not really. Not the way she wants to.

When Glenn tries to talk, Libby begs, "Please don't." She needs no words, just this act and this sensation and to fall, fall, fall into a temporary nothingness.

Afterward, Libby gathers her clothes. "Can you drive me home?"

She can't remember the name of her street, but if she closes her eyes, she can see the white microwave in her kitchen. She recently cleaned it until the turntable gleamed.

Glenn looks around, surprised. "What's wrong with this place?"

He has a thick dark mole on his shoulder that looks like it should be checked by a dermatologist.

"I'm not doing anything," Libby tells the mole.

Glenn looks around. "I'm confused."

"I don't know where my plane ticket is." Libby lifts her shoulders. "And I don't like to fly. Can you just drive me home?"

Glenn fishes through the pile of blankets on the floor until he finds his briefs. They are orange and covered with little white baseballs.

"You're getting cold feet, aren't you?" he asks. "Look, Libby. We've discussed this. I'm doing this story." He stands and shoves one foot, then the other into his underwear. The elastic snaps to his waist. "Why else would I be here?" he says under his breath.

When Libby doesn't answer, he adds, "*You're* the one who started this, feeding me information. I've got you on record. Too bad if you're having second thoughts."

Libby is, and they are especially about sleeping with Glenn again. Already, loneliness is seeping back into her body. Her feet are ice cold.

"It's just—what if *I'm* the story?" she blurts out. "What if I'm the one you're looking for? Then would you drive me home?"

It sounds like a line from a Lionel Richie song—maybe it is?—so she doesn't blame Glenn for looking at her with pity.

"Look," he says, "my divorce isn't final. My wife and I—we could still work things out. And you and I, we barely know each other. We've slept together what, a half dozen times?"

That many? Libby thinks.

"You're a sweet lady," Glenn says, "but I'm not going anywhere until I get this old codger to talk to me."

"This old codger *won't* talk to you," Libby says. "This old codger is sick and depressed."

"Don't worry," Glenn says. "As you've seen, I'm very persuasive."

He disappears into the bathroom, slamming the door.

Libby can barely dress herself. Underwear and socks get shoved into the pockets of her pants. (Has the zipper always been in the back?) Her shirt is mismatched buttoned. The tongues of her sneakers frumple—that's not the right word, is it?—under her bare feet.

In the elevator mirror, her ponytail is nested to one side, and one of her earrings is missing. If she squints past her reflection, Libby thinks she can see her couch at home. On it, Rolf is sleeping.

Libby rides the elevator up and down for several minutes before she remembers to exit. The doors make a *tap, tap, tap* like the tree branches against her windows at home.

~~~

Libby has no idea how to get back to Peanut's house.

She cuts through an alley lined with cardboard boxes and a store that sells toilets and sinks. She winds around streets named after flowers—Aster, Foxglove, Mimosa—then avenues named after trees: Limber Pine, Lodgepole Pine, Piñon Pine.

A calligraphy shop. The train depot. A dentist's office. And then Libby catches sight of a tall spire outlined against the stars. Her heart catches. She would recognize that stately shape anywhere—it's Pompou's.

Libby races toward it. It feels so good to run toward something she loves rather than running away in fear. She leaps off curbs and sprints around corners, never letting the steeple out of her sight.

Not until she is on the sidewalk before it, craning her neck to take in the entire sprawling building washed purple in the moonlight, does Libby realize this isn't a magical toy emporium. It's an old church. And the lights are off, and the heavy wooden doors are smeared shut, and Libby doesn't even *go* to church because there's singing, and she doesn't sing in front of others.

All she can do is lean against the stone wall surrounding the building, laughing at how pathetic she is. *There's reality, and there's imagination*, she chides herself. *Do you even know the difference?*

Inside her brain, the Squirrel Keeper opens the door to the OtherWay only to shriek, *Not you. Not anymore!*

Smack.

He slams the door closed, then opens it again and slams it once more for good measure.

Smack.

It takes a while before Libby realizes the sound is coming from behind the building.

In the parking lot, she sees Buzz on his skateboard, standing outside a set of double doors to the church. Picking up speed, he leaps onto the narrow railing dividing a set of ten stairs but only makes it a foot or so before losing his balance and jumping off.

He limps back up to the top and tries again. This time, he crashes onto the concrete stairs, rolling onto his side and cursing.

Libby sits on the curb, pulling the sleeves of her sweater over her hands, and watches. The falling mesmerizes her, how easily he meets the ground, then stands and goes again.

It hurts; she can hear it: bone against concrete, Buzz cursing "fuck no," and "*cockfucker sucking mother bitcher—*"

But he's smiling.

"How do you make it look so easy?" she finally calls.

If Buzz is surprised to see her, he doesn't show it. "What? Eating shit?"

"*Trying*," Libby says.

Buzz shrugs. "I'm just stoked to be on my board again."

"But doesn't it hurt?"

He uses the bottom of his I-shirt to wipe off his face. "If I stop and think about it, I'm fucked."

He flips his board into his hand and comes closer. "Why'd you let Peanut take you on a wild goose chase? The Greeleys are fucking trouble, their whole family. And you broke into their house."

Libby lifts her shoulders, embarrassed. "I didn't realize we were going to—Peanut thought it would help."

"She's a kid with an overactive imagination! She doesn't know. We looked everywhere for you. You could have been fucking lying in a ditch somewhere."

"I wasn't."

"No, you were with some hipster reporter who banged on my door today, wanting to talk about the 'lead' he's following." Buzz hooks his fingers into air quotes.

Libby suddenly remembers something. She points up at the spire. "This is the church where you got arrested as a kid! When you were six! A Cross Country policeman—"

"Cross Creek."

"—arrested you after you skated down this railing for the first time." Libby pauses, tapping her fingers to her temples. "You did a kickflip frontside broadside."

"Boardslide, but yeah, that's the story," says Buzz.

"And I remembered it." Libby smiles.

He watches her for a minute.

"Why are you here?" he asks.

Libby isn't sure if he means here in general, or here right now. She also can't remember how to get home.

"Come on." Sighing, Buzz steps onto his board. "This way." He motions.

Libby listens to a cricket chirp and a car start its engine, the click of Buzz's skateboard wheels like a dog tagging along. For a second, she thinks she can even smell again. The night air is cool and earthy against her tongue.

"Don't tell that reporter anything," Buzz says as they enter the park. "He and his fucking French tuck don't deserve shit."

"What would I tell him? That I'm sick?"

Buzz pushes on his board so it comes to a stop. "You said you had writer's block."

"Well"—Libby is too tired to fumble her way through a lie— "maybe I'm both."

"What kind of sick?" When Libby shrugs, he asks, "Are you *sick* sick?"

"Yes." That is the perfect way to put it. "I am *sick* sick."

Buzz waits for her to elaborate. When she doesn't, he guesses, "You mean like cancer?"

Cancer would be more dignified.

"Noooooo," Libby says, giving the word a tail. She cups her fingers over her lips to hide the words. "I have dementia."

Buzz pulls her hand away. "Say it again?" This time, he watches her mouth.

"Dementia."

Is this the first time she's said it aloud? It's a cold octopus of a word.

"You mean like Alzheimer's? How? You're not that old."

"No," Libby says. "I'm not *that* old."

"I meant—"

"It's okay."

Buzz rolls his board back and forth against the cement.

"That fucking sucks," he says finally.

Libby agrees. She has waited her whole life to become someone other than the person she is. And now that she's nearing the end, she sees that this "Better Libby" never stood a chance.

Buzz is still holding her hand. When Libby wipes her cheeks, her tears disappear between his fingers.

"Come on." Buzz cocks his head toward the sidewalk, which disappears down a hill. "I'll give you a ride."

"On that? Down there?" Libby isn't sure if he's kidding. "That doesn't look safe."

Buzz shrugs. "Probably not, but whatever."

She doesn't move. "I don't want to fall."

"Like I do?"

Libby thinks of how poorly she's just seen Buzz skate and the hill pitched away from them at a forty-five-degree angle. Her mind reflexively lists a few ways danger is imminent: *concussion, contusion, broken arms, squashed intestines, other painful things she is forgetting.*

Still, Libby allows herself to be helped onto the board. When it tries to roll out from under her, Buzz anchors his hands around her waist. "Relax," he says, pressing his knee against the back of her legs.

"I'm not good at relaxing. I don't know what I'm doing." The worry she feels makes her voice reedy.

"You don't have to do anything." Stepping behind her, Buzz adjusts the board with his right foot.

"Shouldn't we have helmets?" Libby asks. "And mouth guards? And knee pads? I feel like we should."

"At this point, let's just say 'fuck it' and hope for the best."

"Is it too late to change my mind? Because I think maybe I—"

"Yup. Too late," Buzz says cheerfully. Wrapping an arm around her waist, he pushes off from the pavement.

"Can I close my eyes?" Libby asks as they start to roll. "I really want to close my eyes."

"You can," Buzz says, "but why would you want to?"

41

It's over in seconds.

Libby gives names to the things around her as proof that she's still alive.

Cement. Night. Trees. Sky. Things.

Her legs feel like jelly, but they're still attached. Her hands tremble, but they're intact as well.

"How did you do that?"

Buzz kicks his board into his hand. "Don't know. Don't think about it."

But he sounds pleased.

"I can't believe you do that all the time." Libby, not trusting her legs to move anywhere just now, sinks into the grass.

"Not all the time." Buzz looks over at her and smiles. "That's a pretty gnarly sidewalk."

Lying back, Libby feels blades of grass comb the back of her neck. Above her, stars sprinkle like salt.

"I like this place," she says.

"I don't know why." Buzz lies beside her and rests a hand behind his head. "There's nothing to do."

"That's not true," Libby says. "There are—" She tries to think of something but can only think of his arm brushing against hers. "Birds. Don't you like birds?"

"I do," he agrees.

The lights of a plane hum across the sky.

"What's the real reason you're not finishing your book?" Buzz asks. "What are you so scared of?"

"Everything," Libby says truthfully.

"Like?"

"I'm losing the Children."

"You'll think of something. Peanut's got a shitload of ideas."

"I'm losing my mind."

Buzz gestures to the sky. "Somebody out there's working on a cure."

Libby shakes her head. "They won't find one."

"Then maybe they'll grow you a new brain in a test tube," Buzz says. "They can do it with meat."

"It won't happen. Not in time."

"You don't know for sure."

"Yeah," Libby says, "I do."

Buzz doesn't say anything.

"You know what scares me the most?" Libby closes her eyes. "Not dying, but what happens right before, when you know it's coming."

She thinks of her parents on a plane, hurtling toward the ground; Vernice, her lungs full of fluid, fighting to breathe; all the characters she's coaxed to their deaths.

"What goes through your mind? It must be terrifying. You're all alone, just *waiting*."

When Libby starts to cry again, Buzz turns toward her, propping himself up on his elbow. "Since you're already feeling sad," he says, "let's talk about Williwigs."

"What about them?" Libby says, wiping her nose.

"I want to talk about how they're basically lazy-ass teddy bears who throw temper tantrums and fucking whine all the time."

Libby smiles, despite the freight train of sadness traveling through her chest. "You have to get to know them."

"Why? They're assholes. Always mooching off the Unstopping or moaning that their paws hurt."

"He forces them to mine for uncertain magic in dangerous underground conditions," Libby insists.

"He gives them jobs."

"It's grueling work! They don't see the sun for weeks. Their little paws ache, and their fur falls out in clumps. They struggle so much."

"So do I. So do you. Neither of us goes around hurling fucking bowls of butter-rot porridge."

"Bitter hookroot," Libby says, starting to laugh.

"Close enough," Buzz says, but he smiles, too. "God, I hate those fucking bears."

"It's a good thing they're in my books, then," Libby says. She is laughing and crying now. "I'll look past their awfulness and love them regardless."

Buzz doesn't say anything for a minute. And then he gently tucks a piece of hair behind her ear. "Yeah," he says, "you will."

~ ~

Inside Libby's mind, *The Diagnosis* takes a break. The lights go dark on the marquee, and a few letters tumble loose to the sidewalk below. Maybe it's THE DIA NO IS now. Or TH DI AG SIS. Either way, it's a little more nonsensical and a little less scary.

The crowds thin. The concession counter stops making popcorn. And while the lines of ticket holders are sure to return, for now at least the hope that suddenly fills Libby's heart is larger and lighter than the cells dying by the thousands inside her brain.

42

Libby is sitting at the table, an untouched plate of French toast before her, when Peanut comes downstairs the next morning.

"I'm trying to read your books, but here's what I don't get," says Jessie, who is at the stove, adding more butter to a skillet. "You never explain why Lucy Parker fell in love with the Unstopping."

Libby looks confused. "Didn't I?"

"She was smart and talented. And he was this rando outcast."

"That's how everyone saw them," Libby explains. "But they saw more in each other. Lucy was under a lot of pressure to live up to her family's legacy. And no one thought the Unstopping would amount to anything. They were a kind of"—she searchers for the right word—"refuge for each other."

"Oh," Jessie says. "I didn't think about it that way."

"Why do you care about the Unstopping?" Peanut interrupts. "You always say the books are silly. And that grown-ups who read them must not have a real life."

"I'm human." Jessie gives Libby a sideways glance. "I'm allowed to change my mind. Don't look now," she adds, pointing her spatula at the kitchen window, "but your not-so-secret admirer is back."

Walking up the porch steps, a large to-go cup of coffee in one hand and his recorder in the other, is Glenn.

"I'm not here," Libby says, but Glenn isn't looking for her.

"Hey there, kiddo, is your dad home?" he asks Peanut. "I was hoping to catch him."

"Most sadly, he's been captured by the devastatingly cruel pirates of the *Sink Ng* ship," she says.

She closes the door, but Glenn doesn't leave. "I've got all day," he calls. He leans against the mailbox and sips his coffee.

He doesn't need to wait long before Peanut's father comes into view, slowly making his way up the hill.

"Dr. Bixton!" Glenn hurries to shake her father's hand. They talk in the driveway for a few minutes, Glenn nodding intently and scribbling into his reporter's notebook. Afterward, he lifts three fingers in Peanut's direction (Gran Bere's sign of victory, book one) and leaves.

Peanut intercepts her father at the door. "What did you say? You didn't tell him about Libby, did you?"

Dr. Bixton smiles. "I suggested he go make his acquaintance with Annie Yolen, Blue Skies' oldest and most illustrious resident, who is always eager to converse."

"But she doesn't know anything about Libby or the Children!"

"Our reporter friend doesn't know that, does he?" Her father takes off his suit jacket and hangs it on the hook. "I presume two hours of listening to Annie prattle on—three and a half if she opens a new bottle of melon liqueur—will give Libby time to start heading home."

Libby doesn't react. Chin in hand, she is gazing out the window, lost in her own world.

"But we're not done yet," Peanut says.

Her father pats her shoulder. "Then perhaps she'll fare better at home."

"She won't!" Peanut wishes Libby would speak up. "She might not even know where her wallet is. Right, Libby? You don't, do you?"

"We'll loan her money, then get paid back from the million-dollar reward," Jessie says, flipping more French toast in the skillet. This batch is burned.

"What's that supposed to mean?" Peanut puts her hands on her hips.

"It was a joke."

"It wasn't funny."

"Don't talk to me in that tone of voice." Jessie's jaw tightens, and they are facing off now, neither willing to back down, when there's a knock at the door.

"See what you've done?" Peanut hisses. "Now the reporter is back."

"Me? You're the one who—"

"Oh, hush, both of you," their father says as he heads into the front hall. "You sound like a bunch of bone grocers."

Peanut blinks. "What did you say?"

Her father doesn't answer, but Peanut hears him cry out from the front hall.

He gets emotional so rarely that it's hard to tell what this means. Jessie, too, looks alarmed. When their father comes back to the kitchen, he has actual tears in his eyes. Buzz, his hair still wet from the shower, is behind him.

"I told everyone, 'Let the boy heal,'" Dr. Bixton is saying. A smile kites across his face. "That you'd bounce back from this but needed to do so at your own pace." He claps Buzz's shoulder and gestures for Jessie to get another coffee mug. "French toast? Eggs? What can we get you?" He hands Buzz the paper. "I'll even let you read the crime log first."

"Thanks," Buzz says, reddening from the attention, "but I—"

"Have you thought about trying physical therapy again? And listen, when you're ready to go camping, I've been eyeing an induction stove. Solar powered! Stop by the sporting goods store and tell

Merle you want to take a look. Now, eggs or toast? Both? I bet Jessie could even be persuaded to make you some hash."

"No," Jessie says. "I couldn't."

"That's okay." Buzz shifts from one foot to another. "I can't stay. I—"

"Can't stay?" Dr Bixton looks perplexed. "What's the hurry?"

Buzz clears his throat. "I came to tell you," he says to Libby, "that you forgot the noni juice at my house."

"Noni juice?" Libby repeats.

"Yeah. It's in the fridge." Buzz raises an eyebrow. "So maybe you want to come over," he says more slowly.

Libby thinks a minute. "Ohhhhhh," she finally says, letting the word become long and shiny like a ribbon. She lifts her coffee mug, trying to hide a smile.

But Peanut sees it.

So does her father.

And so does Jessie, who dumps the entire plate of French toast into the sink. "Time for school, Peanut."

Peanut looks at the clock. "No, it's not."

"Yes, it is," Jessie snaps. "Go brush your teeth."

"But I haven't had breakfast."

"You can eat on the way to the bus stop. Now go."

Jessie hasn't really read the Falling Children, Peanut thinks as she stomps upstairs. If she had, she would know adults deserve to have secrets kept from them, but children *never* do.

When she comes downstairs again, Libby is outside on the porch swing, smiling to herself like she's heard a good joke. The swing creaks, creaks, creaks.

"Buzz is a bad liar," Peanut tells her. "He just wants you to come over."

Libby blooms with color. "That's okay, though, isn't it?" she asks.

Peanut isn't sure. "When love shifts the ground under two people, the aftershocks can be felt for miles," Gran Bere says.

Peanut likes Libby and she loves Buzz, but she is worried for the Children. Even a faceless trinket from a gumball machine could see that Libby needs fewer distractions, not more.

"Only if you write today," she says. "You can use my room. My stories are on my desk, and you can use anything you want. You can even use my pencils, but please sharpen them when you're done."

Libby doesn't answer. She's watching Buzz through the kitchen window.

Peanut can see him, too, talking to their father. Or well, their father is talking, and Buzz is pretending to listen but mostly sneaking glances at Libby.

Jessie is pretending to wash dishes but mostly watching Buzz watch Libby.

Peanut goes back inside, letting the screen door slam.

"—some health issues which you aren't privy to," her father is saying.

"I am privy," says Buzz.

"No," Jessie counters, "you're up to something."

They stop arguing when they see Peanut.

"What medical issues?" she asks. "Who's up to something?"

"Don't eavesdrop. It's rude," says Jessie.

"It's my house, too," Peanut says. "And Libby is *my* friend. It's mean that you're all sitting in here talking about her."

"Agree. I'm taking her back to my house," Buzz says.

Dr. Bixton lowers his voice. "I don't think we have a lot of time."

"What do you mean 'we'?" Peanut wants to know. "Time for what?"

"He means we can't stay here forever arguing," Jessie says. "I have to go to work. Because apparently that's all I do."

Peanut pulls Buzz's T-shirt sleeve as he passes. "Will you make sure Libby writes today?" she asks. "Please? It's really important if the Children ever want to go home."

"Yeah," Buzz says, not looking at her. "Sure."

43

On the way to first period, Peanut is rereading the part in book three where Everlee is trapped in a carnival funhouse mirror and has to trust Benjamin to help her real reflection escape, when Nancee pulls her into the girls' restroom.

Nancee's silvery-blue eye shadow and coral lipstick make her look like a mermaid, but one that can't swim very well. (Also book three.)

"I talked to Rosemary." Nancee's eyes light up. "The story you told me? How you went to the Murder House in the middle of the night all by yourself? She thought it was awesome."

"You *told* her? I didn't say you could tell her that part."

"It's not like I told some rando. Rosemary's my best friend." At Peanut's expression, she clarifies, "Like you used to be before, you know."

"No," Peanut says. "I don't know."

"She wanted me to invite you to her rally tonight. Which means she is thinking of forgiving you. Which means you totally have to go." Nancee actually dares to tap Peanut's scar. "So maybe do something about this?"

Peanut smacks her hand away. "I don't care if she forgives me or not. I'm not going."

"Are you for real?" Nancee is dumbfounded. "F. T. Goldhero could be there."

"That's a lie."

"No, it's not. You're just jealous. You know, sometimes I think you don't even *want* to be helped." Nancee pauses dramatically on her way out of the bathroom. "Have fun with your imaginary friends."

~ ⌒ ~

Peanut spends the rest of the school day ignoring her teachers, especially Mrs. Hader, who draws a line across her neck and says, "Krrrck!" twice in homeroom. Both times she glowers at Peanut.

Peanut doesn't care. She is too busy staring at the notebook.

Black licorice, pig slop, bitter melon, blood.

Such ugly, sour words. What uncertain magic is the Unstopping planning to do with them? She tries to rearrange them to see if that makes more sense—*slop bitter blood black pig melon licorice?*—but the *scratch-scratch* of her pencil annoys Mrs. Hader.

"Class," she says, "when I am up here, taking time out of my busy day to teach you poetry, I deserve your full attention. And if you choose not to give it to me, you can go sit in the hall."

She folds her arms and waits until Peanut slings her backpack over one shoulder and leaves the classroom.

What is Peanut overlooking? She slumps against the shelves of yearbooks. The answer is so close, she can feel it.

Black licorice, pig slop, bitter melon, blood.

A small kernel of resentment opens inside Peanut's chest. Libby says she can't save the Children, but what if she knows how to—and won't?

Peanut doesn't want to have to choose between Libby and the

Children. But if she must, she knows, deep down, where her allegiances lie.

~ ~

Walking home from the bus stop after school, Peanut can see Buzz and Libby on the porch swing. Libby's knees are hugged into her chest. Buzz's arm is around her, and he is doing all the swinging with his good leg.

"It's making things worse," Peanut hears him say.

"What's making things worse?" she asks, coming up the stairs.

"Nothing."

Peanut grabs the Cream King shake Buzz is holding and takes a long slurp. Buzz lets her, even though it's Suicide, a mix of six different ice cream flavors. It's his favorite, but he doesn't try to wrestle it back.

Suspicious, Peanut thinks.

"Did you write today?" She looks expectantly at Libby, who looks at Buzz.

"We were busy," he says.

Peanut doesn't want to hear excuses. (Which, she realizes with disgust, is something Jessie would say.) "Then we can start now," she says. "I've been thinking of ideas all day."

Or well, *thinking* of thinking of ideas.

She wants Libby to spring up and say, "Hut hut!" like the army of Ten Soldiers in book one. Instead, Libby tucks a strand of hair behind her ear.

"Could we have more time?" She looks at Buzz when she asks. "Please?"

"But I'm ready now," Peanut says.

"Ten minutes, P," Buzz echoes. "Come on."

"But the Children are waiting!" Peanut knows that when adults say ten minutes, they mean thirty or forty minutes or maybe even tomorrow. "They need your help!"

Libby opens her mouth to agree, but the porch swing or the sunshine or maybe it's Buzz, whose shoulder is touching Libby's, has a gravitational pull.

"I'll be there in ten minutes," she says. "I promise."

Peanut slams into the house and up to her bedroom. No wonder the Children are dying.

She's not the only one annoyed. A few minutes later, she hears Jessie clearing her throat on the porch.

"Oh, excuse me," she says loudly. "Am I interrupting something?" And then the front door creaks open, and Jessie, too, thumps up the stairs.

Peanut hears her changing out of her train-robbery skirt and blouse and muttering under her breath when the strings of her corset get stuck. But when she knocks on Peanut's door, Jessie isn't dressed in her usual jeans and tank top.

She's wearing a WHERE'S THE BEEF? T-shirt with rainbow suspenders, jean shorts, and white-and-pink Tretorns with no socks. A red butterfly net is slung across her shoulder.

Like Everlee.

"What are you doing?" Peanut is horrified.

"I'm working a special train robbery tonight because of the rally," Jessie says. "I told you a hundred times."

"But why are you Everlee? You're all wrong!"

"Charming," Jessie says in a terrible British accent. "Love you, too."

The next thing Peanut hears is the front door slam (again). And Jessie saying, "I give up. She's all yours."

As if Peanut is a broken toy no one wants.

She is surprised to find herself blinking back tears.

"Don't you dare," she warns herself. Springing to her feet, Peanut wields a pretend butterfly net overhead, like Everlee in book one when she discovers hundreds of viciously chattering toy teeth have been let loose in the orphanage.

Twelve minutes later, Peanut is still battling imaginary incisors when Libby comes upstairs. Rolf is beside her, panting from the climb.

"I'm sorry," Libby says. "Please don't doubt how important this is to me. There's just so much going on."

Peanut waits for Libby to explain what the "so much" is, but Libby stares out the window. A bird hops along the sill, and she smiles like they know each other.

"Are you ready now?" Peanut demands.

"Ready for—"

"To save the Children's *lives*."

"Oh." Libby bites her thumbnail. "I don't know. No. Maybe tomorrow? There's a lot I'm trying to—think about."

"But if you keep putting this off, you're never going to finish," Peanut says. "I think we should do it right now." She pulls out her notebook. "I made a list of ideas. Like maybe Mean L'il Bebe has a good-hearted doll sister who shows up."

Libby shakes her head.

"Yeah, that is kind of obvious." Peanut scratches it off the list. "What if"—she scans her list, suddenly hating every idea on it—"the Falling Orphanage and Pompou's actually changed places through the Knick in Time so it was the Orphanage that burned down and Pompou's is totally okay?"

Libby lifts her shoulders. "I don't know. Maybe."

Then she says "I don't know. Maybe" to the other half dozen ideas

Peanut suggests. Each time, Libby's voice sounds farther and farther away.

"Maybe we can turn Everlee into a unicorn who has magical pink poop. She can magically pink poop her way to freedom," Peanut says, testing.

"I don't know. Maybe," Libby agrees.

Peanut can't take it anymore. She throws down her pencil. "This relationship is crumbling like the Lair of the Snake-Spider," she hisses.

~~~

Buzz makes macaroni and cheese from a box for dinner because their father has been called to Mrs. Halfchap's house. Her husband is dying, for real this time. Mrs. Halfchap is sure because the Siamese cat across the street said so.

"Then why do you need to be there?" Peanut asks as her father gathers up his medical bag. "You can't save him."

"Don't be callous, Peanut." Her father frowns. "It doesn't become you."

You're only going for Mrs. Halfchap. I've heard you with her, Peanut wants to say.

Her father pauses, even though she hasn't said this aloud.

"A simple lie is sometimes easier to accept than a complex truth," he says. "Wouldn't you agree?"

No, Peanut thinks.

At dinner, Buzz acts bossy like Jessie, commanding Peanut to set the table and fill the water glasses—with *ice*—and go cut purple yarrow from the yard for Libby. Peanut refuses to eat his cooking, especially the broccoli, which he cooked in the toaster oven and is now speckled yellow.

He's trying to show off for Libby, she can tell. Mystifyingly, it appears to be working.

"Aw," Libby says, when Buzz shows her how he taught Rolf to high-five.

It's more than Peanut can take, Libby choosing the real world over her own Children.

Stomping upstairs, Peanut scrubs her teeth and uses a soft little cloth to get the fingerprints off her glasses. When she returns, she finds Buzz and Libby lying on the living room rug, a game of Sorry set up between them.

"Roll again," Buzz is urging. "We're just playing for fun."

He drapes his arm around Libby's back and whispers something in her ear. She smiles.

Peanut clears her throat.

"You want to play, P?" Buzz hastily removes his arm. "We can start over."

"Don't bother," Peanut says in an icy tone. "I'm going to the rally. I have a special invitation to attend from Rosemary Carver."

He looks up, surprised. "You hate her."

"True, but she would like to beg my forgiveness," Peanut says. "And"—she looks at Libby, who is studying the dice in her hand— "I've chosen to support this rally in order to encourage F. T. Goldhero to stop playing games and finish her book already."

"Fine," Buzz sighs. "I'll walk you. Don't go anywhere," he tells Libby as he stands.

That gets her attention.

Peanut waits on the porch, kicking the porch swing so she doesn't have to hear the silence that is them kissing. It reminds her of the Abyss of Nothingness that's about to swallow up the OtherWay.

On the way downtown, Buzz whistles. He says "hey" to two different people Peanut knows for a fact he does not like and stops to pet a pygmy goat. Peanut cracks skinny, dead sticks off the trees they pass and hurls them to the ground.

"Jeez," Buzz says. "Relax."

"I don't like to relax," Peanut says through gritted teeth. "Relaxing is for babies and people who don't read."

Buzz holds up his hands. "Excuse me."

He starts whistling again.

As they get closer to the rally, the smell of buttered fudge fills the air. Peanut can hear the spindly, high-pitched strains of a glass harmonica. They pass the gazebo, which is twinkling with tiny cake-pink lights just like Pompou's. Across the length of the bridge, someone has put up a sign that reads WELCOME TO DARK CREVICE, DESERTED TOY CAPITAL OF THE WORLD!

People are outfitted as Williwigs, giant stuffed dragons, wind-up toys, and *Sink Ng* pirates. There are elaborately made-up dolls, furry bears, bone grocers with their gnomelike caps and bushy beards, and a few not-so-scary Unstoppings, their necks decorated with googly eyes.

Instead of excitement, Peanut bubbles with envy. It's as if someone sneaked into *her* brain, read *her* thoughts, and turned them into a loud, bad party.

Nancee is standing on the front steps of the library, trying to do the Floss to the eerie carnival-like music. But as Buzz gives Peanut the peace sign and turns to leave, she calls, "Wait!"

He turns.

"Do you really like Libby?" Peanut demands.

Her brother chews a loose piece of skin between his thumb and index finger. "What kind of question is that?"

"Because if you like her, you should leave her alone," Peanut says. "You're distracting her. She came here for me, not to listen to your stories and eat your bad broccoli and hear you say the f-word a billion times. You're sabotaging her. The Children are running out of time."

"Don't worry about it," Buzz says. "The Children will be fine."

"No, *you* don't worry about it," says Peanut. "Because you haven't read the books."

He shrugs. "I started the first."

"Lives *depend* on this."

Buzz throws up his hands. "Don't you think Libby should have a life, too?"

"No," Peanut says, emphasizing the word. "This isn't about her. It's about the Children."

She is pushing her way past Mr. Pretzky and his wife, both dressed in dark wigs and itchy horsehair skirt suits like the stern orphanage headmistress, Gladys, when Buzz calls, "What time would Jessie want you home?"

Peanut gives him the same steely stare Everlee gives the Unstopping in book three. "Afraid I can't answer that," she says in a (perfect) British accent. "She never would have let me come in the first place."

~ ⸺ ~

"OMG, you're here!" Nancee says when she sees Peanut. Then she frowns. "Why aren't you dressed up?"

Peanut looks down at the tie-dyed knee socks and black shorts she's wearing, plus the T-shirt she made herself: I LIVE FOR THE FALL-ING CHILDREN.

"I am dressed up."

"I mean as a character from the books." Nancee points to her own long flannel nightgown and tasseled cap.

"The Squirrel Keeper doesn't wear green mascara."

"Well, I do." Nancee unzips her purse and pulls out a makeup bag. "Who do you want to be?"

"Myself."

"God, would you stop being so angry?" Nancee pushes Peanut down on the library step. "I'm trying to help you."

"I don't need your help."

"Please. You totally do."

Rosemary appears behind Nancee. "Why don't you make her a Hide-Behind?"

Like Jessie, she, too, is dressed like Everlee: jeans shorts, a tight T-shirt that reads IT TAKES A LICKING AND KEEPS ON TICKING, Tretorns with no socks, and a butterfly net in hand. She is *not* dressed like a Hide-Behind because Hide-Behinds are eyeless white eels under the control of the Unstopping. They sniff out wherewithal like humans gravitate toward the smell of freshly baked cookies. Then they tunnel fast through the soil, yanking unsuspecting toys into the ground and sucking out that juicy, imaginative part of their souls with forked black tongues.

Peanut will *never* be a Hide-Behind. Ever. And if she were? She would never touch Rosemary since her wherewithal probably smells like—

Nancee pinches her arm. "Oh my God, Peanut. Shut up."

Rosemary rolls her eyes. "Aren't you tired of being called that?"

"Called what?"

"Peanut."

"No." Peanut lifts her chin. "I was dangerously small when I was born. It's part of my origin story. Soon after birth, I was found outside the town's quaint library, buried alive but my tiny heart still beating—"

"*Of course, it's not what it sounds like. My parents were always coming back to get me*," Rosemary says along with her. "I get it. Just like Everlee."

"Yes." Peanut clenches her fists. "I am just like Everlee."

"Totally." Rosemary gives Nancee a sideways look. "It's *wild* how your stories match."

A group of high schoolers dressed in camouflage—Ten Soldiers, although there are only eight and one is too short—walk by. "That makeup's sick, man," says one, pointing to Peanut's scar.

Cupping her hand over her cheek, she turns away.

"Nancee showed me the riddle you couldn't solve," Rosemary says.

"It's not that I can't solve it," Peanut says, glaring at Nancee. "I haven't solved it *yet*."

"So, if I've already figured it out, should I tell you?"

Before Peanut can say no—and she is definitely going to because Rosemary is baiting her, anyone can see that—Nancee instructs, "Close your mouth." She smears greasy white makeup across Peanut's cheeks and chin.

"This night is going to be epic," Rosemary whispers into Peanut's ear. "Just wait."

"Williwigs and Tiny Toys!" booms the mayor over a loudspeaker. "Let the Revealing begin!"

BLUE SKIES RED VINE RALLY

Join us to celebrate The Falling Children and
convince F. T. Goldhero to finish the last book!
Help us make this the BIGGEST Red Vine Rally ever!
$5 suggested donation AND a pack of Red Vines
(Twizzlers are okay)

Come for the

- Adult and children's costume contests
- Falling Children trivia contest
- Magical games
- Raffle (Win a trip to Harry Potter World!)
- Falling Children temporary tattoos
- T-shirts & hoodies for sale (cash only)
- Photo booth
- Face painting
- Snacks and drinks
- Live performance by Creative Ability,
  Blue Skies' newest cover band
- Special tribute to sixth-grade cancer survivor
  Rosemary Carver
- Routine by the Cross Creek Chickpea
  Cheerleaders
- OtherWay-themed Great Train Robbery
  (one night only!)
- And more!

Will we have A VERY SPECIAL GUEST???
Only time will tell!!!
Please do NOT park in front of the Pig-n-Pancake
or you will be towed.

All proceeds go to the Carver family.

44

By nine o'clock, crowds of Falling Children fill the streets. Peanut sees Benjamins chomping on Red Vines; freckled and ponytailed Huperzines, cheeks painted with glittering tears; and Everlees in '80s-era T-shirts, butterfly nets at the ready.

Rosemary keeps recording updates on Instagram. "Y'all, we're totally going viral tonight!" She has to shout to be heard over the mash-up of carnival music and '80s rock.

Ricky McAvoy, wearing a gray Gran Bere wig and carrying a worn medical bag, waves from across Main Street.

Peanut doesn't wave back. "You're wearing glasses," she cups her hands around her mouth and yells. "Gran Bere's glasses got broken at the end of book one."

"Sexy nightie." A tall boy with greasy hair and a T-shirt that reads I Can't Believe I Ate the Whole Thing nudges Nancee.

"It's not a nightie, it's the Squirrel Keeper's protective sleepwear," Peanut says. "Without it, he'd be turned back into a toy. Have you even read the books?"

The boy scowls. "Chill, freak."

"You're the freak if you think the Squirrel Keeper would wear a nightie," Peanut calls after him.

Once he's been swallowed back into the crowd, Nancee turns on her, her cheeks flushed red. "Why are you always embarrassing me? What is wrong with you?"

"This is all wrong." Peanut flings out her arms. "There's no such thing as vegan buttered fudge. 'Children' is spelled wrong in the banner by the bike shop. And why are they selling raffle tickets for Harry Potter World? Harry Potter doesn't know the Children! If this were my rally—"

"Well, it's not," Rosemary interrupts. "You didn't think of it. I did."

Her tone, and the way it makes Peanut feel, reminds her of the Depths of Despair in the OtherWay. When the Children try to cross it in book one, at first, they don't think it's that bad—maybe a little like wading through a cranberry bog that smells like a pigsty. Then, suddenly, they are up to their necks, unable to move, except to cry.

"Seriously?" Benjamin shouts as the dark slop of melancholy starts to pull them down, down, down...

(Luckily, he threw out a Red Vine, and a Knock-Knock pulled them all to safety.)

Peanut has encountered her own Depths of Despair once before—at the beginning of the summer, when Jessie felt compelled to sit her down and talk about What It Means to Grow Up.

"There are things that you're probably ready to know..." Jessie said haltingly.

"Seriously?" Peanut shouted as Jessie's clumsy explanations about puberty and teen pregnancy attempted to pull her down, down, down.

She covered her ears and ran from the room, successfully escaping into the Falling Children books. But now, even surrounded by people who can tell jokes in Williwig, even with the ability to drink Gran Bere's warm and nutritious honey-mud milk, and even knowing the real F. T. Goldhero is *at her house*, Peanut feels her toes unexpectedly touch the claggy edge of Despair again.

In the window of the pet store, she catches sight of her white lips and cheeks. Covered with makeup, her scar resembles a slug.

"Welcome, Blue Skytonians!" the mayor, an older man shaped like a dumpling, cries into a microphone. "F. T. Goldhero, if you're out there, this is for you!"

He leads the crowd of thousands in chanting, "*Fin*-ish the book! *Fin*-ish the book!"

Peanut watches as they punch the air with their fists.

"*Fin*-ish! *Fin*-ish!"

As they shout, Peanut can feel the night air around them thicken. A sour taste scratches at the back of her throat.

"Something bad is going to happen," she tells Nancee. "I can feel it."

Nancee isn't listening. She is chanting now, too.

~ ~

For the next hour, groups step onto the stage to act out their favorite scenes from the Falling Children books: Everlee, Huperzine, and Benjamin meeting in the orphanage for the first time. Gran Bere calmly pulling out a musket and shooting an entire pack of wild-eyed jack-in-the-boxes, then taking time to mend their springs. Oh! And the part in book three where Benjamin, fearing Everlee will be wiped off the map in a real-life game of Risk, assures her, "There's always an OtherWay."

Peanut mouths the words she knows by heart. Still, dread oozes around her ankles. No one understands or loves the Children like she does. No one *needs* them like she does. And they need her, too, she is sure of it.

"Now *that* is the best costume ever." Someone whistles.

Peanut turns to look. Balancing on the edge of the cowboy fountain, scanning the crowd, is the Unstopping.

He's wearing his ragged black hoodie and dirty loose pants. And like the Unstopping in the books, he lifts his hands, pressing the rings on his fingers together to summon uncertain magic.

Everyone watches as he hastily pours a bottle of black liquid into the cooler of dry ice at his feet, shrouding himself in a heavy dark mist. When it clears, everyone claps.

Then one of the Unstopping's eyes lasers through the crowd and hooks directly onto Peanut.

It's time we talk, he mouths.

Claps and whistles from the crowd drown out the sound of Peanut's heart.

"Niiice," someone says.

"That's next level," another agrees.

"You know why I'm here," the Unstopping says to Peanut.

She hears his voice clearly in her head.

"We need to go," Peanut tells Nancee. She pulls her backpack tighter onto her shoulders.

"What? No way!" Tilting her head back, Nancee drops a handful of Skittles into her mouth. "Rosemary and I are up next."

"I mean it." Peanut looks back at the Unstopping, now striding toward her through the crowd. "My life may be in danger. Or the life of someone I know."

"Oh, please." Nancee rolls her eyes. "You never like when things aren't about you."

"What's that supposed to mean?"

"Exactly what I said!" Nancee has to shout to be heard over another round of applause, and then Rosemary grabs her hand, and together they climb onstage.

Peanut can hear the train whistle and gunshots from the special train robbery up in the mountains. She thinks of Jessie in her Everlee costume and wonders if she'll still shout, *Please! Don't hurt my baby!*

"In case you guys didn't know," Nancee says into the microphone, "my best friend, Rosemary, organized this. She is the biggest fan of the Falling Children in, like, the universe."

Someone blasts an air horn. Peanut glances behind her. She can just make out the top of the Unstopping's head, bobbing closer through the crowd.

Peanut pushes her way toward the stage, hiding in front of a stout woman in a yellow-feathered Knock-Knock costume. "What do you call a dream about soda?" she asks no one in particular, flapping her wings.

Rosemary approaches the microphone, waving a piece of paper above her head. "You guys, I want you to hear this. F. T. Goldhero wrote me a letter."

She pushes her hair off her shoulders, blinks back tears—they are fake, everyone can see that, Peanut thinks—and reads in a crystal voice:

"My dear Rosemary,

"I am besieged with letters from fans every day, but yours is the first I have felt compelled to respond to.

"You, my dear, who planned the world's largest rally while recovering from cancer, are clearly my number one fan. I am touched by your fortitude.

"Everlee, Benjamin, and Huperzine Falling would never exist without your imagination and loyalty, which is why, in my final book, I have chosen to name a character after you."

"What?" Peanut feels as if all the air has been sucked from her lungs.

"A Fanta sea, get it?" crows the outsize Knock-Knock behind her. "Aw! Aw!"

And then the Unstopping lunges at Peanut, his dirty fingernails wrapping around her arm, his fishy breath striking her ear. "Let's go somewhere," he says, holding tight as she squirms. "Just you and me."

"Hey." The Knock-Knock nudges him with the plastic cup of beer she's holding. "What do you call it when you have a dream about soda?"

"Begone, birdbrain," the Unstopping says.

"Rude!" The Knock-Knock gives a little burp and flaps its wings faster. "Rude! Rude!"

It is just enough distraction for Peanut to pull free of the Unstopping's grip and hoist herself onto the front of the stage. Tucking her elbows and head, like Buzz does when he falls off his skateboard, she rolls toward the podium. Her backpack makes it difficult, but Peanut still manages to leap to her feet with a little *sproing*.

Rosemary covers the microphone when she sees Peanut. "What are you doing? Get off the stage, dwerp."

Peanut will not let herself be bullied, not by Jessie or the Unstopping and definitely not by lying Rosemary Carver, whom the Children would *never* want in their books.

Moving forward, Peanut grabs the letter from Rosemary's hand.

"This is a counterfeit!" she shouts, ripping it into confetti. "You don't know F. T. Goldhero. You don't know anything about her! This is all fake, everything here!"

"My letter!" Rosemary wails.

A collective gasp rises from the audience.

Peanut, not sure what to do next, stands there, panting slightly, her fists full of paper.

"Get off the stage!" Nancee warns. "I mean it, Peanut."

From the crowd come phrases like, "Yeah," and "Get the eff off," and "*Boooooo*."

Peanut sees the Unstopping beckoning to her from the edge of the stage steps. When he smiles, the strange lone baby tooth in his mouth catches the light.

"We can do things the easy way, or we can do them the hard way," the Unstopping warns Everlee in book one.

Naturally, Everlee chooses the OtherWay.

Peanut rummages through her backpack. She will not bow down to the Unstopping. He will not capture her. He will not fling her wherewithal to the disparate corners of the universe. Imagination will win. It *has* to.

Peanut lifts her bear spray. But before she can remove the safety clasp, Nancee yanks the can from her hand.

"You're ruining everything!" she says. "I'm sick of you and your games!"

The notebook lies exposed in Peanut's backpack. Nancee scoops it up and waves it, threateningly, in Peanut's face.

"These words are just more crap you made up. They mean nothing," she says.

"That's not true. I haven't figured them out yet!"

"Like you still don't know who your mother is? Please. Everyone in town knows! They don't say anything because your dad's their doctor, and they feel sorry for you," Nancee says. "But you know what? I don't anymore because all you think about is yourself."

"That's not true!" Peanut cups her hand over her scar. It's cold, but the skin around it feels hot.

"Girls." The mayor is back onstage, holding out his age-spotted hand for the microphone. "Come on now. Now is not the time or place."

Nancee doesn't move.

"You think you're smarter than everyone else, but if you're such a genius, how come you never guessed that Jessie is your mom?"

LIBBY LOST AND FOUND

Peanut is crying, and she hates to cry.

"And now?" Nancee gestures to the Unstopping, who is already retreating into the crowd. "I bet we all know who your freak dad is, too. You've got his ugly evil eye."

Peanut will not cry. She will *not*.

She clenches her fists, ready to punch Nancee, but her feet won't move. She is stuck fast in the Depths of Despair, she knew it!

"If you ever want to read the last Falling Children book, you better be nice to me," she shouts.

"Please." Rosemary crosses her arms. "What's that got to do with anything?"

Peanut grabs the microphone and hears her voice reverberate through the town. "I know who F. T. Goldhero is. She's at my house right now." The words rise from her, like the blood-soaked sword Everlee pulls from Gran Bere's chest in book four.

Except, of course, that Gran Bere still dies.

45

"I can't believe you let her go." Jessie's cheeks flash with anger. "The one thing you're supposed to do is watch her. The one thing! And you—"

"Take it easy." Buzz checks the clock on the dashboard of the car. "She's only been there a couple of hours. And she's with Nancee."

"You still don't get it, do you?" Jessie says, but she looks at Libby when she says it.

It's too dark to make out anything but the reflective paint on the road. The lane dividers look like ellipses.

And then...

And then what?

Orange-and-white barricades block the streets downtown. Buzz has to park on the outskirts, in front of Whippity Jim's. Jessie doesn't wait for him or Libby but stalks right up the street, elbowing her way through the crowd.

"You didn't have to come," Buzz says as he opens Libby's door.

"I did," she hears herself insist, although she's already forgotten why they're here and what the fuss is about. Around them is every nightmarish version of Falling Children characters that Libby can imagine.

There's a much older Everlee with a swastika tattooed on her forehead, packing a handgun in the waistband of her shorts. A Gran

Bere with a bladder of Chardonnay shoved into her sports bra, a tube leading into her mouth, screaming at her crying toddlers. ("God, I fucking hate you!") A zombie Williwig, with (fake?) blood running from its glassy eyes. ("Grrrr…brains.") It slicks its lips as they pass.

Jessie makes a beeline to a food cart, where a girl wearing a white nightgown like the Squirrel Keeper is paying for a corn dog.

"Where's Peanut, Nancee?" Jessie demands.

"I don't know," Nancee says, taking small fast bites of the corn dog. "I haven't seen her."

Even Libby can tell she is lying.

"Busheknos," Nancee says, with her mouth full of corn dog.

"What?" Jessie snaps. "Is that some Falling Children garbage? What does that mean?"

Nancee swallows. "She knows about you," she says. "Peanut knows."

Color swims from Jessie's face.

"Happy now?" she says to Buzz. She has to raise her voice over the thumping music.

They go from tent to tent. In the first one, a leather-skinned woman dressed like the Seer airbrushes prophecies onto cheeks.

Everlee is the password.

Furry Williwig ears and feet are sold inside the second tent. After that is a beer garden.

Libby is reminded of the Hall of a Thousand Doors.

Thirteen to get you trapped forever, one to get you home.

Which is, of course, one of the Unstopping's tricks, because thirteen of the doors *trap* a visitor for eternity while only one (number thirteen) can lead the Children home.

The last tent, in front of the library, sells Falling Children posters, bookmarks, key chains, stress balls, hoodies, yoga mats, and—of course—stuffed animals. No Peanut.

"Maybe she went home," Buzz says.

"No." With a desperate look, Jessie runs toward the library.

Buzz and Libby follow her around the old building. The back parking lot, surrounded by a grove of trees, is deserted except for an old rusted dumpster. Libby is surprised at how quickly noise from the rally recedes.

"Peanut? Are you back here?" Jessie calls.

There's no answer.

Libby hears water running. Did she leave her kitchen sink on again? *Focus*, she tells herself.

"Peanut!" Jessie calls. "Come on. Please? Come out."

"She's not back here," Buzz says.

But he's wrong. When Jessie lifts the plastic lid of the dumpster, there is Peanut, curled among the bags of trash.

Her cheeks are smeared with greasy gray paint, and her hair is ratted. One eye stares at the ground, the other at Jessie. Both droop with tears.

"What are you doing in here?" Jessie asks, although it's clear from her voice that she already knows the answer. "It's not safe."

Peanut launches a handful of trash in her direction. "Why? Are you worried I'll die?"

Jessie opens her mouth. "Peanut—"

Leaping to her feet, Peanut shouts, "Don't call me that! And don't talk to me—not ever, ever again!"

She hurls herself over the edge of the dumpster and tears back to the rally.

"Peanut!" Jessie calls. "Wait!"

Buzz pulls Libby along as they make their way back by the tents, the thumping music, the cart selling Marvelous Marbled Mayberry Melts. The crowd is as thick and slow-moving as the stretchy candy, yet strong enough to break Libby's hand free of Buzz's.

326

In an instant, he is gone—*Was he ever there?* part of Libby questions—and instead, she faces a girl with shell-colored lip gloss and a glossy sweep of blond hair, a bandage placed just so on the bridge of her nose. "Why are you looking for Peanut? Who are you?"

"Libby Weeks." She says it automatically, as if the girl is with the police and has asked for her driver's license and registration.

"Are you staying with the Bixtons?"

Libby looks down at her hand, but Buzz is no longer holding it. *Is that a bad sign?*

"Yes," she says, answering her own question.

The girl is invading Libby's personal space now, looking her up and down. "Is anyone else there with you? Like an old man from England?"

"No." Libby takes a step back. "Just me." Warning bells sound in her head, but there's so much noise already in there that they only make a soft tinkling sound, no louder than a kindergarten xylophone.

"Then is it really—you? Seriously?"

"Me as in—" Libby's unsure what the girl wants to hear. She looks around for Buzz. The music goes *thump, thump, thump.*

The girl places a hand over her heart. "Are you—F. T. Goldhero?"

No is all, really, that Libby needs to say. There are many ways to do so:

Of course not!

No.

A shake of her head.

But Libby has never thought fast in emergencies, and this is no exception.

"No one's supposed to know."

The girl's blue eyes brim with tears. "I knew you'd come tonight. Your books are, like, the best thing that ever happened to me. They got me through cancer. And when a bully tried to break my nose."

She gives Libby a beautiful wide smile. "I love the Children so much."

"Then could you please not say anything?" Libby looks around. "I'm really not—"

"There you are," Buzz says. "It's like a fucking mosh pit in here." He takes Libby's hand, then stops when he sees Rosemary. "What are you staring at?"

"OMG. Squill Boy and F. T. Goldhero?" Rosemary lifts her phone. "I am *so* breaking the Internet."

~⁓~

Once the car begins moving, Libby closes her eyes. She needs to think about what to do, what just happened, and why. But all she can register is embarrassment.

She is an adult, not a child. Why can't she act like one?

"I was going to tell you," Jessie is saying. "I was waiting for the right time. You don't understand how hard this has been on me."

Peanut, who's been slumped against the car door, sits upright. "Don't talk," she shouts. She kicks the back of Jessie's seat, punctuating her words. "I. Hate. You."

The car slows around a curve.

"What's wrong?" Libby asks. "What's happening?"

No one answers. Buzz squeezes the steering wheel so tightly, his knuckles ghost. Peanut curls herself into a ball, her head buried between her knees.

Libby fumbles to roll down her window. She needs air, so much air. Something ominous is racing toward them, she can feel it, and when it arrives, she will not be able to breathe.

"Peanut," Jessie says in a measured voice, "Listen to me. You have to understand—"

"I don't want to understand! I don't want to understand anything about you."

"Understand what?" Libby asks.

They both talk at once.

"She left me for dead," Peanut sobs.

"I was scared," Jessie insists. "I didn't know what else to do."

Later, Libby will wish she handled this moment differently. That she undid her seat belt and slid closer to the girl. That she put her arm around Peanut's slight shoulders and said something reassuring, even "shhhh," the white noise that emanates naturally from mothers, even ones of fictional children.

Instead, Libby stays silent, her hands in her lap, while neurons in her brain crackle like Pop Rocks. *I can use this*, she thinks. *This is it. I can use this.*

Buzz meets her gaze in the rearview mirror.

"I'm sorry," Libby says.

She means it. She is a horrible person.

A police car roars up the hill in front of them, its lights flashing. They are coming for her. The jig. The rig? Is up. They're on to her.

"Perfect. Annie Yolen's stuck behind her fridge again." Jessie thumps the dashboard.

But Annie Yolen isn't wedged onto her side on the cold dust-balled linoleum in her kitchen. At least, not right now.

The Bixtons' street is lined with news trucks and reporters. Fans clutch Falling Children books or stuffed animals. Some hold hastily drawn posters.

GIVE US THE CHILDREN!

FINISH THE BOOK OR YOU'RE FINISHED!

WHERE ARE THE CHILDREN?

As they pull into Buzz's driveway, cameras and phones rise toward them.

"Libby!" Glenn yells from the crowd. "Remember! You know whose story this is!"

Google "F.T. Goldhero Falling Children"

TOP STORIES

Falling Children frenzy descends over town

By late September, Blue Skies, Colo., a cross between Stars Hollow
and a Wild West movie set, is typically down to the dregs of its
tourist season. Today, the streets are clogged with news trucks,
millennials dressed as teddy bears, and tired, teary children holding
signs that read, "Reveal Yourself!" This tucked-away mountain town
is believed to be home to the beloved author of the...

NYT, 1 minute ago

F. T. Goldhero: We know the "where"; now we need the "who"

The feeding frenzy around the "Falling Children" intensifies. Groton
& Sons, publisher to the bestselling fantasy series, has confirmed
that the series' anonymous author is indeed finishing their last book
in the remote town of Blue Skies, Colo. (Pop: 403). Yet now that we
know where they are—down to the unimposing yellow farmhouse
in which they're puzzling out the Falling Children's fate—the "who"
remains a mystery. According to local tax records, the 1888 home is
owned by...

The Washington Post, 3 minutes ago

Falling Children author "not who you think"

Groton & Sons, publisher of the bestselling Falling Children series,
has a message for fans: "Don't believe everything you read."
"F. T. Goldhero always has tricks up his sleeve," notes editor
Merry Jaminsky. "He's a clever man and won't allow himself to be

revealed until he's good and ready." This statement is in response to a TikTok video, now viewed over 6 million times, that...

Chicago Tribune, 7 minutes ago

17 people I hope AREN'T F. T. Goldhero because—sad

I've been intrigued by who writes the Falling Children since I was a zit-faced tween and still had toys of my own. I want the FaChi to end in a big, colorful way but even more, I want F. T. Goldhero's identity to blow me away. "But alas and abut," as Everlee says, that may not happen. Click through for the saddest possible FTG reveals— besides, you know, Arie from *The Bachelor*.

BoredPanda, 9 minutes ago

HELL YESSS: Baron McBroom wants Falling Children fans to fight back

FaChi Army, I stand with Baron McBroom! Someone is trying to SLANDER the real F.T. Goldhero by pretending to be him. Don't fall for it! We all know a boring fugly woman past her prime cannot write the best, most important books in the world. THIS IS A SCAM! Like McBroom, I am organizing a mission to "Blue Skies" to FIND THE TRUTH. Brothers, who's with me?

Reddit.com > Falling_Children, 12 minutes ago

EXCLUSIVE: "Did I just have an affair with F.T. Goldhero?"

A dog park in Princeton, New Jersey, may not sound like a pick-up spot. Or where F.T. Goldhero, the most famous (and sought-after) author in the world, would be hanging out. But on a steamy August morning, while exercising my Welsh corgi, Bruce, I crossed paths with a middle-aged woman in active wear who revealed her mutt was named Rolf—yes, like *that* Rolf. In a thinly veiled bid for my attention, she left *without her dog*, then waited for me to track her down and...

Buzzfeed, 18 minutes ago

46

Jessie and Buzz pull curtains and lock doors, but Libby doesn't feel safe. Rolf won't stop barking.

Danger, he warns in dog language. *Everywhere. Danger.*

"I don't get it," Buzz says. "How do they know it's you? Who told?"

"Private property, folks," Freddie, the police chief, bellows outside. "Back into the street."

Libby kneels on the floor of the living room in between the couch and coffee table. *Breathe*, she tells herself. She imagines herself as a scuba diver, a tank of extra air on her back, swimming past schools of tropical fish. . . .

Empty tank, foot caught in seaweed, approaching shark. . . .

Buzz sits beside her. He rests his phone against her knee, and they watch a live stream of the swelling crowd outside.

Libby's apartment in Princeton is surrounded, too.

"Hold up, you're saying we share a wall with F. T. Goldhero?" a skinny college kid in square black glasses is saying to a reporter. "The old lady with the dog?"

On X, #FTNoHero is trending.

Is my child the only one crushed by this? reads one tweet. It includes footage of the video that Rosemary took. In it, Libby looks confused and on the verge of tears.

Danger, Rolf barks. #DangerEverywhere.

But Rolf knows Libby better than anyone, so why is he growling *at* her?

~~~

It only takes another hour for Merry to track down Libby. Buzz has to show her where the phone is in the kitchen. The cord whorls around her arm.

"Is 'whorls' a real word?"

Merry doesn't answer. "Do you understand Groton could take you to court? Have you even *read* your contract?"

"A long time ago," Libby says. "Maybe? I didn't think—"

Merry doesn't want to hear it. She reels off legal-sounding phrases like "disregard of contractual progress updates," "failure to deliver required manuscript," and "violation of nondisclosure agreement" before adding, "You're in a world of shit, Libby."

"But I'm almost done," she says.

Merry doesn't believe her. "Marketing is shitting themselves. Do not speak to anyone else. And if I were you," Merry says before she hangs up, "I'd hire myself a good lawyer."

Buzz replaces the receiver. "Why'd you let her talk to you like that?"

"This is my fault." Libby's not sure he can hear her over the chants of "*Re-veal yourself! Re-veal yourself!*" carrying through the window.

"How is it your fault? They need you."

The panic that stings her lungs like nettles is so familiar, it's almost soothing.

But it's not Merry or Groton & Sons or even her fans Libby is worried about disappointing. It's the Children, *her* Children, who are still lost in the forest.

47

Peanut wakes the next morning feeling like her mouth is lined with cotton and her head is splitting in two. It's not until she sees Jessie looking out the window that Peanut remembers she doesn't have the flu, that there is a worse reason she feels sick.

She pulls the covers over her head.

"Go away," she says.

"What if I want to talk to you?"

At another point in her life, Peanut might have answered, "*It's past time to make amends. The mere timbre of your voice hardens my resolve against you.*" (Everlee, speaking to the Unstopping, book two.)

But not today. Today she lies in bed and lets herself sink deeper into the Depths of Despair. No one knows how deep it goes or what lies on the bottom, but today Peanut will find out.

"You're going to have to talk to me sooner or later." Jessie places a hand on Peanut's shoulder, but Peanut shakes it off.

"Leave me alone!"

She repeats the words, louder and louder, until Jessie finally does.

A cross-stitch of Pompou's mocks Peanut from the wall. YOUR FAMILY CHOOSES YOU, reads the woolly red lettering. Jessie gave it to her last Christmas, the liar.

Peanut yanks the hoop from its nail. Using the spine of book five as a hammer, she smashes the wood, then opens her window and flings the shards outside.

A sea of reporters is gathered outside, many holding microphones or bulky cameras to their shoulders.

"Little girl!" one of them shouts. "Hey, kid!"

"Can you confirm—"

"Where's F.T.?"

"Tell us about F.T.!"

"Is the last book finished?"

Peanut slams the window shut. She crawls underneath her bed and covers her head with her hands.

If only her father were back from Mrs. Halfchap's, she thinks. He'd know how to get these bone grocers to leave.

But then Peanut thinks about Jessie getting pregnant in high school and her father—a *doctor*—never noticing. Or how he pretends no one in town knows he and Mrs. Halfchap are in love, while Mr. Halfchap lies dying, right in front of them. And Peanut realizes her father hides when he is scared, too.

~

Peanut isn't sure how long she's been lying under her bed, amid a few wayward pencils and forgotten planets of dust, when a knock comes on her door.

She doesn't move. She is Everlee encased in amber (book three).

Buzz comes into her room anyway. "Why are you under there?"

He doesn't understand her. No one does.

"Go away."

"Brought you food." He drops a bag of Funyuns on the floor, but

Peanut ignores it. Instead, she pulls book one of the Falling Children off her shelf and drags it toward her. She already knows the first page by heart:

If you are reading this book, you—like Everlee Falling—need a place to hide.

Buzz lowers himself to the ground beside her.

"You could have told me," Peanut says, her eyes still trained on the page. "My whole life so far, you knew, and you didn't say anything."

"I kept telling Jessie to tell you. It wasn't my story to tell."

Everlee needs her hiding spot quickly. As she tears around the corner of Fifth and Main, here comes the orphanage headmistress behind her. Gladys has a cruel mouth and black hair slicked into a topknot. She reeks of sauerkraut and mustache bleach. But even dressed in an itchy horsehair skirt-suit, even wearing wooden clogs that are two sizes too small, she is a fast runner.

Sighing, Buzz opens the bag of Funyuns and offers one to Peanut. It's a kind gesture, but Peanut doesn't want kindness. She needs anger to pull out of Despair.

Unlike Everlee Falling in the next paragraph, there is no squirrel who will point out impatiently to her, "Oh for pity's sake, girl. Go the OtherWay!" There is no alley, streetlights flickering with secrets, that will suddenly appear, and no magic toy store to spring from the ground and open its door to hide her inside.

You, the store seemed to say to Everlee. I've been waiting for you.

No one is waiting for Peanut. She does not have a special destiny. She does not have special parents. She will live an ordinary life, become an ordinary adult, and then she will die an ordinary, sad death.

"Look," Buzz says, his mouth full. "When you love someone, you have to see the person they want to be, not who they are now."

It's a quote from book two. It does not make Peanut feel better that he's quoted it verbatim.

Outside, cars honk and Freddy warns, "Back it up, people. Come on." The leaves on the trees outside the window churn as a news helicopter sounds overhead.

"What the fuck are they doing?" Buzz limps to the window. "They should leave her alone already. What the fuck is wrong with people?"

He is finally as angry as Peanut wants him to be, but it's not about her and how she's been lied to. It's because of Libby.

Squill Boy, she thinks. She suddenly *wants* to watch Buzz fall off his skateboard and almost die. And not once. She wants it on autoplay. She wants to watch him get hurt over and over and over again.

"She doesn't fucking deserve this," Buzz is saying. "Why can't they—"

"I was the one who told," Peanut interrupts. "That Libby's F. T. Goldhero. I told everyone."

"What?" Buzz turns around.

"That's right. It was me." Peanut raises her voice. "The Children are my family—my *real* family—and she's killing them."

Deep inside, the words are also meant to wound him and Jessie, her father, the Unstopping, maybe the entire world.

"We are standing here in Blue Skies, Colorado, a Rocky Mountain boom town once known for its gold and now allegedly the home of F. T. Goldhero, the highest-grossing author in the world," a reporter says outside.

"Libby didn't ask for this." Buzz gestures to the window. "All she wanted was your help."

But Peanut's anger has latched on to Libby like a magnet. It was Libby who came here. Libby who wrote the Children into a dead end. This is all Libby's fault.

Sliding out from underneath her bed, Peanut yanks open the door and runs from the room.

Libby's suitcase is on the floor in Jessie's bedroom, and the perfect idea comes to Peanut: she will take the manuscript and burn it. The children will be in limbo forever, but that's better than dying slowly and painfully, forgotten in a forest.

"Peanut, come on," Buzz calls.

She can hear him limping down the hall and slams the door, putting her back against it in case he tries to come in. "Leave me alone!"

"Whatever you're doing, stop."

Peanut slides the dresser in front of the door. After digging through Libby's suitcase—how many gray cardigans does she have?—she pulls the manuscript from the bottom and stuffs it under her T-shirt. There are matches in the kitchen. She'll get them, then sneak into the woods and start a bonfire.

"If the fire inside you dies out, strike a match against your soul and start another" as Gran Bere says.

Peanut's eyes light on two giant bottles of Tylenol.

How many pills would she need to make everything around her go away?

"Open up," Buzz says, trying the doorknob. "Come on."

The lids say they're childproof, but the first one twists off easily in Peanut's hand. A full glass of water waits on the nightstand, and Peanut gulps to wash down one, then two, then three capsules.

She feels nothing.

"Peanut, come on. I mean it."

"Go away," she says with her mouth full. The pills knock against her teeth. "*I* mean it!"

Peanut hears cursing, followed by Buzz's uneven steps on the stairs. He's going to tattle on her to Jessie, she's sure of it. She moves the dresser back and opens the door so she can hear what he says.

"I told you," Buzz says to Jessie. "For fucking years, I told you to tell her."

"You literally fall off a skateboard for a living. Why would I listen to you?"

Peanut takes a handful of more pills. It will serve them both right if she dies. At least then she can be with the Children and not stuck with the worst family in the world.

When she is up to twenty smooth little capsules, the front door slams.

"What in God's name is going on?" bellows Peanut's father, who is not really her father but an *accomplice.*

Twenty-one, twenty-two, twenty-three. Peanut sits on Jessie's bed and swallows the pills dry.

48

If only Libby could crawl inside Pompou's and stay there forever. There would be chess pieces to dispense shrewd advice and stuffed animals to climb into her lap and purr. *But Pompou's has burned to the ground, remember?* she reminds herself. *Thanks to you.*

Libby runs her hand over the Bixtons' overstuffed sofa, its printed yellow flowers softened with age. She stares at the water stains on the coffee table and Dr. Bixton's shelves of medical reference books. What will she do to this family?

Libby has an uneasy feeling she's done it already.

Although the sun rakes the crowds outside, Libby can't stop shivering. Even under a blanket, even holding a mug of tea that she can't remember sipping but which Buzz occasionally refills.

Liquid sloshes onto the couch cushion. Libby can feel the wetness seeping into her pants. She's embarrassed to ask for a towel. It's easier to not move.

Reporters scratch closer to the front door. A few have found their way into the woods behind the house. Light reflects off their camera lenses and makes Libby see spots.

When Buzz opens the back door and steps onto the deck, fresh sunshine streaks into the house.

"What are you doing?" Jessie raises her voice. "They'll see you!"

"So?" Buzz says. "We can't stay here forever."

Grabbing a bag of cookies shaped like circus animals from the pantry, he steps outside and shuts the door.

Jessie sinks into a chair opposite Libby and puts her bare feet on the coffee table. Her toenails are painted violet.

"He's going to get sick eating all those cookies," Jessie says after a while.

Libby doesn't answer.

"I'm not a villain," Jessie says. "I was a scared kid."

Libby tries to move out of the puddle of tea—*Have I been sitting in it all night?*—but Jessie mistakes her silence as an invitation to keep talking.

It is not a complicated story, but it is a sad one: A lonely girl. A sad, odd boy, abused by his father and bullied at school.

"Mrs. Hader? Peanut's teacher? She was the worst," Jessie says. "The day Orson showed up with cigarette burns all over his neck, she called him 'Ashtray.'"

One night, Jessie stumbled across Orson in the woods, a gash in his head the size of a quarter, bone flashing underneath.

"I was going to be a doctor," Jessie points out. "I knew I could help him."

They sneaked into Dr. Bixton's clinic, and she stitched up the cut.

"Then, I don't know, one thing led to another." She sighs. "He was different back then. Sad, not scary."

When her period was late, Jessie asked Buzz to steal her a pregnancy test. "If I'd gotten caught," she says, "my dad would have locked me in my room until I was forty. Buzz got arrested, and he got a 'now, son' talk and a camping trip."

Libby swirls the leftover tea leaves in her mug. In her head, Jessie's words slosh, too.

Orson Child.

Orson Unstopping Child.

"I was so scared, I didn't tell anyone," Jessie is saying. "I barely showed. Although my dad had the nerve to tell me I was 'letting myself go.' Can you believe it? Those were his exact words."

Unstopping Secret Child.

"People think I bombed the SAT," Jessie goes on, "but I'd like to see them get through the math section while having contractions. I waited so long, I didn't have time to go home, just out back of the library, into that little wooded area."

Unstopping Children Woods.

Jessie describes the umbilical cord wrapped around Peanut's neck, the slick feel of her skin, the stillness of her chest.

"She was dead," Jessie says. "I swear she was. What was I supposed to do? I was fifteen!"

Unstopping Children Woods Dead.

"I was going to go back," she says defensively. "It wasn't just Buzz's idea. I needed to think."

Abandoned children. Lost Children.

"But why didn't you tell Peanut?"

Jessie looks at her incredulously. "Would you want to know your mother buried you alive? Or that, oh, I don't know, the freaking Unstopping is your father?"

Libby looks down at her hands. They are trembling, as if they are writing without a pen.

What if she's having a seizure? Or a stroke?

"Stop," she tells them. "That's enough."

Jessie thinks Libby is talking to her.

"Oh, pardon me." She stands, hands in the air. "I didn't realize I was boring you with my life."

~ ~

Libby is not used to being handed other people's feelings. She feels like a coat check girl in an old-timey movie, sinking under the itchy weight of vicuña and mink.

She craves her lonely bed and cockeyed crocheted blankets, her desk confettied with Post-its, her predictable and quiet runs with Rolf to the dog park. Being alone, being *lonely*, is easier than figuring out what to say to others.

I'm sorry is all she can think of.

It's true: She's sorry for Peanut. Sorry for Jessie. Sorry for Orson, even as the Unstopping. And sorry for herself because, quite literally, she is forgetting something.

Libby is not sure how she will get home. Still, by late afternoon, she decides to pack.

When she sees Peanut curled on top of Jessie's covers, at first she thinks she's walked into the wrong bedroom.

"Sorry," Libby whispers and tiptoes out, shutting the door behind her.

She retraces her steps down the hall.

Bathroom. Linen closet. Dr. Bixton's bedroom. Peanut's bedroom. Libby steps back into Jessie's pink room. It is a little like being inside a baking cupcake.

Peanut is sleeping on the bed.

"I'll just be a minute," Libby says, mostly to herself.

She packs her suitcase, making sure to check every surface and even under the bed, among shoeboxes and photo albums. She wants no trace of her to stay here.

Libby can't remember if the lipsticks and hair ties on Jessie's dresser are hers. She sweeps them into her hand anyway, then zips her suitcase and rumbles it to the stairs. She'll write Peanut a letter when she gets home and thank her for trying to help. There's no point in waking her.

Yet, even as she's thinking this, Libby goes back to the room and lightly touches Peanut's head. "I'm leaving," she says.

Peanut doesn't move. Her scalp is clammy. Again, there is the nagging feeling that Libby is forgetting something.

She scans the room. No underwear left on the floor. No socks under the bed. No wallet or phone because those are long gone. She spies an open canister of Tylenol on the nightstand and scoops it up, replacing the cap. That would be a bad thing to leave lying around.

Downstairs, Libby is snapping on Rolf's leash when it hits her. Her manuscript is missing.

Rolf in tow, Libby heads back upstairs. The draft of the last book isn't on Jessie's dresser or in the closet or the nightstand or confused in the magazines on the floor or camouflaged among the framed pictures—it's disappeared.

Libby gives Peanut a gentle, apologetic shake. "Peanut?" she whispers. "Wake up."

She doesn't.

Libby rests her hand on the girl's cheek. "Peanut?"

Peanut's face and neck are cold. So are Libby's socked feet, and she realizes she's standing in a puddle of vomit.

Libby needs to call someone, but panic blurs her thoughts. After minutes of searching for her cell phone, she finds an old rotary dial in the hallway and dials "9" but can't find "11" on the number pad. Frustrated, she hangs up. Minutes stretch as she stares at the phone and thinks what should happen next.

Outside, people cheer and chant and boo. Maybe one of them will know how to help. Libby is struggling to open the window in the hallway when Jessie comes upstairs.

"What are you doing?"

"She's not moving," Libby says, tugging at the window sash. "Can you help me get this open? It's stuck."

"It's not stuck. You didn't unlock it." Jessie twists the locks, and the window rises easily, a warm breeze smiling in. "Who's not moving?" She scans the crowd, which has turned toward them in one synchronous motion, like a flash mob preparing to dance.

Libby points to the bedroom.

And then Jessie is flying past her, and Dr. Bixton and Buzz are there, too, and where did Mrs. Halfchap come from? Because here she is, taking Libby's arm and pulling her out of the way.

"I don't know what happened," Libby says.

She sits with Mrs. Halfchap on a bench in the hallway with Rolf on his leash and her suitcase next to her and listens to herself cry and her brain go *hmmmmmmm* like an idling car.

"Shhh, shhh," Mrs. Halfchap says and pats Libby's shoulder.

And then an ambulance crew—where did they come from?— trundles downstairs with their scritch-scratchy black bags and blue-gloved hands and Peanut, strapped into an aluminum stretcher with a mask of oxygen hooked over her nose.

Jessie and Buzz leave, too.

"They're taking her to Cross Creek," Dr. Bixton tells Mrs. Halfchap. "We'll run some tests and try to figure out what's going on."

He turns to Libby, handing her the manuscript. "I believe this is yours."

His tone is accusing. Libby tries to shove the papers into her suitcase, but something's in the way. Turning the suitcase onto its side, Libby unzips its belly. Once she moves the Tylenol bottles—or, well, Dr. Bixton snatches them up—the book fits just fine.

Show all history

Clear recent history

Restore previous session

Recently closed tabs

Recently closed windows

Inbox (4,322) ftgoldhero@gmail.com—Gmail

Falling Children books FT Goldhero—Google search

How write a happy ending—Google search

Prevent panic attack—Google search

TRAIN ROBBERS BROKE THIS DUDE'S IPAD! Hilarious video of
     Blue Skies's Great Train Robbery—YouTube

Buzz skateboarder—Google search

EPIC wipeout Squirrel Keeper eats skater's LUNCH—YouTube

How people fall in love—Google search

How fast can you fall in love—Google search

Clam Box Blue Skies, Colorado "Try Our Rocky Mountain Oysters."

Can Your Brain Fool You into Thinking You're in Love?—Psych
     Pearls

How long does hope last—Google search

New treatments for dementia?—Google search

Dementia Research: What we still don't know I The Cognitive
     Council

How much Tylenol can kill you—Google search

The Web Doctr I Tylenol Poisoning (Acetaminophen Overdose)

How to say you're sorry when it's complicated—Google search

You've Hurt a Friend. How to Make Amends. I FriendshipFaqs.com

Am I a bad person—Google search

49

Libby doesn't want to be here. She doesn't trust hospitals and the growling, snapping machines leashed to their walls. She doesn't want to think of Peanut trying to end her life.

This isn't happening, she tells herself.

Nurses go past, their pants rubbing their inner thighs.

A doctor across the ICU glances at Libby. His placid expression—or maybe it's his glasses—reminds her of Dr. Whatsit. She wonders if he misses her. How long has she been gone?

"Here," says Mrs. Halfchap, patting Libby's arm when they reach Peanut's room.

She goes inside first and makes it look effortless, an Olympic figure skater executing a triple axel. Libby freezes in the hallway.

Go, she orders her feet. *Go witness what you've done.*

Nothing happens.

It's like being at her computer, staring at her screen, and not knowing what to write.

When Buzz comes into the hall, Libby doesn't ask if Peanut will be okay. She doesn't want to know if the answer is no. And if someone's already told her, how could she have forgotten?

"That was supposed to be you, right?" Buzz asks, gesturing to the room. "Taking all those pills?"

A monitor inside the room beeps.

"Is she going to be okay?"

Buzz scuffs his sneaker against the floor. "We don't know yet. No one's told us."

Dr. Bixton steps into the hallway, holding the door open for Jessie.

"Go home for a while," Dr. Bixton is saying. "Take a shower, get some food—I'll stay."

"But what if she wakes up? I want to—"

Jessie's eyes narrow when she sees Libby. "This is your fault," she says. "You put this idea in Peanut's head. You and your books."

"I'm so sorry." Libby can only bring herself to tell this to Jessie's shoes. They are cheap flats, shoe-colored, but she can't think of the word.

"Are you? I don't think you give a shit," Jessie says. "To you, she's just another character who serves a purpose and then, 'Oh, look at that! Let's kill them off for more drama.'"

"Shut up, Jess," Buzz says, but Jessie isn't done.

"You didn't come here to finish your book," she says, tapping her finger in Libby's chest, right over her heart. "You never wanted Peanut's help. You're only here because your real life sucks. You're lonely and pathetic and scared."

Although Libby's cheeks are hot, and her heart is slamming inside its cage, she doesn't reply. She's reminded of the afternoon in sixth grade—*Nice remembering*, she observes—when a classmate pushed her against the lockers in the school hallway. While Teresa Holly raged and spit and slapped, Libby stared at the open door behind her. Outside stood the school playground, blue sky, warm sun—a clear escape route. Yet she never considered running, or even walking, toward it.

This has always puzzled Libby. Why can't she help herself?

Even decades later, Libby often thinks of that doorway, the cloudless sky showing through, and imagines what would have happened, who she would have become, if she'd gone through it.

"Go." Jessie points now down the hallway to a red EXIT sign that appears lit through with blood. "Go away and leave us alone."

Dr. Bixton peers at Libby over his glasses. "Perhaps it's time."

Buzz reaches for Libby's hand, but she pulls away. "Pity is the tip of the spear," Gran Bere says, and Libby can't bear the excruciating pain when it runs through her.

She walks past the nurses' station, past open doors where patients are well enough to turn their heads and side-eye her. Past a vending machine, a set of bathrooms, a painting like Dr. Whatsit has in his waiting room: wilting flowers.

"Libby." Buzz limps after her. "Hold up."

But she doesn't. She walks faster. And then she runs, her eyes trained on the EXIT sign. It gets bigger and redder, and then it is above her, and finally, as she pushes open the door into the stairwell, it is gone, and so is she.

~~~

Not until she reaches the parking lot does Libby remember she has nowhere to go. No car, no working phone, no plan. No Children. She chews the tip of her thumbnail until it bleeds. No Band-Aid.

Just like that day on the playground, the sky is the color of an eye. Libby sits on the warm curb in front of the hospital and watches it back.

Okay, I'm here, she thinks. *What next?*

At the far end of the parking lot, a group of TV trucks and reporters lies in wait. A news anchor, suit off and shirtsleeves rolled up, wipes his brow and gestures to the hospital sign with his microphone.

Here we are at Colorado's Cross Creek Hospital, where the world's most famous author has reportedly been admitted after suffering what sources say is an emotional breakdown.

When a hearse purrs into the parking lot, the gaggle of reporters rushes toward it, cameras and microphones outstretched. They quickly lose interest when a pale balding man in jeans, a black hoodie, and white Velcroed sneakers climbs out. He's holding a shiny silver balloon that reads GET WELL SOON!

Without makeup, contact lenses, hair extensions, and his dirty tailcoat, Orson is unremarkable. The soles of his shoes squeak against the pavement.

"I don't get it," Libby says when he reaches the sidewalk.

Orson stops next to her, the balloon bobbing above him. "Get what?"

"Why would anyone want to be the Unstopping?"

He gestures to himself. "Would you pay attention to me like this?"

"The Unstopping is cruel. He tortures toys for no reason. He wants the entire world to suffer. He's almost killed the Children a dozen times."

"Stop," Orson says. "You're making me blush." He smiles, revealing the small baby tooth where his left canine should be. In the daylight, Libby can see that it is a harmless nub of plastic.

He gestures at the colorless stucco hospital, the skinny trees planted too close to the sidewalk, a chewed and discarded lump of green gum in the gutter. "Call me whatever names you want, but let's be honest: Reality is boring. It goes on and on and on. I'm the most interesting thing in this shitty little town. People love to hate me. I make them feel alive."

Libby is startled when Orson sits beside her on the sidewalk, so close that she can see the dozens of eyes on his neck and cheeks are still there. They are just closed.

She puts her head into her hands. *Stop imagining things.*

Or does she just need to imagine different things?

"You look like you could use some help."

"The Unstopping never helps anyone," says Libby.

Orson shrugs. "Maybe I've had a change of heart."

As Libby watches, he reaches into a pocket of his hoodie and pulls out a wad of napkins from the Cream King. At first, Libby thinks it's an actual heart.

Orson looks pleased when she recoils.

"A change of heart, get it?" he says. "It's the only way I could see the Unstopping coming here. I like to walk the walk."

"Don't worry." He lowers his voice. "It's a rump roast."

Using Libby's shoulder, Orson pulls himself into a standing position.

"Why are you even here?" she asks.

Orson returns the cut of meat to the pocket of his hoodie. He looks surprised. "I found out I have a fucking kid. Where else would I be?"

After pulling open the door to the hospital, he disappears inside.

Libby stares at Orson's hearse in the parking lot. She hears the warble of an ice cream truck and dank rumble of an air conditioner. Her mind feels like a train struggling up the side of a mountain.

Black licorice. Pig slop. Bitter melon. Blood.

Why was this the one page she saved in her notebook? What is it supposed to mean? Other random words crowd out the question.

Orson Unstopping Child Children—

Deep inside her head, a door opens, and a voice calls, "Libby?"

She automatically stands, thinking Dr. Whatsit's nurse is calling her into an exam room.

Mrs. Halfchap pats her shoulder. "Someone's looking for you, dear."

353

~⁓~

Painted on the far wall of the hospital cafeteria, which is called "Doctor's Orders," is a chorus line of vegetables in top hats and tap shoes. They are all smiling except for the tomato, which appears to have stage fright. Libby is wondering how she can help it when a voice calls her name.

At the back of the otherwise deserted cafeteria is a table crowded with people. They're not dressed for Blue Skies. The men are in suits. The women are in black.

On the center of the table is a sheaf of papers held together with binder clips.

"There she is." A woman with curly hair waves. "Over here!"

Libby moves toward her slowly, trying to remember who she is—or any of these people are. A revelation doesn't happen. Still, the woman grabs Libby's arms and air-kisses her on both cheeks.

"How *are* you," she wants to know.

"I'm—"

"Libby," the woman keeps going, "I'd like you to meet—"

She runs through a gauntlet of names. There are two esquires from legal, and someone from marketing whose necklace resembles a picture frame, and a young assistant with fingernails as ravaged as Libby's.

"And," Curly says, "of course, you remember Rowena."

She gestures to a large woman wearing bright red glasses. A streak of red separates her severe gray bob. A pink birthmark, the shape of a heart, spreads over her nose and right cheekbone.

It's Libby's publisher.

"Good to see you again, Libby." Rowena gestures for Libby to take a seat next to one of the esquires, a thin man with razor burn and a solemn expression.

"I know this meeting's a bit last minute," Rowena apologizes, "but we felt a face-to-face was necessary. This week alone, someone's attempted to hack into Groton's server twice. It wasn't prudent to do this over video."

"And we've had a difficult time reaching you by phone," Curly says.

This is her editor, Merry, Libby realizes.

"I thought you were the police about to arrest me," she confesses.

Everyone laughs.

Then Libby looks around the table again.

Two lawyers.

One marketing person with purple acrylic nails tap-tap-tapping on her phone.

One assistant.

Merry.

And the *publisher*, who usually just sends Libby bottles of expensive champagne when the Falling Children win an award. Libby has thirty magnums or so on top of her refrigerator at home. She is thinking about donating them to charity, but does the Salvation Army want Dom Perignon?

"Are you suing me?" Libby hears herself ask.

No one answers at first.

Then Merry says, "Look, Libby. We haven't lived your personal experience, and clearly, if we're meeting in a hospital in Tiny Town, USA, things must be challenging right now for you." She sounds apologetic. "But you're in violation of your contract, and we're all very, very concerned."

"Me?" Libby says, startled. "What did I do?"

She likes to follow rules. It's really the only Everlee thing about her.

"You've missed the last seven of your deadlines," Merry starts.

"Seven?" Libby repeats.

"Plus not showing up for our conferences or scheduled Zoom meetings, not returning emails. For weeks, I had literally no idea where you were."

"I haven't been feeling well," Libby starts to say, but one of the pale esquires—it's hard to tell which one since they share the same neck rash and receding hairline—interrupts.

"Here," he says, opening a leather portfolio. "Maybe it's easier if I—" He slides out a sheet of paper and, when Rowena nods, reads aloud in fluent and damning legalese:

"Repeated disregard of mandatory meetings and progress updates.

"Unsatisfactory completion of deadlines.

"Violation of nondisclosure agreement via unauthorized interviews to the media."

"I didn't grant an interview," Libby says quickly. "We slept together."

She hopes the esquire will take that off the list, but he continues reading all the other things Libby has done wrong.

Never made any friends, she hears.

Never had your own family.

Preparing to die alone.

"…which brings us," he says, "to proceed with termination of your contract in order to protect the Falling Children brand."

"The—brand?" Libby doesn't know where to put her hands. She clutches them in her lap, smooths her hair, twists the buttons of her shirt.

"You're such a talented writer," Merry goes on. "Low ego, very easy to edit."

"But time is of the essence," says Rowena. "We have a lot of moving parts to consider. After some careful thought, we've decided we need to pivot."

"I don't know what that means," says Libby.

"If we're going to move the needle, we need to transfer the Children to another writer."

"Don't worry," Merry adds quickly. "You'll be compensated for your work. Our team has worked up a really lovely deal. I think you'll be pleased."

Libby's face feels like it's on fire. "You're taking the Children away from me?"

"You've done a terrific job," says Merry. "We know you've given a hundred and ten percent. But—"

"F. T. Goldhero's reputation is at stake," Rowena finishes. "His mystery's always been as crucial as the books themselves, but now, because of you, that's in jeopardy."

"But I haven't finished!" Libby can feel panic hatching in her lungs like so many larvae.

Not now. She taps her sternum. *Later. Not now.*

"You'll adore the writer we have in mind." Merry hands Libby a napkin to dry her eyes. "She's a machine. Once we get your draft to her, my guess is she'll be able to pump out the ending we need in days. A week at most."

Libby hates many things about herself. How she bites her fingernails, for one thing. The dementia, of course. And how she does not like cats when, truthfully, they've never done anything to her. Here's something else: she does not do well under pressure.

Or has she admitted that already?

Everyone at the table stares at Libby, waiting for her to agree, applaud, ask questions. Or, on the other hand, maybe she will complain, argue, or fucking defend herself and her life's work. Instead, Libby watches her tears fall onto the contract someone has pushed in front of her along with a Groton & Sons pen.

"Look," Merry says gently, tapping a number on the first page. "You've totally earned that."

Rowena agrees. "It's important to us that you feel compensated."

"And if you ever want to try to write anything else"—Merry rubs her arm—"of course, I'd be happy to have a look."

Libby pretends to read the first page of the termination agreement, but the words swim before her. "I sign and it's over?" she asks.

"Sign and initial," corrects one of the esquires.

"And date," says the other.

Libby stares at the line for her signature. They've spelled her name wrong. A tear splats onto it, and "Weaks" begins to bleed.

"And while we have you," Merry says. "Do you have contact info for that sweet little girl who threw the rally last night? How cute is she? And she's a cancer survivor. That might be a narrative we can use."

"How wild would socials go if a kid had been writing these amazing books?" the woman from marketing chimes in. "We'd score millennials and Gen Z for sure. Even Boomers would be like, 'That could be my granddaughter!'"

"Online would love," Merry agrees.

"And imagine," Marketing says, dropping her voice, "if she really *does* die."

Libby can't hear anything other than her heartbeat. "Would you—" She points to a hallway that may or may not lead to a bathroom. "I just need—"

"Take your time," says Rowena.

The elderly man at the cash register gives Libby a sympathetic smile as she goes by. "Take a right at the water fountain," he calls.

But Libby takes a left into the stairwell, heads downstairs, then takes a right at *that* water fountain, and pushes through a set of heavy double doors.

She finds herself in an atrium filled with a forest of tree sculptures, their branches reaching toward the angled glass ceiling. Dozens of painted birds cover the walls. If Libby stares long enough, they seem to soar past her.

Like her thoughts, she thinks. Falling away. Like the Children, being pulled away. Like Peanut, fading away.

Libby presses her palms over her eyes. Her breath goes in and out like a broken accordion.

We know you've never given us trouble before, Libby.

As if she were a child.

But the mystery of F. T. Goldhero is more important than the books themselves.

As if the Children don't matter.

If you ever want to write anything else, of course we'll take a look.

What else *could* she write?

Libby can't write anything but the Children. She can't write anything without the Children.

Do something! she wills herself.

But Libby is not a fighter. She is not a complainer. She is not a stand-up-for-your-selfer.

I am! a voice inside Libby shouts, exasperated.

At first, she thinks it's Everlee. Then Libby realizes the voice sounds far more like Peanut.

Closing her eyes, Libby imagines Peanut at the table with Merry and the esquires and the marketing lady with thingy nails.

This is as nonsensical as the pile of bumblecock Everlee found in book two! Peanut would say, pushing the contract away and crossing her arms. *No one gets to finish the book but Libby. And as the biggest fan there is of the Falling Children, I can tell you exactly what your readers want.*

It's true. Peanut can.

Ante up.

In a corner of the atrium sits a plastic bin filled with crayons and drawing paper. Libby takes them all.

Then, sitting cross-legged on the floor, her back against one of the fake trees, Libby does the only thing she knows how to do well: she writes.

Finally, Peanut thinks. She is exactly where she wants to be.

As quietly as she can, she scrambles down the slippery tree roots to the entrance of the OtherWay, but the Squirrel Keeper is already waiting for her.

"Just look at that costume." He bristles. "I've asked you before, and I'll ask you again: Do you take me for a fool?"

"Don't get huffy." Peanut holds up the little red notebook and points to the words—To Save—on the cover. "I'm here to help."

The Squirrel Keeper unlocks the ancient wooden door that leads to the OtherWay.

"Have it your way," he snaps. "But If I hear screaming, I'm not coming to save you!"

The door slams behind Peanut with an ominous, otherworldly thud.

The forest where the Children have been abandoned is worse than Peanut imagined, nothing more than dead trees and sniggering clevervines that creep around her legs as she walks. Her eyes sting with anger when she spies Pompou's. The magical toy emporium, the Children's best friend and protector, home to so many lost souls, is nothing but ashes.

If only it were still alive, this destruction would stop.

When she spies flames in the distance, Peanut knows she has found the Unstopping.

It's not trees he's burning. It's Everlee. But even trapped in the Depths of Despair and lit through with fire, even with a gap in her chest where her wherewithal should be, Peanut can see Everlee's lips move: "Ante up," she says. "Ante up."

The Unstopping notices, too.

He roars in frustration, stripping the sky with his teeth, and Peanut knows it's time to speak.

"You can't kill her!" Peanut throws a rock to get the Unstopping's attention.

With the flick of a finger, he throws Peanut backward against the ground.

"I can do anything I want," he threatens, and to prove his point, the Unstopping lifts Everlee out of the infinite gooey sadness and high into the air, spinning her like a carnival pinwheel. Iridescent flecks of despair splash onto the ground.

Ante up, Everlee mouths.

"Do you want to know why you can't kill her?" Peanut scrambles to her feet. "Because I know."

"You know nothing."

The dozens of eyes on the Unstopping's neck shoot daggers at Peanut. She ducks and covers her head as they glance past.

"That isn't true. I don't do well in school only because they don't talk about the Children enough. But I know this for a fact." Peanut points to Everlee. "She's your daughter."

For a moment, the Unstopping freezes, considering this possibility. Then he lunges for Peanut. "Liar."

"I'm not lying." Peanut darts just out of reach. "In book one, you tell the Children, 'You don't know everything about me. Not even I know everything about me.'

"In book two, you trap the Children in the abandoned funhouse, where the mirrors show their deepest fears. But when you sneak in to hunt them, the reflection you see is Everlee looking for her parents. In book three, we learn about you and Lucy Parker—"

"Silence!" The Unstopping grabs Everlee by her scalp and winds up, preparing to fling her clear across the OtherWay and into the Abyss of Nothingness.

"I'm telling you, it won't work," Peanut says, although she's not quite sure anything can withstand the hungry gray waves of Nothingness. "She will always be part of you." She points to Lucy Parker's shriveled conscience pinned to his lapel.

The Unstopping is more furious than Peanut has ever seen him. He slashes the ground until it bleeds.

"Here's where you give her wherewithal back," Peanut demands.

Instead, the Unstopping rips open the sky.

"Find it yourself," he snarls. And before Peanut can stop him, he catapults into the real world. Out there, he can hide for infinity in the feelings no one wants: loneliness, disappointment, shame, regret.

Peanut runs to Everlee, lying face up on the ground, a Wiffle-ball-sized hole in her chest. Where could the Unstopping have hidden the juiciest part of her soul?

She is checking inside tree trunks and abandoned Williwig holes when she gets a sense that she's being watched.

Turning, she sees a scavenged baby doll with chewed fingers and plucked hair. Its eyes have been x-ed out with black marker and its mouth sewn shut. It's the doll from the Greeleys' house.

"What are you doing here?"

It doesn't answer.

Some toys, Peanut knows, can only speak when asked the exact right question at the exact right time. She waits until the hands on her watch reach the next minute, then asks, "Do you want me to help you?"

The doll nods.

Peanut finds a sharp-enough stick and saws away at the wire holding the doll's lips shut. She tries to be careful, but the stitches are tight. When she is done, a fine pink mist pours from the doll's mouth.

It takes Peanut a moment to understand why. Inside the doll's mouth isn't tongue or teeth or even a plastic tape recorder that calls, "Mama." It's...Everlee's wherewithal.

Safe, and protected, and syrupy as ever.

Cupping it gently in her hands, its warm, wet pulse between her fingers, Peanut isn't sure what to do next. She's not a doctor.

For the first time in her life, Peanut wishes Jessie were there. She would know what to do.

"Don't overthink it, honey." A small bear wearing a gingham apron appears next to her. It's not the real Gran Bere but a wispy figment that lives in Everlee's imagination. "You take a toy out to play with, it goes back in the chest when you're done, you know what I'm sayin'?"

Peanut looks down at her hands. "But this isn't a toy."

"Potato, po-tah-to," Gran Bere says.

"Are you sure?" Peanut starts to ask, then sees Gran Bere's expression. No one questions Gran Bere.

Peanut stands over Everlee, trying not to look directly at the gaping wound in her chest. That makes it hard to aim just right, but Peanut thunks Everlee's soul back into her chest and hopes for the best.

Sometimes that's all it takes.

As if by magic—because it is!—Everlee's chest cavity seals, the rip in her T-shirt closes, and her eyes flutter open.

"Well, would you look at that." Gran Bere whistles as it slowly fades away. "It actually worked."

Everlee sits up and pats her hair like she's awakened from a long nap.

When she notices Peanut, Everlee looks at her fondly. "Right," she says in a British accent. "Shall we save the others, then? It's practically teatime. Benjamin will be famished."

Peanut follows Everlee to where Benjamin and Huperzine have collapsed, from hunger and frustration, nearby. The splinter from Pompou's has turned Huperzine's foot craggy and gray green. Angry sparks shoot from it.

"You'll need this," Peanut says and hands Everlee the notebook that reads, "To Save." "At first, I thought it meant 'To Keep,'" she confides.

Everlee nods. "Yes, I can see why."

Together, they lean over the Depths of Despair where the Unstopping

LIBBY LOST AND FOUND

imprisoned Everlee. Peanut stirs the tar-black liquid with a stick, and a chewed watermelon rind burps to the surface.

"Black licorice, pig slop, bitter melon, blood," she recites.

"It's ingenious, really." Everlee takes the stick from Peanut and stirs faster, keeping an eye on her pink Swatch watch. "People hate the way despair feels, so they don't bother paying attention to what it can do."

Beneath the stagnant darkness, vivid magenta threads of uncertain magic—the most powerful kind—are already forming.

Once they are the size of fat caterpillars, Everlee carefully collects them in a gourd and carries them to Huperzine's lifeless body. Peanut expects her to gently open Huperzine's mouth and drop the wriggling things onto their tongue like medicine. Instead, Everlee lets the threads crawl onto the infected splinter in Huperzine's foot.

"As Gran Bere would say"—Everlee smiles at Peanut—"bottoms up."

The magic they've created from despair foams like hydrogen peroxide on an open cut, although hydrogen peroxide doesn't turn every color of the rainbow and smell like roast chicken.

Huperzine lets out a terrible cry, their foot kicking and thrashing.

Peanut starts to move toward them, but Everlee holds her back.

"Give it a moment," she says.

It is hard to stand by and watch Huperzine grieve alone. They gnash their teeth and pull at their hair. At one point, they curse uncontrollably, using words Peanut has only heard from Buzz.

Then, finally, with a loud, satisfying pop, the splinter dislodges from Huperzine's foot and lies, in a puddle of slime, beside them.

"Ugh," says Peanut.

"I know, right?" Everlee's eyes shine. She shakes her head in wonder. "It's positively magnificent."

That's not the phrase Peanut would use, but she stands next to Everlee and watches as the newly freed splinter wriggles and leaps like a fish on dry land. Then, with a high-pitched squeal, it suddenly explodes, throwing Peanut against a nearby gimcrack tree.

When she gets to her feet, a tiny red building sits on the scorched ground beside her.

It is only the size of a jewelry box but already splendid with a tall, thoughtful spire and rows of four-paned windows that are good for looking out, not in, and a gilded gold "P" above its fancy wooden door with decorative metal hinges...

"Oh my gosh." Peanut laughs. "It's Pompou, a baby Pompou."

Carefully, Everlee scoops the toy emporium into her arms. "Shhhh," she soothes it as it starts to cry. "You'll be back to normal size soon."

When the Squirrel Keeper ambles over to assess the fuss, Peanut can't resist telling him, "I told you I would save the Children. I saved everything!"

The ugly baby doll claps shyly. Benjamin stands and yawns and stretches. "Is it dinner?"

"I had the saddest dream." Huperzine sniffs.

The sun is rising above the forest for the first time in months, and the birds are back, and they are singing full-throated duets—and look! Here comes a weaselly little bone grocer, hunched on top of his wagon heap, calling, "Femurs! Fresh femurs! Cost you an arm for a leg!"

"Thanks to you, I get to work a thousand more years," the Squirrel Keeper complains, shaking his tail at Peanut. But he allows a smile as he says this and motions for the ugly baby doll to follow him.

"I suppose I'm going to take you in and grudgingly nurse you back to health until we become family." He sighs.

Benjamin comes forward to shake Peanut's hand. "Nice rescue," he says. He peers into her face. "And you look so real."

"That's because I am." Peanut laughs.

It's such a Benjamin thing to say!

The Children exchange glances.

"What's that look?" Peanut asks. "I know that look."

Everlee is about to speak, but Huperzine does first. "You were our secret plan," they pipe up. "A good one, too."

"What secret plan?" Peanut asks, confused.

"Don't look at me." Benjamin catches a clever-vine and drops it, still wriggling, into his mouth. He points to Everlee, who is looking both proud and a little ashamed. "She's the mastermind," he says, chewing. "The quick study. The deep thinker. Huperzine and I, we never make decisions—well, good decision—without her."

"What plan?" Peanut asks again.

"It's easier if I show you." Taking a stick, Everlee scribbles something in the dirt.

"There's some complicated uncertain magic that I'll save for the book, but think of it this way: if we Children have a motto, a call to arms, a secret verbal handshake, this is it."

ANTE UP, she writes.

"I know that." Peanut still doesn't understand. "What does that have to do with me?"

"The best way to make something real," says Everlee, "is to give it a name. Even better, a story."

She moves the letters around. "Now do you understand?" she asks.

Peanut takes a step back. "Oh," she says. Her fingers tingle and her stomach flips.

How did she miss this?

Rearranged, the letters spell out P E A N U T.

50

Buzz is slumped against the wall outside Peanut's hospital room, speed-eating Red Vines, when Libby returns. "You came back." He looks relieved. "She's awake."

Libby stares down at the papers in her hand. "Is she okay? She is, isn't she?"

"Okay enough to be pissed and not want to talk to anyone. Jessie brought her books—your books—from home."

A clock in the hallway ticks, ticks, ticks. Libby finds it comforting—it's the same sound she makes at her laptop when her writing is going well.

"Do you think she'll talk to me?" Libby asks.

Buzz opens the door for her. "Try."

~ ~

Peanut is sitting up in the bed, gripping a copy of book one. She looks exhausted, her eyes swollen, her lips chapped. An IV glugs colorless liquid into her arm.

"I'm so glad you're still here," Libby says.

Peanut presses her mouth into a line. Her eyes don't lift from the page.

Libby wishes she knew what to say. In awkward situations, Vernice always made things worse before she made them better. Libby has a feeling she is the same way.

She sits in the chair next to the bed and watches Peanut turn pages.

Silence nibbles at the space between them.

(Libby does not like the word "nibble," but she will switch it out later.)

"Did you know that, for years, I kept a notebook of ideas about the Falling Children?" she finally asks. "I probably started it when I was your age. That's when I started writing stories about them in the first place. After my parents died."

Peanut doesn't answer.

"I remember that there was a character who read the thoughts of animals and a talking pull-string doll who can decapitate other toys just by going like this." Libby draws her finger across her neck. "Oh! And an enchanted gas station with funny candy no one's ever heard of. But I didn't understand how to sew those things together," she says, "so I didn't use them. And then I got really angry at myself and threw all those ideas away. Or, well, most of them."

Peanut lifts her head. One eye glares at Libby, while the other stays trained on the book. "Why are you telling me this?"

"I guess because sometimes we don't understand right away how things—or people—fit into our lives." Libby twists the buttons on her shirt. "It takes some time to make room."

Peanut returns to her book, but Libby doesn't leave.

She waits and listens, and there it is, the sound of the clock in the hallway again.

Tick, tick, tick.

"I'm sorry," Peanut finally says.

"Sorry? Why are you sorry?"

"Because I told everyone you were F. T. Goldhero." Peanut grips the book. "And I was going to burn your manuscript." A tear rolls down her cheek. "I don't blame you if you hate me."

"I don't hate you!" Libby drags the chair closer to the bed. "You're okay. That's the important part."

"But it's not! Saving the Children is. That's why you came here, and I haven't helped with that at all."

Libby looks down. At first, her brain sees the crush of drawing paper and red crayon in her lap and thinks her hand is bleeding again. Then she remembers.

"But you did help." Libby hands the dozen messy papers to Peanut. *Hot off the press,* she means to say. It comes out as, "Hot of the thing."

Tick, tick, tick.

After skimming the first sentences, Peanut looks up, startled. "You put me in the book?"

"Keep reading."

Libby watches Peanut's eyes flicker back and forth, left to right, past to present, here to there. She *is* a fast reader.

"Ta-da!" Libby can't help saying. "You saved the Children! You saved the OtherWay. You saved Pompou's. You saved everyone!"

But Peanut isn't smiling.

"No one will understand this. I shouldn't be in here. I'm not a character."

"I'll go back and take you out," Libby promises. "I'll use something else to help the Children figure out that the Unstopping can't kill Everlee. But he won't be able to get away from the truth, now that we know it. The Children are okay. They're safe! They rescued themselves, just like Huperzine said they would. Remember? At the very beginning? And everyone laughed?"

Peanut plays with the edges of the papers, curling them like a tongue.

"I'm not real, am I?" she whispers.

Tick, tick, tick.

"What are you talking about? Of course, you're real. You're very real." Libby wants to touch Peanut to reassure her but can't decide where. She squeezes her leg through the blanket.

"I'm real to *you.*"

"No, to—everyone! To Jessie, and Buzz, and this town. To everyone here." Libby gestures to the hallway, but it's deserted, save for a UPS driver passing the doorway with a dolly stacked with boxes.

"Why don't you shut your eyes and get some sleep?" Libby says to Peanut. "A lot has happened. Do you want me to get your—Dr. Bixton?"

Peanut shakes her head. "I said I would do anything for the Children, and it's true." She nods, wiping her cheeks. "I meant it."

Libby takes the girl's hand, surprised at how small it is.

"You'll be okay, Peanut. I promise." Libby swallows the ship of guilt bobbing into her throat. "I won't let anything happen to you."

Peanut looks around the hospital room, her eyes glassy with tears. "You already did."

"But I—" Libby doesn't finish her sentence.

What has she done?

"Let me fix this," she pleads. "Please. I have an idea."

And then, so she won't forget, Libby fishes a Post-it note out of her pocket.

I AM F.T. GOLDHERO! she scribbles.

F. T. Goldhero, guardian of the Falling Children. F. T. Goldhero, bestselling author in the world. F. T. Goldhero, changer of lives.

She hands the small square of paper to Peanut.

Google "F.T. Goldhero Falling Children"

TOP STORIES

Let the revealing begin!

It's the moment Falling Children readers have been waiting for. Tomorrow, after four long years, Groton & Sons will reveal the author of the bestselling fantasy series. An estimated 21 million viewers are expected to tune in to the announcement, which will be aired live across all television networks. "You will not be disappointed," says Merry Jaminsky, senior editor at Groton & Sons...

CNN, 1 hour ago

EXCLUSIVE: The biggest F. T. Goldhero clue yet

We don't yet know the true identity of F. T. Goldhero, but Buzzfeed has exclusively learned that the author's real name is hidden in each of the Falling Children books. "How it's done is really ingenious," says our anonymous source. "If you're wondering if it will live up to the hype, the answer is *yes*." It is unclear whether the author's name is hidden in an anagram, a popular literary device in each of the five books, the name of a toy, the answer to a riddle, or perhaps all three...

Buzzfeed, 3 hours ago

Alleged F. T. Goldhero dispute ends as secretly as it began

The identity of F. T. Goldhero, author of the Falling Children series, is a closely guarded secret, so it's fitting that a reported disagreement between Goldhero and their publisher has ended

as mysteriously as it began. One month ago, a rumor surfaced that Groton & Sons was trying to replace the beloved author. Outraged fans took to social media—and the streets surrounding Groton's New York headquarters. "The FaChi community is very passionate, and we respect that," says a Groton spokesperson. "When F. T. Goldhero is revealed, you will meet the *real* author. You have our word. We are hopeful now that our employees can safely return to the building..."
NPR, 4 hours ago

Fans demand the *real* F. T. Goldhero

Boxes (and boxes) of Red Vines continue to gum up the U.S. postal service, but now they're being sent to the New York headquarters of Groton & Sons, publisher of the globally beloved "Falling Children" books, for a new reason. Fans of the fantasy series aren't, ahem, kidding around. They want Groton & Sons to reveal the *real* F. T. Goldhero—not, as a leaked document suggests, a carefully curated option selected by a marketing committee. A confidential list of candidates, posted online, shows that Groton & Sons considered paying millions to big names like Kim Kard...
The Guardian, 8 hours ago

Hello, Unstopping—is that you?

In the Falling Children books, the Unstopping is the Children's mortal enemy. Strutting around in a grimy tailcoat, a borrowed (damaged) conscience pinned to the lapel, he cuts a terrifying figure. But as the countdown begins to reveal the books' author, fans can't get enough of this murderous villain. That works out just fine for Blue Skies, Colorado, local Orson Greeley. The Unstopping impersonator, who has modified his appearance to match his fictional hero, has nearly 4 million followers on TikTok. He has become a fixture on TV shows like *The View* and is in demand to appear at birthday parties, weddings, bar mitzvahs, and a recent christening...

NYT, 2 days ago

51

The morning of the press conference, there is some arguing over what Peanut will wear. Jessie has bought her a navy-and-white polka dot dress with a small pink embroidered heart over the chest, which Peanut refuses to even consider. Same with the navy tights. Same with the navy Mary Janes.

"I'm wearing my own clothes!" Peanut stomps upstairs. When she returns, she has on a faded Falling Children T-shirt, black terry cloth shorts, striped knee socks, and worn sneakers.

"*That's* what you're wearing?" Jessie makes a face.

"I think it's relatable," interjects the stylist Groton & Sons flew in from New York. "Here you are, a normal everyday kid who also happens to write the best books in the world."

Without being asked, the stylist scrunches scented oil into Peanut's frizzy hair and swipes a fingertip of Vaseline over her lips. "I adore your writing," she shares. "How'd you come up with such amazing characters?"

"They're my family," Peanut says.

She doesn't look at Jessie, but after the stylist is done, Peanut allows Jessie to take off her glasses and wipe the lenses on her shirt before placing them back onto Peanut's nose.

"How's that?" Jessie asks. "Any better?"

Peanut considers this. "Maybe the smallest, infinitesimal bit," she says.

"Five minutes," calls Merry, power walking into the living room and nearly tripping over Rolf. "This is it, folks."

"This was quite an act of generosity," says Dr. Bixton, coming to stand beside Libby.

"Is it?" She lifts her shoulders. "It's really not. Peanut was born for this."

It's an awkward choice of words.

"What I meant was—"

Dr. Bixton waves off her apology. "We all serve a larger purpose now, don't we?"

Before heading outside, Peanut scoops each of the Falling Children books into her arms. They reach her chin. "Okay," she announces, her arms full. "I'm ready."

"What are you doing? You can't hold those the whole time," says Jessie.

"Yes, I can," Peanut says stubbornly. "They're my lucky charms."

"They'll get in the way. You can't—"

"Libby," Peanut interrupts. "Is this okay?"

"Sure," says Libby. She looks over at Jessie. "If it's up to me to decide."

Jessie sighs. "Fine." She waves. "Go."

"You're like a proud little mama," the stylist clucks at Peanut, but it's Libby who answers.

"I am."

Libby watches Dr. Bixton pat Peanut on the back and whisper something into her ear. Peanut smiles and stands a little taller, even as Jessie prompts, "Don't forget to stand up straight. And smile. But not an 'I'm better than you' smile, but a real 'I'm lucky' one."

"Luck is just a stirred pot of hard work," Peanut replies. "That's what—"

"Gran Bere tells Benjamin in the first book," Jessie says. "Yes, I know. We all know."

At Peanut's surprise, Jessie says, "Look, I'm trying, okay?"

Peanut pauses. For the first time, Libby can't read her expression, can't guess what she's thinking or what she'll do next.

"Okay," Peanut finally says.

And then with great effort, as if using one of Benjamin's Red Vines to climb out of the Depths of Despair, she says, "If you want, you can borrow my 'Falling Children' CDs to listen to because you're a slow reader. But you can't lose them or get them mixed up," she warns.

Jessie nods. "I promise."

"One minute, people!" Merry calls.

Peanut pauses in front of Libby. "I won't let you down," she says.

"Of course, you won't," says Libby. She gives her a hug, even though the stack of Falling Children books creates a wall between them. "I never thought I'd make such a good friend."

"Best friend," Peanut corrects. "I know you're close to Rolf, but he can't really talk."

"This is true," Libby agrees.

Merry brushes by Libby without acknowledging her. "Come on, little Goldhero," she says, steering Peanut toward the front door. "It's time to meet the world."

~~~

Libby goes outside, too. Not to the front yard of the Bixtons' house, where the press conference is being held, but out back with Rolf. She wants to preserve her last few minutes here.

Remember this, she begs herself.

Remember the golden light tracing paths between the trees, and the warm September breeze against her neck, the crunch of dirt beneath her feet, and hundreds of miles below, although Libby will never be able to prove it, the OtherWay.

She breathes in, imagining the lavender and damp grass she's no longer able to smell. Sitting on a fallen log next to Jessie's garden, which bursts with turnips and lettuce and green frilly things she can't name and maybe never could, Libby closes her eyes and thinks, *Goodbye, Children.*

A melody of applause comes from the front yard.

After a while, Buzz comes and sits next to her. "You okay?"

"How was it?"

"She crushed it. Especially when Baron McBroom stood up and said he didn't believe a seven-and-a-half-year-old girl could start coming up with such good stories, and she answered in Williwig."

He plays her the video on his phone.

"She said," Libby translates, "'We are all more than one story.' And then"—she laughs—"she called him a bone grocer."

"People liked how 'ante up' is an anagram for Peanut."

Libby nods. She likes that, too.

Buzz moves closer so he can catch a string of her tears on his index finger. "Second thoughts?"

"No." She shakes her head. "I just don't like goodbyes."

"So don't say them." Buzz pauses. "Listen."

Libby can barely make out a lisping, off-tune bird call.

"Bushtit." Buzz scans the trees for a few minutes before pointing to a stream of drab tiny birds erupting from a tree.

Libby still doesn't get it. "They're so—nothing," she says.

"That's what you think now. You'll come around."

He kisses her for a long time.

"A year from now, I might not know who you are," Libby says.

"I'll show you videos."

"It could be six months or six weeks," she says.

Buzz shrugs. "Or six years."

"There isn't a cure."

"But there could be. Shit happens all the time. Aren't you the one who writes happy endings? Write one for yourself. Stick around." He nudges her. "Don't you want a front-row seat to the Jessie and Peanut Show? That's gonna be a riot."

"You hate it here," Libby insists.

"Yeah, but where am I going?" Buzz gestures to his leg. "Think about it. The Sky is yours," he jokes. "We'll go to the Clam Box on Fridays and get food poisoning again. You'll rent a video, and twelve fucking people will tell you the ending before you get home. Tourists will ask you to take their picture, then complain it's out of focus. There's seven feet of snow in the fucking wintertime, which should start any minute now. And you've never been on the train," he adds. "That really blows."

It's such a neatly delivered speech that Libby asks, "Have we had this conversation before?"

"Maybe." He smiles. "But I always convince you."

When Libby starts to cry, Rolf comes and sits on her foot.

"See?" Buzz says. "He wants you to stay, too."

From far away, Libby can hear the sounds of her real life—the whirr of her apartment air conditioner, the thunk of boxes delivered outside the front door, the ping of her microwave, although she can't remember what is being reheated.

"I've been thinking about that question you asked me," Buzz says.

Libby doesn't remember.

"You asked what people think of when they know they're about to die. You know what I think?"

He doesn't wait for her to answer.

"I think," he says slowly, "they imagine the people they love." He shrugs. "They don't have to be real."

"Is that supposed to make me feel better?"

"Yes," he says, meeting her eyes. "So stay already."

Libby takes a deep breath. She imagines herself writing this scene and watching the words come to life on her computer screen. The hope that rises inside her is exquisitely real, so much that she has Buzz say it again.

"Stay," he says.

Stay, she types in her head.

And so she does.

Google "F. T. Goldhero last Falling Children book"

The Children are no longer lost in the forest

In the final installment of F. T. Goldhero's beloved Falling Children fantasy series, the most poignant insight comes not from one of the titular orphans, but the nihilistic villain who has spent years terrorizing them. "Reality is boring," points out the Unstopping. "It just goes on and on and *on*." And therein lies the profound magic of the books. We all need to escape reality for a short while, don't we? And in doing so, we find ourselves.

NYT, 1 year ago

The book we've been waiting for lives up to the hype

In *The Falling Children Find Their Way Home*, we at last learn the fate of imperturbable Everlee, easygoing Benjamin, and empathic Huperzine. For the past five books, author F. T. Goldhero has teed up enough cliffhangers to fill Pompou's Toy Emporium: Will the OtherWay be overtaken by Nothingness? Who are Everlee's parents? Can the Children defeat the Unstopping once and for all? In the last 676-page installment, we receive satisfying answers to each of those questions.

Los Angeles Times, 1 year ago

F. T. Goldhero, you are one of us

In retrospect, it could have been a disaster: A marketing campaign that hinged on readers becoming as deeply invested in a living, breathing author as the fictional books they created. But Groton & Sons knew what they were doing. The revelation that F. T. Goldhero is a precocious adolescent who crafted the books as a way to process her own tragic past surpasses any and all expectations Falling Children readers, fans, and skeptics like myself could have had.

The Atlantic, 1 year ago

Beloved Blue Skies doctor announces retirement

After 48 years in medical practice, Jim "Dr. B." Bixton is retiring. "Now calm down, I'm not fading away," he told this reporter. He has camping trips planned, although his companion, Trudy Chapman, Blue Skies' animal communicator, has made him promise he will not fish or hunt. Dr. Bixton's daughter, Jessie, will take over the management of Bixton Family Medicine, including hiring a new doctor. "Jessie knows what she's doing," Dr. Bixton said. "She'll do a fine job."

Blue Skies Gazette, 6 months ago

The Falling Children live on (whew!)

In movies, TV shows, podcasts, the recent opening of Universal Studios' OtherWay®, and a just-announced Broadway musical, the beloved Falling Children aren't going anywhere. But author F. T. Goldhero, a.k.a. Pandora "Peanut" Bixton, wants everyone to know why. "Baron McBroom rudely said that everything I do is a 'money grab,' but like Gran Bere told the Squirrel Keeper in book two, "Don't tell me I'm eating a pie if *you're* eating a pie," the eleven-year-old author said on a recent episode of *Hot Ones*. "I just love the Children. I don't want them to go away."

Variety, 4 months ago

The F. T. Goldhero Foundation makes record-breaking donation

The F. T. Goldhero Foundation has made a jaw-dropping gift of $175 million to four health organizations dedicated to finding a cause and cure for dementia. "Someone out there—and most likely a child like me since we have the best imaginations—can find a cure," said F. T. Goldhero, a.k.a. Pandora "Peanut" Bixton. "And the sooner, the better, so chop chop."

Hollywood Reporter, 2 months ago

Red Bull spends the day in Blue Skies with Buzz Skovgaard

Buzz is back, baby. Watch as he lands a backside 5–0 down 35 face-melting stairs, no squill in sight. Sit back and enjoy the show.

The Berrics, 2 weeks ago

The Falling Children find a new home

Descend the steps to the OtherWay. Wander a lush life-size forest of gimcrack and geegaw trees. Haggle with bone grocers. Help a Williwig get to work on time! Author F. T. Goldhero, aka Peanut Bixton, had a hand in every decision that went into building the state-of-the-art interactive Falling Children Museum, tucked away in Blue Skies, Colorado. (Indeed, you'll need to solve a riddle and two anagrams to find it.) Since the museum opened last week, one local fan (who preferred not to give her name) admits that she's stopped in every day. Sometimes by herself, sometimes with her partner and his family, always with her dog. "It's home," she said.

Time, 1 day ago

READING GROUP GUIDE

1. How long would you wait for the release of a book from your favorite author? How much patience would you have?

2. Libby thinks about the things that tether her to life despite her despair: Rolf, her dog, and her book series. What are your tethers?

3. Is it important to prepare for death? Why does there seem to be a reticence to talk about death in general?

4. Do you see the characters from your favorite books in your dreams? Can you imagine them standing next to you? What would they say?

5. Why would someone want to write under a pseudonym? What are the reasons someone would want to keep their identity a secret?

6. How important are book or series endings to you? Does a bad ending ruin a good book? Does a good ending enhance an overall uninteresting read?

7. Peanut idolizes the writer of the Falling Children series. How do you think about your idols? Would you be upset or angry if someone insulted them?

8. Dr. Bixton says this about Libby's dementia: "You didn't cause this, and you can't cure it. But you sure can't deal with it alone." What other parts of life does this statement apply to?

9. There is the constant assumption throughout the book that F. T. Goldhero is a man. What does that say about people's preconceptions?

A CONVERSATION WITH THE AUTHOR

Libby has such a devotion to her characters in this book. Do you see your characters in the same way?

Yes! They feel very real to me, so it was incredibly hard to watch them struggle. Looking back, that's probably one reason why I began writing this from different perspectives. Peanut has energy and optimism when Libby feels depleted. And Libby finds inner strength when Peanut has sunk into her own Depths of Despair.

Considering the main trouble of the book is that Libby can't figure out how to end her series, do you find writing endings difficult?

My issue (so far) hasn't been *how* to write an ending but the emotional toll that endings take on me. I'm saying goodbye not only to characters I love but a world that I've been living in for the majority of my waking hours. I think I cycle through all the stages of grief.

There are many difficult themes in this book: death, suicide, grief, and so on. Was it difficult to write about such heavy topics? Why is it important to write these topics into stories?

Writing about heavy topics is difficult, but I really believe that reading about them can help us all feel less alone. As a journalist,

I've spoken to so many people who are going through tremendous challenges. Time and time again, they've shown me how it's possible to experience tough things and difficult emotions without getting dragged under by them. And what a gift it is to be reassured of that.

But I also wanted Libby and Peanut to live in a benevolent universe, where Everything Will Be Okay, even if it's not a neatly wrapped-up "okay." And knowing that helped me too.

What do you want readers to take away from this book?

That the parts of ourselves we perceive as weaknesses, those secrets that we're most ashamed of, are really our biggest strengths. That just because you're going through something difficult doesn't mean you have to go through it alone. And that imagination can sustain us in the most lovely, unexpected ways.

Also, dogs really do make everything better.

What are some of your favorite books?

This is a really hard question! I tried to whittle it down to just a few titles and quickly gave up. I love so many books for vastly different reasons: because I adored them as a kid or read them over and over to my own kids. Maybe because I saw myself in the characters or wished I could live in their world. There are also books I adore because years later, I *still* can't wrap my head around the amount of research or craftsmanship or candor that went into creating them.

But I think it is fair to say that all my favorite books share one quality: the power to transport me out of the real world, even for a short while. And when I return to it, I've changed for the better, even in infinitesimal ways.

ACKNOWLEDGMENTS

A downside to being a gushy person is that I lose the element of surprise. I don't think anyone on this list will be surprised to hear (again) how grateful I am. I do hope they realize I mean it each time I say it.

Thank you to Jeff Kleinman at Folio Literary Management for your steadfast encouragement, insight, and willingness to entertain my off-the-wall ideas. This book simply would not exist without you. Infinite thanks to Shana Drehs at Sourcebooks Landmark—from your extraordinarily thoughtful edits to your cheerful support, you are my dream editor. I love that you immediately understood what this book was about and knew how to make it better.

I wrote these words, but many people at Sourcebooks worked hard to get them to you. I'm so grateful to Manu Velasco for copy editing, Kelly Burch for proofreading, and Jessica Thelander for heroically catching every last inconsistency. Thank you to Stephanie Rocha and Erin Fitzsimmons for the luminous cover design, Tara Jaggers and Rosie Gaynor for perfecting the internal design, and Erin LaPointe for manufacturing. To put this book on shelves and in hands, I'm so appreciative of Cristina Arreola for heading up publicity, Molly Waxman's marketing expertise, and the entire Sourcebooks sales team. Alev Neto, thank you for dreaming up the beautiful cover illustration.

For research assistance, thank you to the Alzheimer's Association, as well as Trace Longo of Longo Communications; Carlos Uquillas, MD, orthopedic surgeon and sports medicine specialist at Cedars-Sinai Kerlan-Jobe Institute; and Noami Halsey McClure, MD.

Many characters in The Falling Children series are named after or inspired by real-life toys. I'm grateful to the toymakers for unintentionally firing up my imagination. The quote ("May your belly never grumble") on the downtown Blue Skies statue is not mine. Although I see it all over the internet, sometimes referred to as a cowboy blessing, I have been unable to track down its original source.

I'm in awe of authors who ask friends to read multiple drafts of their work. I should really try that. I owe big thanks to the following, all of whom never read one word of this book but still cheered me on: Danielle Centoni, Gillian Freney, Angie Holt, Elona Landau, Emily Petterson (who also generously shared her PR savvy), and Nikki Zeman.

A thank you to Dan Zevin for many years of friendship and support. And to Esther Crain for all that *and* carrying on an email correspondence for the ages.

Thanks to Marguerite and Sarah Booth, especially when I show you this and ask, "Do you think it sounds okay?" after it's too late to change. (Please say yes.) And to Christopher, Max, and Maddie, who politely pretend they don't see the half-drunk cups of coffee I forget around the house: thank you for giving me such a lovely real-life family to return to after spending countless hours in my head.

Lastly, if life feels really hard right now and you or someone you know is having thoughts of suicide, please text or call 988 to reach the 988 Suicide & Crisis Lifeline.

ABOUT THE AUTHOR

Stephanie Booth is a writer in Portland, Oregon. Hundreds of her articles and essays have appeared in print and online, including in *Cosmopolitan, Real Simple, Parents, O: The Oprah Magazine, Washington Post,* and *Los Angeles Times.* She has a master of fine arts degree in creative writing from Emerson College and a master of arts degree in English from the University of New Mexico.